Oh Wicked Escort

D. L. Robinson

Published by
Satin Romance
An Imprint of Melange Books, LLC
White Bear Lake, MN 55110
www.satinromance.com

Oh Wicked Escort ~ Copyright © 2015 by D. L. Robinson

ISBN: 978-1-68046-169-5

Names, characters, and incidents depicted in this book are products of the author's imagination or are used fictitiously. Any resemblance to actual events, locales, organizations, or persons, living or dead, is entirely coincidental and beyond the intent of the author or the publisher. No part of this book may be reproduced or transmitted in any form or by any means, electronic or mechanical, including photocopying, recording, or by any information storage and retrieval system, without permission in writing from the publisher.
Published in the United States of America.

Cover Art by Stephanie Flint

Dedicated to my husband Dan, the most romantic of men—my love and my inspiration.

Chapter One

Lightning flashed across the black sky, heralding the arrival of the storm that had been threatening the city since late afternoon. Bennett Kirkwood impatiently pushed the heavy draperies aside and stared out into the dark wet night. How could he have left himself so open, so vulnerable? Bitter curses fell from his mouth as, frustrated, his fist slammed against the wooden sill of the window. Sighing heavily, he swallowed the bitter wave of despair that threatened to consume him before turning back to meet the anxious faces of his friends, reading concern for him in their eyes. After replenishing their empty glasses with more of the strong amber liquor, a weak smile flitted across his face as he once more sat down, his pride unconvincingly trying to conceal his inner turmoil.

Restlessly running a hand through his black wiry hair, a look of puzzlement crossed his countenance as he once more reviewed the events of the day in his mind. The morning had begun so well…

A note from his closest friend, Braxton Kane, had arrived with the morning post, announcing his return from the West Indies. Without hesitation, Ben had sent off a speedy reply, extending an invitation to join him and the Chambers brothers for the evening at a fashionable gaming house where they could enjoy a few games of chance before returning to Silverwood House for a late supper.

And so, the richly tailored foursome had met, and while the three had gambled moderately, Ben had signed yet another chit to the smirking proprietor. His run of bad luck continued to plague him, as it had for the past few months. Allowing himself to finally be persuaded to leave, the four had made their way back to Ben's home where a delicious repast of roasted meats, fresh bread, and a bottle of fine wine awaited them. His three companions, aware that their friend had fared poorly earlier in the evening, worked hard to distract him from his woes. Their banter was lively as they reminisced about their shared school days, by unspoken agreement avoiding any serious topics while the servants hovered about.

At last, appetites sated, the small band of revelers retired to the library, a room no servant in Silverwood House would dare enter unless bidden to do so and where an assortment of liquor bottles and sparkling crystal glasses awaited them. Lamps had been lit, casting a warm glow over the room as they collapsed onto the overstuffed sofas and chairs scattered about.

Curiosity consuming him, Teddy Chambers, a man who delighted in being the first to know any juicy tidbits of gossip, wriggled in his chair, unable to contain himself any longer.

"Where has that bastard half-brother of yours disappeared to, Braxton?" His fair eyebrows were raised inquiringly. "Despite hushing the scandal somewhat before you sailed, I doubt he'll have the courage to show his face in these parts ever again." Conversation faded as discomfited but questioning eyes turned to the one addressed.

The tall, black-clad figure had stiffened, annoyed at the unexpected prying. Grey eyes brooding, Braxton laughed derisively, hoping to disguise his irritation at the reminder of such a family skeleton, a skeleton he would rather keep in a securely locked closet. *But*, he mused, *perhaps I should talk things over with these three, my trusted friends. Who knows, they might even be able to offer some advice, should Patrick dare return to these shores.* He shrugged his shoulders almost imperceptibly before speaking, a melancholy frown briefly touching upon his handsome features. As was his habit when agitated, he began to pace about, hands clasped tightly behind his back as his long legs carried him the length and breadth of the room. As he spoke, he retained his affability, but there was a distinct hardening of his eyes.

"I know you're all aware of my brother's fascination with cutting up small animals, especially any creature that had the misfortune to become a pet of mine. This went on for years until finally, at his wit's end, my father felt perhaps a career in medicine was the place for his eldest son.

Oh Wicked Escort

But after serving less than two years as an apprentice at St. Guy's Medical School right here in London, Patrick withdrew, claiming the instructors were treating him unfairly. By coincidence, Father died within days of my brother's return. His will named me as administrator of the estate, a fact which infuriated Patrick who was, after all, my senior by a few years. I rarely saw him after that." Braxton paused to draw a breath, resuming his seat before taking a small sip from the glass before his story continued.

"And then, of course, the scandal." He stood, his powerful, well-muscled body returning to restless pacing about the room, his distress obvious. "As you have already pointed out, Teddy, I...somehow I was able to hush it up before it became common knowledge throughout London that he had slashed a prostitute's throat, one who somehow and against all odds survived the brutal attack. With the able assistance of my solicitor, I convinced the magistrate that Patrick would leave the country, never to return. And since his victim had no one to speak up and protest on her behalf, Patrick was released into my custody. We set out immediately for the West Indies, which is where I had planned to leave him, hoping to never hear of or from him ever again."

"But it seems Patrick had his own plans, jumping ship before we reached our destination. I haven't heard from him since that time, and God willing, I never will. I set out to remove him from England, and at least I have accomplished that."

Recalling the humiliation visited upon their friend, the others raised their glasses in silent commiseration, praying that the matter was indeed at an end.

Hoping to lift the pall that had descended onto the cozy little group, Braxton's deep-timbered voice broke into his companions' thoughts, congratulating the two brothers on their respective marriages some months ago.

"And both of you now married—two brothers wed to two sisters! I am most sorely vexed at missing your nuptials. I can only imagine the trials to which you are subjecting your brides. But tell me, my friends, do your ladies not object to your spending the evening in the company of two bachelors, worrying perhaps that we might lead you astray?"

Teddy, the younger of the two brothers by a little more than a year, flushed as he looked across the room at Braxton. His blond hair hung in dull limp strands around his pale face, his slight frame in direct contrast to his brother's robust build.

"Of course, gentlemen, I can speak only for myself, but in truth, she wouldn't dare. My Miranda knows her place and recognizes who is master." His pale cheeks colored fiercely at this empty boast, hoping none of them discovered that his wife had extracted the promise of a new gown in exchange for his night of freedom. The fire crackled in the hearth, breaking the stillness that followed this avowal of mastery over one's spouse.

Julius, his great mop of brown hair spilling onto his forehead, glanced sideways at his brother, wondering how the young whelp thought he fooled anyone with such posturing. His own marriage to Minerva Penrod was nothing short of a disaster, and he didn't care a fig who knew it.

"Truth be told, Braxton, Minerva was quite happy to see the back of me, even if it is just for a few hours. That most fearsome, nay, loathsome of guests, my mother-in-law, the despicable Letitia Penrod, has been staying with us since our vows were spoken and is, I might add, quite the most malicious gossip and vainest woman I have ever met. I've dropped great hints in my brother's ear that it might perhaps be his turn to take in the Widow Penrod, but my words must have been too subtle as the old harridan continues to haunt Shelton Hall."

Turning his troubled face away from the gathering, he stared into the fire before continuing. "I never imagined that when I agreed Minerva's mother could 'visit', it would be a never-ending occurrence."

He turned his eyes upon their host. "Let my unhappy experience guide you, Ben. If Miss St. Martin's father makes any noise, however faint, about moving in, you must stand firm."

At this piece of unsolicited advice, all eyes fell once more on their host, who scowled at his friend's words. "I'm afraid your counsel, Julius, though welcome, comes too late."

"As they only have each other, my intended does indeed expect her father to make his home with us. At first, I too thought she meant it to be a temporary situation, but unfortunately that does not seem to be the case." He ran his fingers impatiently through his wiry black hair once more.

"Do not misunderstand me, gentlemen. I'm not in love with the girl, at least not yet, but I believe I could very easily be." He gave them a bleak, tight-lipped smile, causing them to wonder what troubled him.

Thinking to distract his friend from the melancholy that seemed to threaten him, Braxton refilled his glass. "Ben, your Miss St. Martin seems to be a veritable paragon of virtues. I'm half in love with her myself, and I've yet to meet her." His words amused the others and, as he had hoped, the sadness that seemed to fill the room began to lift.

As Braxton finished speaking, a grinning Julius raised his glass, proposing a toast to their friend's good health and fortune. As the glasses were emptied, he glanced at Braxton.

"You must join us for dinner tomorrow evening, old boy. Teddy's Miranda and my Minerva are simply aching for a chance to form their own opinion of the delightful Miss St. Martin…and I must confess to some curiosity myself." He paused, lost in thought for a moment but then continued.

"Though I feel it only fair to warn you that once the Widow Penrod and her daughters realize they have a bachelor in their midst, well, it's really only a matter of time before they start parading any and all unmarried women of their acquaintance before you."

Braxton threw back his head and let out a great burst of laughter. "My friend, let me assure you that many a lady has been tempted to play matchmaker, but I have always managed to avoid any serious entanglements. I am content with my bachelorhood and plan to remain so, at least for the present."

It was at that moment a firm knock resounded on the door. Bennett, irritated with the interruption, barked a command to enter. The door opened just enough to admit Mrs. Dixon, housekeeper of Silverwood House. Her prim manner was marked by small, piercing eyes, which quickly surveyed the state of the room and the men occupying it, coming to rest on the bottles whose contents were much depleted. Her short, round figure stiffened in censure, and with thin lips pressed tightly together, she wordlessly registered her disapproval.

When she spoke, her words were clipped as she addressed her employer. "Your pardon, sir, but there's a Mr. Mordock Peckworthy asking to see you on what he claims to be a matter of great urgency."

Puzzled glances passed between the four, their curiosity instantly aroused. They all remembered the unlikeable Peckworthy as a boy, for he had also attended school with them, though it was doubtful that his memories of their shared school years were recalled with the same degree of fondness as their own.

Mordock Peckworthy had been a thin, gangly boy with a shock of ginger-colored hair who, on his arrival at school, immediately became a target for pranksters, chief of whom had been Bennett Kirkwood. They had been in their final year when word of the sudden death of his father reached the young Peckworthy. He had left school that very day, never to return. The only news that had reached the ears of the foursome concerning their former schoolmate was that, being an only child, he had inherited an enormous fortune, becoming one of England's richest men. And now here he was, just outside the door, demanding entrance into their company. Intrigued, Bennett Kirkwood directed the housekeeper to show him in.

Mordock Peckworthy strode confidently into the room, the once nervous and stuttering schoolboy gone, replaced by a tall, cadaverous man, copper hair thinning and slightly faded. He conveyed an air of authority, one who was accustomed to receiving instant and unquestioning obedience. A finely woven black cloak was draped casually over one arm, a beaver hat clasped loosely between long, tapered fingers. The rich fabric of his jacket and trousers bore silent witness to great wealth, although he displayed no sense of style and wore his clothes awkwardly. A black mourning band contrasted starkly against the pale grey sleeve of his jacket. His eyes were dark and unfathomable as he bowed his head curtly to the four.

A second man followed him quietly into the room, his nondescript coat stretched across a squat but well-muscled body. Dark-complexioned with thick black eyebrows, the stranger conveyed a menacing air as he quickly scrutinized not only the inhabitants but the four corners of the room also. Crossing to the window just beyond the cozy circle of friends, he peered out into the inky black wetness of the night. His profile was strong and rigid, giving the other occupants of the room the impression of a wild animal, ready to spring should even a hint of danger to his master be perceived.

"Gentlemen, do forgive me for intruding, but I've had to wait some time to find all of you gathered together and, shall we say, away from inquisitive eyes." There was no hint of the boyhood stutter as the taller of the two new arrivals spoke, drawing attention back to himself, his expression a mask of stone.

Their collective curiosity was now piqued beyond imagination but with it came wariness and an unaccustomed feeling of disquiet. The four glanced about the dimly lit room, drawing little reassurance from its comfortable familiarity.

Bennett Kirkwood, suddenly remembering his obligation as host, indicated the bottles of liquor, his eyebrows raised inquiringly.

"Just a small sherry, Kirkwood." Answering his host's unspoken question, he shook his head. "Nothing for Leopold. He never imbibes while on duty."

Assertively, he positioned his chair so he faced his seemingly mesmerized audience, glancing at all of them before sinking down into the chair's upholstered depths. Taking a small sip of his drink, he studied the four, his eyes sharp and assessing. The ticking of a clock suddenly seemed to echo loudly within the four walls of the room, the storm outside having passed from deafening rolls of thunder to a soft whisper of rain against the windowpanes.

His voice, when he at last broke the silence, was cool and impersonal. "Well, Julius and Theodore Chambers, you have both married—recently, I believe?"

Teddy bristled at the use of the name he detested but for the moment chose to ignore it. Both brothers, uncomfortable at being singled out, nodded. Julius spoke, more stiffly than he had intended. "Yes, we married four months ago—the Penrod sisters, Minerva and Miranda. Perhaps you're acquainted with the family?"

With a dismissive shake of his head, the newcomer's eyes moved on, falling on Braxton Kane.

"And you, Braxton, have just returned from the West Indies. If my information is correct, you have spent these past months disposing of your family's remaining interests on the other side of the Atlantic."

Braxton, astonishment written across his handsome features, was momentarily speechless. He looked across at his friend, but Ben could only shrug, staring wordlessly back at him.

Mordock Peckworthy's look was one of faint amusement as he turned to face his host. He took another small sip of sherry before turning his full attention on Ben, regarding him thoughtfully until the other, his expression stiff and distrustful, shifted uncomfortably in his chair.

"And you, Ben, have recently become affianced to a Miss Claire St. Martin, a young lady who has spent her life in the country under the loving but protective eye of her father, tucked safely away, until very recently, from the wicked ways of London. The nuptials are just a few short weeks from now, if I'm not mistaken?" Nodding in surprise, Ben confirmed the statement.

"And so here we all are, old school chums, reminiscing about bygone days and anticipating a bright future." He laughed softly but his eyes were filled with contempt as he gazed about him, smugly satisfied at their expressions of unease as their eyes continued to dart back and forth between the two interlopers.

"But perhaps, Ben, before I divulge my reason for calling, you could send that odious creature lurking just beyond the door and whose ear, I fancy, is pressed to the keyhole hoping to hear some juicy tidbit to share with the other servants, for some tea or coffee. For I fear, gentlemen, that you will need all of your wits about you this night."

As he spoke, and with an almost imperceptible shake of his head which kept the vigilant Leopold standing at his post beside the window, Mordock Peckworthy had noiselessly crossed the room. He pulled the door open to reveal a much embarrassed Mrs. Dixon awkwardly attempting to straighten her rotund frame.

Ben, a look of annoyance on his face, regarded his housekeeper coldly. "A pot of coffee, Mrs. Dixon, and then you can make your way to your bed, for you won't be needed again this evening."

An expression of consternation filled her eyes as she spun about, retreating hastily toward the kitchen. As the men awaited her return, they realized the intruder had now become the host, making it clear he had no intention of enlightening them further until the errant servant had delivered the tray. Desultory small talk about the doings of other school friends occupied them until the squeaking wheels of a tea trolley, competing with the rattle of china, alerted them to the housekeeper's return. After depositing the cumbersome cart within reach of her employer, a much discomfited Mrs. Dixon beat a speedy retreat to her bed.

❀ ❀ ❀

Waiting for the hot brew to be poured, Mordock Peckworthy impatiently brushed at a tiny thread, which marred the rich fabric of his jacket, until as they all settled back, cups of hot coffee in hand, he cleared his throat and began to unfold his wicked scheme of revenge.

"Gentlemen, before I reveal my reasons for intruding on you, I must have your assurance that what you are about to hear will be held in the strictest of confidence." His eyes seemed to rest mockingly on Teddy, that lover of gossip, seconds longer than the others. Under such scrutiny, Teddy shifted uncomfortably.

Glancing around the tight circle, each man nodded guardedly as the newcomer's eyes swept over them. His voice was like an echo from an empty tomb, without inflection, as he continued.

"No doubt you are aware that Ben here, and his father before he departed this world, had legendary quarrels, which were gossiped about by all of London society." He smiled coldly as Bennett Kirkwood bristled and made as if to rise. "Steady there, Kirkwood, it won't do to interrupt me, for I am determined to have my say." Ben, with Braxton's steadying hand on his shoulder, settled back once more.

"Now, where was I? Oh yes, those quarrels—the elder Kirkwood considered his son a reckless spendthrift and womanizer, a profligate of the first order, one who would soon squander the fortune he and his forebears had so carefully amassed over the years. So certain was he in fact, that the old man tied up the entire estate until the day his son reaches the ripe old age of thirty years, which unfortunately is still some three years from now. I believe the senior Kirkwood's reasoning was that by that time his son would hopefully be married and raising a family, a responsibility, which would encourage a more steady hand. At present, the cost of running both Silverwood House in London and his country estate, Bindley Park, including a monthly allowance for our friend here, is paid through a trust, which is controlled by the family's bankers and one other."

Ben felt himself flush as his friends turned to him, silently willing him to refute what they had just learned. Restlessly, he crossed to the fireplace, stirring up the embers before adding another log. Looking up, he saw all eyes were on him. He sighed with exasperation. He gave the intruder a glacial stare.

"See here, Peckworthy, what exactly do you hope to gain by revealing details of my personal fortune, or lack of it, to my friends and to your creature who continues to skulk about in the shadows?"

Mordock Peckworthy, his voice stern with no vestige of sympathy in its harshness, barked out an order. "Sit down, sir. All will be revealed, but it will be done as I dictate, with no assistance from you. And don't fret about Leopold gossiping—he's been a mute since the day of his unfortunate birth." Ben, nodding gloomily, regained his chair.

The intruder crossed his legs as he gazed about the room. "The long and the short of things, gentlemen, is that our friend here has found this stipend—this allowance—simply not enough. He has left notes in various gaming houses throughout the city, plus other sundry debts such as his tailor, whose patience, I might add, is wearing thin. The cheeky fellow has had the audacity to threaten Mr. Kirkwood with debtors' prison."

As the others stirred uncomfortably, unwilling witnesses to their friend's public humiliation, a derisive snort of laughter rang out.

"Unfortunately, gentlemen, your friend, laboring under the mistaken belief that the family possessed great riches, proposed marriage to Miss Claire St. Martin shortly after her arrival in London. It had been rumored the St. Martin family, when they fled France during 'The Terror' all those many years ago, was somehow able to smuggle their wealth out of that country. But sadly this fortune, which Bennett thought would be the solution to his financial woes, was only ever a modest one and is now all but depleted."

Leaning forward in his chair, he continued his narrative in a cold voice. "In turn, Pierre St. Martin thought he was securing a rich husband for his daughter. A few months ago, he was forced to sell what little property he had left to satisfy his creditors. The wily old fox did manage to tuck away just enough from those who hounded him to outfit his daughter in the hopes of launching her into London society, optimistically confident of finding a rich husband. Bennett and Claire met, and a marriage now looms on their horizon. If only the old man hadn't been so ill—his doctor doubts he'll see the end of the year. No matter. If he had been a healthier man, he might have exercised caution and at least visited Silverwood House. As I have already said, he was, before falling ill, a wily old fox. He would have immediately noticed the missing paintings, don't you agree?"

At these words, both of the Chambers brothers and Braxton Kane glanced around, observing for the first time the empty spaces on the walls where paintings had once hung, before turning their attention back to Peckworthy.

"No doubt you're asking yourselves why the engagement couldn't be broken. Think about it, gentlemen. There is the enchanting Miss St. Martin, who seems in a very short time to have cast a spell over most of London society, and who, some love-smitten swains have already declared, is the most beautiful woman in the realm. She is everything a man could want in a wife—beauty without equal, charming, kind, intelligent—I could go on but I won't, or you'll think I too am besotted with the girl. Suffice it to say that were Mr. Kirkwood to abandon her to the penury that awaits her on her father's death...well, I can only assume that those who rule London society would likely cut him cold, something he simply would not be able to tolerate. As you are all no doubt aware, while it is acceptable to marry for money, you must not be blatantly flagrant about it. And so they are both caught, like flies in a web."

He remained motionless, savoring the moment before pacing the narrow confines of the room, his eyebrows knotted in a deep frown. A muscle quivered in his jaw as he met the eyes of his reluctant audience.

"No doubt you have been wondering how I came to be so well informed about all of your lives. Well, gentlemen, for the past year I have had my agents gathering as much information as they could, especially about you, Ben."

A shadow of annoyance crossed Ben's face at being singled out. He rose from his chair and faced the man who had so quickly become his adversary, his voice lashing out, demanding an explanation for such behavior.

Peckworthy crossed to where Ben stood and the two, unmovable and unbending, faced each other, almost snarling their hatred of the other. Peckworthy's voice was heavy with sarcasm, his words cold and exact.

"Sit down! I'm just getting started." Ben regained his seat with an angry thump, casting a scathing look at the man.

"Do you remember a young girl, Kirkwood, by the name of Elizabeth Manning? Think, man! She was an innocent until she had the misfortune of crossing your path." His words were loaded with derision. "You robbed her of that innocence with no thought of anything but your own selfish needs."

As a faint memory niggled its way into Bennett Kirkwood's brain, his fingers tapped the arm of his chair apprehensively. "I admit knowing the girl, Peckworthy. What of it?"

Mordock Peckworthy's voice was like an echo from an empty tomb. "Elizabeth, before she fell under your evil spell, had consented to be my wife, Kirkwood. Our families had neighboring estates in the country. I fell in love with her when we were both still children, and I watched her blossom from a sweet, lovable child to a radiant young woman." He began to stride about the room again, his anguish apparent to all.

"Our marriage had the blessing of both families, although, because she was still so young, her parents asked us to wait a year. We married on her seventeenth birthday. Can you imagine my shock when on our first night spent as man and wife, I discovered that she was not the sweet, pure angel I was in love with, unsullied by any man. When confronted, she tearfully confessed that she had had a dalliance with you."

"She pleaded with me to forgive her and I…well, I confess that I loved her so much, I assured her it didn't matter." His words were harsh and raw with pain.

"But I was wrong!" He paused in his oration, a sudden icy contempt flashing in his eyes as he cast his gaze once more on the man he blamed for his troubles. "It did matter, and she knew it. You were a shadow between us, Kirkwood. I was in torment every time I sought her bed, torturing myself, wondering if she was imagining it was your caress, your kiss." Sighing, he met the other's eyes. "I admit it freely, my jealousy was a poison that crept into our marriage and destroyed Elizabeth, my sweet love. With the passing months, she slowly faded, becoming quieter and sadder. But then she rallied when the fates offered her hope of a new beginning."

"She was with child, *my* child. But from the beginning, it was a difficult pregnancy and her labor long and hard. Neither my wife nor son survived." His voice faded to a haunted whisper. "And so you see me here, a mourning band on my arm and ice where my heart once rested."

Ben's head shot up in surprise. "You're blaming me, Peckworthy? I admit to having met her when I was visiting an elderly aunt with my father. And yes, I encouraged her to meet me secretly, but we were both so very young. Believe me when I say that I had no knowledge of her being spoken for, by you or anyone else."

A snort of disgust sounded from the other as he flew into a rage at the words that dismissed the entire episode as a youthful flirtation. "You ruined both Elizabeth's and my life, you immoral bastard."

He raised a clenched fist, prepared to lash out at this most detested of men, but cool reason returned before any blows were struck. Leopold, instantly alert, straightened his misshapen body as much as was possible, ready to defend the man he loyally regarded as his master. The other occupants of the room, prepared to fly to their friend's rescue, had also risen from their chairs but slowly resumed their seats. Bennett, seeing the threat disappear, moved away, not wanting to provoke violence in either of his unpredictable and thoroughly despicable visitors.

Giving an impatient shrug, he locked his hands behind his neck and his voice, when he at last spoke, was unyielding with no vestige of sympathy in its hardness. "All right, Peckworthy, you are determined to lay the blame for your unhappiness at my door. I accept some of the responsibility but not all."

He rose and stepped toward the door. "And now, if you're finished embarrassing me in front of my friends…"

"But I'm not finished, Kirkwood. Indeed, this is only the beginning." Mordock Peckworthy's words, though spoken softly, had an ominous, chilling quality.

"I must once again insist that you be seated and let me finish." Speechless at the man's gall, Ben resumed his seat.

Chapter Two

Mordock Peckworthy, with an impatient shrug of his bony shoulders, spread his hands out and studied his fingers, the faint chiming of an unseen clock seeming to fill the room. Abruptly, he looked intently at the foursome.

"I'm certain that I now have your complete attention, gentlemen, and so will reveal my plan, my revenge on our friend here, Mr. Bennett Kirkwood of Silverwood House. I trust you are all familiar with the phrase—'an eye for an eye'?" At their cautious nods, his lips twisted into a contemptuous smile. "Good, good. For that is precisely what I'm proposing."

At their perplexed expressions, his face became a marble effigy of condescension. "Surely at least one of you has some inkling!" He frowned, frustrated into a cold fury at their blank expressions.

"Must I spell it out?" He sighed in exasperation. "Kirkwood here stole my wife's virginity, therefore I claim the right of *'Prima Nocta'* or, if you prefer, *First Night*, a fine old medieval custom, with Miss Claire St. Martin or, as she will have already exchanged vows but little else, Mrs. Bennett Kirkwood." The stunned silence that followed his pronouncement filled the room.

There was a sudden threatening rumble of voices as the four rose to their feet, crowding menacingly around him, all of them momentarily forgetting the very real threat of Leopold who was already moving silently toward them. Signaling the servant to return to his post, Mordock Peckworthy stepped back, raising his hands in an attempt to placate the very real threat before him, his voice hardening ruthlessly as he again began speaking.

"Gentlemen, heed my words! I have thought long and hard on this matter, and I seek your agreement. Kirkwood took what was mine so I will in turn take what is his. But it will happen most discreetly, I assure you. With skill and a little luck, his bride, assuming she's as innocent as she looks, won't even be aware of anything amiss."

"My plan is a simple one—replace the bridegroom with another man! And please, before you state the obvious, I am not such a simpleton to think a woman, no matter how besotted or perhaps even frightened she might be on such a night, would fail to notice the physical difference between her new husband and myself. No, that deed would require another—someone who bears a strong physical likeness to the groom, both in build and height, someone such as Braxton Kane." At the mention of his name, all eyes looked speculatively at Braxton. A burning log crashed noisily into the embers of the fire, startling the reluctant conspirators.

"Are you insane, Peckworthy?" Braxton's deep voice filled the room. "Why would any one of us agree to such a preposterous plan? And in case you haven't noticed, although I admit we are similarly proportioned, the poor girl would have to be a simpleton not to notice I'm not Ben."

"Of course I've considered that—a mere stumbling block, nothing more." His long fingers met as he paused in his discourse, seeming to weigh his words before continuing on.

"Firstly, you will have to familiarize yourself with the layout of the bridal chamber. As Ben escorts his bride upstairs after the wedding festivities, he will instruct her to leave no light burning in her chamber. The weather will likely be warm and a fire would, hopefully, not be needed. He claims her modesty as the reason for this odd request, and she, in her innocence, considers her new husband a most thoughtful man, a true gentleman above all others."

Julius Chambers, his own voice cracking from such a prolonged silence, spoke up. "Have you, in your depraved scheme, considered the difference in voices? Braxton's voice is low and smooth while Ben's words are usually crisply spoken."

"Another barrier easily surmounted. Braxton must take care not to speak above a whisper. One man murmuring sweet words of love must surely sound much like another."

Braxton, fists clenched, rose and stood threateningly before Peckworthy, but the man was not to be intimidated. "Sit down, Kane. You're already aware that I wasn't foolish enough to enter this lion's den and make such a proposal totally unarmed!" All eyes again turned to Leopold who, unblinkingly, met their stares.

As Braxton attempted to spy out a weapon, Peckworthy laughed, a hollow, mirthless sound. "I'm under no illusion regarding my ability to defend myself against any one of you, hence the faithful Leopold. No, gentlemen, my weapon is power!"

"I sense your disbelief, but I am sure Mr. Kane will soon be willing to fall in with my plan." Catching Braxton's eyes he smiled, a cold gesture that offered no comfort. "I understand your half-brother accompanied you when you sailed from England?"

Braxton, taken aback with both the sudden shift in conversation and the man's knowledge, nodded suspiciously.

"Yes, I thought so. But, after crossing that wide ocean together, he chose to part company at the ship's first port of call. And you, dear fellow, feeling only relief at his disappearance, made no effort to find him." He sighed dramatically. "If only you had, a young lady's life might not have been so cruelly snuffed out."

Braxton's expression became one of mute wretchedness. Silently, he cursed the day his brother was born.

Pursing his lips into a smirk, the man smiled coldly. "Oh dear, have I let the proverbial cat out of the bag? Surely, your friends know that your half-brother is a monster, a depraved fiend! For the good of mankind, Braxton, you should have tossed him overboard when you had the chance. From what my agents have been able to learn, Patrick's uncle suffered from a similar affliction. Tell me, Braxton, when did you first suspect that your only sibling wasn't quite normal?" His words taunted Braxton. Glancing about the room, Mordock Peckworthy smiled coldly when he saw the four men regarding him with total abhorrence.

Peckworthy's voice hardened ruthlessly as he moved closer to his prey. "Enlighten me, Braxton! Were you relieved when you learned that Patrick's mother had died bringing the monster into the world and all you shared was a father—and that you had none of the strange cravings that seemed to consume him:" His voice faded to a whisper. "And what have you done to ensure he never returns to these shores?"

Braxton, ashen-faced and hands visibly trembling, looked up in disbelief. No, it wasn't possible! He had given him his share of the estate and in return, Patrick had sworn never to return to these shores.

"Your brother is currently languishing in a jail cell in New Orleans, a city on the other side of the world." He spoke in a tense, clipped voice that forbade any questions. "His freedom, or rather the lack of it, will depend on your cooperation in my little scheme."

Before Braxton could form a reply, Ben stood, jaw clenched and eyes slightly narrowed. His expression was tight with strain. "When you first laid out your proposal, Peckworthy, I thought you insane—now I am convinced of it. You should be locked away in Bedlam. If Patrick Kane is a monster, you are but another, you just wear a different guise. Leave my house this instant!"

Mordock Peckworthy turned and regarded his host, his expression contemptuous. "You, my friend, are being somewhat hasty. I have yet to reveal the final element of my plan."

His heart racing, Ben felt a sense of dread and foreboding fill his very being. He backed away from the man who had so quickly become his enemy, almost falling into a chair. The others followed his lead, regaining their seats and regarding the devil now standing before them.

As he sat there, he studied the distance from where he sat to his desk, knowing a loaded pistol rested in the middle drawer, trying to judge his chances of retrieving it before Leopold could react. Could he casually walk over to it without either of his unwelcome guests becoming suspicious? As he started to rise, Peckworthy spoke.

"You wouldn't be planning anything foolish, would you, Kirkwood? I really must insist you stay where you are." As Ben fell into his seat with a dull thud, the gaunt man strolled casually to the desk, quickly opening and closing drawers until he found what he had surmised would be there. Lifting out the pistol, he held it up. "Would this be the reason you were staring at your desk so intently?" He once again nodded to Leopold to remain where he was, assuring him that he had everything under control.

"Now, where was I? Ah, yes. As I mentioned earlier, Ben, you have been careless, leaving a number of signed notes around the various gaming houses that you frequent, not to mention that pesky tailor and others of his ilk. I, charitable soul that I am, have bought all of these notes and paid your outstanding debts, including this evening's debacle. You, my friend, now have only one creditor—me! A collective gasp escaped the four men as they stared in horror at the Machiavellian fiend standing in their midst.

Both Chambers brothers stood, ready to restrain Bennett Kirkwood or Braxton Kane, should either attempt to throttle the rogue for the effrontery he had thus far displayed. Slowly the tension eased as Ben assured the others he was in control of himself. Once more all eyes fell on the stocky, malevolent figure who continued to stand apart, muscles taut and fists clenched, waiting for a signal from his master that would launch him into battle.

Watching Ben closely, Peckworthy's pale face was marked with loathing. "Did you think to escape unscathed from your lecherous inclinations?" He held up a pale, bony hand to stop the protestations that threatened to pour from his captive audience.

"Should you decide not to participate in my plan, gentlemen, your friend will be thrown into debtor's prison. That would surely come as a shock to your social circle." A smirk continued to play about his thin lips as he faced his nemesis. "I'm not sure, Ben, that you would ever recover your position in society after release, assuming of course anyone even remembers you! And don't consider borrowing from your friends—I've maneuvered it so that I'm on the Board of Governors that administers your estate. The money to repay me must come from your pocket, no other!"

Once again, he surveyed the small party, his expression cruel and unnerving. "Well, Kirkwood, do we have an understanding?" His voice, though quiet, had an ominous quality.

Ben's voice was naught but a gravelly whisper as he nodded woodenly. "Yes."

The others, not totally surprised at his acquiescence, began arguing, but Bennett Kirkwood, shoulders slumped in defeat, knew he was beaten. He would have to dance to the tune that Peckworthy was playing. With an exhausted sigh, he stood up.

Teddy, incensed for his friend spoke, his tone contemptuous. "And

Oh Wicked Escort

what happens if the girl should fall pregnant? Is Ben expected to accept a babe possibly not his own?"

Peckworthy snapped his fingers together. "Oh yes, we have to be prepared for the unexpected. Should your bride prove to be fertile, it would be best if there was no doubt as to the babe's father."

"Braxton, I trust you will take every precaution. As for you, Kirkwood, I would suggest that you refrain from exercising your husbandly rights until you know for certain that your bride did not conceive on her wedding night. And if in spite of our planning, Miss St. Martin does prove to be in a family way, well, I leave it to you gentlemen to sort it out."

The intruder, knowing he had won, gave a slight nod of his head. "Kirkwood, I look forward to your wedding day, probably with less trepidation than you and Kane, not to mention your young bride." He chuckled softly at his drollness as he disappeared through the library door, his minion following closely on his heels. Scant seconds later, the sound of the front door closing behind the pair was heard.

The brothers had immediately burst into excited chatter, dispensing words of advice and promises of discretion should Bennett choose to challenge the bastard to a duel.

Characteristically, Braxton remained quiet and reflective, agonizing over the anguish he felt for not ensuring his brother never had the opportunity to harm anyone else, while trying to find a way out of the calamity that threatened his friend. Discarding the wilder ideas, the four men had sat, despondent at the lack of options open to them. It came down to obey or face the consequences.

Although it seemed many hours had passed since the despicable pair of rogues had departed, in truth it was little more than a single hour, and just when Ben thought he could bear no more discussion on the matter, his guests prudently took their leave, each vowing not to rest until a solution was found.

Not unlike one who carries the weight of the world on his slumped shoulders, Bennett Kirkwood slowly made his way up the stairs to his bed, where despite his exhaustion he spent the night tossing even as sleep claimed him, still seeking a solution to the very great problem of Mordock Peckworthy.

Chapter Three

The day had begun worryingly when Claire entered the breakfast room and saw that her host, Lord Magnus Jennings, was dining alone. An inquiring glance brought forth the somewhat hasty explanation that her father continued to feel unwell but hoped to join them for lunch. Sensing that Claire was about to retrace her footsteps back upstairs to her father's chamber, Lord Jennings quickly assured her that it was surely nothing more than a minor indisposition. Somewhat reassured, she slid gracefully onto the cushioned chair he held for her, and the two nibbled on the light breakfast set before them, chatting companionably until the last sip of tea had been swallowed.

Lord Jennings, a lifelong friend of her father, watched as the slender figure left the room, musing on the memory of Claire's mother. Elaine had been a beautiful woman, but he thought Claire surpassed her with that cloud of deep auburn hair curling softly around her face. And those eyes—such a rich deep brown, ringed by thick black lashes, eyes that seemed to look out on the world in wide-eyed innocence. He was aware that wherever they went, men's eyes followed her, captivated by the perfect oval of her face, which in turn emphasized the dusty rose of her cheeks and her exquisitely dainty nose. She had such a delicate, fragile air about her…it just made you want to protect her from any harm that might come her way. He shook his head, trying to clear his thoughts. Ah yes, he sighed, it was well that she was already engaged to be married.

As Claire made her way back to her bedchamber, she once more silently thanked the good graces of Lord Jennings for extending such a generous invitation to both his old friend, Pierre St. Martin and his daughter.

Reaching the top of the stairs, she smiled fondly as she looked down on the balding head of her host as he paused to give instructions to his housekeeper before setting out. Pondering on the kindness of the man she had known since her birth, she reflected on how much he had eased her entry into the whirl of London society.

Reaching her bedroom, she sat at her dressing table, absentmindedly brushing her auburn curls. Her thoughts wandered back to that darkest of days—the day that her home, a small manor buried deep in the Kent countryside, had been sold by the sheriff at auction to satisfy their creditors' demands.

Claire recalled her struggle to hold back her tears at the final humiliation, leaving their home for the last time—in a hired carriage! The St. Martins had indeed come down in the world. The mud-spattered windows of the carriage had failed to conceal her father's bowed head as he tried to ignore the curious looks of former neighbors who were witness to the departure of the once-proud St. Martin family. Salty tears had traced pathways down her pale cheeks as she caught a last glimpse of her former home. She had felt her father's loving hand stroking the rich auburn tresses that framed her face, the hair he had always declared was identical to her mother's, the woman who had died giving birth to her.

But it was also the day Lord Magnus Jennings' reply had arrived in answer to her father's frantic letter to him. He had apologized for the delay in responding but explained that he had been away in France on business. He invited—no, he had *insisted*—that both of them come immediately to London, declaring they would find that he, a lonely old widower, was just rattling around Romford House by himself. Since his daughters were both now married with young families, they preferred a rural life rather than the hustle and bustle of London.

Laying her hairbrush down, Claire wandered over to the casement window, happy to see the sun peeking cautiously out from behind a cloud. Smiling, she watched as two squirrels chased each other up and down the branches of a tree, scant inches from her. It brought to mind her only serious suitor, Edward Fisher, son of one of the wealthiest farmers in Kent.

She had known who he was of course, for all that he was almost ten years her senior, but their paths had often crossed on market days. Poor Edward. Papa had been pitiless in his blunt refusal to allow the man to court his daughter, claiming that such an exquisite beauty as Claire was destined for a much higher position in life than one spent milking cows and breeding babies. Word of the callous treatment meted out to the young man soon spread, and no other suitors were willing to feel the sharp edge of the elder St. Martin's tongue.

Claire was confused by her own emotions. True, the manor had been her home, one she shared with her father, and before she died, her maiden aunt Marie. Claire sighed as she thought of her recently deceased aunt. She had stressed to Claire that, though they might not have the servants or entertainments of the rich, Claire must learn the basics of managing a staff of servants and how to conduct oneself among the rich and privileged.

She had rarely mixed with the younger residents of the village, especially after the fiasco involving Edward Fisher. The elder St. Martin had soon found himself rebuffed by most of the villagers, those inhabitants suddenly recalling that the St. Martins had once been French aristocrats, living a privileged life, until they, like many other families of the time, had been forced to flee as crazed hordes battered down the gates of their chateau in France. The St. Martins had joined other desperate émigrés, all fleeing to England, all seeking sanctuary from Madam Guillotine.

But the move from Kent to London had been further blighted by her father's health. Claire had at first blamed the disastrous condition of their finances and the upheaval they had been forced to endure, but his cough and increasing weakness continued to worsen, the doctor Lord Jennings had sent for unable to affect a cure.

Since their arrival in the great city, her father seemed even more determined, desperately willing to go to any lengths to accomplish the task he had set for himself. He knew that he had shocked his beloved daughter when he confessed their poverty, having kept the state of their finances concealed from her while she was growing up. As he had crustily explained after watching the last of their holdings in the country sold, the money he had been able to squirrel away from the grasping fingers of their creditors would be used to find someone worthy of her.

"Indeed," he had spoken in his croaking voice, "if it's a rich husband we seek, we must travel in the same circles of society that he does. So, my dear, it's a new wardrobe for you and a tiny dowry, thereby putting to flight any rumor that might arise accusing us of being paupers or fortune hunters." He couldn't entertain the thought that a hint of gossip or scandal might touch his precious offspring.

Claire had attempted to dissuade him from his obsession of finding her such a man. She had brought out all of her arguments, reminding him once again that this was 1888, not the Middle Ages, desperately trying to make him understand she wanted to fall in love with the man she married. Sadly, this thought was dismissed as "a female weakness," and she merely a victim of Miss Jane Austen's romantic novels that she was always reading, filling her head with unseemly thoughts. Frustrated with herself for yielding to his plans, she prayed that it would all somehow work itself out, but with each attempt she made to reason with him, he would be seized with a fit of coughing, reminding her that it was cruel of her to upset him when he was so weak.

A small clock in the hallway chimed the hour of noon when Claire tapped lightly on her father's door. A muffled voice, much weaker than usual, bid her enter. Alarmed, she pushed the door open, her slippers whispering softly as she crossed the carpeted floor. The drapes hadn't been opened and no lamp was lit, but even in the dim light, Claire fought back a sense of unease as she gazed at the slight figure huddled beneath the covers.

"Papa…should I call the doctor?" She gently placed her hand on his forehead, her brow furrowed as she again brooded over the unknown cause of the malady that continued to plague her beloved parent. A claw-like hand reached out and grasped her fingers.

"Child, I've caught a slight chill, nothing more. I'm sure I'll be myself by tomorrow. A maid is fetching a cup of beef tea, and I plan doing nothing more strenuous than sleeping the day away." Smiling weakly, he patted her hand reassuringly.

Oh Wicked Escort

"Leave me to my rest, child. Lord Jennings' servants will attend me, and tomorrow you can regale me with the details of your evening. Please convey my apologies to Mr. Kirkwood."

Claire, seeing his weariness, kissed his forehead before tiptoeing from the room. Returning to her own bedchamber, she distracted herself with the selection of a gown for the coming evening.

Slender fingers plucked nervously at the folds of her velvet cape as Claire stole furtive glances at the man seated across from her. His aloof manner invited no conversation as he stared out at the dimly lit streets they were passing through. Once more, she pondered the decision of her beloved parent. He had been so ill of late. Was his determination to marry her off to the scion of the rich and respected Kirkwood family a wise one? A nagging voice in the back of her mind refused to be stilled from the worrying feeling that her fiancé was holding part of himself back from her. Bennett's manner seemed to be more distracted each time they met, and now, when she was about to meet his friends, he seemed totally unconcerned about her or her apprehensions.

Her musings were interrupted as the carriage slowed and then stopped, the door quickly opened by a servant who waited patiently to offer his assistance should either of them need it in their descent. Brushing the man brusquely aside, Bennett, at last aware of both her and their arrival at Julius's home, Shelton Hall, climbed down and turning, offered her his hand.

Tucking her arm through his own, they slowly mounted the steps just as the door was opened by a second servant, casting a welcoming light onto the new arrivals.

Chapter Four

After surrendering their cloaks to a hovering servant, Bennett caught Claire lightly by the elbow, guiding her toward a pair of paneled doors that stood slightly ajar. The hum of conversation from within the room drifted out toward them.

As he pushed open the door, the subdued chatter inside the room slowly came to a halt, and all eyes turned expectantly toward them. One of the men broke away from the small assembly and hurried forward, a welcoming but curious look on his face as he determinedly brushed back his mop of unruly brown hair.

"My dear, allow me to introduce an old friend of mine, Julius..."

Nodding a brief greeting at Ben, Julius didn't wait for the introduction to finish, enveloping Claire's dainty hands in his own larger ones.

"And you have to be none other than the exquisite Miss Claire St. Martin, the beauty who has all of London society talking. Welcome to Shelton Hall, Miss St. Martin." He hesitated briefly before continuing. "Shall we dispense with formalities, which can be so very tedious, and just address each other by our first names?" Not waiting for a reply, he continued. "I for one am very happy to make your acquaintance, Claire."

A faint blush colored Claire's cheeks at his words. He cocked his head jauntily to one side before taking her arm from the proprietary grasp of her escort, advancing toward those already gathered with a determined smile on his face.

Leading her to the three women who frostily watched their approach, he patted her hand familiarly, as if to reassure her that she was not alone. Claire drew back imperceptibly from the women who remained motionless, all of them unabashedly assessing her from top to toe. Claire suddenly felt uncomfortable, as if she had been appraised and found wanting.

"Miss Claire St. Martin, may I present my wife, Minerva, her sister Miranda, and their mother, Letitia Penrod." The three women nodded their heads in the briefest of acknowledgements. "Miranda is married to my brother Teddy, who understandably of course, seems to be utterly mesmerized by you."

At this comment, all eyes turned to the younger Chambers brother who flushed at being caught gawking like a schoolboy. His wife sniffed indignantly, her eyes promising serious reprisals when they next found themselves alone. Claire's voice, as she acknowledged the introductions, was soft and clear, her words warm and friendly, an enchantingly shy smile touching her full lips.

Silver hair piled in an elaborate coiffure, the tall and daunting figure of Letitia Penrod stepped forward, dwarfing both her daughters and sons-in-law by some inches. She peered down her very patrician nose at Claire before extending a few icy words of greeting.

"So pleased to meet you, my dear." Her words, delivered in such a cool and patronizing tone, left no doubt in Claire's mind that meeting her was giving the older woman no pleasure whatsoever. Turning, the Penrod matriarch imperiously beckoned her daughters forward.

The two stepped into the small circle, nodding their blond heads in greeting, envy and curiosity unbridled as they coolly eyed the newcomer. Claire felt somewhat overdressed as she returned their collective stares.

Recalling how she had agonized over what to wear before finally settling on a gown of blue velvet with the sleeves and skirt trimmed in a paler shade of blue satin, a choice motivated more for warmth than fashion on this cool spring evening, she realized nothing she possessed would have been acceptable. The three women were clothed similarly in black crepe with small touches of white lace at the necks and sleeves. Both daughters also wore their pale blond hair piled in elaborate coiffures, replicas of their mother's greying tresses. Noting her questioning glance, the elder of the two daughters spoke.

"We're still in mourning for our dear papa, Miss St. Martin...I mean, Claire." Suddenly unsure of herself, she paused and then smiled hesitantly. "He died several months ago." Flushing, she glanced at her mother.

"Now, now, Minerva," she chided. "We don't want to bore Miss St. Martin with our personal tragedies." The older woman turned back to Claire, her lips twisted into a disdainful smile. She regarded the girl with a degree of cool haughtiness before remembering her manners, and with a regal flourish of her hand, motioned the other two men in the room forward.

Teddy Chambers, glancing uneasily at his sharp-eyed wife, edged out the second man and hastily seized Claire's fingers in his own, kissing them in what he optimistically hoped was a suave, continental manner. Letitia Penrod glanced contemptuously down at her slightly built son-in-law. "And this, Miss St. Martin, is my Miranda's husband, Theodore, who for some reason known only to himself, insists on being addressed as Teddy."

A blushing Claire attempted to retrieve her fingers from his eager grasp. "Teddy, behave yourself. Claire is spoken for, and you, sir, already have a wife—the lovely Miranda." Teddy Chambers flushed at the joking admonishment as Bennett Kirkwood took his place beside his fiancée.

Drawing the one person forward she had not yet met, Bennett spoke. "Claire, may I present Braxton Kane, my oldest and dearest friend."

She once again had her slender hands enveloped in a stranger's grasp. His voice was resonant and impressive. "Miss St. Martin, it is indeed a pleasure to meet you at last."

As her hands were released, Claire found herself gazing into warm grey eyes. A tall, handsome man returned her gaze, successfully disarming her with his smile, a smile she found impossible not to return. Turning to her betrothed, her deep brown eyes met his blue ones, eyes that seemed to be mocking her. Suddenly unsure of herself, she smiled tremulously, her white teeth flashing between lush pink lips.

The butler, standing stiffly in the doorway, announced that dinner was served. Letitia Penrod, grasping Braxton's arm tightly, led the way into the dining room where servants hovered. Over the tinkle of silver cutlery scraping delicately against sparkling china, talk of the upcoming wedding dominated the conversation until, steered by Letitia, it suddenly centered on Braxton Kane's bachelorhood and thinly veiled but very

Oh Wicked Escort

probing questions concerning his assets.

Braxton, with tendrils of dark hair falling onto his forehead, laughingly protested, declaring himself unworthy of any matchmaking efforts on her part. "In point of fact, Mrs. Penrod, I fear Ben, and of course your two sons-in-law, have captured the best that London has to offer, and so I am quite content to remain a bachelor, at least for the time being."

Much giggling could be heard from the two sisters at such an extravagant declaration while Claire, blushing prettily, bowed her head in acknowledgement of the compliment.

As the last course was removed from the table, the moment that Claire had been dreading arrived. Mrs. Penrod, assuming the role of hostess over that of her daughter Minerva, excused the ladies, leading them to the drawing room while the gentlemen remained at the table to enjoy their brandy and cigars. As the door closed behind them, Minerva Chambers unobtrusively took Claire's arm and steered her toward a comfortable sofa, smilingly talking of weddings and such, making a half-hearted effort to put the younger woman at ease. Claire glanced apprehensively across the room, watching as the other two women continued their whispered conversation, casting many a dark glance in her direction.

Mrs. Penrod at last approached them, and with a nod toward a piano standing in the corner, fixed a cold smile on her face as she addressed Claire. "Do you play, Miss St. Martin?" Not waiting for a response, she nodded to her daughters who obediently made their way to the instrument. Minerva sat down, fussing with the folds of her dress while Miranda quickly leafed through sheets of music. In whispers, the two sisters agreed on a selection and ever so softly, music filled the room. Miranda's voice trilled out in song, a pleasant but uninspiring sound.

At last, the men joined them, leaving their lively discussion of politics and the like in the dining room. As all drew near the crackling fire, a silence fell over the room as Braxton Kane raised his wine glass, toasting his friend and Claire.

Accepting the group's good wishes, Bennett paused before he spoke. "I know all of you wish the best for us, but it has just struck me that our wedding would indeed be a sorry occasion if you, my friends, were absent. True, it will be a very small affair due to the extreme age of my relatives, most of whom have no wish to travel, even across the city. There is also a lack of family on Claire's side, not to mention the poor health of her father, but surely Mr. St. Martin will not find it too disturbing to have all of you in attendance."

As his eyes swept the room, he was surprised to see Claire looking at him in astonishment. He suddenly became uncomfortably aware that he should have discussed this with her beforehand, but the idea had been both impulsive and inspired. It solved any problem of explaining the presence of Peckworthy. Tentatively, he took her arm as everyone looked on.

"My dear Claire, I do so hope this meets with your approval." Flustered at being thrust into such an awkward position, she could only smile, assuring him that it was a lovely idea, one she should have thought of herself.

The evening wore on until wraps and cloaks were at last fetched and the final good-byes spoken, everyone assuring the affianced couple of their intention to attend their nuptials in three weeks' time. As she was helped into the carriage, Claire felt as if the silken bonds of matrimony were quickly turning into shackles of steel.

Chapter Five

The days leading up to the wedding passed in a flurry of activity, for if Claire wasn't serving tea to an acquaintance of the Kirkwood family, Bennett was whisking her about London, meeting those relatives who were too frail to travel any distance. *At least I haven't had to suffer the company of Letitia Penrod or her daughters*, she thought, *although seeing Braxton Kane hasn't been too much of a hardship.* It was indeed a much more cheerful outing whenever he joined them. Despite enjoying his small attentions when Bennett seemed preoccupied, which seemed to be almost always, Claire couldn't help but wonder why Braxton, a handsome and most charming man indeed, seemed so willing to accompany them on what must seem to him to be very tedious and inconsequential visits. And when at last her day was done, she would return to Romford House, hastening to her father's side, only to find his condition unimproved.

Lord Jennings, meeting her at breakfast one dismal morning, sat and chatted with her. He no longer tried to assure her that the illness her father was suffering from was a minor indisposition. Many doctors had been consulted, and all agreed that every possible avenue of treatment had been exhausted. They had advised him to get his affairs in order.

Claire, thinking out loud that dismal grey morning, mentioned that she was considering postponing her wedding, but Lord Jennings insisted that might hasten her father's end, sure that he was clinging to the threads of life so he might see her safely wed. And so Claire, with many misgivings, allowed the preparations to proceed.

Less than a week before the nuptials, Lord Jennings invited Bennett to join Claire and himself for lunch at Romford House. He had been hearing rumblings for some time about young Bennett Kirkwood that cast a shadow over his character, and so the well-intentioned gentleman now sought to know the younger man better, hoping the rumors would prove to be without substance. Assuming the role of protector of Pierre's charming daughter was the least he could do for his old friend.

Pierre St. Martin, a pale, wizened shadow of his former self but feeling fitter than he had in some weeks, joined them as they were having tea and dessert. He was helped to a chair beside the crackling fire, the room being cool and damp from the rain that had fallen that morning. A steaming cup of tea was placed on the table beside him. Smiling into his daughter's worried eyes, he patted her hand reassuringly.

Looking at his old friend, his tired eyes twinkled. Holding Claire's chin gently, he spoke. "Magnus, look at her. Isn't she the very picture of her mother?" Claire blushed at being the center of attention but was delighted to see her parent in such good spirits. Lord Jennings nodded his agreement, recalling the beautiful woman who had died some seventeen years ago giving birth to the young girl now standing before him.

Remembering the presence of their guest, Lord Jennings beckoned Bennett into their intimate circle. It had been some time since Ben had seen the old man, his inquiries to Claire regarding the health of her sire being met with worried looks and brief reports of what the doctors had said on their infrequent visits. A sudden flash of inspiration struck the younger man.

Barely managing to speak in a low, composed voice, he addressed the others. "Lord Jennings, Mr. St. Martin, if I might beg your indulgence by suggesting that Claire and Mr. St. Martin take up residence in Silverwood House before the wedding? I am painfully aware that society might frown at such a move, but sir, you have been unwell. In your weakened state, you will need time to recover from such an upheaval." He paused, giving both men little time to consider before continuing. "That is, if you plan on attending your daughter's wedding."

Claire, surprised at his suggestion but touched at her fiancé's concern hesitantly agreed, adding her support to his proposal. The two older men looked doubtfully at each other, both weighing the benefits of such a proposition. Pierre St. Martin fell back against the cushions of his chair, his hands held up in a gesture of surrender.

"Well, children, when shall we make this move?" Lord Jennings softly patted his friend's thin shoulder, silently assuring him of his support. Bennett, his mouth spreading into a thin-lipped smile, spoke in a voice full of authority.

"Then it's settled. Claire, will tomorrow be too soon to expect you? Mrs. Dixon, my housekeeper, has been bustling about for days, preparing Silverwood for its new mistress. I doubt she'll need much notice, but there are a few loose ends I must attend to. Claire, gentlemen, I bid you a good day." He nodded his head in deference before disappearing through the doorway.

The three stared at each other as the door closed quietly behind him, astonishment written across their faces. A decision had been made, but it somehow felt as though they had no part in it, a feeling that was becoming all too familiar to Claire.

As Bennett mounted his horse, he had already begun planning. Deciding that Braxton Kane had to be at the top of his list, he nudged his mount in the direction of his friend's home. A short time later, Ben found himself facing a very reluctant Braxton.

"What do you mean you're having misgivings? Braxton, you agreed!" Ben's angry voice held a note of panic.

Braxton's grey eyes darkened warningly. "I don't know how I can make it any clearer, Ben, but yes, I am having second thoughts. When it was a stranger we were talking about, I thought I could go through with it, but I've met Claire now. Somehow, that changes things. How can I be party to such an enormous deception on one so trusting and innocent?"

"You know Peckworthy was probably hoping for this very thing to happen, for you to back out. He knew I would trust no other in such a delicate situation!" He paced about the room, both despair and desperation weighing heavily on him. "He'll ruin me, Braxton." His mind began to frantically clutch at straws. "And what of his threat concerning your brother, released onto an unsuspecting world?"

Bennett's voice was pleading as he stood in front of the man he had thought of as his ally, the same man who now held his future in his hands, his only chance to avoid the ruinous scandal that threatened. In desperation, he grasped the lapels of Braxton's jacket, his blue eyes fixed intently on the face of his old friend. Finger by finger, Braxton pried the other man's hands free.

He stared at Bennett Kirkwood, a man who suddenly seemed a stranger rather than someone he had shared so many boyhood adventures with, someone with whom he had grown up. How could he truly contemplate letting another man, no matter who that man was, share his wife's bed, especially on that most momentous first night, or, he paused in his thoughts, what was it Peckworthy had called it? Oh yes, *Prima Nocta!* He sighed heavily. "All right, Ben, stop carrying on so! I'll do it."

The change in the other's face passed from incredulous disbelief to unrestrained joy mixed generously with waves of relief. "Oh, thank you, Braxton, thank you." The transformation in Ben's demeanor was swift as he struggled to gain control of himself, almost sobbing as he expressed his gratitude. "I'll make it up to her somehow, Braxton, you'll see. But hopefully she'll never find out."

Feeling himself master of the situation once more, he turned toward the door, pausing in midstride when he realized his friend wasn't following him. Looking across the room questioningly, he spoke.

"Braxton? Are you coming?" His voice was again rough with anxiety. "One piece of advice that scheming bastard gave me was sound—you, my friend, have to learn the layout of the master bedroom. And since Claire and her father are moving in tomorrow, we only have tonight." Shrugging his shoulders in resignation, Braxton followed him from the house.

Pierre St. Martin had indeed needed time to recover moving from Lord Jennings' home to Silverwood House, but Claire, taking her breakfast with him each morning, had found him determined to attend the ceremony. She felt a momentary rush of gratitude toward Bennett, for it was he who had suggested the marriage vows be spoken right here in the manor, thus avoiding any undue strain even the short carriage ride to the nearby church would impose on the old man.

Oh Wicked Escort

And Bennett has certainly proven to be a stalwart supporter, thrusting himself into Mrs. Dixon's domain, insisting on her heeding both his and my own wishes for the wedding supper itself. Smiling, she pictured the inflexible housekeeper retreating in defeat when faced with Bennett's stubborn determination to have his way on this most important of days.

But, she mused, *if he's so wonderful, why do I continue to have misgivings about him?*

A breathless Betty Sims, carrying a small bouquet of flowers, rushed up the stairs to her new mistress's bedchamber, a sprinkling of freckles clearly evident on her flushed face. Smiling as she opened the door, she crossed the room to where Miss Claire so very patiently waited. She presented the flowers to the bride and was rewarded with her shy, sweet smile. Betty's hand reached out and felt her mistress's hair, satisfied that it was indeed dry enough to begin arranging it. Yesterday evening Betty had washed her mistress's lustrous auburn tresses, and now the talented maid swept it up into a cluster of ringlets, weaving a string of pearls through the curls.

As she worked, Betty had chatted, hesitantly at first but was soon going on nonstop, confiding to her mistress the sad tale of her sister Rosie, who had recently been deserted by her husband, a man who had proven to be not only a drinker but bone idle as well. The scoundrel had left Rosie with a son, small for his age and sickly, with no money for food or rent except that which Betty could spare. Desperately in need of cheaper lodging, Betty had taken her unfortunate sister and nephew in hand, packing their few meager belongings and moving them to Whitechapel, that area of London where the poorest of the poor struggled to eke out an existence. The sad tale had captured enough of Claire's attention to distract her from the relentless ticking of the clock.

But, as it must, the hands of the grandfather clock in the main hall of the house chimed out the hour. Claire, knowing there was less than an hour before her life would be changed forever, felt her heart flutter, unsure if it was from nervous excitement or apprehension. The clatter of carriages arriving followed by voices raised in greeting floated up to the two women as they began to put the finishing touches to Claire's toilette.

Her mother's wedding gown lay draped across the bed. It had been lovingly packed away almost twenty years ago and luckily had needed little in the way of refurbishment. A wistful smile played about her lips as she tenderly stroked the satin gown, tracing the delicate roses embroidered on both the bodice and skirt. Her mind flew back over the years to all those times when her father had heeded his child's plea and told the story of the day he married her mother, recalling how beautiful his bride had been. And when Claire and Bennett had announced their intention to wed, both she and old Pierre had been thrilled beyond words to find the dress a perfect fit for her own wedding day.

Slipping the gown over her head, Claire waited patiently while the maid fastened the bodice and fussed with the skirt. Just when she thought she couldn't remain still a minute longer, there was a soft knock at the door.

"Claire, it's time." Lord Jennings' voice was hushed. Betty skipped over to the door to admit the man who would walk Claire down the aisle. Pierre St. Martin had made that painful decision the day before the wedding, at last admitting to himself that his feebleness might possibly mar this most important of days. Unwilling to risk it, he had asked his old friend to stand in for him.

Lord Jennings stood in the doorway, a broad smile signaling his delighted approval of the vision that stood before him. Claire, murmuring her thanks to the maid, smiled shyly up at the man before taking the arm he extended to her, the two moving ever so regally down the hallway to the staircase.

A flicker of apprehension again coursed through her as they slowly descended the circular stairs, causing Claire to grip Lord Jennings' arm even tighter as she ignored the tiny voice that whispered to her, a voice that urged her to flee before it was too late.

Glancing down at those assembled below, she searched the sea of faces until at last she found the one she loved above any other. Seated near the improvised altar, her father's twinkling eyes and glowing smile held her as Lord Jennings led her to the waiting groom.

Bennett, resplendent in a blue frock coat with a deeper blue waistcoat and trousers, stepped forward and took her hand, barely glancing down at her as they both turned to the waiting vicar. Vows were exchanged, his delivered in a crisp, clear voice but those in attendance could only assume she had spoken, for her voice was little more than a soft and tremulous whisper. After the clergyman had intoned the final benediction, the guests surged around the newlyweds, all clamoring to be first in extending their congratulations and good wishes.

Claire felt the minutes tick by as she was embraced by people she barely knew, slowly making her way to where her father sat, his smiling face beaming up at her as he watched her graceful approach to his chair.

Taking her hand, he stood up, a trifle unsteady but doggedly determined to enjoy the day he had long anticipated. Lord Jennings appeared at his side, ready to lend an arm should the need arise. Both men kissed her lightly on her flushed cheeks, hoping they could keep this enchanting creature to themselves, at least for a few minutes, but Bennett chose that moment to seek her out.

"Gentlemen, I do apologize but there's someone…an old school chum…who's most interested in meeting my bride."

Claire, too startled by the brusqueness of his words to resist, allowed herself to be led away. Both men stared after them, recalling the bits of gossip about the bridegroom that Lord Jennings had heard and, out of concern, had discussed briefly with the bride's father. In the end, they had decided it was just that—idle gossip. A flicker of apprehension coursed through Pierre St. Martin, wondering if his obstinacy on the subject of his daughter's marriage would be her undoing.

Choosing to ignore the shocked expressions on the faces of the two men they had just left, Bennett held his bride's arm tightly, hurriedly steering her through the knot of people, paying no heed to greetings from well-wishers, single-mindedly intent on reaching a figure that stood, almost menacingly, in the furthest and most secluded corner of the room.

Stopping in front of the stranger, Claire noticed the sheen of perspiration on her new husband's forehead and marveled at the effect this stranger seemed to have on him, for Bennett was definitely on edge, the tension almost palpable. His blue eyes darkened as he held her gaze for a brief second.

"Claire, may I introduce you to…" he hesitated ever so slightly before continuing, "an old school chum, Mordock Peckworthy."

Claire shivered almost imperceptibly as haunted eyes pierced the distance between them as he coldly studied her. He reached out and drew her toward him, his cold hand carrying hers to his lips for a fleeting second. The man was almost skeletal, his copper hair slightly longer than fashion dictated.

"Mrs. Kirkwood, I am most truly delighted to meet you at last. Bennett has indeed been remiss in his duty to introduce you to London and his old friends."

Awkwardly she cleared her throat. "I'm very pleased to meet you, Mr. Peckworthy." She became increasingly uneasy under his scrutiny and glanced up at Bennett, who seemed to be hovering anxiously over her.

Glancing around, Claire smiled uncertainly at the man. "Is Mrs. Peckworthy with you?" She heard a sharp intake of breath from Bennett at her innocent question.

A grim smile flitted across the man's face. "Unfortunately, madam, my wife died some months ago in childbirth."

It was only then that Claire spied the black mourning band on his arm. She stiffened, momentarily flustered. "Oh, I'm so very sorry, Mr. Peckworthy. Please forgive me."

He sighed heavily, his voice filled with anguish. "Please, gracious lady, don't let my heartache spoil your day." Derision and sympathy were mingled in his glance, leaving Claire blinking with bemusement.

It was at that moment that dinner was announced. Guests began forming into pairs, waiting for the newlyweds to take the lead. The young couple, excusing themselves from this most peculiar of guests, took their place at the head of the line and led the small procession into the dining room where servants patiently waited to begin serving the meal.

As Bennett held the chair for her, he felt some sort of explanation was necessary. Clearing his throat, he began speaking, his words as cool and clear as ice water. "I take it you didn't care for Peckworthy? Have no fear, my sweet, for you'll never be in his company again after this day ends. I wouldn't have invited him had he not been so insistent and very,

very persuasive."

Sensing something vaguely disturbing in her new husband's manner, she watched him pensively as he sat down beside her. Her hands, hidden from sight, twisted nervously in her lap until her attention was caught by the recently widowed Letitia Penrod leading a reluctant Lord Jennings to the table. Noticing Claire watching him, he loosened the grip the older woman had on his arm and made his way to the young couple.

"Claire, your father was exhausted by the excitement of the day and decided to have his meal in his room. He didn't want you to worry so he just slipped away." Seeing her distress, he patted her arm, reassuring her that all was well and her father would see her in the morning. He bowed to the couple, and stiffening his shoulders in resignation, returned to the waiting widow.

As the guests found their chairs, the servants began setting platters of steaming food before them, the sound of cutlery tinkling against china soon prevailing over the chatter, which slowly subsided, replaced by delicate smacking of lips and appreciative grunts as appetites were appeased.

Braxton stood, wine glass raised, as he toasted the newlyweds. "I have only known Claire for a few short weeks but am already aware that Bennett Kirkwood is indeed the luckiest of men. He has, without a doubt, captured not only the most beautiful but the sweetest woman in all of England. Raise your glasses, ladies and gentlemen, to the very exquisite Claire Kirkwood."

Blushing in embarrassment at his words, Claire's eyes met Braxton's, startled at the smoldering flame she saw there—the very air around her suddenly seemed electrified. She reluctantly became aware of everyone joining Braxton in wishing her good health and happiness. Rising gracefully, she stood beside Bennett as he drank deeply while she did little more than sip, her heart still beating wildly within her breast.

Mentally she stood back and shook herself. *What's wrong with me? I've just married one man and am flirting with another—and that man, my husband's best friend!*

Finally, after many more toasts extolling the virtue and beauty of the bride or the shrewdness of the groom for claiming her before anyone else knew of her existence, the supper, which had seemed interminable to

Claire, at last ended. Slowly the guests dispersed into small groups, the women chatting, the men making ribald remarks as they all slowly wandered into the sitting room where a maid and footman stood ready to serve tea, coffee, or something a little stronger. Conversation was desultory, and yawns were being politely hidden behind fans, the wedding and dinner having taken up the whole of the evening. The elderly guests were the first to leisurely saunter toward the entrance hall where servants stood waiting to fetch wraps.

Claire found herself embraced once more by Lord Jennings, who planted a fatherly kiss on her brow before wishing her a good night. A smirk on Bennett's face made him realize his words were being misconstrued, and he harrumphed in embarrassment before stepping into the brisk night air where his carriage and driver awaited.

As he stepped outside, a small group of well-wishers, consisting of silver-haired old ladies who were still lively enough to travel about the city, pinched the cheeks of the bridal couple, singing bawdy ditties as they recalled their own lost youth as they made their way out.

Letitia and her daughters, bestowing light kisses of farewell and promises of future visits, once again wished the young couple well. Julius and Teddy smiled down at her, amusement playing across their faces. Bennett, seeing their leers and knowing what must be going through their minds, scowled fiercely, his cobalt eyes hooded like those of a hawk. Warned, Julius turned away, but Teddy, a casualty of too much liquor, foolishly continued to ogle her, his interest plainly evident for all to see.

"Teddy!" It was Miranda's voice that cut through the awkward silence, her contemptuous tone sparked with anger. He sighed in exasperation, knowing she would not be happy until she had delivered a bitterly jealous harangue, touching on all points of his appalling behavior before allowing him to seek the peaceful haven of his bed.

How can I placate this carping shrew so I might have some peace? Following her through the door, his mind was already spinning, for Teddy, as well as loving to collect gossip, was equally content sharing it. *I could give the bitch a hint of what's going to happen tonight, not the whole story, just a tidbit. That might earn me some peace and quiet.* He stopped in midstride. *What am I thinking? Ben and Braxton would kill*

Oh Wicked Escort

me if I told anyone about their dirty little secret. I'd better promise Miranda a new gown—that'll keep her quiet.

As the door closed behind the last of their guests, Claire realized she hadn't said good night to Braxton or the very peculiar Mr. Peckworthy. Voicing her concern, Bennett assured her they hadn't left, but since both were too far under the influence of the numerous toasts and whatever else they had to drink, had begged to spend the night. Since she was busy with the Chambers brothers and Mrs. Penrod, he had asked Mrs. Dixon to show them to rooms in the same wing that her father occupied. Both men had asked him to convey their very good wishes to her and promised they would apologize to her personally at breakfast.

Shrugging in puzzlement at this odd turn of events, Claire met the brooding eyes of her new husband. "I'm just going to look in on my father, Bennett."

Seizing her arm as she turned away, he whirled her back toward him, his gaze falling to the creamy expanse of her bosom. He peered at her intently, his compelling eyes riveting her to the spot. She caught a faint whiff of wine and cigars clinging to him.

His voice was tender, almost a murmur. "I'm sure your father has long been asleep, Claire, but check if you must." He turned away but just as quickly turned back. "Don't be long, my dear. I'll come to you shortly. And please, Claire, trust me when I say to have no lamp lit in your chamber. You'll find yourself less self-conscious in a darkened room, at least on this, our first night spent as man and wife."

Cheeks flushed with embarrassment, Claire nodded, eyes downcast as she quickly climbed the stairs, her skirt swirling with each step she took.

Chapter Six

Reassured after noiselessly peeking in on her peacefully slumbering parent, Claire quietly entered her own bedchamber. A flustered Betty had jumped up, trying to hide the fact that she had fallen asleep awaiting her mistress's return. Laughing nervously, Claire barely glanced at the maid. "Unfasten me, Betty, and then seek your own bed."

If Claire were to be truthful, at least to herself, she desired nothing more than to be alone. She was nervous about what was to come and wanted no distraction. Sitting in front of the mirror, brushing her auburn curls, she wondered about the night ahead. She had lived her entire life in the country, her only companions the village children, all of whom were quite willing to share their own scant knowledge with her. Blushing at her own thoughts, she glanced in the mirror, wondering if she would look any different on the morrow.

As she clambered into what suddenly seemed like a huge bed, she remembered Bennett's request. *Is darkness a normal request or is he just being exceedingly thoughtful?* Blowing out the single candle that still burned, she burrowed under the covers, her eyes roaming the now-darkened room. A muffled noise alerted her to the door that led to a smaller bedroom adjoining the master bedroom. The sound seemed to echo through the room. Claire's heart suddenly started beating rapidly as the door opened fully. Her ears followed what her eyes could not see.

The connecting door whispered shut, and footsteps quietly crossed the floor. The mattress sagged with the weight of someone sitting down. Claire strained her eyes but the blackness that enveloped the room was total. The one who had joined her whispered her name as he lifted the covers and stretched out beside her.

He gathered her into his arms, murmuring into her hair, his breath hot against her ear. Softly, as his breath fanned her face, his lips pressed against hers, gently covering her mouth, gradually becoming more demanding, forcing her lips open with his thrusting tongue. She was shocked at her own eager response as his hungry mouth seared a path down her neck, his kisses sending spirals of excitement through her.

Claire felt her nightgown being torn from her, and blushing, knew he was in a like state. Gently his hand outlined the circle of her breasts, his tongue tantalizing the buds, which had swollen to their fullest. She clutched at his shoulders, stroking the strong tendons in the back of his neck as she felt his caress, light and teasing. His lips continued downward, exploring her soft ivory flesh.

Sensing the awakening flames within her, his expert touch sent her instinctively arching toward him, shivers of delight following his every caress. His hands explored the soft lines of her back, her waist, her hips, his lips slowing tracing a sensuous path to ecstasy. She struggled for breath as he lowered his body over hers, bare chest meeting bare chest, gasping in sweet agony and then, together, they found the tempo that bound their bodies together.

She was filled with an amazing sense of completeness as she felt him fall onto the bed beside her. He picked up a lock of her hair and caressed it gently. Whispering as if afraid of being overheard, he rose from the bed. "I must leave you for now, my love."

Shocked and bewildered, she heard him shrugging into his dressing gown. "Why do you have to leave?" Her words were harsh as she waited for some sort of explanation. Impatiently, she repeated the question. "Why do you have to leave, Bennett? Surely everyone expects us to share a bed now we are wed."

"I'm sorry, my love. I'll see you at breakfast."

His words were whispered so softly, she wasn't sure he had spoken. Pensively she stared into the blackened room, trying to see his face, but the only sound she heard was the soft closing of a door.

I've acted like a harlot! I've disgusted him by behaving like some wanton slut! Illogical thoughts chased each other around in her head as she desperately sought to grasp some understanding. *Why did he leave?* Tears slowly coursed down her cheeks as, trembling, she slipped on a fresh nightgown. Another thought dawned on her, one that made her smile. *Of course, he could just be overly considerate of my feelings. Perhaps he thought I might find it awkward this first morning if he were in my bed.* The sun was already peeping over the horizon before she at last fell into an exhausted slumber.

❀   ❀   ❀

As Braxton made his way quietly down the hallway, a door opened and a freckled hand beckoned him to enter.

"Well, is the deed accomplished?" Braxton, recognizing the demanding, caustic voice of Mordock Peckworthy, stepped into the room.

Spitting out his answer, Braxton looked about before spying Ben sitting on the corner of the unused bed, a hangdog expression on his face, his entire being slumped in dejection. Braxton, his own face flushed with humiliation and anger, paced the room.

"I have to go, Ben," he choked out. The other, wrapped in a cloak of misery, nodded.

A cackle of glee came from the author of their mutual misfortune, his florid self-satisfied face mocking both of them. "I'm afraid I also must take my leave, Kirkwood, for I'm off to Winchester in the morning."

Turning to Bennett as he donned cloak and gloves, he paused, a soft chuckle barely audible. "Chin up, Kirkwood. You'll soon get used to the idea that another stole your wedding night from you. And if not, well…" His voice trailed off as he left the room, maniacal laughter following him as he made his way down the stairs. Braxton, not wanting any further contact with the man, went to his own room to dress before he too fled, his anger slowly evaporating, leaving only confusion in its place.

❀   ❀   ❀

Bright sunshine streamed into the room as Betty pulled the heavy drapes apart, the smile on her face suddenly replaced by a worried frown as she saw the lonely figure struggling to sit up. Looking at her mistress's downcast expression, she wondered what had transpired during the night. As Claire climbed out of the rumpled bed, the sharp-eyed maid caught a glimpse of a stain on the white sheet. *Well, at least he was here for part of the night, and if they've had a lovers' spat, well, they'll soon make it up.*

"We'll have to hurry, madam. Your husband and father await you downstairs. According to Mrs. Dixon, that very peculiar Mr. Peckworthy left in the middle of the night, laughing like a madman. She says it sent shivers down her spine just hearing it. And that nice Mr. Kane left at the same time. Mrs. Dixon told me neither of their beds had been slept in. She thinks it very odd indeed."

It was sometime later that Claire, deep in thought, found herself at the dining room door. She hesitated, suddenly shy at the thought of greeting her new husband and her father. *Well, I have to face them some time.* Chin held high, she pushed the door open.

"Claire." Her father's voice, weak but adoring, greeted her first. She smiled affectionately at him just as her attention was caught by Bennett. His lips were twisted into a mocking smile, his expression almost aloof. Hesitantly she stood there, uncertainty slowing her steps. As if just becoming aware of her presence, he stood, a spark of some indefinable emotion in his eyes.

"Good morning, Claire." Bennett, face flushed, rose and moved toward her. Holding her elbow almost possessively, he escorted her to a chair.

She smiled shakily at her father who, lost in the misery of his illness, had failed to notice the demeanor of his son-in-law. "Father, did you sleep well?" Fortunately, neither of the men noticed the tremor in her voice.

His watery eyes looked lovingly at his daughter. "I fear, my darling daughter, that in spite of a night spent slumbering, undisturbed though it was, I must once again seek my bed."

Claire, glancing at his untouched breakfast, felt a deep sense of foreboding. Mrs. Dixon, who had been waiting to serve her new mistress, quickly called for two servants. There was a brief stir as they helped the old man stand, and supporting him on either side, slowly and cautiously made their way to his bedchamber.

Rising gracefully, she started to follow her father but Bennett also stood, and touching her arm lightly, met her worried eyes. "Let him get settled before you go to him, my sweet. Eat something, if you can, or at least a cup of tea."

Claire sat down, suddenly grateful for her husband's presence. She sipped at the tea but ignored the plate set before her. Feeling enough time had elapsed, she rose once more, surprised to see Bennett also rise. Together they left the dining room, but only Claire made her way upstairs.

❀ ❀ ❀

Claire spent most of the day in her father's room, refusing all offers of assistance. Lord Jennings, having received word of his friend's rapid deterioration visited, offering what comfort he could to Claire. Meeting the freckle-faced Betty in the hallway, he inquired as to young Kirkwood's whereabouts.

"Oh, sir, Mr. Kirkwood left the house earlier this morning, and no one's seen him since. And the young mistress is so concerned about her father she hasn't even noticed her husband's absence." Her blond curls bobbed up and down in emphasis. "Mrs. Dixon declares it a disgrace that he's not at the young mistress's side, with them just married and all." Sighing heavily, Magnus Jennings climbed the stairs, intending to sit with Claire for the rest of the afternoon.

It was later that evening that the wayward Bennett Kirkwood returned home. Seeing no change in his father-in-law's condition, he studied his wife thoughtfully for a moment before exerting his husbandly authority, insisting that she get some sleep. It was only after he promised that a servant would stay with her father for the night, calling her if there was a need, that she agreed. Escorting her to the door of the master bedroom, he kissed her chastely on the forehead before continuing down the hallway. An exhausted Claire, lacking the energy to mull over his choosing to spend the night in another chamber, collapsed onto the bed, swept into the arms of Morpheus as soon as her head met the pillow.

❀ ❀ ❀

A soft but persistent knocking on the door aroused Claire, a man's voice calling to her, urgently, insistently. "Mrs. Kirkwood, Mrs. Kirkwood."

Her dark eyes flew open. Sitting up, she saw that she was still dressed. Futilely brushing the wrinkles from the skirt of her dress, she stumbled to the door. Claire recognized the short, portly figure of the usually imperturbable butler of Silverwood House, standing motionless in the hallway, hair askew and expression somber.

"I regret having to disturb your sleep, madam, but you had best come to your father's room."

Claire, heart beating rapidly, was already darting down the long hallway. Calling to the butler to fetch Mr. Kirkwood, she hardly noticed as he hurried off as speedily as his short legs would allow.

Coming to a standstill outside the doorway, she leaned forward, hoping to hear sounds from within but was met with a hollow silence. Hesitantly she pushed the door open, her eyes slowly adjusting to the dim light of the candle that flickered on a small bedside table. Making her way to the bed, she could distinguish the shrunken outline of her father as he lay in the bed, still, so very still. Taking the claw-like hand that rested outside the covers, she squeezed it lightly as tears rolled silently down her cheeks. Leaning over the bed, she kissed his brow. "Adieu, dear Papa."

Sensing that someone had entered the room, she turned and saw her husband, his eyes puffy with sleep, hastily tucking his shirt into his trousers. He stepped forward, awkwardly patting her shoulder, murmuring words she couldn't absorb. Claire stared up at the man she now called husband. *Is this the most you can offer me, Bennett? My father has died and you pat my shoulder as you would a maiden aunt, not someone with whom you have shared a night of passion.*

Bennett, knowing he was disappointing her, couldn't explain to his young wife that which he himself didn't really understand—a mother who had died when he was just a small boy, leaving him with a cold and distant domineering father and a succession of indifferent governesses until he was finally old enough to be sent off to boarding school. He had never had to think of anyone but himself and was therefore unfamiliar with the needs of a young, grief-stricken wife, thus unable to provide little in the way of comfort, not because he was a cruel man but rather a thoughtless and selfish one.

Perhaps, he thought regretfully, *if I had been the one who had introduced her to love our first night, I could now hold and comfort her through the long and lonely hours.* He stiffened at this unexpected softening. *No! Absolutely not! Without knowing if there was to be an unwelcome result of that first night, I can't chance it. I certainly don't want my name given to some other man's get, even if that man is Braxton Kane.* And so, almost effortlessly, they drifted into a pattern of separateness.

"I've sent for the doctor, my dear, but I doubt it will change what we already know. Go back to bed, and I'll send Mrs. Dixon in with tea." He hesitated, struck by a thought. "Unless you'd prefer something stronger. At a time like this, brandy might be the very thing...?"

Wordlessly, Claire turned and walked numbly back to her bedchamber. Time passed slowly, distant doors opened and closed, and whispering, unseen figures hurried past her door. Mrs. Dixon, hair sticking out of her nightcap at odd angles, brought in a tray and silently poured a cup of hot tea. Patting the girl's shoulder in a gesture of sympathy, she left the room. After a few sips, Claire set the cup down and sat, huddled in the blankets, remembering the man who had always been there for her, guiding her through life.

Already I feel so alone without him. What will happen to me now? I'm not sure the man I call husband will be as concerned with my well-being. Tears flowed unchecked until, mercifully, sleep overtook her.

The day they buried Pierre St. Martin was cool and overcast, reflecting Claire's mood perfectly. She and her husband stood apart as the coffin was slowly lowered into the waiting grave. Several of Bennett's friends attended, offering words of sympathy to Claire, all of them wondering at the aloofness that seemed to exist between the two.

On the return to Silverwood, the mourners rushed to get inside and escape the cool dampness of the day. Bennett, not one to stand on ceremony, made his way to a cabinet that held an assortment of liquor bottles. Claire, shocked at his disregard for her or their guests, shook her head, slender fingers playing nervously with the strand of pearls around her neck. Hoping to disguise her annoyance in front of so many, she dismissed him from her thoughts as she turned to welcome some late-arriving guests.

Oh Wicked Escort

The unflappable Mrs. Dixon calmly directed the servants as they threaded their way through the gathering with trays laden with food and cups of tea, although, most of the men were clustered around Bennett, who was liberally pouring something a little stronger than that which was being offered by the servants.

Braxton, ignoring the clamor surrounding his host, lounged casually against a door frame, studying both Claire and Ben, pondering on their avoidance of each other. He watched as Claire hesitantly approached her husband who, glass in hand, now stood slightly apart from his cronies. She spoke a few words and then drew quickly away, her cheeks flushed in embarrassment at the brusqueness of his reply. Braxton, not missing the significance of the gesture, stiffened slightly. He continued to watch her as, struggling to regain her composure, she moved among the crowd, graciously attentive to each guest, ensuring no one wanted for anything. Many minutes passed before she finally slid gracefully into a wingback chair. Crossing the room, he bowed his head to the new mistress of Silverwood House before taking the chair next to her.

"I trust you're keeping well, madam?" He leaned forward, looking at her intently, his voice deep and soothing.

Claire, who had earlier sensed an undercurrent between this man and her husband but was unable to understand the cause, nodded. Glancing up, she saw Bennett, jaw clenched and his face clouded with anger, glaring at the man now sitting beside her, a man he had always called his most trusted friend. Her brow creased with worry as she faced Braxton Kane, his grey eyes lingering on her, an unspoken question in them.

"I'm keeping well, Braxton. Thank you for asking." There was a soft gentleness in her voice. It was at that moment that Mrs. Dixon approached, and bending down, whispered in Claire's ear. Murmuring an apology, the two women disappeared in the direction of the kitchen, intent on solving a domestic crisis.

Bemused, Braxton sat there until he felt the presence of another. Ben, glass in hand, sat down in the chair so recently occupied by his wife. His tone was low and laced with sarcasm when at last he spoke, grinding out the words between his teeth.

"Stop sniffing around her skirts! You had your night and now it's over!"

Startled, Braxton quickly looked around to see if anyone was within earshot, but in his haste, he failed to notice Letitia Penrod slowly edging her way toward them. She had overheard just enough to realize there was something very much amiss between the two men.

"What are you going on about, Ben? This whole thing…you begged me to help you, or have you conveniently forgotten that fact?" His voice, though quiet, had an ominous quality. "How much have you had to drink?"

A glazed look of despair began to spread over Bennett's face. *What have I done? This is my friend, my lifelong friend, the man I turned to when my back was against the wall.* Beads of sweat broke out on his forehead.

"Braxton, forgive me. I don't know what came over me." There was an edge to his voice.

The other man cuffed Bennett's shoulder lightly, relieved that a crisis had been averted. "Ben, don't dwell on these kinds of thoughts—they're deadly. You'd be giving Peckworthy not only the revenge he was seeking but a kind he never dreamt of."

There was a moment of silence before Braxton spoke again. "But I must ask, Ben, is she becoming someone of importance to you?"

Disconcerted by the question, Bennett Kirkwood crossed his arms and looked pointedly away. When at last he answered, it seemed his words were spoken hastily, perhaps too hastily. "It's not that I love her, Braxton, at least I don't think I do. It's having a woman, and such a woman, so close at hand—one I don't dare touch, at least for the time being."

Torn by conflicting emotions, Braxton Kane could only nod in sympathy, refusing to acknowledge the feelings that were gnawing at his heart. So intent were they on their conversation, both failed to notice Letitia Penrod standing scant inches away, puzzling over what she had been able to overhear. The tiniest of smiles played about her mouth as she planned a chat with her son-in-law Teddy, a man with a penchant for gossip. *Yes,* she thought, almost purring in anticipation, *Teddy is just the one to indulge in a bit of tittle-tattle about the newlyweds and their secrets.*

The two men, soon joined by others, stood talking until at last the women began to make noises about leaving. It wasn't long before the only ones left in the room were the servants, bustling about, efficiently restoring the room to its former order.

As the door closed behind the last of the guests, Claire, moving away from her husband's side, requested the very busy Mrs. Dixon to have a tray sent up to her room, leaving a perplexed Bennett watching as she glided gracefully up the stairs.

Chapter Seven

Claire stared into her mirror, wondering if she had done the right thing when she agreed to an evening at the theatre with Bennett and his friends, followed by everyone returning to Silverwood for a late supper. He had put pressure on her, claiming that her mourning was putting him in a despondent frame of mind. No visitors, no outings, no entertainment of any sort, until Claire, anxious for this bizarre marriage to work, had hesitantly fallen in with his plans.

She knew that the past weeks had been hard on him but couldn't escape the feeling that he was waiting for some inexplicable something to happen. He hadn't returned to her bed since that first night and she wondered, not for the first time, if he had a mistress. Indifferent to the possibility, she shrugged her shoulders, wondering if she even cared.

Rising from her dressing table, Claire rang a second time for Betty. Where was the girl—it was unlike her to dawdle when summoned. A sharp rap at the door interrupted her thoughts. On opening it, she was surprised to see Mrs. Dixon standing there. With a nod from her mistress, the housekeeper stepped inside and closed the door.

Taking a defensive stance, Mrs. Dixon, in a querulous voice began to speak. "I've had to dismiss your maid, madam." Claire, dumbfounded, could only stare uncomprehendingly at the woman.

Encouraged by her mistress's silence, the housekeeper continued her discourse. "She was observed consorting with loose and unsavory women in Whitechapel, that part of London that absolutely teems with those odious creatures. Oh yes, she offered me a tearful, garbled explanation but I closed my ears to her, reminding her that rules were rules." The housekeeper paused, becoming uneasy at the silence, but like the proverbial bull, she plowed on, plucking nervously at her stiffly

Oh Wicked Escort

starched apron.

"I had to remind her that anyone accepting a position at Silverwood knew that the first sign of a questionable nature meant instant dismissal, the guilty party leaving immediately and without a character!"

Claire's brows drew together in an agonized expression, her voice shaking with emotion. "Oh, Mrs. Dixon, what have you done? Betty isn't some wanton creature of the streets. She has a sister who's fallen on hard times. Betty gives her money for food and lodging for herself and her sickly child."

Hand flying to her cheek, Mrs. Dixon paled, her eyes falling to the floor. "Oh, madam, I had no idea," she sputtered, then quieted for a few seconds, desperately seeking a way to shift the blame. "Why didn't she tell me?"

Exasperated, Claire interrupted her. "I'm sure she was trying to tell you but you refused to listen." Pausing, she stopped herself from hurling accusations but when next she spoke, her voice rang with command. "You must send one or two of the men out to search for her."

"Madam, that isn't possible." The housekeeper snapped her mouth shut, surprised at her own impertinence. "I can't send anyone to that…that place." Her lips curled in distaste at the very idea.

At Claire's puzzled expression, she went on. "If I let," she paused, thinking swiftly, "no, not let, if I should instruct someone else to go there, who will obey the rules of the house, I ask you?"

About to explode at the woman's insolence, Claire stopped as she saw the door swing open, both women seemingly frozen in a stunned tableau as a startled Bennett stood there, having heard the tail end of the housekeeper's line of reasoning.

"Trouble, my dear?" He spoke with a deceptive calmness in his voice.

Claire's mouth flew open, ready to explain and defend her position but he held up a hand, forestalling her. "Please, Claire, spare me the details of any domestic dispute." He stepped back in astonishment as he eyed her state of undress.

"I trust you're not wearing that!" Claire, glancing down at her lace wrapper embroidered with pink rosebuds, hugged it tightly to herself. Tiny curling tendrils escaped the heavy silken cloud of auburn hair as she shook her head. The enticing scent of her perfume filled his nostrils, reminding him once more of her exquisite and fragile beauty. "We have to leave in less than ten minutes." He ripped out the words impatiently as he turned to the housekeeper. "Quickly, Mrs. Dixon, help your mistress dress."

Turning toward the door, he hesitated, knowing he had come to his wife's bedchamber for a reason. "Oh yes, I wanted to remind you that I leave tomorrow for Bindley Park with Braxton and the Chambers brothers for a few days of hunting." Not expecting a reply, he bowed his head in her general direction, speaking more to himself than anyone as he hurried down the stairs. "I'll call the carriage around."

As the door closed behind him, Claire raised finely arched eyebrows as if daring the housekeeper to speak. "We'll discuss this matter tomorrow, Mrs. Dixon! Help me fasten my gown." Her usual warm tone was chilly, and no further words were exchanged between the two women.

It was some hours later that the Kirkwood carriage returned, following the winding driveway to the front entrance of the house. The butler, having waited patiently for some time, opened the door and stepped out, clutching several umbrellas to protect the theatergoers from the rain that had been falling since earlier that evening.

Letitia Penrod alit from her son-in-law's carriage holding her umbrella aloft, caring nothing for the well-being of the other passengers. She arrogantly made her way into Silverwood House, following closely behind Bennett Kirkwood and that mousey little woman he had married who seemed to have charmed everyone except herself.

We'll see if everyone thinks her quite so wonderful after I reveal what I know. It will absolutely ruin her. Her smile was cold and forbidding as she anticipated the tumult her revelation would bring about. *When should I divulge my little secret? Now? No, not now! Everyone is too concerned with the emptiness of their bellies. After we eat? Yes, when the men join us!*

Standing in front of the fire as she waited for everyone to gather, her eyes met those of her son-in-law, Teddy. His expression was one of desperate pleading as he gazed intently at his mother-in-law. Taking his linen handkerchief from his pocket, he dabbed at the droplets of perspiration that had appeared on his forehead.

The butler appeared, and after a brief word with his employer, announced dinner. Men linked arms with the women, escorting them into the dining room. Conversation was light, the play they had just seen being the main topic. Laughter rose above the tinkle of china and silverware. The time passed pleasantly until, seeing appetites had been sated, Claire stood, nodding to Letitia and her daughters. As the women left the room, a footman entered, presenting Bennett with a box of cigars and a bottle of brandy which he quickly passed on to his friends, taking little notice of Teddy's sickly demeanor.

Claire led the way into the sitting room. Heart beating furiously but head held high, she glided across the room to the chaise lounge and casually arranged herself over its curving surface, refusing to allow the three women to intimidate her. Minerva and Miranda glanced at their mother, pausing as they waited to follow her lead.

There was an inexplicable air of nervous tension about them, their mother having dropped the tiniest of hints that she would be taking "that insufferable Claire Kirkwood" down a peg or two this evening. Letitia glanced about the room before choosing the richly brocaded sofa that was positioned opposite Claire's chaise lounge, subtly motioning her daughters to join her there.

Claire and the two sisters chatted, or rather Minerva and Miranda gossiped about people she had never met as she tried, to no avail, to introduce other topics of conversation.

Letitia, with a smug look on her lined face, seemed content to sit and let the conversation flow about her. After what seemed like innumerable hours later, although in truth it was less than thirty minutes, Claire could hear the men, laughing and talking, making their way toward the sitting room. Looking around the room, Bennett and Braxton quickly rearranged the chairs into a circle so all were facing each other, although Teddy seemed more content to lean against a wall, refusing almost rudely to join them.

At first, the men dominated the conversation, politics being their chosen subject, but both Minerva and Miranda quickly expressed their boredom, looking to their mother for the promised dressing-down of the woman they both secretly envied. Letitia straightened her shoulders and cleared her throat, a sure sign that she was about to speak. No one heard the small groan that escaped Teddy's lips.

"Has anyone heard about a most bizarre marriage that took place right here in London a few weeks ago?" Her seemingly innocent question had an ominous quality to it. Suddenly wary, Bennett stiffened before glancing at Braxton, a question in his eyes. Teddy, wishing the floor would open up and swallow him, turned even paler. Letitia's daughters gazed at their mother, wondering what she was going on about but listened intently, always eager to hear any gossip. Julius, feeling the sudden tension, sat quietly, waiting.

"I must admit that at first I couldn't lend credence to such a tale, but I had it on the best authority." She paused, savoring the moment as she glanced at Claire who sat listening politely. Claire, so sweet, so innocent! The woman almost purred out loud as she continued.

"It seems that after the ceremony, the bride, unknowingly, or so it is claimed, was bedded by one of the groomsmen, and the groom is now left cooling his heels, unable to assert his husbandly rights until he knows if there is to be fruit from that night, that *Prima Nocta*."

Shocked gasps escaped all the occupants of the sitting room but it was the men who turned as one to face Teddy—Teddy the gossip and now Teddy the coward, who had begun to cravenly edge toward the door and escape. Eyes bulging with fear, he glanced at Bennett and Braxton, knowing these could be his last moments on this earth.

It was Claire's voice ringing out and calling Bennett's name that saved Teddy from receiving the thrashing he so richly deserved. All eyes turned to her, some in shame and some in absolute delight.

Her face had a deathly pallor, and her voice when at last she spoke was a broken whisper, willing her husband, the man who had so recently vowed to care for and protect her, to deny it. But deep inside she knew he couldn't. "Is she speaking of us, Bennett?" Her voice was becoming shrill. "Did you send another man to share my bed that first night? Is that why you haven't returned, you had to be sure I wasn't carrying another man's child?"

Even as she heard herself utter the accusation, her voice seemed to come from a long way off. Swaying as she stood there alone, she knew all eyes in the room were focused on her. Fiercely, she willed herself not to faint—not now, not with everyone watching—but finally, mercifully, she lost that battle and would have fallen, unconscious, to the floor if Bennett had not caught her in his arms.

❀   ❀   ❀

Claire awoke slowly, gradually becoming aware of everyone gathered around her. She was most aware of Bennett, who was kneeling beside her and softly rubbing her hand.

Eyes fluttering, she fought to return to that land of nothingness but it wasn't to be. "Claire, sweetheart…" She snatched her hand back, physically divorcing herself from the man who was her husband.

The small sea of faces continued to watch her intently. Her eyes scanned each face, wondering who…no…she refused to speculate about who she had shared her bed with. Her eyes fell on Letitia Penrod, smirking down at her. If ever she wished someone to disappear forever, it would be the malicious Widow Penrod.

The woman moved away from the others, silently enjoying the havoc she had created, a smug smile of satisfaction playing about her mouth. Basking in her private moment of glory, she slowly became aware of how deathly quiet the room had become. Casting her eyes on the other occupants, Letitia Penrod suddenly felt weak and vulnerable, realizing her position had become as precarious as her son-in-law's seemed to be. Both Bennett and Braxton were glowering at her, mayhem and murder in their eyes.

Teddy looked into Claire's deep brown eyes, his expression one of mute wretchedness, knowing full well that his friends would become like hounds, baying for his blood. Even Julius had distanced himself from his own brother, his face flushed with anger and humiliation.

Incredibly, both of Letitia's daughters had been momentarily struck speechless. They gawped in wide-eyed skepticism at Claire, wondering how she could have allowed such a scandalous incident to happen. Miranda was the first to break the interminable silence.

"Surely, Claire, you must have known, or at least suspected, who you spent your first night of married life with." There was a muffled groan from one of the men as all, including Letitia, wondered at the tactless and unfeeling remark.

Claire, eyes downcast, pushed herself to a standing position until, raising her chin, she assumed all the dignity she felt capable of mustering. Bennett stepped forward, an almost imperceptible look of pleading in his eyes. Sniffing her disdain, she ignored his outstretched hand and walked with rigid dignity toward the door. A movement caught her eye, and she found herself looking into the one face she had instinctively avoided. She remained absolutely motionless for a moment, an unwelcome blush creeping into her cheeks. Braxton Kane, a glazed look of despair spreading over his face, held the door open for her, stepping back as she passed him, her scent filling his nostrils. For a long moment, the only sound to be heard was the tapping of Claire's shoes as she fled up the stairs to the sanctuary of her bedroom.

Ignoring the women, a desperate Teddy herded the other three men into a far corner of the room. Inching toward Bennett, he haltingly offered his apologies. "Bennett, this is all my fault. Letitia overheard you and Braxton talking after the old man's funeral. She tricked me into believing she had heard more than she had, digging at me until finally I divulged everything that happened here the night Peckworthy made his proposition. She vowed she would tell no one, but I think even at that moment I knew it would all come out."

Bennett, looking at the cringing, hand-wringing figure before him, spoke brusquely. "Teddy, I've always known you to be a gossip, but now I suspect Mordock Peckworthy was counting on it. If you'll recall, he said he had to wait some time to find all of us gathered together away from inquisitive eyes."

"His plan was more fiendish than I thought. The three of us Teddy, you, Braxton, and me were the essential elements—Julius's presence or absence didn't really matter to him." The four men's eyes met, and they realized they had all played right into Peckworthy's hands.

Bennett pressed his lips together in frustrated anger before he continued, ignoring the women still huddled together at the other end of the room. "That night I regretted that you were part of the conspiracy, Teddy, but there was nothing to be done but forge ahead, trusting in your discretion but not altogether too hopeful."

Oh Wicked Escort

He paused as he gathered his thoughts, running his fingers through his hair in frustration before meeting Braxton's questioning look. "Gentlemen, I propose we proceed with our plans and head out to Bindley Park tomorrow. There are partridge and grouse aplenty, just waiting for us." He smiled, trying to convince his friends that he was in control. "My absence will give Claire time to think things through, and once I've returned home, I'll explain everything to her. She'll understand that Peckworthy had me backed into a corner. She'll understand that one night of our married life was sacrificed for our financial well-being...she'll understand." He almost whispered his last words. "Oh please, God, she must understand."

The others, if surprised by their host's plan to carry on as if nothing untoward had occurred, nodded in silent agreement, promising to meet in the morning for the long ride to Bennett's country estate.

Silently, the guests found their wraps and jackets. As Letitia passed uncomfortably close to Bennett on her way out, she braced herself for some sort of scathing comment and wasn't disappointed.

"You've had your moment, madam, and you've hurt someone who has never done anything to you that would warrant such treatment." There was a silken thread of warning in his voice.

"My mother, in the few years we had together, taught me to never strike a woman, but let me assure you it took everything I had not to throttle you on the spot. And please, don't take that as a sign of weakness, for there will be retribution. I'll bide my time and wait for an opportunity, when there are no witnesses." His words, though spoken quietly, held an ominous warning. He then looked right through her, as if she had ceased to exist. The woman paled as she digested his words, hugging her wrap tighter, certain that he would follow through on his threat.

The daughters followed their mother out, wondering what words had been exchanged between her and Bennett Kirkwood. They both looked speculatively at their host as they walked out into the night, thinking about the man they had thought they knew so well. Giggles were smothered until they were safely tucked inside their carriage, taking no notice of the unnatural silence of their mother.

Julius looked at his four travelling companions with deep, stomach-wrenching disgust, wishing for the umpteenth time that he had chosen another for his wife and had never made the acquaintance of the accursed Penrod family. He nodded gloomily at Braxton as he galloped by, idly contemplating the guilt the man must be feeling for his part in the whole sordid affair.

Chapter Eight

Claire was awakened by the sound of crockery being set down in her room. She opened her eyes slowly and saw Mrs. Dixon standing in front of the window, about to open the curtains.

"Please, Mrs. Dixon, leave the curtains drawn." The room was light enough for Claire to distinguish the housekeeper's features, making her certain that the woman was positively smirking. *She knows! She was probably hiding behind a door and listening to the whole ugly incident. Bennett warned me of her penchant for eavesdropping.*

"Mr. Kirkwood left early this morning for Bindley Park." The housekeeper's tone was almost chatty as she moved about the room. "Will madam need anything more? Shall I send one of the maids to help you dress? And what of Betty, madam? Do you still insist on sending out a search party to Whitechapel?"

Claire's hold on her temper was fragile and her voice shaking as she tried to control the scream she felt building inside her. "No, Mrs. Dixon, to all of your questions! Please leave me!"

Sniffing her disdain, the housekeeper nodded her head curtly as she withdrew, a self-righteous smirk on her face. *There, the high and mighty aren't quite so high anymore, are they?*

As the housekeeper pulled the door closed behind her, Claire threw a pillow at it, regretting that it wasn't something breakable and much more satisfying.

Oh God, what am I supposed to do now? What a horrid catastrophe this marriage has become. As she thought, she paced back and forth, nightgown swirling with each turn she made. *Dear Papa, you thought you had found somebody special but even you were fooled.* She sat down at the small table that held her breakfast tray. Not hungry but wanting something comforting, she sipped at the hot tea. *At least I'm spared Bennett's company for a few days.* Tears welled up as she thought once more of the satisfaction that vile Letitia Penrod had taken in her disgusting revelation.

Desperately seeking a solution, she began pacing again, despondently exploring avenues of escape. *Escape...I can't even escape! I have no money and almost everyone I know in London is Bennett's friend, not mine. I can't even go to Lord Jennings—he just sent a note yesterday saying he was travelling to France for at least a month and would call on his return.*

Halting in mid-stride, she turned to the mahogany writing desk tucked into a corner of the room. She did have money—not much, true, but it was better than nothing. Excitement began to course through her, as fingers trembling, she drew out her tiny horde of coins from the drawer and counted them. *So few coins—how far would that take me? I could leave this marriage that is no marriage.* Her mind raced. *I would have to find some kind of employment.*

What had been the seed of an idea suddenly burst into flower...Betty! She would go to Whitechapel and hopefully find Betty. Practical Betty. Betty could advise her about employment and lodging.

She sat down, sipping her tea, anxiously recalling everything Betty had told her. She and her older sister Rosie had been raised by their widowed father, a vicar in a small village. He had seen to it that both girls knew how to read and do sums. Rosie had married and been whisked away to London by her new husband, and the two sisters, once so close, had lost touch. Sadly her father had died, leaving Betty to look after herself since that time. The one bright spot was the two sisters had been reunited, the scoundrel of a husband having deserted Rosie and their child.

Claire pulled an afternoon tea gown from the wardrobe—nothing too ostentatious, not for where she was going. As she pulled the dress over her head, she realized she would have to have someone fasten her, hopefully not the arrogant Mrs. Dixon. She tugged on the bell pull, impatiently hooking her shoes while she waited for her summons to be answered. A quiet knock signaled that help had arrived. Opening the door, Claire smiled brightly as she admitted Betty's replacement and not

Oh Wicked Escort

the obnoxious housekeeper.

After fastening her new mistress's gown, the maid looked around the tidy room. "Will that be all, madam? I mean, will you be needing me again today? Mrs. Dixon has given us a half day, and we're all going to the fair." The girl was twisting her bony fingers anxiously, her plain face breaking into a broad grin when her mistress assured her that her services would not be needed for the rest of the day.

Smiling, Claire watched as the girl almost danced out the door. *Everything is falling into place. The servants will be gone so I'll only have to contend with Mrs. Dixon.* Wrapping her shawl around her shoulders, Claire cautiously made her way down the stairs, holding her breath in trepidation. Excited voices and giggling drifted up from the kitchen. Realizing her opportunity was now, she opened the heavy door and slipped outside, pulling it quietly shut behind her. The sun shone brightly down on her—surely that must be a good omen—as she lifted the hem of her dress and ran down the driveway, terrified that she would be seen and forced to return to Silverwood and Bennett Kirkwood.

Reaching the roadway, Claire slowed her pace. Looking about, she realized she had no practical idea as to which direction one would take to reach Whitechapel. *Am I doing the right thing?* She shook herself, angry at where her thoughts were leading. *No! Don't you dare get cold feet now, my girl. This is no ordinary tiff—he betrayed me and I'll never forgive him, never!*

Peering down the road, she could see only one wagon lumbering along, pulled by a plodding dusty horse, the memory of fresh sweet hay to eat and a dry stall being the creature's only incentive to continue its journey. Reluctantly, she faced the road and waved at the driver of the heavily laden wagon.

Unbridled curiosity prodded the stubble-faced man to warily come to a halt, his load of wooden crates and boxes barely shifting. Leaning down, he displayed a cautious smile, which quickly turned into a cheeky grin as he got a closer look at the beauty that had beckoned to him. *The lads at the pub will never believe this.*

To prove he knew how to act with a toff, he touched the brim of his hat, his impudent grin widening. "Oi! What do yer want wif' old Billy Marple, Missus?"

Wondering what she wanted indeed, Claire smiled up at him. "Mr...er, Marple. I need directions to get to Whitechapel."

Black bushy eyebrows shot up in surprise. "Whitechapel! Are you barmy? What'd a leddy like you be wantin' in Whitechapel?"

Claire straightened her shoulders in an effort to appear more imposing than she felt. "What I want, my good man, is none of your concern. I just need directions."

Exasperation sharpened his tone. "Missus, I'm tellin' you, Whitechapel's not a place for your sort. It's full of pickpockets and foreigners and worse—oh my word, yes—much, much worse. Why, Whitechapel would swallow you up and no one'd even know you'd been there." He was sputtering in his efforts to convince her to change her course.

"Thank you for your warning, Mr. Marple, but I am indeed going to Whitechapel and if you can't help me, I'll simply wait here by the side of the road until someone comes by who will."

Stiffening her spine, she put her nose in the air, obviously dismissing him. Turning, she glanced up the empty road.

"All right, missus, I can see you be determined to go." Her mouth twitched slightly as she realized she had won, although she wasn't sure exactly what it was that she had won. He clambered down, positioning himself by her side. Standing in such close proximity, she saw that his girth more than made up for his lack of height, and although his clothes were well worn, they had a look of regular laundering.

Sighing heavily, he reached across her, pulling down a wooden box that had been tucked into an unoccupied corner of the wagon. "All right, me darlin', climb up and I'll take you to Whitechapel, although I don't know what me sainted mother would have said if she knew I was even thinkin' of doin' such a daft thing."

Cautiously, Claire stepped onto the box, and holding her skirts as high as she dared, climbed up to the driver's seat, a wooden bench barely wide enough for two. Returning the box to its resting place, Billy Marple efficiently used his work-roughened hands to pull himself up. Standing directly behind her, he hesitantly nudged her toward the far end of the driver's seat. Startled, she froze, wondering what was coming until she saw that he had pulled a large red handkerchief from the depths of some hidden pocket and was fastidiously dusting the seat before gesturing to her to sit down.

Taking up the reins, Billy turned to his passenger. "Before I sets off, I needs to know why you be wantin' to go to such a place. And don't bother handin' me any lies. Me and my old woman has raised three daughters—I know all there is to know about female trickery."

Claire looked down at her hands, wondering what to say. Deciding that half a truth would probably sound more believable than an outright lie, she raised her eyes to find him watching her.

"It's really just a silly mistake my housekeeper made. She's of a rigidly intolerant nature, unwilling to admit she might have been mistaken. My personal maid, Betty, was seen on the streets of Whitechapel, an unforgivable lapse of moral judgment in Mrs. Dixon's eyes. Betty was dismissed immediately, without my knowledge. She was given no chance to explain that her sister, abandoned by a drunken husband and left with a sickly child, was forced to move to cheap lodgings. Betty's been helping her out but now, thanks to Mrs. Dixon, she's without employment."

She twisted her hands, anxious for the wagon to move, but Billy Marple sat there, turning her story over in his mind. At last, deciding her story was true, he joggled the reins and the long-suffering horse resumed its journey.

"I'll take you there, missus, but you must promise to be gone from there before the sun sets. I do have a question though—why are you the one out looking for this 'missing' maid? You must have a husband or brother…"

Claire blushed, suddenly angry for not having prepared an answer to such a reasonable question. She licked her lips nervously. "My husband was called away to his brother's sickbed just before I was told about Betty, and so I decided to go in search of her myself. And of course, Mr. Marple, I'll follow your advice and do exactly as you say."

They continued on in silence, Claire's mind racing. Surely, she could find Betty before the end of the day. *And what if Betty can't help you, Claire, what will you do then?"*

More wagons were now sharing the road, all funneling into streets already crowded with people, more people than Claire had ever seen. Billy Marple gestured with the reins toward the mass of moving humanity as the wagon slowly worked its way down the road. The cries of costermongers calling out their wares plus a multitude of other voices in just as many languages were deafening. *How will I ever find one person in such a throng?*

Billy cleared his throat, his voice becoming gruff. "Listen to me, my girl. You're in Whitechapel now. Do you really believe you can find your maid? All alone? I think you should go home and ask your husband when he gets back home, or a brother, or somebody, anybody, to give it a go."

Stubbornly, Claire shook her head, knowing he was probably right but then he didn't have all the facts. He had no way of knowing how desperate she was.

He continued on, shouting to be heard above the tumultuous noise of the streets. "Listen missus, I'm just down here on Hanbury Street—Dabney's Freighthouse. In fact, missus, I now be one of the owners." He preened, full of pride at such a feat before pointing toward a building farther along the cobblestoned street. "If you need help, go there. They all know me and can fetch me in no time. And if it's the end of the day, you'd probably find me at The Blind Beggar."

Seeing her quizzical look, he elaborated. "The Blind Beggar—it's the tavern where I likes to do my relaxin' before I makes my way home to my missus."

Just as he finished speaking, Claire, who had been studying the throngs of people moving slowly down the cobbled path, suddenly gripped Billy's arm. "It's her, Mr. Marple, it's Betty!" She pointed at a blond woman who was shuffling along the crowded walkway, eyes downcast.

"Betty!" Claire, trying to attract her former maid's attention, waved her arms frantically, jumping up and down in the precariously narrow space of the driver's box. "Betty!" The slightly plump woman kept moving, unaware that anyone was calling to her.

Claire turned to her escort, who had already decided on his course of action. "Stay here, missus. I'll fetch her." He clambered down and

Oh Wicked Escort

moved off into the crowd, his short but powerful legs propelling him forward. Reaching his target, he laid a hand on her shoulder. The woman spun around, prepared to do battle with whoever had dared accost her, but Billy shouted something and pointed toward his wagon where Claire stood, waving madly at the two of them.

Betty, eyes wide with disbelief, followed Billy as he cleared a path through the crowd. Once again, he lifted out the wooden box and stood on it, holding out his muscled arms to Claire. She felt herself being lifted and deposited safely on the ground, facing her former maid. Both women, tears flowing, hugged each other, babbling unheard words to the other, ignoring Billy, who stood waiting patiently, unwilling to leave until he had spoken to his passenger one last time.

"Excuse me, missus, but I has to be goin'." Claire nodded, brown eyes sparkling as she gazed warmly at this most unanticipated knight in shining armor. "But first, I has to know your name, just in case you was ever to come callin'."

There was a spark of some indefinable emotion in her eyes as she quickly studied him. "My name is Claire, Mr. Marple...Claire St. Martin."

Nodding to both women, he hoisted himself up to the driver's box. As he took up the reins, the horse, sensing the nearness of the stable, broke into a trot that belied its years, pulling the wagon quickly down the road.

As Claire watched Billy drive off, she felt Betty's eyes on her. She knew the girl had heard her introduce herself as Claire St. Martin, not Mrs. Bennett Kirkwood. *How much should I tell her? I can't admit to her, to anyone, how I was betrayed on my wedding night—and by my husband, the man who had vowed that very day to love and protect me.*

Reluctantly, Claire met the eyes of her former maid and read both puzzlement and concern. A couple, deep in conversation, jostled past her, almost causing Claire to lose her balance. Betty, using her elbows rather forcefully, led Claire to an open space in front of a shop.

"What's happened to you, madam, and if I may be so bold, why are you calling yourself Claire St. Martin rather than Mrs. Bennett Kirkwood? And why are you here in Whitechapel of all places?"

"Calm yourself, Betty. There's an explanation but I will need your understanding—not your sympathy, mind you, just your understanding."

She suddenly noticed two rough-looking men eyeing them, and recalling Billy Marple's warning about the nefarious population of Whitechapel, moved closer to her former maid.

"Betty, is there somewhere we can go to speak privately and get ourselves off this street?"

The maid, having also noticed the louts ogling them, steered her into the dubious shelter of a shop doorway, all the while trying to recall if she had ever seen such a thing as a tearoom in Whitechapel.

Suddenly unsure of herself, Claire spoke, her voice holding a note of desperation. "Betty, for reasons I'd rather not go into, I'm leaving Mr. Kirkwood—today. I was hoping you could advise me about finding employment and lodging."

The blond woman's head snapped up, her eyes wide with incredulous disbelief. She had never heard of such a thing. *What are you going on about…wives don't leave husbands, especially not in the upper classes.* Looking at the younger woman's grim but determined face, she knew her reason must be shockingly dreadful and in that instant, her practical side took over. Whatever her former employer's reasons were, they were her business and hers alone.

"Madam, I…I simply don't know what to say. What sort of position would suit you? A governess? I'm at a loss to suggest how one goes about finding such a post. Any other position—well, I'm afraid I know of nothing that would suit you. And jobs are scarce, especially without a character. Why, I've just got myself a position this very day, and that's only because Mrs. Henderson remembered me mum."

Claire, with a strength born of desperation, grasped Betty's wrist. "You've found a position? Do they…is there a need for another maid?"

Betty looked at Claire as if she had gone mad. "A maid! You can't become a maid, you're…why, you're quality!" She struggled for additional words to describe the absolutely scandalous idea of Claire becoming a maid.

"Why can't I, Betty? I certainly know what such a position entails. And if not a maid, then what? I certainly can't cook but I could wash dishes." Her voice trailed off as she faced Betty, despair in her dark eyes.

Betty, massaging the wrist that Claire had been squeezing, was beginning to understand the anguish of the other. "All right, we can at least ask Mrs. Henderson, but how do we explain someone who looks and talks like you..." She stumbled in her search to find the right words. "I mean, like the gentry, looking for a domestic position?"

Relieved, joy bubbled in her laugh and shone in her eyes as Claire impulsively hugged Betty. "What if we say I've recently been widowed, without a farthing to my name, and my husband left me penniless so I must seek employment? I will become *Mrs.* Claire St. Martin! And Betty, you must begin, this minute in fact, to address me as Claire, your friend, and forget I was ever your employer."

Betty giggled at the thought of having such a friend but sobered quickly as she studied their surroundings and the interest they seemed to be attracting. Shyly she spoke. "Claire, there's a bit of luck that goes with the position. Mrs. Henderson prefers that her domestics live in the building—she owns the whole lot and it's been done over—ladies' rooms are on the second floor and the gents' rooms are on the third."

Hugging excitedly, the two linked arms and turned off the high street, a three-story brick building down the road being their goal. As they drew near, Claire read the sign, large and imposing, hanging inside the front window.

Henderson's Domestics
Daily Rates
A Christian Establishment

A smaller, hand-lettered sign had been placed in the corner of the window.

Help wanted
Apply Within

Chapter Nine

As they pushed the door open, a dark figure stirred in the dimly lit room, someone who slowly rose from behind a wooden desk. The girls stood at the counter, which served as a boundary for any who entered the building, and which, apart from the desk and three chairs, were the only pieces of furniture in the starkly furnished room. Along the inner wall were three doors, all firmly closed with no indication of where they led.

Betty stepped in front of Claire and sketched a quick curtsy. "Good afternoon, Mrs. Henderson. It's me again, Betty Sims." Her voice squeaked in nervousness.

A flicker of apprehension coursed through Claire. She felt almost as fearful as Betty as they both watched the dark figure draw closer. Mrs. Henderson, a tall woman of perhaps fifty years or so, towered over both of her callers. Her figure was thickset and sturdy, her hair dull brown with streaks of grey running through it and drawn tightly back into a chignon. Her face, though plain, had a freshly scrubbed look, in fact her entire person gave the impression of having been scrubbed clean. Thick, dark eyebrows hovered over pale eyes, which intently studied her unexpected and uninvited visitors. Her nose was oversized, her mouth tight and grim. Glaring at the one she had hired less than an hour ago, the woman wondered if perhaps she had been too hasty. After all, the girl had arrived without a character from her previous employer.

Clearing her throat anxiously, Betty started talking, her words tumbling out hastily. "You said you were looking for another maid, Mrs. Henderson." She glanced at Claire, crossing her fingers superstitiously in the hope that she wasn't jeopardizing her own position. She gently nudged Claire forward.

"This is Mrs..." Betty paused, collecting her thoughts. "Mrs. St.

Oh Wicked Escort

Martin. I met her when I was a maid at Silverwood House, my former position. It seems Mrs. St. Martin has also fallen on hard times, for she has suddenly found herself a penniless widow. She must find a position immediately."

Turning slowly and deliberately, the imposing figure studied the prospective employee. Claire, refusing to be intimidated, held her ground. Seeing something that apparently satisfied her, Mrs. Henderson smiled, nodding her thanks to Betty.

She spoke with authority, her words clipped. "And exactly what experience have you had, Mrs. St. Martin?" As she spoke, she took both of Claire's hands, turning them this way and that before finally releasing them.

Claire floundered for an answer, unsure whether she should make claims of experience she didn't possess.

"I've never held a position, Mrs. Henderson. But my aunt ensured that I learned all there was to know about the running of an estate and dealing with servants. My position in life might have changed but those early lessons will prove valuable, I'm sure. I promise you'll find me both a willing worker and a quick learner, if given the chance of course."

"Normally I would send you on your way, girl, but I find myself short of two additional servants for a formal dinner at the Spanish Embassy tomorrow night, and the week to come promises to be just as busy."

Sighing loudly, the proprietor of Henderson's Domestics looked intently at both young women. "I suppose Betty has already told you that I prefer my employees to live on the premises? And that each employee must be of good moral character. Each and every employee is responsible for the upkeep of this building. That includes laundry, sweeping, and dusting. Cook prepares all the meals, but everyone takes turns cleaning up the kitchen."

"And, Mrs. St. Martin, I have a strong suspicion that you're running from something or somebody. Betty says you're a widow, but I think there's more to you than meets the eye. I trust we won't find the law on our doorstep because of my charitable nature."

Without waiting for a response, she ushered both girls into the room, moving quickly toward one of the doors Claire had noticed earlier. A narrow staircase was revealed, bordered by stark white walls, winding its way upward. Mrs. Henderson led the way, talking matter-of-factly as they climbed.

"The building has been remodeled and now has three bedrooms each on the second and third floors—the ladies on the second and the gents on the third. You and Betty will be expected to share a room and will take your meals downstairs. You will each receive one black dress with white lace trim, two white aprons, and two white mob caps. You will be expected to keep these garments neat and clean. When you're not actually working, you may wear your own clothes, thus preserving your working attire. There will be a work schedule posted in the dining room downstairs."

Reaching the second floor, Claire marveled at the woman's ability to climb stairs and continue to talk nonstop. She led them into the bedroom nearest the stairwell, stopping in the middle of the room before turning to face her newest employees. "Ladies, your new quarters."

Two single beds stood opposite each other with neatly folded sheets and blankets at the foot of each. A small table holding a washbasin and water jug sat just below a curtained window. A large wooden wardrobe that seemed to dwarf everything else in the room occupied almost half a wall. Despite the sparsely furnished room smelling strongly of carbolic soap, both Claire and Betty felt they had found a haven, temporary though it might be.

Mrs. Henderson picked up the threads of her conversation. "Mrs. St. Martin, as I have already explained to Miss Sims, Henderson's Domestics provides a service to the upper class and well-to-do. They all have enough servants in their employ to suit themselves, but there are those occasions, whether it's a ball or perhaps a large dinner party, when extra, well-trained hands are needed, just for that one instance. They contact me with their needs, and I provide the temporary solution they are looking for."

Claire nodded, her admiration for the woman's business sense growing. She looked around the room, feeling that surely this would give her time to decide which direction her life would take.

"My staff is, on the whole, not particularly well educated, which is of little consequence to me. They are rarely required to speak while serving, nothing beyond 'very good, sir' or 'no, madam'. From the few words I've heard you utter, and I do have quite a good ear for this, I suspect that your diction is probably much more than passable."

Content with the appearance of both women, she continued her discourse as she led the way downstairs. "Because of your lack of experience, Mrs. St. Martin, you will be paid less than Miss Sims...£8 for the year. This includes the cost of your room and meals. Prove yourself valuable and...well, we'll discuss that later. *All* of my people attend Sunday services with me, no exceptions. You will have one afternoon off every week and every second Sunday." She looked up at the ceiling, silently reviewing everything she had just imparted.

"I assume you both have your belongings to collect. You'll begin your training tomorrow." Nodding her head in dismissal, she held the door open, a thin-lipped smile crossing her face as she bid them good-bye.

Claire and Betty, both dazed by the speed with which all of their respective problems had been solved, hugged each other excitedly.

Betty was the first to speak. "I have to tell my sister. She'll be relieved that money will be coming in. Her landlord has been complaining about me staying there, promising her a prompt eviction on rent day if there's no money forthcoming." She started off down the crowded street, turning and shouting her good-byes. "Good-bye Claire. I'll see you back at Mrs. Henderson's later this afternoon." She gave one last wave before hurrying away.

Claire watched as the crowd swallowed Betty up. She stood for a moment, lost in thought, before noticing the street sign. Hanbury Street...Dabney's Freighthouse! Billy Marple! *Oh, please, please,* she prayed to an unseen deity, *let me find Mr. Billy Marple and let him be willing to earn a shilling or two.*

A quick study, she used her elbows as she had seen Betty do, making her way through the never-ending mass of people, walking as quickly as she could down Hanbury. A sign, now faded with age and grime, had been painted on the side of the building—Dabney's Freighthouse. *Oh, bless you, Billy Marple, for making sure I knew where to find you.*

A bell tinkled overhead as she pushed the door open, her eyes quickly adjusting to the dim interior. A faint odor of horses drifted in from the stables, which were attached to the building. A balding man with an enormous red moustache stood leaning on the counter, eyes full of curiosity at the entrance of a woman, unescorted and most definitely of a higher class than any he was used to dealing with.

A gold tooth glinted in the smile that played about his mouth as his voice, deeper than any she had ever heard, bellowed out a greeting. He tucked in his shirttails, all the while wishing he had taken the time to shave that morning. Stepping out from behind his scarred wooden counter, he pulled a chair from a darkened corner of the room, offering it to her with a sweep of his hand. Shaking her head, Claire wished that Betty was still with her.

"Good afternoon, madam. What can I do for you this fine day?"

"I'm looking for Billy Marple. He told me he worked at Dabney's Freighthouse." Warily she remained standing beside the door but met the man's eyes, refusing to be cowed by anyone ever again.

"Why, indeed he does, miss. But old Billy only worked a half day today." He rubbed his whiskered chin thoughtfully. "He might still be down at The Blind Beggar. It's just a couple of doors down the way. I'll send a boy to fetch him—it's no place for a lady such as you."

Declining the man's offer, Claire almost flew out the door. She scanned the other buildings nearby, finally spotting The Blind Beggar. Lifting her skirt slightly, she hurried along the dusty path, the great masses of people from Whitechapel Road having thinned down to a trickle.

A boisterous din coming from the tavern ushered her along the walkway until, standing outside the building, she was suddenly hesitant. Fortunately, the publican chose that precise moment to throw a rowdy customer out onto the cobblestoned footpath. As he stood there dusting off his hands, the man looked up and spied an unfamiliar figure determinedly making her way past the inebriated fellow who continued to lie where he had landed, his drunken snores filling the courtyard.

"Are you lost, miss?" His voice, though raspy, was courteous.

"I'm looking for Billy Marple. He told me he sometimes stops here before making his way home." Feeling quite awkward, Claire continued to stand there, aware that those inside, attracted by the publican's

Oh Wicked Escort

question, were now crowded round the two windows that overlooked the courtyard. Nervously she moistened her dry lips, patiently waiting while the man pondered her question, unsure whether he should admit Billy was indeed inside. A voice rang out, taking the decision out of his hands.

"Oi! Hold on just a tick, Rafferty, that's the little leddy I been tellin' you fellers about." Billy pushed the man aside and stepped out, his cheeky smile a welcome sight to Claire. Taking her arm, he steered her inside and led her to an empty table, all the while strutting like a peacock to have such a beauty on his arm, especially in front of his mates. "Well, miss, or is it *Mrs.* St. Martin? I never expected to lay eyes on you again. What you be needin' from old Billy? Would you be wantin' a pint?" Claire shook her head, declining his offer. He sat back and waited.

"Mr. Marple, I have just been hired by Mrs. Henderson of Henderson's Domestics on Brick Lane." Seeing his mouth gape open in surprise, she hurried on. "I'm in need of transportation back to where you first picked me up. You would have to wait for me to pack my belongings and then deliver me to Mrs. Henderson's. I'll pay you for your trouble, of course. And if such a trip is not possible, could you direct me to someone who would be willing?"

Billy sat across from her, flabbergasted, but when he at last regained his voice, she could hear anger in it. "What do yer' mean, you've taken a position? Leddies like you don't work, especially not as servants. What game would you be playin' at, missus? And don't forget, I've raised me own daughters and can recognize a lie a mile off!"

It was Claire's turn to be thunderstruck. No one had ever spoken to her in such a rude manner. "Mr. Marple..." Her tone was frigid. "Why I have taken a position of any sort is simply none of your business. And if you don't want to help me, that's just fine. Good day, sir." She stood, preparing to march out.

He spoke grudgingly, his hand on her arm. "All right, missy, if you don't have an inclination to tell old Billy, that's fine. And I'll take you back for your belongin's, so don't go lookin' round for someone else."

As soon as he finished speaking, Claire smiled and leaned across the table to hug him. Laughter and cheers burst through the room as his cronies looked on, pleased that someone such as her seemed so fond of one of their own. Billy, cheeky grin in place, rose and bowed to the room in general before taking Claire's arm, guiding her through the doorway.

Once outside Billy, speaking more to himself, wondered how he would get his boss and new partner to agree to his taking out a wagon on a personal matter. Claire, following behind him, nodded when he gestured to a recess behind the door, indicating she should stay out of sight while he was gone. Hitching up his trousers, he pushed the warehouse door open, strutting forward as if he owned London itself.

❀ ❀ ❀

"Is St. Martin your real name?" His voice now contained a compassionate tone. They had ridden in silence for most of the trip.

Claire wanted to explain to him why she was leaving her husband, but she couldn't bring herself to reveal that the life her father had sought for her had been so quickly broken into tiny pieces, like a shattered mirror.

"It's the name I'll go by now, but my married name was Kirkwood—Mrs. Bennett Kirkwood." Tears shimmered in her eyes as she faced him. "Please, Billy, I can't talk about it, but you must believe me when I say I shall never return to Silverwood House after today."

As she directed him up the drive to her former home, Billy sat back in surprise, scratching his head thoughtfully. He had guessed that she was gentry, but the house spoke of money and power, neither of which had ever been his. He looked at her again. "Are you sure, miss, that you wants to leave what looks to me like a soft life, especially if you was to compare it to a life in service?"

"I don't have a choice really, Billy. I have no family and the one person who might help, an old friend of my father, is out of the country. And to tell the truth, I'm not sure what he would make of all this."

They had pulled up to the front door. Claire had been holding her breath, waiting for the door to be opened by the butler, but it remained closed. *The servants must still be at the fair. Now I only have to get past Mrs. Dixon.*

"I'll be as quick as I can, Billy. When I'm done, will you carry my trunk out?"

Billy had already jumped down and was holding out his hand to help her alight. "You just give me a whistle, missus." He watched as Claire gently pushed the door open and slipped silently inside. *Well now, I better make a change or two to this old wagon.* He pulled the large packing blanket from the floor of the wagon and draped it casually over both sides, covering the sign Dabney's Freighthouse—Hanbury Street, London. *No one will guess where to even begin looking for her now.*

Climbing the staircase, Claire wondered where Mrs. Dixon was. *Perhaps she's taken a half day also. Could I be that lucky?* Holding her breath, she crept up the steps agonizingly slowly, hoping to avoid creaking stairs, floorboards, or any other noise that would alert anyone who might be in the house to her presence. Once inside her bedchamber, she crossed to the small alcove where her trunk had been stored. Flinching at the scraping sound it made as she dragged it toward the bed, she paused to listen for footsteps but the house remained still. Moving quickly, she emptied drawers and the large wardrobe, folding items haphazardly in her frenzy to be gone. She retrieved her small bag of coins and tucked it into her trunk, keeping two coins out to pay Billy. Intent on finishing the task she had set for herself, she was unaware of the bedroom door slowly inching open.

"Mrs. Kirkwood, why are you packing...?' She couldn't finish her question.

Claire spun around, a guilty blush suffusing her face. "Mrs. Dixon ...I didn't think you were in."

"I must insist that you answer my question, madam. Does your husband know your intention?"

Claire made a heroic attempt to face the housekeeper down. "How dare you question me! Why, I'm shocked, simply shocked, at your insolence. When and where I travel is none of your affair." Moving to the window, she opened it, and leaning forward, called out to Billy to come upstairs.

Mrs. Dixon, thin lips almost disappearing in her disapproval of the situation, took a stance before the open trunk. "You're not going anywhere, Mrs. Kirkwood. As soon as I discovered your absence, I sent a message to your husband. He's probably on his way back as we speak."

Billy entered the room, eyes round at the luxury and riches that surrounded him. "Oi, missus, here I be. Would that be the trunk you be takin'?" He advanced a step in the direction of the housekeeper who had crossed her arms and stood glaring at the audacity he was demonstrating to his betters. "S'cuse me, leddy, but I was hired to haul a trunk and that's exactly what I plans to do." Boldly he removed her from his path and heaved the trunk onto his shoulder. "Missus, you comin'?"

"Yes, Billy, I'm right behind you." Meeting the piercing, angry eyes of the housekeeper, Claire looked around, satisfied she had missed nothing. Turning her back on the woman, in a final defiant gesture, she removed her small gold wedding band and laid it on the dresser. Mrs. Dixon listened to their footsteps as they made their way down the stairs and out the door before she roused herself enough to walk over to the window.

Watching as the occupants of the wagon made their way down the drive, she peered at the wagon itself, hoping to spy out a name, but a scruffy blanket hung over the side, thwarting any chance she had of identifying the owner. Frustrated, she stomped downstairs, praying that Mr. Kirkwood was indeed on his way.

The housekeeper's frantic note had indeed reached Bennett Kirkwood who was even now racing back to London, his friends riding with him. Shocked at the girl's unexpected show of spirit, one and all wondered where she would seek shelter, for they were all aware of her total dependence on Ben, the man who was her husband and their friend. No, she had no one else and no money. Even that old fussbudget, Lord Jennings, was away, somewhere in France, Claire had told him. Both Ben and Braxton, aware of the danger she might be facing, urged their horses on.

Ben's thoughts tumbled about in his head as he rode, seeking to lay blame anywhere but at his own door. *Why did my friends let me leave without talking to her, try to explain...at least a note? We all knew she was shocked—what woman wouldn't be? If ever I see that swine Peckworthy again, I'll put a bullet through his head.*

Another mile passed, another mile closer to London. *And why did Braxton agree to such a preposterous plan? The bastard was probably already lusting after her and I unwittingly helped him.* He spurred his

Oh Wicked Escort

horse on, momentarily oblivious to the rain that had started to fall. *I was shocked that Braxton went along with Peckworthy's mad scheme. He should have been delighted that the Yankees were solving the dilemma of what to do about his brother. And if I was sent to debtor's prison—that would leave the way clear for him to court my wife.* Ben swiped angrily at raindrops that fell on his face as he continued his silent tirade. *He's probably ready to crawl on his knees to Claire once she's found, begging her forgiveness for his own part in that pact with the devil.*

He looked behind him at the Chambers brothers. A bitter laugh escaped his lips as he scanned their faces. *Julius keeps staring at his brother with murder in his eye but I doubt he has the nerve.* Ben looked down the muddy road, calculating how much longer before he reached the warm haven of Silverwood. *And I wonder how much longer he'll allow that vile mother-in-law Letitia Penrod to remain under his roof.*

His eyes fell on Teddy, that tittle-tattler, that gossipmonger! Ben's hands clenched the reins tighter as he fought to control his rage. *That damn Teddy! If only he hadn't let Letitia know the goings-on of my marriage.* His horse, sensing his rider's unrest snorted beneath him, forcing Ben to grip the reins even tighter. *The little worm probably can't wait to fill her ears with the latest happenings.*

Ben paused, his thoughts turning to his much abused bride. His mind awhirl, he envisioned every horrific possibility that such an innocent might encounter on her own. *She was blameless in all of this. Let me find her, safe and unharmed and I'll spend the rest of our days making amends. After all, they say time heals all wounds—she'll forgive me. Oh Lord, she has to forgive me.*

The Chambers brothers rode along with their friends, silent and not quite as introspective, although Julius vowed, not for the first time, to have nothing more to do with his brother, sister-in-law, and most especially his mother-in-law, the loathsome Letitia.

Teddy, as he followed the others, wondered if he dare tell his mother-in-law of this latest development. *Imagine the little twit running off on her own.* Even now, he was reluctant to admit his part in this nightmare, knowing that although he was temporarily out of favor, he had heard it said that time healed all wounds.

And the rain continued to fall, almost unnoticed by the somber quartet who rode toward London.

They arrived back in the city in the early evening, their horses exhausted and the men in a like condition. Falling in behind Ben and Braxton, the Chambers brothers started to accompany them to Silverwood, but Ben told them to go home to their wives. He and Braxton had trotted along the cobblestoned roads, both wondering what awaited them when they reached their destination, both hoping that Claire had returned, repentant but safe.

The despondent butler, his bearing dignified but his manner morose, stood at the door, waiting for them to enter.

"Has Mrs. Kirkwood returned?" A negative shake of the servant's head gave Bennett his answer.

"Bring us something to eat and a bottle of wine. We'll be in the library. And don't look so glum, we'll find her." The servant merely nodded his head, knowing that the girl, if she was clever and determined not to be found, could hide forever in London. "And have Mrs. Dixon join us immediately!"

The plump housekeeper entered the room moments later, her stiff demeanor daring them to find any fault with her. Taking the chair indicated by her employer, she perched prudishly on the edge, defiantly meeting the cold blue eyes of Bennett Kirkwood.

"Mrs. Dixon, although I am most grateful that you alerted me about my wife, I must ask you a few questions and try to sort out what exactly happened here. My first question must be how do you know, in fact, that she has fled? Or why? She could merely be out visiting." His voice trailed off.

The housekeeper thought for a moment. *Should I tell him about Mrs. Kirkwood being so upset when she found out Betty had been dismissed after being seen in Whitechapel? No, wherever she's fled, I won't give this pair any sort of direction to look for her.* She took a deep breath, knowing her position was at an end and thus making her feel almost invulnerable, and delivered her answers in a clipped, brusque manner.

"The 'why' she fled, sir? It's common knowledge below stairs, Mr. Kirkwood. All of us know that it wasn't you that shared her bed on your wedding night. And might I add that if servants know, it's most likely known far and wide. Did you expect anything less?" Both men flushed guiltily at the servant's frank accusation.

"And I do indeed believe Mrs. Kirkwood has left Silverwood permanently. After I sent you the note saying she was nowhere to be found, she returned. I had given the house staff the afternoon off—that was before I knew she was gone—and so was in the house alone, or so I thought. I heard some bumps and bangs coming from upstairs and crept ever so cautiously up the stairs. Her door was open, and I could see her moving about, packing her trunk. She called to someone below her window to come up after I confronted her."

"Did you recognize this person?" It was Braxton who spoke, his voice filled with hope.

She pressed her thin lips primly together. "No, Mr. Kane, I'd never laid eyes on the likes of him before. She called him Billy and told him to take her trunk down. When I protested and tried to block the way, he forcibly moved me to one side as if I were a child and then carried the trunk outside. She followed right behind him. I looked out the window but all I saw was an old wagon. If there was any lettering on the side of the cart, it was covered by a scruffy, tattered blanket, just as shabby as its owner. And this Billy, such a common, vulgar man, why, I could barely understand anything he said." She nodded her head for emphasis.

Ben stood up, preparing to usher her out of the room when she spoke once more, in a tart voice that forestalled any questions.

"I regret, sir, that with all your troubles, I must inform you that I'm leaving Silverwood House, tomorrow morning in fact. I find it most distasteful to work in a house with the sort of goings-on that seem to be happening here. I would appreciate it if you would write a character for me but if you choose not to, well, that's your business. I'm going to my sister's cottage in York. She's a widow now, so it would be just the two of us."

Bennett held up his hands in a gesture of surrender. "Enough, Mrs. Dixon! I'm sorry you're leaving, but I'll manage just fine without you. I must say you have some nerve asking for a character." He saw her blanch at his words and felt some small bit of satisfaction as he grasped her elbow firmly and escorted her to the door, closing it decisively behind her exiting figure.

"Well, Braxton, you know as much as I do. Any ideas?" The other shook his head, knowing that the vague description of the wagon and its driver probably fit half of London's carters.

The two talked awhile longer but finally decided they were too tired and the hour too late for anything to be accomplished today. They would meet in the morning and form a plan.

Chapter Ten

The sun had only just risen when Claire was shaken awake by an excited Betty, eager to begin learning about her new position. Claire took less time than she normally would in performing her toilette, for she was also learning, not only about her situation but about her new station in life.

As she dressed, Claire recalled the previous evening and her nervousness as Billy's wagon had halted in front of Henderson's Domestics. She hadn't expected it to be so late, and Mrs. Henderson, as she opened the door, mentioned the lateness of the hour.

After Billy had bid them both a good evening, her new employer had led the way to the dining room, explaining that the evening meal was over but the cook had saved something for her if she was hungry. Betty, who had also missed dinner, was cautiously spooning hot soup into her mouth when they entered the dining room. Mrs. Henderson left them to chat, admonishing them to tidy up after themselves, which included washing their dishes. They giggled as the imposing figure left them, presumably making her way to her own bedroom.

Neither of the girls was aware that after they had left Henderson's that morning to collect their belongings, Mrs. Henderson had entered the dining room where her other employees—four women and seven men, which included Mr. Smith—had just finished lunch and were still sitting, enjoying a second cup of tea. The driver of the omnibus, Mr. Smith, transported the servants to their engagements around the city and was just making his way to the door when she called out to him, asking him to stay for a few more minutes. She had caught the attention of all of her staff, for meetings were rather uncommon unless it was to admonish them for some slip-up in serving.

"Everyone, if I might have your attention." She waited for the buzz of conversation to die down before speaking again. "I have just hired two young ladies to fill our vacant posts." Smiles appeared on all of their faces, for they had all had to work harder to fill the void.

Holding up her hands to stop any comments, she regained their attention. "They are both young, probably under twenty years old. One of them, a Miss Betty Sims, is the daughter of an old friend and seems to be of a pleasant disposition. The second woman is a Mrs. Claire St. Martin. She is a recent widow, fallen on hard times." The woman paused, wondering how to phrase what must be said. *I might as well just come out with it—there's no way to put this delicately.*

Licking her dry lips, she smiled at the upturned faces. "I don't know how to say this, so I'll just come out with it. Mrs. St. Martin is a very striking young woman…" She paused again, ignoring the surprised gasps that swept round the room. "But she appears to be modest and unpretentious. I believe we'll find that she is just like all of us—she needs employment in order to survive, and I expect all of you, without exception, to give her your friendship. If her prettiness proves to be a problem among you for any reason, well then I'll have to dismiss her, which would be harsh treatment based on looks alone."

She was quickly rewarded for her candor as all present declared their willingness to judge her on merit and help her fit into their tight little circle. She quietly voiced her gratitude and left them to discuss it amongst themselves.

And now, as Betty and Claire descended the stairs the following morning, the first person the two girls encountered was Mrs. Henderson, nodding her head in greeting just as their feet touched the main floor.

Her stern expression relaxed into a smile as she indicated the two newcomers follow her down the hall. As the three entered the dining room, the hum of conversation stopped abruptly, the seasoned employees quietly appraising their new colleagues from top to toe. An excited buzz arose from the men's end of the table as all of them, both young and old, gawked at Claire's stunning beauty. Taking the two vacant chairs, the girls sat down, their youthful appetites whetted by the aroma of the breakfast fare, plain but nourishing though the meal proved to be.

There was a momentary lull as introductions were made, and Claire, looking at her fellow employees, counted six men and six women, including Betty and herself. The conversational thread was slowly picked up and was similar to the meal, basic and unexciting. As breakfast ended, everyone carried their dishes into the kitchen where two of the women rolled up their sleeves to perform scullery duties. The others, with similar household tasks to perform elsewhere in the building, disappeared just as Mrs. Henderson entered, carrying a bundle of neatly folded clothes.

Smiling at both of them, she sat down and indicated that they join her. "We don't have enough time to outline your duties before services but that will be attended to this afternoon. I trust you have both remembered that this is a Christian household and since it is Sunday, we will all be attending St. Bartholomew's together. I prefer the early service."

She separated the clothing into two piles, each bundle containing a serviceable black dress, two starched white aprons, and two mob caps. She pushed the piles toward the girls. "We'll begin your training as soon as we return home, Mrs. St. Martin. As I mentioned yesterday, Henderson's Domestics has been hired to serve at a formal dinner tonight at the Spanish Embassy."

As the woman arose from her chair, Claire felt overawed as she became aware of the height and the enormous bosom of her employer, formidable attributes that had somehow escaped her notice earlier. There was a faint shadow of a moustache above the thin lips that were now smiling down at her.

"Ladies, I suggest you fetch your bonnets and shawls. We'll be leaving shortly." As she turned away, Claire sensed the woman deliberately presented as imposing a figure as possible.

Dismissed, Claire and Betty ran up the stairs to their room, carrying their newly acquired wardrobe. They could hear chatter coming from the occupants of the other rooms as everyone rushed about, all reluctant to draw the attention of Mrs. Henderson by appearing late.

D. L. Robinson

Claire and Betty were the last to arrive outside. As they looked about, a horse-drawn omnibus drew up, the kind that was seen on the streets of London transporting shoppers to the high street or workers to their places of employment. Painted on the side of the wooden vehicle, in dignified black lettering, was almost the same legend as in the front window of the building.

Henderson's Domestics
Brick Lane - Whitechapel
Daily Rates

At the sound of Mrs. Henderson's voice, they turned toward her. She was smiling, obviously proud of her novel solution to a problem. "Do you like our mode of transportation, ladies? The city was selling it as scrap, so my late husband purchased and refurbished it. The driver, Mr. Smith, escorts all of Henderson's Domestics to and from whatever grand house they happen to be working in, thus I am doubly able to ensure that no person of questionable morals is in my employ. And when he's not escorting my staff around the city, he makes himself useful, delivering firewood in the winter, shoveling snow, keeping weeds down, whatever might be needed."

She nodded her head as if she was gathering her thoughts before continuing. "And would you believe it, he even makes a little extra on the side. He drives a hearse to local cemeteries when the funeral parlors are overrun with business, paying me a percentage of his earnings for use of…a conveyance, if it's needed. Oh yes, our Mr. Smith is a most industrious and resourceful man." She lowered her voice. "Don't be put off by his appearance though. He might seem a little odd, but he certainly does his job efficiently." Having dispensed this last piece of advice, she moved off, leaving both young women puzzling over how "odd" Mr. Smith could possibly be.

The male servants were standing beside the omnibus, waiting to assist the six female employees up, each hoping to be the one to lend a hand to the delicate beauty that had just entered their lives.

Inside the conveyance were long wooden benches on either side of the vehicle with narrow windows running the length of the wall above, allowing some light inside. The newcomers, following their more experienced female colleagues, somehow managed to squeeze themselves onto one of the benches. The men, as they entered, followed suit on the opposite side. Claire could hear the unruffled tone of Mrs. Henderson's voice as she conversed with the as yet unseen driver but was soon distracted by the surreptitious flirting between the two benches, accompanied by much muffled giggling as the cumbersome wagon plodded its way along the bumpy road.

The more perceptive among the group had already decided that Claire was not a servant by profession, no, not of their station at all. The few words she had spoken at breakfast revealed that her speech was too refined, her voice too soft, and her words too cultured, more the sort to work *for* rather than work *with*. Bessie Marigold, a morose individual with bright apple-red cheeks, made it her business to keep her eyes on those under her, reporting any indiscretion or misstep to Mrs. Henderson. She decided that this young girlie was just the sort to cause trouble, and she'd be watching her double hard.

The carriage had come to a stop, and the doors were flung open as the men climbed down first, again vying for the privilege of being the one to help the young widow, Mrs. St. Martin, to alight. The other women snorted their distaste at such apparent lack of good manners, but even Bessie Marigold admitted that the woman had done nothing to invite such attentions, at least not yet.

Claire looked around as she stood with the others, apparently all awaiting their employer to lead their small company into St. Bartholomew's. As Mrs. Henderson emerged from the other side of the carriage, Claire caught her first glimpse of the driver who had been described as odd and was now walking toward them.

The man was of average height but seemed dwarfed as he stood next to the formidable figure of Mrs. Henderson. He appeared to be of mature years with a muscular frame, a fair complexion, and under an unremarkable nose was a neatly trimmed moustache and beard. His black leather coat was shabby and cracking with age. A threadbare deerstalker cap was pulled slightly forward, almost but not quite hiding his bushy eyebrows.

Claire shivered, almost in foreboding, at her first sight of Mr. Smith.

She chided herself for being so fanciful—she wasn't usually the sort given to such girlish silliness. The circle of passengers drew back slightly as the two passed, but whether this was a mark of respect or wariness of Mr. Smith, she couldn't decide.

Mrs. Henderson, pausing in front of Claire and Betty, introduced them to her driver who, as she liked to point out to all newcomers to Henderson's Domestics, was the man who would transport them to all of their working engagements by the scheduled hour and be on hand to see them safely home. The man barely tipped his hat in acknowledgement, his eyes olive black and unfathomable in their murky depths as they fell on her and lingered, making her very uncomfortable. Claire could barely suppress another shudder.

"How do, ladies," he murmured, mockingly raising his hat. "I am assured by Mrs. Henderson that both of you will not only be obliging but prompt. I abhor late arrivals, don't you?" A faint lisp was barely discernible when he spoke. He took Claire's and Betty's arms assertively, compelling them to enter the church just steps behind their employer, the others quickly falling in behind them like a covey of quail.

As Mrs. Henderson strode up the aisle to sit with her lady friends, Mr. Smith led the servants to pews that could contain all of them, nudging Betty into the first one, followed by himself, and then Claire. Bessie Marigold, intent on monitoring the goings-on of her fellow employees, followed closely on Claire's heels, the others taking their seats as the vicar of St. Bartholomew's began the service.

Bennett was drinking coffee when his friend was announced. Braxton strode in and, after refusing his friend's offer of breakfast, took a chair and stared intently at the man he had always considered to be a close friend, his fingers drumming an impatient rhythm on the table.

"Well, Ben, were you able to get anything further from your housekeeper?" The look on the other's face answered the question. "What about Lord Jennings?" His voice got lighter. "Could she have found her way to Romford House?"

"Forget that one, Braxton. I thought I had mentioned that Claire had a note from him a few days ago, saying he would be out of England for a few weeks." His words became vague. "I think he went to France or some such place."

Braxton stood, his grey eyes hard and cold as glacial ice. "I can't sit around here all day, wondering where she spent the night, knowing that I'm partially to blame for her fleeing Silverwood. I'm going to ride through a few boroughs of the city. Who knows, I might even see her. Will you join me, Ben?" The other man rose, glad to be doing something and, even if it proved pointless at least it was something, which had to be better than nothing.

Sometime later, having ridden down the high streets of some of the districts of London, searching for a familiar face, they paused at the corner of Brick Lane in Whitechapel, trying to decide which direction to take when an omnibus came abreast of them. All were soon trapped in the congestion caused by an overturned wagon further down the road. Both Ben and Braxton, caught up in their quest, paid no heed to the vehicle or to the legend *Henderson's Domestics* painted on the side of it, but the driver immediately became aware of them, pulling his hat lower over his brow and hunching his shoulders, almost as if he would disappear if he could.

The driver caught enough of their conversation to know that they were searching for someone. *Did they say Kirkwood's wife? When did he get married, and why were they searching for her?* The man, known to his passengers as Mr. Smith, stroked his moustache nervously before he dared take a quick look and saw his half-brother Braxton Kane astride a horse, not an arm's length away. *I could plunge a blade through his deceitful heart before he knew what was happening,* the man reflected, sniggering quietly to himself at the thought. Mrs. Henderson, sitting beside him, heard the soft laughter and wondered, not for the first time, what went on in the man's head.

Inside the omnibus, though their words were unclear, Claire recognized their voices and was barely able to control her gasp of surprise. Her body stiffened in shock, her breath coming in quick, shallow gasps. Betty, chatting amiably with one of the other maids, noticed immediately that all was not well with her former employer.

"My dear, what's wrong? You've gone white as a sheet."

Claire, not wanting Betty to become aware of who was outside just a few feet away, smiled at the woman who was fast becoming a cherished friend.

"It's nothing, Betty dear, really. It just seems so stuffy in here, that's all." Her fingers fanned her face, trying to cool her flushed cheeks. Unconvinced, the freckled face frowned, her gaze falling by chance on the two men on horseback outside their carriage. She turned, wide-eyed, to meet the frightened eyes of Claire, and the two clasped hands until at last the congestion outside began to clear. The horsemen moved down the street to carry on with their fruitless search, unaware of how near the object of their quest had been to them.

The carriage, continuing its journey from St. Bartholomew's, turned onto Brick Lane, moving at a snail's pace in the crush of humanity toward home and what had become a haven to two of its residents.

As they rode along, each lost in their own thoughts, Bennett Kirkwood suddenly turned to his companion. "Would you think me mad if I said I was going to visit Peckworthy tomorrow?" Braxton stared at him, unsure if he had heard Ben correctly.

"I'm serious, Braxton. If anyone might know where Claire has gone, it would be that spawn of the devil. He had all of us watched for months, and we never suspected a thing. Maybe he's continued to watch," his voice was full of hope as he continued, "and Claire just became one more to keep an eye on."

"Well, Ben, if you're willing to talk to him, the least I can do is to go with you." Nodding in mutual agreement, they each turned in the direction of their respective homes, plans made to meet on the morrow.

Peckworthy kept his two unexpected and uninvited visitors cooling their heels for a short space of time before he designed to join them. Ben paced restlessly but Braxton preferred to sit, wishing the coming interview was already ended.

Footsteps alerted the pair to the arrival of the man they were seeking, but it was Leopold, his mute bodyguard, who crossed the threshold first, sniffing his contempt at the intruders before taking up his customary stance in front of the window. Peckworthy then entered the sitting room, his gaunt frame clothed in costly fabric, mourning band still prominent on his arm, and his thinning ginger hair neatly combed. Curiosity was evident on his face, doubtless overcoming any reservations he might be having about seeing them.

"Gentlemen." He dipped his head slightly. "I thought our business dealings complete."

Ben studied his adversary, looking for any hint that he knew the reason for them being there. "Do you know where she is?" He spat out the words contemptuously.

Mordock Peckworthy's eyebrows shot up in surprise, his manner changing from curiosity to annoyance. "Who is 'she', and why would I know 'her' whereabouts or anyone else's you might have misplaced? Have a care, Kirkwood, and choose your words wisely."

Leopold casually laid his hand on the pistol in his belt when Braxton stood up and began pacing the room. He had watched Peckworthy's face and was already convinced he knew nothing. Laying a hand on his friend's arm, he quietly counseled Ben that they should leave, but his advice was ignored.

"My wife is missing, sir, and I for one am not convinced that you're innocent of any knowledge of her whereabouts. You had all of us watched for months, you bragged about it at our first meeting. Why would I not think you might have continued to watch us, just expanding your spider's web to include Claire?"

A cautious smile played about the man's mouth as he gazed at his uninvited guests, seeming to take a perverse pleasure in their accusations. He laughed, an evil laugh that chilled both of them, a shadow of annoyance crossing his face.

Speaking more to himself than the others, he absentmindedly rubbed his chin. "So the bride has fled. I didn't think she had that much gumption." He paused for a moment, lost in thought. "The question I must ask is...how did she find out?" He held up his hand. "No, don't tell me, let me guess...Teddy Chambers!"

Bennett, snarling his rage, faced his nemesis. "You bastard! You knew Teddy Chambers loved to gossip, in fact you counted on it. And his mother-in-law, it couldn't get any better, could it? I suspected Teddy was as much a part of your 'revenge' as Braxton and myself."

Smiling in delight, Mordock Peckworthy looked at the rival for his dead wife's affections, whether real or imagined. "And now you're in my home, to accuse me of...what, exactly?"

Bennett Kirkwood stood, shoulders slumped in defeat. "Never mind, Peckworthy. Sorry to have bothered you."

Braxton also rose, his grey eyes filled with icy contempt. "Peckworthy, I agree with Ben, you're worse than a bastard. You chose to lay the blame for your sorry marriage at Ben's door, and you sought revenge. I admit we all had our own selfish reasons for carrying out that ridiculous farce without one thought ever given to Claire. But she found out! And now she's wandering the streets of London, homeless, friendless."

"As I have already stated, gentlemen, our business is finished. Good day."

Braxton, seeing the mocking smile on Peckworthy's face, turned and stormed out of the house, followed closely by Ben. The one thing that had been accomplished was that they were both satisfied that Peckworthy knew nothing of the girl's whereabouts. *And where will I find her, that auburn-haired beauty with the deep and soulful brown eyes?* He sighed glumly as his thoughts continued to wander. Anger directed at himself rose to a crescendo as the two rode down the road.

What's wrong with me—was Ben right? Am I sniffing around the skirts of another man's wife? And if I should find her, what then? She would still belong to another. Shoulders slumped in dejection, Braxton nudged his horse forward.

Ben guided his horse to Braxton's side. "I think we're finished, Braxton. There's no way we'll find her, not with the whole of London to hide in. Perhaps the best thing we can do is to wait for her to become desperate enough to return to Silverwood."

Astonishment crossed the other's face. "You're giving up? Just leaving her to her fate?"

"She chose to run. I don't know where to begin looking." Ben lifted his chin defiantly, meeting his friend's hostile gaze straight on.

The bonds of their friendship had never before been so strained. Wordlessly, Braxton tipped his hat in a gesture of farewell and turned his horse in the direction of his own home, his anger so great he dared not spend another moment in the other's company.

Ben watched the other man ride off, relieved that a greater rift between the two had been avoided. *This whole thing is Peckworthy's fault. I'll find some way to get even. And I'm sure Braxton will fall in with any plan I come up with. He hates the man as much as I do.* Satisfied with his own twisted reasoning, he spurred his horse on, suddenly anxious to be in his own surroundings.

Chapter Eleven

Claire hurried up the steps to the front entrance of Henderson's Domestics. She should have set off earlier that morning but had had no idea what sort of time to allow. It was a long trip to the docks and then she had to do a lot of walking. Intent on finding Berwick Shipping Lines, she ignored the distraction of the sailors and other men who called out to her as she passed by. Before leaving home, she had memorized the address from an advertisement in the newspaper, pausing occasionally to ask directions from anyone who appeared respectable.

Her plan had been forming in her mind for some time—she was going to sail to either America or Australia, whichever proved cheaper. She hadn't shared her secret with anyone, not even Betty, for she was sure her friend would attempt to dissuade her. *But Betty has been quite occupied lately with her gentleman, James Forrester. I doubt she'd even notice my absence.* She hurried up the stairs to her room, barely avoiding the dreaded reprimand from Mrs. Henderson about punctuality.

As she hastily slipped on her serviceable black dress and crisp white apron, thoughts flew around in her head. *The cost of passage to America was high at 6/6, even in steerage it was £4, a lot of money...and I'd still have to pay for a train or coach to Southampton. But if I'm very careful, I could leave England before too many more months pass. And I'm sure I could get another position wherever I go, thanks to Mrs. Henderson's exacting standards and training.*

The panic she had felt those many weeks ago still haunted her. *What if Bennett or Braxton had glanced inside and seen me?* She had considered leaving London, but to go where? England was no longer the safe haven her family had always thought it to be.

Her mind wandered back to her first days in the employ of

Henderson's Domestics. Mrs. Henderson, who could be somewhat of a bully, had pushed Claire hard, training her to carry a tray of glasses or food without spilling anything, curtseying respectfully when spoken to by her betters, and above all, never voicing an opinion, no matter what the provocation. A servant was expected to serve and to be almost invisible while doing so.

Claire had proven to be a quick learner, pleasing her employer with her aptitude. Eloise Henderson had also noticed that many of her employees turned to the younger woman for direction in performing their duties, recognizing that she came from a privileged lifestyle. *Claire blessed the memory of her Aunt Marie, and her insistence that Claire learn how to conduct herself in the ways of the rich and privileged.*

Taking Claire aside one day, Mrs. Henderson had spoken decisively, making the girl a proposal. "You, Claire St. Martin, are obviously of a different class of people. Your talents are being wasted passing glasses of champagne around. I think you would be more effective behind the scenes, overseeing that the champagne is poured into clean glasses, canapés are hot, and no one is shirking their duties. Yes, you have a definite flair for organizing the chaos that seems to accompany these events. I'll even raise your wage by £1 a year."

"And Claire, I don't know who or what you're hiding from, but I think there is less chance of discovery tucked away in a kitchen than moving among the elite. With a face as striking as yours, someone is bound to recognize you eventually."

Claire, at first dumbfounded at the woman's shrewd judgment, could only babble her thanks, for she too had worried about coming face to face with someone who might recognize her. But now she need never expose herself to a chance meeting. And more money! She had hugged her employer, surprising that decidedly reserved woman with such a show of emotion before running up the stairs to her bedroom.

And now, many weeks later, she had actually spoken to someone about boat passages and thus taken the first step in her plan to leave England and sail across the ocean, into a new life. She was glad she had finally decided to take Betty into her confidence, but unfortunately they had been overheard and word had quickly spread. It seemed everyone knew with the possible exception of Mrs. Henderson.

Skipping down the stairs, she saw that all were assembled and she was the last arrival. After inspecting the crisp white shirts and aprons against the black dresses of the ladies and the white shirts and black suits of the men, Mrs. Henderson clapped her hands for everyone's attention before speaking.

"Well, now that everybody is here, you can be on your way. Tonight's event is a ball with a late supper. Most of you will be passing out wine and canapés until it's time to serve dinner. Remember to be a credit to Henderson's Domestics." She nodded her dismissal but just as Claire was reaching the door, her voice called out, "Mrs. St. Martin, might I have a word?" There was a short silence before the chattering resumed as the last of her fellow employees went out the door to where Mr. Smith and his omnibus waited.

"The others already know this, Claire, but I won't be accompanying you today. I know you'll do just fine." Smiling at her in encouragement, she gave the younger woman no chance to voice any objection as she escorted her outside, holding up a finger to stop any protests. "You'll be fine, Mrs. St. Martin, though perhaps you should ride up front, beside Mr. Smith. That's where I always ride, and it will lend your new position more authority. Good-bye, my dear." She stepped back inside and shut the door, effectively ending any arguments the younger woman might have had.

As soon as Claire appeared, the male servants began assisting their female counterparts onto the omnibus as she made her way to the front of the vehicle, where Mr. Smith stood stiffly at attention. "Evening, mum. There'll be rain tonight." His words were spoken slowly and deliberately, knowing that his lisp , slight though it was, on occasion provoked fits of giggles from some of his passengers.

His mouth spread into a thin-lipped smile as she neared, his hand outstretched to her. Once again, Claire tried to hide her disquiet of the man, not noticing the scowl of disappointment that crossed his bearded face as he handed her into the seat usually occupied by Mrs. Henderson, holding onto her hand a trifle longer than necessary before at last releasing it.

"Good evening, Mr. Smith." She looked at the black sky worriedly as she settled herself into the seat. "I, for one, hope it doesn't rain." She then looked straight ahead, optimistically hoping to discourage any further attempts at conversation.

"Oh, you needn't worry, mum. Should it start to come down, we'll be right cozy up here under this big umbrella I've got tucked away under the seat."

They rode in silence through the city toward the elegant manor that was their destination for the evening. Claire, nervous at being in charge completely for the first time, ticked off in her mind the tasks to be performed and the order in which to do so. *I'm not sure I'm ready for this.* A wave of apprehension swept through her when she realized they were pulling up at the servants' entrance. Mr. Smith climbed down and stood waiting to assist her, help she reluctantly accepted. The others were also clambering out, brushing at wrinkles in their clothing and patting their hair in a rush of last-minute primping.

The door swung open and a thin, middle-aged woman stepped out, holding her lamp high as she searched the arrivals for the familiar face of Mrs. Henderson. Claire stepped over to the woman and introduced herself, explaining that her employer had been unable to come but that she, Mrs. St. Martin, would be in charge of those servants provided by Henderson's Domestics.

The beanpole of a woman stepped back and sneeringly looked Claire up and down. "You look far too young to be handed such authority. Well, it will be Mrs. Henderson that gets a dressing down if anything goes awry." Dark eyes snapping, she stepped back inside, gesturing for the temporary staff to follow her. Walking through the kitchen, the cook and her helpers had no time to look up, but the serving staff stared curiously at the newcomers. The housekeeper, who had finally introduced herself as Mrs. Redding, gathered the newcomers around her.

"You must not only look impeccable...your skill in serving must also be flawless tonight, without any mishap. There will be guests from abroad, and Lady Bestwick is most anxious that everything run smoothly." Her voice grated harshly on Claire's nerves.

"None of the guests have arrived yet, so let me give all of you a quick tour of the dining room and ballroom so everyone knows their posts and the route back to the kitchen." Claire followed them, her anxiety lessening as she realized that not only was she prepared to do the job of organizing and directing the servants, but she need have no worries about anyone from her past noticing her, a lowly maid. The upper classes never ventured beyond the kitchen doors.

They were herded into the servants' small dining room off the kitchen where wine glasses had been filled and set on trays. The footmen slowly dispersed to various positions, ready to offer liquid refreshments to the guests who had now started to arrive. The maids stood waiting impatiently for the hot canapés to be arranged on platters so they too could begin the task of serving their betters, all the while stealing quick looks at the costly gowns and jewels that seemed to float around the ballroom, listening as refined and educated voices called out greetings to newly arriving acquaintances.

Claire, unmindful of the milling guests, kept the kitchen maids busy filling more wine glasses to be ready whenever a footman returned with an empty tray. All of the staff, permanent and temporary, were performing faultlessly. Strains of music drifted out to the kitchen, reminding Claire of another time, another life. Pushing those thoughts from her mind, she performed her own duties without a flaw, impressing Mrs. Redding into a grudging, silent respect.

The evening wore on, and Claire, wisps of auburn curls escaping from her lace-trimmed cap, became aware that the late supper was at last being served. Soup tureens, perched on small wheeled tables, were being cautiously pushed toward the dining room by the footmen, followed by maids bearing baskets of bread. The minutes ticked by as bowls of vegetables and platters of meat were being readied in the kitchen, until the quiet hum of voices was broken by a sudden cry of pain, immediately followed by the sound of shattering china. Mrs. Redding, followed closely by Claire, entered the dining room, immediately assessing the cause of the turmoil.

Molly, one of the Henderson maids, a plump, sweaty girl with a bent toward the dramatic, held her reddened arm up, sobbing noisily as two of the Henderson footmen, Arthur Tucker and his brother Gordon, worked quietly and efficiently clearing the broken pieces of the soup tureen which, unfortunately, had not been totally empty when Molly bumped into it. Moving toward the maid, Claire put her arm awkwardly about the stocky girl's shoulder, softly urging her toward the kitchen.

As the fuss subsided, all but one of the diners resumed eating, the majority chattering about the clumsiness of the help and other domestic crises being currently experienced by them.

Braxton Kane sat, stunned, as bits of conversations floated around him. Apologizing to those seated nearest to him, he rose in one fluid motion, and lithe as a cat, moved slowly in the direction of the kitchen, his face clouded with apprehension.

It couldn't be this easy, not after all this time. Who could have predicted I would be sitting at the table of someone with hopes of ensnaring me in a marriage to a daughter or niece, when in walks the face that has haunted my dreams these past months.

Pushing the door to the kitchen slowly open, he saw the only occupants were concerned with the meal being served. His presence was noted with little more than mild curiosity and surprise, the kitchen staff too busy to question his being there. It was at that moment that Molly again broke into loud sobs, the sound of those sobs leading him to the servants' dining room off the main kitchen. Claire's back was to him as she applied a salve and a dressing to the girl's burn but Molly, facing the doorway, spied the grand gentleman as he entered the room and stopped her wailing abruptly. Claire, curious as to who or what had the power to stop the girl's moaning, turned around.

Claire stood there, tongue-tied, surprise draining the blood from her face. Leaning on the wooden table for support, she heard, as if from a great distance, his quick intake of breath. The tenderness in his expression startled her, and she continued to stare at him, speechless. Rationality slowly returned to her as Molly, equally awestruck, croaked out a greeting of sorts, inviting him into the small room. The walls seemed to shrink as he pulled the door closed, ignoring the curious stares of those in the kitchen.

"Molly, back to your duties. Hurry up girl, they'll be shorthanded. Go!" Molly, curiosity raging, reluctantly left the room, pouting in resentment at being sent away. Slamming the door as loudly as she dared, Molly hurried off, eager to impart a bit of gossip about the mysterious Mrs. St. Martin.

Claire licked her lips nervously, a feeling of fear and anger knotted inside her. *What right does he have to come in here?* A wave of apprehension swept through her as she considered her options. *I could run—but where would I go? No, I'll try to reason with him, beg him not to give me away.* As she steeled herself inwardly, Braxton's deep voice reverberated through the room.

"I've been searching these many weeks for you, Claire. I won't be boorish enough to ask why you ran..." His handsome face flushed as he recalled his own despicable behavior that night.

Claire, reminded of her wedding night, seethed with anger and humiliation. "I have nothing to say to you, Mr. Kane. The past is just that, the past! But now that you've found me, my question must be what do you plan to do about it?"

His long frame leaned against the wall as he gazed at her, his expression unreadable. There was a sudden, sharp rap on the door, followed by the appearance of Mrs. Redding, disapproval evident as she spied an unknown man.

"Excuse me, but you're not allowed visitors while you're working. The gentleman will have to leave." Arms crossed forbiddingly, the woman stood there, determined there would be no immoral behavior of any sort while anyone was under her care, even those that were there only temporarily.

A shadow of annoyance crossed Braxton's face but he held back a retort. Turning to Claire, he grasped her hand and brought her fingers to his lips. "We have to talk. When can I see you?"

Struggling to maintain her badly shredded dignity, she snatched her hand back. "Please, just go! I can't afford to lose my position."

Glancing at the disapproving Mrs. Redding, he sighed, and when at last he spoke, his voice had an infinitely compassionate tone. "All right, Claire, I'll go. But I'll be back and you will listen to what I have to say." He was whistling softly as the door closed behind him.

Mrs. Redding, with a sniff from her beaked nose, watched him leave the kitchen before turning to Claire. "Mrs. St. Martin, I will have to report both incidents to Mrs. Henderson—first that clumsy girl breaks a valuable soup tureen and now this." She strode off, muttering something about not understanding what the world was coming to.

It was more than two hours past midnight when the last dish was

Oh Wicked Escort

washed and put carefully away. Those from Henderson's Domestics gathered their wraps and stumbled tiredly outside to the patiently waiting Mr. Smith and his omnibus. Claire would have climbed into the more sheltered part of the vehicle but again Mr. Smith came up and stood beside her, waiting to hand her into the driver's box.

The man seemed on edge as he seated himself beside her, puzzling Claire slightly. He was usually so cool and composed. Bending down, the man picked up a tattered blanket from the floor of the driver's box. "Care to cover up, Mrs. St. Martin? It's a cool night—been raining off and on all evening." Claire shook her head, wondering what species of bug might be lodging within its folds.

The darkness that enveloped them couldn't hide the tension that seemed to emanate from the man and, uncomfortably, Claire edged over on the small bench they shared until she could go no further.

One of the Tucker brothers shouted through to their driver. "What's all the to-do about, Smith?" Receiving no reply, he persisted. "Wasn't that a copper's whistle?"

As the omnibus bumped steadily over the cobblestones, Claire and the other passengers could hear whistles being frantically blown and frenzied shouting in the distance. Those inside the conveyance began peeking through the windows, chattering nonstop, everyone speculating what might have happened to cause such a furor so late at night. Sensing that the driver was watching her, Claire shifted uncomfortably, the disturbance that had attracted everyone's attention fading into the distance. The horses, knowing there was a warm stable and fresh hay waiting for them, were soon the only creatures to be seen or heard as they clopped along the uneven road.

Braxton couldn't sleep that night, his thoughts refusing to leave Claire. *In some way, she has not only left her husband but somehow has managed to land on her feet.* He shook his head in amazement. *She's not only found employment but is obviously well thought of. Her position seemed to be one of some authority.* Feeling suffocated in bed, he kicked the covers off and began striding about his bedchamber, soon falling into a pattern of staring pensively out the window into the black night and then walking the length of the room before returning to the window once more.

Will I tell Ben? Should I tell Ben? She never asked for my silence but I think she was about to before that carping shrew appeared. I must see her again! I'll go round first thing tomorrow morning to Lady Bestwick's. Having settled on a course of action in his mind, he crawled back into bed, soon drifting into a deep, dreamless slumber.

It was midmorning when Braxton, astride his horse, studied the manor of Lord and Lady Bestwick, deciding finally that it would be best to ride around back to the servants' entrance. *After all,* he reasoned, *she's posing as a servant, so where else would one look for such a person?*

Arriving at the rear of the manor, he dismounted, tying his horse to a small post. A young freckle-faced boy sat shelling peas into a bowl. He nodded a greeting to the youngster, who in return could only stare at the well-dressed gentleman in awe.

"I wonder if you could help me find someone…" Braxton hesitated, unsure of how one dealt with young children, and this one couldn't be more than seven or eight years, surely. "What's your name, lad?"

Realizing the visitor was talking to him, the boy roused himself from his perch, almost up-ending the bowl and its contents. "I'm Peter, sir. And just who you be looking for? I knows everyone what lives here."

Encouraged, Braxton smiled, warming to the subject. "I'm looking for a young woman, a real beauty, Peter! Lustrous, auburn hair, deep, brown eyes with thick black lashes, a short, charming nose, a delightful but firm chin, and oh yes, she's very slender but not very tall." There was a trace of laughter in his voice as he continued, "She looks delicate, Peter, but don't be fooled." He shook his head before continuing. "I think she's one of the strongest people I've ever met. Probably less than twenty years old."

He saw the puzzled look on the boy's face and wondered if he had given too much detail. *After all, he's just a child.*

The lad looked at the man, regret written on his face for the lack of help he was able to give. "There's no one here like that, sir. Any of them what works here is all very old, at least thirty, maybe even forty. And my old granddad says there's not a beauty in the lot."

Braxton gave the boy a sidelong glance filled with disbelief.

"You're mistaken, lad. I was here last night and met her in a room just off the kitchen."

"I knows for sure there's no one here like that, but I could go and ask Granddad. Everyone says he can sniff out a bit o' fluff…" He started walking toward the door. "And anyway, I wasn't even here last night. I was helping George in the stable."

Grabbing the boy by the shoulder, Braxton swung him around. Frustration flashed across his handsome features. "Fetch that scrawny woman that seemed to be in charge of things. Do you know the one I mean?" The boy shook his blond head vigorously, wanting only to escape from the stranger's sudden anger. "She'll know who I'm talking about."

Worried that he might get in trouble for not being of more help to the caller, the boy beat a hasty retreat into the house, calling frantically for the housekeeper who, upon appearing, sternly admonished him for creating such a disturbance. He pointed toward the door, saying there was a fine gentleman outside wanting to talk to her.

Mrs. Redding, spine ramrod straight and pointed chin held defiantly high, stepped outside. Recognizing the gentleman who was asking for her, she suddenly became fretful that she might have jeopardized her position, should he decide to go to Lady Bestwick with a complaint.

"Sir, you wanted to see me?" Her eyes peered nearsightedly at the man she had previously regarded as an intruder. Chewing nervously at her lower lip, she was prepared to fall on her knees and plead with him not to involve Lady Bestwick in their little scrap the previous evening.

"Yes, I do, Mrs…" he paused.

"Mrs. Redding, sir. Housekeeper for Lord and Lady Bestwick these past eleven years—with nary a complaint, I might add." She saw that his eyes were a stormy, thunderous grey and doubted he would show her any pity. "And you are…?"

Braxton seemed quite surprised by the question. "I, madam, am Braxton Kane of Pennygrove Hall. Now, Mrs. Redding, I've already spoken to young Peter who tells me anyone employed by Lady Bestwick is quite ancient, at least by his standards. That being said, what about the young woman I was speaking to last night before you so rudely interrupted us?"

The housekeeper's sharp mind seized immediately on what this despoiler of women was after, and remembering her own youthful experience, had no intention of allowing it to happen to that nice Mrs. St. Martin. *After all, it wasn't her fault this rake came seeking her out. No, I'll protect her, from both him and herself.*

Smiling smugly, Mrs. Redding shook her head. "I'm sorry, sir, but that young lady was hired only for last night. She did her job satisfactorily and was paid her wages, and quite frankly sir, I don't expect to ever see her again." *Not a lie, just not the whole truth.*

Braxton shot the woman a hostile and disbelieving glare. "Surely you have some idea where Mrs. Kirkwood went? She can't have just walked off into the night!"

"Mrs. Kirkwood! Who's Mrs. Kirkwood? It certainly wasn't that young lady's name. Perhaps you mistook her for someone else?" She spat the words out contemptuously.

His tone was relatively civil in spite of his anger. "Madam, she was no stranger to me. And if she no longer calls herself Mrs. Kirkwood, what name does she go by? Surely somebody must—" Feeling an acute sense of loss, his voice trailed off, his jaw clenched in frustration. Nodding at the woman curtly, he mounted his horse, unable to accept the dull ache that engulfed him as he turned his steed toward the road. Just as he reached the corner of the manor, he heard a shout.

Turning in the saddle, he spied young Peter and an older, grey-haired man standing at his side. He rode back to where they stood. "Were you calling me, Peter? And might this be your granddad who you say can sniff out a bit of fluff?"

The older man smiled, playfully cuffing the boy at this assessment of his talents. Peter nodded, anxious to return to his bowl of peas before Mrs. Redding found him gone. "Yes sir. I asked Granddad and he says there was extra servants here last night."

Braxton's head snapped up, instantly alert, his eyes fastening on the man. "Mrs. Redding led me to believe the lady I seek was engaged just for the night. I never thought there would be a number of them hired on a temporary basis."

Peter's granddad nodded his head warily, hoping the housekeeper didn't step outside and find him talking to a toff. "Yes sir, there must have been a dozen or so extra servants hired, just for last night, mind. And I can guess which one you're asking about, a real beauty she was. I heard it mentioned that Mrs. Redding hired them from somewhere in Whitechapel."

Braxton grinned briefly at the boy and his granddad with no trace of his former rancor. Digging in his pocket, he pulled out a few coins and handed them to the old man.

"Buy yourself a pint, sir, and make sure young Peter gets a treat as well. And know that you have my deepest gratitude."

He was whistling cheerfully as he nudged his horse in the direction of Whitechapel. At last, he had a starting point, and with a bit of luck, he'd find the elusive Miss St. Martin or Mrs. Kirkwood, or whatever she chose to call herself.

After a night spent tossing sleeplessly, Claire felt it a relief to get out of bed. *Braxton, why did you have to come back into my life? I was trying so hard to forget...*

Her misery was almost a physical pain. Shaking her head, she tried to push him to the back of her mind while she readied herself for the day ahead, knowing she would have to report the events that had transpired at Lady Bestwick's and she had better do it before Mrs. Redding reported on the happenings herself.

She woke Betty, and with few words spoken waited patiently while her friend performed her brief toilette. About to leave their bedroom, there was a sharp thump on the wall, causing both girls to jump in surprise.

A look of annoyance crossed Betty's freckled face, and there was more than a hint of exasperation in her voice. "Why is that Bessie Marigold banging on the wall? We've hardly spoken a word since we woke up."

Looking at Claire, the two started to giggle as they made their way downstairs. On reaching the dining room, they were surprised to see Bessie already eating, scowling at everyone as each new arrival sat down. The girls looked at each other, both framing the same question in their minds. *How did she beat us down here?* Shrugging, they took their accustomed places at the long wooden table, not giving the incident another thought.

Despite everyone suffering from lack of sleep, they all sat chatting amiably, wondering what had happened the previous night to cause police whistles to be heard.

Mr. Smith, the last to arrive for breakfast, greeted no one and sat down at what had quickly become "his place" at the end of the table, almost as if he was trying to be as inconspicuous as possible.

His presence puzzled Mrs. Henderson. *He never joins in any conversation, he just sits there, occasionally lifting his head and glancing around the table, as if assuring himself everyone was present and accounted for. The man is such a recluse, why has he suddenly decided to endure the company of his fellow employees at mealtime?*

Had she asked any of the others, they would have told her that their driver seemed to be developing a fondness for Mrs. St. Martin, not that she ever encouraged him in the slightest, they would have been quick to point out.

Seeing the meal was at an end, Mrs. Henderson sent them about their daily duties, beckoning Claire to join her in her office, and just as Claire had expected, she was less than happy about the events of the previous evening.

"Molly will have to go. She's too clumsy and always ready to flirt with any man that crosses her path." Speaking more to herself than Claire, she continued to grumble. *And who will pay for the broken tureen? Not Molly—she wouldn't earn enough in a year to cover the cost.* Sighing, she stared out the window, regretting ever hiring her dead husband's niece. She'd have to explain her actions to the girl's mother, something that made her both uncomfortable and irritable. *Oh, let her stay...she'd have no chance at all if she were to be sent home.*

Claire, unaware of her employer's inner battle, knew she couldn't argue with her reasoning, for the girl did seem to be all thumbs. She sat waiting, for she had also confessed that an acquaintance from her past had somehow discovered her, but before there was an opportunity to take any sort of liberty, Mrs. Redding had interrupted and sent him on his way.

Mrs. Henderson sat silently, lost in thought, until Claire finally stirred. "This man, was he somebody special? More importantly, girl, will he try to find you again?"

"He was a friend of my husband's." She tried to hide her inner misery from the woman's probing stare, giving a choked, desperate laugh. "He has no reason to seek me out."

The older woman, after a final piercing look, shrugged her shoulders as she dismissed the matter. "You've done well, Claire. Since neither incident was of your doing, I'm more than pleased with your performance." She hesitated before speaking again. "I've decided to give Molly another chance. She'd just become some tavern slattern if I was to send her back to her mother." She nodded to herself, satisfied with the decision she had reached.

She opened a ledger, which Claire interpreted as a signal to leave the room, but just as she reached the door, Mrs. Henderson called out to her. "Claire, just a moment, dear. Since this is the first day of September, perhaps we should look at the schedule for the month."

She was already leafing through her well-thumbed appointment book until she reached the month of September. "We'll be busy this month—every Saturday is already taken, and there are a number of afternoon teas. And there's a ball at the American Embassy on September thirtieth." She sat thinking for a moment. "I wonder if they'll require our services." Claire sat down and the two women talked about the various dates and problems that might arise until quite late in the morning.

It was during lunch that one of the men casually mentioned the commotion of the previous night, wondering aloud what all the fuss had been about. Had anyone been watching, they would have noticed Mr. Smith stiffen at the turn in conversation. It was Gordon Tucker's guess that some disreputable burglar had been caught in the act. His brother Arthur had merely laughed, shaking his head at all of them in their innocence.

"I walked up to the butcher's this morning. You know Ollie, he 'ears everything that goes on in these 'ere parts. Seems there was a 'orrible murder over on Bucks Row..." He paused delicately for a moment before continuing, "an 'unfortunate' got 'er throat slit, and so it's said, even 'er stomach was ripped open." He saw horrified looks on some of the faces, but others regarded him with blank expressions until he smilingly enlightened them. "You know, ladies of the evening, prostitutes."

"Mr. Tucker." Mrs. Henderson ground out his name between her teeth, her voice coolly disapproving. "Those poor women you're calling prostitutes—most of them never planned to sink so low. In fact, many of them were forced into it when husbands deserted them or parents died, leaving them with hungry mouths to feed any way they could. I think we could all show some Christian charity toward them, for they're really nothing more than victims themselves."

Hoping she had given her employees something to think about, she spun on her heel and disappeared down the hallway, but hers wasn't the only departure. Mr. Smith, with much sullen muttering, went to see to the horses. Stifled giggles were heard around the table, and for a few short moments, they pondered Mrs. Henderson's words before once more speculating on whether the coppers would catch the culprit. But with so little known, the diners soon lost interest and began making plans for their afternoon off.

The meal ended and the washing up was soon taken care of. Claire laughingly called out to Betty that she would fetch their bonnets as she lightly ran up the staircase to the second floor. With a free afternoon, most of the Henderson employees had made plans to attend a fair that had arrived in Whitechapel two days earlier.

Unlocking her bedroom door, she skipped across the room to where the two bonnets hung, lifting each from its hook. Turning, she stopped abruptly. On the pillow of her bed lay a single red rose. Puzzled, she picked it up, feeling a moment of panic. *Silly, it's not for you—it's for Betty. Somehow, James had managed to make his way into the women's quarters.* Still carrying it, she made her way downstairs and handed it to Betty who stood waiting for her. Betty smiled at her friend but her expression was one of curiosity.

"Why have you given me a rose, Claire?"

"I found it on my pillow." She lowered her voice, not wanting anyone else to hear. "James must have slipped in and somehow found our room. He just mistook which bed was yours."

"Claire, James isn't in London." There was a nervous edge to her voice. "He's gone to Bath. His Mr. Beaton wanted to take the waters. Don't you remember me telling you? He won't be back until Thursday or Friday."

As casually as she could manage, Claire looked at her friend. "Of course, I remember now, Betty dear. Well, someone left this rose…I wonder who was foolhardy enough to dare enter the women's quarters."

"If it was on your pillow, dear, perhaps it's for you." She was sorry as soon as the words left her mouth when she saw the effect they had on her friend. The color drained from her face as the rose fell to the floor, unnoticed by either of them.

A flicker of apprehension coursed through Claire. *It's impossible. He can't have found me, much less located my bedchamber. Someone would have noticed a stranger creeping about.* She forced herself to draw a deep breath before speaking again.

"It was probably meant for…someone just made a mistake." Handing Betty her bonnet, the two linked arms and went out into the sunshine to join their friends, neither noticing a shadowy figure step out from the darkest corner of the room and pick up the forgotten flower, breathing in its sweet scent before crushing it beneath the well-worn heel of a boot.

Chapter Twelve

The small party had reached the footpath leading to the fairgrounds when, one by one, they became aware of a horse and rider keeping pace with them. It was Molly who spoke first.

"Oooh, Mrs. St. Martin, it's 'at fine gentleman what was looking for you t'other night." Her words became lost in a fit of giggles. "Oooh, ain't 'e a 'andsome bloke?"

Claire halted, shocked at Molly's words. Looking at the man who sat atop his horse, she was too surprised to do more than stare. "You!" An unwelcome blush crept into her cheeks.

"Good afternoon, Claire, and also a good afternoon to you lovely ladies and to you gentlemen." He spoke to all of them but gazed only at her.

Giggling and shuffling of feet prevailed except for Betty who stood back, not knowing what to do. *How can I stop someone, obviously a rich someone, from taking what he wants?* She positioned herself protectively beside Claire as they watched him dismount.

"Good morning, Mr. Kane. Whatever are you doing in these parts?"

"Ah well, Betty, is it? I've been searching all of London for the lady you seem so intent on protecting." Reaching past Betty, he extended a red rose to the woman he couldn't put out of his mind. In fact, if he was to be totally honest, he didn't want to forget her, ever.

Spying the flower, Claire's deep brown eyes flew open. She retreated a few steps, as if he held a poisonous viper.

Her soft voice trembled with emotion as she turned to her friends. They had had to step off the footpath as small clusters of pedestrians passed them, all intent on reaching the fairgrounds but finding a moment to stare curiously at them.

Oh Wicked Escort

"I will have to beg you to excuse me." At the bewildered look from the faithful Betty, she nodded. "Don't worry, Betty, I'll be fine." She watched as the others reluctantly left the drama that was unfolding before them and continued, albeit ever so slowly, toward the fair.

She could feel an imperceptible flicker of hysteria coursing through her as she turned to meet this most unwelcome visitor's curious gaze.

"Mr. Kane, I haven't the faintest notion why you have suddenly re-entered my life, and truth be told, I don't care in the least." As casually as she could manage, she asked the question that had been haunting her every waking moment since their chance meeting at Lady Bestwick's. "Have you told Bennett where I am?" Her voice had drifted into a hushed whisper, her composure a fragile shell around her.

He stared at her, totally baffled. "Madam, until last night's chance meeting, I didn't even know where to find you, although I won't deny I've been looking for you. By the greatest good fortune, I was led to Whitechapel, and upon inquiring where I might hire temporary servants, the lady who sold me this rose told me to try Henderson's Domestics on Brick Lane."

She felt herself shrinking from the grey warmth of his watchful eyes and suddenly was furious with him. Rancor sharpened her voice.

"If you have any regard for me, leave me in peace to make a new life for myself." Lifting her chin, she took a deep breath, ignoring the faint light that twinkled in the depths of his eyes. "Leave me alone, Mr. Kane. I never want to see either you or Bennett again, at least not in this lifetime." Her voice was cold, her words precisely delivered and exact. "And if you're waiting for me to fall to my knees and beg you not to tell Bennett my whereabouts, you will be sadly disappointed, but that will have to be your decision. Good day, sir!" Triumph flooded through her when she saw him wince at her words.

Gathering her skirts, she turned away, not waiting for a reply. Shoulders stiff, she turned back toward the building that so far had afforded her a safe haven.

Braxton, speechless, watched her flounce down the path, not noticing when the rose he still held dropped to the ground, soon trampled by the restless hooves of his horse.

As Claire drew near to what was now her home, she saw a familiar face studying her progress. "Billy Marple, whatever are you doing here?" Even as she spoke, she experienced a sense of alarm. Has anyone else from her past tracked her down? Her apprehension must have shown in her face.

"Steady now, my girl. I've just come round to be sure that all was well with you."

Relief evident, Claire stepped forward, and much to his surprise, affectionately hugged him, leaving him temporarily speechless. "Oh, Billy, thank you for your concern, but I'm doing well."

Shyly, she smiled at the man she would always consider her knight in shining armor. "I've decided, Billy, to leave England. I should have enough saved in a year or so to pay for my passage to America or Australia." Her words tumbled over each other in her excitement. Billy smiled at her, uncertain about the wisdom of her plan.

Standing there, they both became aware of a horse being tied up and the rider approaching them. Billy heard her sudden gasp of astonishment as she faced the intruder.

Her voice rose in controlled anger, her words thrown at him like stones. "Mr. Kane, was I not clear enough when I said I never wanted to see you again?" She stamped her foot in frustrated emphasis. "Never, never, never!"

Exasperated with the man, Claire failed to notice Bessie Marigold, the self-appointed guardian of morals at Henderson's Domestics, appear at the open window, drawn there by Mrs. St. Claire's voice raised in anger. Bessie, who had chosen to stay home, local fairs being of no interest to her, listened for a moment before she withdrew and quickly went to summon her employer.

She heard his voice, chuckling and hearty. "Why Claire, I did indeed hear you, but I thought your words lacked..." he paused, as if searching for the right word, "a certain conviction." Smiling, he turned his attention to the man he had seen Claire impulsively embrace.

"Are you going to introduce me to your friend, madam, although I have a strong suspicion this might be the mysterious Billy that Mrs. Dixon was going on about? I, sir, am Braxton Kane of Pennygrove Hall." He held out a hand in greeting, and somewhat taken aback, Billy offered his own as the two men took each other's measure.

"Might I inquire the purpose of your visit, sir?" His question shocked Claire into speechless indignation.

"How dare you question anyone concerning me?" She spat out the words contemptuously.

"Oi, missy, the gent only wants to know you're not bein' taken advantage of." Billy turned and faced Braxton. "And you be right, sir, she needs protectin' but not from the likes of old Billy Marple." He shook his head for added emphasis.

"The fact of the matter is that I told my missus about Mrs. St. Martin and now she wants to meet her, never havin' the opportunity to invite quality in for tea before. My Maybelle admires women who refuse to be pushed round by husbands, fathers, or the like, oh my, yes. Why, she's even started to attend meetins' about the rights of women, not that she's ever felt threatened by the likes of me, oh my, no." He scratched his head in momentary puzzlement. "Oh my, yes, that's why I been sent round…to invite this here young lady to tea, whenever she has a free afternoon."

It was at that precise moment that the door of Henderson's Domestics creaked open to reveal the formidable Mrs. Henderson standing there, quickly assessing the situation. "Mrs. St. Martin, is there a problem?"

Nervously, Claire glared at Braxton. "No, Mrs. Henderson, there's no problem. This gentleman was just leaving."

"Why Claire, I am indeed surprised at your lack of manners." He turned to the imposing figure. "I, madam, am Braxton Kane of Pennygrove Hall." Taking the woman's hand, Braxton bowed over it before lightly brushing it with his lips. Blushing furiously, Mrs. Henderson almost giggled. "And this other gentleman is Mr. Billy Marple, who has come to invite Claire and myself to tea with his good wife, Maybelle, and himself, of course. All that remains is for you to tell us when Claire will have a free afternoon."

The proprietor of Henderson's Domestics barely had time to recover from her first encounter when he swooped down again, intuitively assessing her weakest point.

"Might I also take this opportunity to compliment you on your business acumen…Mrs. Henderson, is it? What a clever scheme. Extra servants for hire, whenever needed, well trained and well groomed. Do you perhaps have a card or pamphlet I might pass around to friends?"

Giggling like a schoolgirl, Eloise Henderson became putty in his hands. Turning, she saw the morose face of her least popular female employee. "Bessie, fetch me a business card for the gentleman." The servant, afraid of missing anything, was back in a flash, handing a white card to her mistress.

"Here you are, Mr. Kane, my card. And I believe Mrs. St. Martin has Wednesday afternoon free." She fluttered her eyelashes. "Will that suit you?"

With a nod of approval from Billy, Braxton confirmed his agreement, taking almost no notice of Claire who stood listening as everyone but her decided how her free time would be spent. About to voice her objection, she spied Bessie standing just inside the doorway, listening to every word being spoken. Not wanting to add to the woman's already extensive collection of gossip, she nodded her head in agreement as a time was agreed on between Braxton and Billy.

Braxton, giving her no opportunity to do more than send him a withering glare, smiled at both her and Eloise Henderson. "I'll call for you at two o'clock Wednesday, Claire. Good day, ladies." He bowed his head, his expression that of a cat that had swallowed a canary, making Claire wish they were alone so she could slap the smug look from his handsome face.

Not wanting to allow her any opening to call off the arrangements, Braxton took Billy by the arm, pausing just long enough to retrieve his mount's reins. The two strolled down the cobbled road, barely glancing at the omnibus as it rumbled into view, its driver suddenly hunching over as Billy and Braxton ambled by.

The two women, distracted by the arrival of the omnibus, watched as Mr. Smith expertly turned it onto the Henderson property. Ensuring there was no chance of them being overheard, Eloise Henderson spoke, concern in her voice.

"I can only assume that this Braxton Kane is not the man you are hiding from, my dear. Will he keep your whereabouts a secret, do you think?"

Oh Wicked Escort

Claire could only nod her head as the two women entered the building. With a mumbled apology, she hurriedly crossed to the stairway leading to the second floor. Flying up the stairs, she stumbled through the doorway of her bedroom and fell onto her bed, wrapping herself in a cocoon of misery, tears of frustration slowly tracing pathways down her pale cheeks.

❊ ❊ ❊

The following day, after dutifully attending morning services at St. Bartholomew's, the staff again boarded the omnibus, having been hired to serve at an afternoon function in the drafty halls of Pegborn House. A benefit tea was being held for the Orphans of London, overseen by a collection of ladies possessed of a charitable nature whose goal was to improve the plight of orphans who somehow managed to survive on the streets of London.

The work, while lighter than serving a dinner, was no less demanding, but all of the employees of Henderson's Domestics sailed through the afternoon, performing their duties flawlessly. When the affair ended, they once again climbed onto the waiting omnibus. There were a few half-hearted attempts by Arthur Tucker, the more gregarious of the two brothers, to stir the others into conversation, but even discussion of the murder of the "unfortunate" two nights ago failed to arouse much of a response.

As snippets of conversation drifted through to Mr. Smith and the young woman who occupied the seat beside him, he tried in vain to engage her into voicing an opinion about the murder. Claire wondered at the change in the man, for on the ride to Pegborn House he had been unusually quiet. He had handed Claire out of the vehicle without comment, but now on the return journey, his manner was proving to be quite the opposite.

At last recognizing that she had no desire to join into a conversation with him, he lapsed into a sullen silence until they were nearing home. He cleared his throat before speaking. "I've been curious, Mrs. St. Martin, about your gentlemen callers yesterday."

Stiffening, Claire turned in her seat to rebuke him for his insolence. She would not be questioned about her private life by anyone, most especially one hired to escort them to and fro. "Mr. Smith…" She got no further.

Smiling almost shyly, yellowing teeth peeking out from under his moustache, his dark eyes meeting hers, he spoke, his lisp barely evident. "I know it's none of my business, but are you well acquainted with either of them?"

"I hardly think that any of your concern, Mr. Smith." Spots of color had appeared on her cheeks.

Bobbing his head, the driver hesitated before speaking again. "I meant no harm, madam. I merely thought the taller one was a gentleman of my acquaintance. Is his name Robert Thomas by chance?"

No, Mr. Smith, his name is not Robert Thomas. I hope your curiosity will be satisfied to learn that the gentleman's name is Mr. Braxton Kane of Pennygrove Hall."

Silently snickering to himself, he mockingly touched his hat in a gesture of deference. "Aye, Mrs. St. Martin, my curiosity is indeed satisfied."

※ ※ ※

As much as Claire wanted time to stand still, Monday and Tuesday flew by, Monday serving at yet another tea and Tuesday a dinner at Lord and Lady Chitham's London manor.

Mrs. Henderson had added to her stress by smiling warmly at her whenever they chanced to meet, complimenting her on her capable performance at both the tea and the dinner, confiding that Lady Chitham, always one to find fault with temporary servants in an attempt to reduce the fee charged, had been impressed.

But no matter how one might dread the passing of time, it did eventually go by, and in due course Wednesday morning dawned, bright and sunny. As she entered the dining room, all conversation stopped, and Bessie Marigold, who had been whispering in Molly's ear, flushed guiltily as she returned to her own chair. Everyone looked askance at Claire, for Bessie had quickly spread the happenings of Claire and her two gentlemen callers. Claire, having no intention of discussing her private life with anyone, kept a tight rein on her thoughts, not missing the smug look on Bessie's face.

It was immediately after lunch that Betty, a worried look on her freckled face, brushed her friend's rich auburn tresses into a mass of shining ringlets, all the while chewing at her lower lip to stop herself from blurting out a plea to her former mistress to stay at home, thus avoiding the company of that devilishly handsome Braxton Kane. She helped Claire choose a simple, striped green frock from her trunk, not wanting to present too fine a figure to the eager eyes of Maybelle Marple.

The minutes turned into hours and it was only when they heard the sound of a carriage stopping outside, closely followed by a firm rap at the door, that Claire, pale and trembling and with a last hug for Betty, glided through the bedroom door and down the stairs.

As her feet touched the main floor, she looked across the room and saw Braxton standing, hat in hand and seemingly unperturbed, as he chatted with Eloise Henderson. She took a moment to study him, seeing at a glance that the man, broad-shouldered and tall, would set any maiden's heart beating faster. The fact that he was handsome and obviously a man of means made him doubly desirable, if one were looking for a husband. Claire felt her cheeks flush at her thoughts. The embarrassment quickly turned to annoyance as he, spying Claire, inclined his head in a short bow, his eyes glowing warmly as he studied the picture she presented.

"Mrs. St. Martin, you are a portrait of incomparable beauty." She paused, unsure of the wisdom of going anywhere with this man. Seeing her hesitation, he crossed the room and taking her hand, brushed it softly with his lips. Straightening, he tucked her arm into his, and bowing to Mrs. Henderson, was about to leave when the older woman laid a hand on his arm.

"Perhaps, Mr. Kane, you'd be interested to know of another service which I provide to my employees, keeping their safety and well-being in mind." She turned and gestured to the man who had just entered the room. "Mr. Smith, would you come over here please."

The man, who had been deep in thought and oblivious to the three standing at the door, looked across the room and twitched his shoulders nervously. Nodding in deference to his employer, he pulled his hat lower and stumbled clumsily across the floor.

"Mr. Kane, this is William Smith, the man I rely on to see to the safe and prompt transport of all of Henderson's Domestics, both to and from their temporary positions."

Braxton attempted to see the man's face, but the other man only buried his chin deeper into his chest. "How do you do, Mr. Smith?"

The man made an unintelligible response, leaving the others at a loss for words at such boorish behavior. Just as he turned away, intent on making his escape, Braxton's voice rang out.

"Mr. Smith, have our paths crossed before today? I get the distinct impression that I know you." He paused, awaiting either confirmation or denial.

Without lifting his head, a muffled raspy voice, seemingly coming from the depths of his chest, replied, "No, I'd remember such an event." Without so much as a nod, he reeled across the room, moving at a pace that surprised even the unflappable Mrs. Henderson.

Flushed, she faced the other two. "I'm so sorry, Mr. Kane. Mr. Smith has always been a man of few words, but today he seems to have outdone himself." Smiling, she shrugged. "Oh well, he wasn't hired for his conversational skills."

She stepped back as Braxton opened the door and ushered a speechless Claire into his waiting carriage. Glancing back at the front window of the building, Claire saw a number of pale faces watching in fascination as she was assisted into the brougham and a world they could only dream about.

Claire sat stiffly as the carriage eased into the cobbled street, once more wishing she had followed her instincts and declined Billy Marple's invitation. *Oh well, there's no help for it now. I'll make the best of the day, and may the Lord help Braxton Kane if he has anything else in mind.*

They rode slowly through the crowded streets of Whitechapel, Braxton's attempts at conversation being met with little more than a yes or no from his travelling companion. He watched her as she glanced outside, perplexed by her curtness. The carriage, unable to avoid a bottleneck of traffic, was forced to stop and wait for the congestion to ease.

"Claire, I know you're angry with me..." She whirled around, amazement written across her face.

Her mouth opened but it took a moment before words began to pour out. "Why, Mr. Kane, whatever would make you say such a daft thing?" Her words were full of sarcasm, her eyes reflecting her befuddlement.

There was a slight tinge of wonder in the deep timbre of his voice. "Surely you must have some idea of my feelings, madam. After all, I've been searching for you." He paused before speaking again. "I would have declared…"

She held her hand up as if to stop his words. "Enough! I refuse to listen to anything you might have to say." Her voice rose an octave, causing a passing pedestrian to stare up at her in astonishment.

"You acted the role of a friend before that sham of a wedding, but it is now quite evident you were merely planning my seduction." She turned toward him, tears sparkling like diamonds on her thick black lashes. "What could make two grown men behave so abominably? Did you have a wager? Were you the winner or loser?" Tears were now flowing freely down her soft cheeks.

Braxton ached to take her in his arms but wisely only took out his handkerchief and attempted to wipe her tears away. She slapped the offending hand away, her eyes challenging him, daring him to try again. "Please Claire, let me explain."

She glared at him with burning, reproachful eyes, amazed at his audacity. "Explain! There is no explanation possible." She spun around and stared out of the carriage window, ignoring the tableau of humanity that slowly shuffled past the coach window. His hand grasped her arm, forcing her to meet his eyes.

"You must listen to me. Please!" There was a note of desperation in his voice. Two families were walking past them, their eyes alive with interest as voices from the halted carriage drifted out to them. The conveyance at last began to slowly inch forward.

"Braxton, there's nothing to say." She swiped angrily at the tears that continued to fall. "But before we arrive at Billy's home, I have to know…have you…? Her words stumbled out of her mouth. "Will you tell Bennett where I am?" Her anguish was overtaking her control. Swallowing the sob that rose in her throat, she looked up into his stormy grey eyes.

He smiled derisively at her. "Madam, it's been some days since I've been in the company of your husband, and as I've only just learned where you've been living, that question is rather pointless, wouldn't you think?" He suddenly glowered at her, his tone relatively civil in spite of his growing anger.

"Do you seriously believe that I would give your whereabouts away to Bennett or any other who might ask? You must believe me when I say I would do anything to change the course of events that occurred on the night of your marriage." He paused, a gamut of emotions crossing his striking countenance. "Do you honestly think so little of me?" His angry retort hardened his eyes.

"You fooled me when you acted the part of my husband. Surely you didn't think I would be eagerly anticipating another meeting after that horrible Letitia Penrod publicly exposed your duplicity." The words poured from her mouth belligerently. With a moan of distress, she turned away, her only thought to escape to the hopefully safe haven of Billy Marple's home.

"Why did you agree to this outing, Claire?" His words were suddenly soft, raising her ire once more.

She almost snarled her reply. "You cornered me into it. I couldn't very well refuse with Mrs. Henderson falling all over herself to please you. Believe it or not, Mr. Kane, some people have to make their own way in this world!" Her words stung him but she, unwisely, didn't stop.

"I have no intention of looking over my shoulder for the rest of my life, Mr. Kane. As soon as I have enough money saved, I'm sailing across the ocean, away from England, away from Bennett Kirkwood, and away from you."

Chapter Thirteen

His eyebrows shot up in surprise, and Claire knew immediately she had said too much. She turned and stared out of the window once again, unmindful that the carriage was turning onto a narrower road.

"Claire, I believe we're about to arrive at Billy Marple's. Can you put away your hostility and act like we're actually friends? Billy has your best interests at heart and if he suspects you're unhappy, I can't say how he's likely to react."

Not wanting to cause Billy any distress, Claire, still sniffling, nodded. Braxton offered her his handkerchief once again which she gratefully took, dabbing at her eyes and nose before absently tucking it up into her sleeve. She fussed with her hair and face before reluctantly turning to Braxton for his opinion on her makeshift toilette. As he nodded his approval with a warm smile, she prayed that neither Billy nor his wife would notice anything amiss. As the carriage came to a stop, the door of a neatly tended cottage opened and out stepped a much-scrubbed Billy Marple, wearing his familiar cheeky grin, his arm around the shoulders of a tidy, plump, blonde woman, welcoming smiles on both of their faces.

Billy stepped forward and opened the coach door, hands extended to lend aid to Claire as she stepped down. He frowned as he took note of her reddened eyes, turning to Braxton Kane with a searching look. Braxton shrugged noncommittally as he noticed the stir of interest the brougham was drawing from the neighboring houses. Curtains were being pulled aside to afford a better view, with the more daring stepping outside to boldly scrutinize such an unprecedented event, excited voices wondering aloud who the Marple's visitors were.

Billy, taking his wife's hand, urged her forward. "Maybelle, I want you to make the acquaintance of Mrs. St. Martin and Mr. Kane." Turning his head slightly toward his guests, he continued speaking. "Folks, this is my Maybelle, oh my, yes."

Claire, stepping forward, grasped the older woman's hand and pressed it warmly between her own. "Mrs. Marple, I'm so very pleased to meet you. On the few occasions that I've been in Billy's company, he has spoken most highly of you and your daughters."

Braxton, not one to be outdone, took one of the woman's work-roughened hands and brought it upward, brushing it with his lips. "Madam, it is indeed an honor to be invited into your home."

Maybelle could do little but sigh at the gallantry of the gesture, suddenly pleased that her neighbors were witnesses to such an occurrence, although it took great control on Claire's part not to snort in derision. *Why does he have to charm every woman he meets with such gestures, and why am I the only one to see through him?*

Maybelle, having rubbed elbows with women of both higher and lower social standings at her meetings concerning women's rights, was not intimidated by the couple before her. "Both of you are most welcome to our home. Please, do come in."

Billy, taking charge of the gathering, politely ushered them in, leaving the neighbors to speculate on the happenings inside the Marple cottage. Maybelle excused herself while she went to fetch the tea, leaving them with Billy in the tiny parlor, a room that smelled faintly of soap and beeswax. As the young couple sat down, he fixed them with a penetrating stare.

"Well, I see the ride over gave you no time to settle whatever it is that vexes you, missy, but if you were to be seekin' my thoughts on the matter, I be of the opinion that Mr. Kane means you no harm." He moved gingerly about the over-furnished room, as if it was a place he rarely visited, with its miniature curio cabinet and a small table filled with delicate porcelain figurines. Shaking a finger at them, he spoke in more of a whisper than the brash voice he usually employed. "And I caution both of you that I'll not tolerate anythin' that will spoil my Maybelle's little tea party, oh my, no."

A much-chastened Claire realized that her feelings were more transparent than she had realized. Rising, she kissed Billy on his cheek.

"Oh, Billy, I am sorry. You're right, I am vexed and it's none of your doing. I promise to behave, if Mr. Kane will promise likewise." Braxton only had time to nod as the tinkle of china heralded the arrival of Maybelle carrying her very best tea service on a large tray.

The remainder of the afternoon passed pleasantly with conversation ranging from Maybelle's interest in women getting the vote to Braxton regaling them with tales of his boyhood visits to the West Indies, and Billy voicing his opinions and dissatisfaction with the politicians who were at present running the country.

Claire was surprised to find she was enjoying herself, something she hadn't been able to do for far too long. It was with regret that the afternoon ended and she and Braxton were once more riding through Whitechapel.

Braxton was lost in thought, which suited Claire, who was content to watch the unending masses of people they were passing, wondering at the varied expressions of joy and sadness, anger, and sometimes what looked like madness playing across the anonymous faces, all of them seeming to be moving in all directions.

As they pulled up in front of the building on Brick Lane, Braxton roused himself and smiled at her. "Well, Mrs. St. Martin, we seem to have arrived at your door. I apologize for not being good company on the ride back, but you have given me much to mull over."

Claire looked at him in surprise. "What have you to 'mull over' where I'm concerned, Mr. Kane? We have shared a pleasant afternoon, but I have not changed my mind. You are a ghost from my past, and that is where I certainly intend to keep you—in my past!"

Smiling, Braxton stepped from the carriage and turned to assist her in alighting. "Oh no, my dear Claire, I am just as certain that we are meant to share not only the past but the present and the future."

Her brown eyes flashed warningly as he lifted his hat and smiled impertinently at her before taking her arm and leading her to the door where a smiling Eloise Henderson awaited them. "I enjoyed our outing, madam." Bowing courteously to both women, he returned to the carriage that stood waiting to whisk him away.

Descending the stairs that evening for dinner, Claire could hear excited chatter coming from the dining room. All eyes were focused on her as she entered the room, ranging from the friendly and interested to the curious and somewhat hostile. Ignoring them all, she took her seat, giving no hint as to what transpired on her afternoon away from Henderson's.

❀ ❀ ❀

Just as breakfast was ending, a flustered Mrs. Henderson called a meeting of the staff. "Thursday…I mean today of course, Henderson's Domestics has been hired by a Mrs. Grant to serve at a luncheon for the annual London Garden Party, held in nearby Gainsby Hall."

Claire, listening to her employer, thought she was not quite herself. She couldn't decide if the woman was annoyed or just what it was, but she gave her employer her full attention.

"Usually, Mr. Smith drives all of you to any engagement we have and is also responsible for seeing you safely back here to Brick Lane." She paused, trying to gather her thoughts. Curious as to what was to follow, everyone glanced at the reserved man who had so recently started joining them for most of their meals.

"He has volunteered to drive the hearse for the funeral of that poor unfortunate who was murdered last Saturday night." Her voice was almost apologetic and two bright spots of color appeared on her cheeks. "And while I think it commendable that he wants to assist the poor and downtrodden, it does inconvenience us somewhat."

There was the hiss of whispering as they were reminded of the murder, all wondering how this could possibly affect them. Lifting a hand to stop the chatter, Mrs. Henderson continued.

"Mr. Smith will be able to escort you to Gainsby Hall but will be otherwise occupied for the rest of the afternoon. The funeral itself is scheduled for three o'clock, but I very much doubt he will have returned by the time the garden party ends, sometime around half past four. I thought, since no one here has experience driving such a cumbersome wagon, that you could all walk back home. I most strongly admonish you to stay together, taking care there are no stragglers. Mr. Smith assures me that it's not very far and should take less than thirty minutes."

There was another outbreak of chatter but all hushed as Arthur Tucker stood and met his employer's eyes. "What I think, ma'am, is walking back 'ere will be a doddle, and speaking for me and my brother Gordon 'ere, we will be most 'appy to escort the ladies safely 'ome." Gordon, surprised at being volunteered, could only nod his head in agreement. Mr. Smith quietly pushed back his chair, pausing to listen to the exchange between Arthur Tucker and their employer, before he quietly left to tend the horses.

"Well, thank you, Mr. Tucker. I'm sure the ladies will also feel safer, knowing their well-being is in your capable hands."

Claire was skeptical that the younger brother Gordon's motives were selfless, for she had heard Molly and Grace, the youngest female members of the staff, gossiping about his penchant for trapping them in dark corners, kissing and fondling them until only the threat of a scream convinced him to release his prey. He had left both Betty and herself alone, so far at least, most likely because Betty had a steady gentleman caller and, curiously, he seemed to be somewhat intimidated by Claire, at least for the present.

Leaving the dining room, she and the others hurried up the stairs to change, for it would soon be time to leave for Gainsby Hall.

Bennett Kirkwood was announced just as Braxton was finishing his breakfast. The ever-efficient Mrs. Henfield, housekeeper of Pennygrove Hall for the past seventeen years, entered from the kitchen carrying a second cup and saucer, pausing just long enough to fill both cups. Nodding his thanks to her, Braxton invited Ben to sit down. Stirring the hot liquid, both seemed lost in quiet reflection until Ben, unable to bear the silence, began to speak.

"There's been no word of her." His mouth spread into a thin-lipped smile but it was a smile devoid of humor.

Braxton, unsure of what was coming, answered in a voice that contained a strong suggestion of reproach. "Does that surprise you, Ben? After what we did…"

Bennett held up his hands in mock surrender. "Enough, Braxton! You can't possibly point out any one of my multitude of shortcomings that I haven't already flayed myself with. And I have to admit to a certain feeling of desertion in my hour of need by one I always called friend."

Braxton nodded his head, preferring to remain silent. He studied the familiar face across the table and saw the petulant expression that he had seen so many times before but had always chosen to ignore. His conscience was quiet. After all, he had been out there, combing the streets of London for any sight of Claire while Ben had chosen to continue frequenting the gambling dens, especially since Peckworthy had kept his side of the bargain and paid all of his debts.

There were snippets of desultory conversation touching on mutual acquaintances such as the Chambers brothers, their wives, and the evil and much-abhorred Letitia Penrod, but the old, easy camaraderie was missing. After what seemed an eternity, Ben stood, ready to depart. A puzzled look crossed his face as he gazed at the man he had known since their shared school days.

"What's happened to you, Braxton?"

Surprised, the other looked up, suddenly cautious. "What do you mean?"

Bennett shrugged, unexpectedly at a loss for words. "You're not the same. I can't quite put my finger on it but you've changed somehow." He circled his friend, looking him up and down, searching for a clue. His eyebrows lifted and there was a snap of his fingers, a smile playing about his mouth.

He paced the room, his delight far reaching as he contemplated the man who had such a short time ago declared himself quite content to remain a bachelor. The pleasure he felt quickly turned to determination as he sought to discover the name of the woman who had captured Braxton Kane's heart.

"Braxton, have you met somebody? And by somebody, I mean a woman!"

Flushing, Braxton turned away. "Don't be ridiculous, Ben." Any embarrassment he felt quickly turned to annoyance as Ben continued to circle him, demanding a name. Recalling the woman he had spent yesterday afternoon with, he knew that love would always transcend the bonds of friendship. Thoughtfully he paused, surprised that he was using the word *love* but quickly realized it was the only word that could even begin to describe the overwhelming emotions he felt whenever his thoughts turned to Claire. *I wonder how he would feel if I suddenly shouted out that her name was Claire, Claire St. Martin Kirkwood, Mrs. Bennett Kirkwood, formerly of Silverwood House.*

Ben's badgering carried on until, in a fit of pique, he threw his hands up in mock surrender. "Very well, Braxton. Keep your secrets, but be warned, I will find out one way or another."

Braxton listened as his uninvited guest, in long angry strides, opened the door to the outside world, slamming it angrily as he wordlessly took his leave. Feeling somewhat relieved to be alone, Braxton couldn't help but contemplate what lengths Ben might resort to in order to discover the woman's identity. He knew, through long years of friendship, how relentless the man could be and should he discover her name, how disastrous the consequences would be. Wisely he decided that, at least for a few days, he would avoid Whitechapel altogether.

Walking back from Gainsby Hall had proven to be not quite the "doddle" that Arthur Tucker had envisioned. The day had been overcast, forcing those hosting the garden party to move their event indoors, and after Mr. Smith had transported them to the hall, the dreary weather had turned to rain. The downpour continued most of the afternoon, leaving large puddles along the road and the footpath, unexpectedly stopping just as the employees of Henderson's Domestics finished the last of their serving duties.

Claire, acting as Mrs. Henderson's representative, listened politely to Mrs. Grant, hoping her impatience to be off didn't impart itself to the organizer of the affair. The woman chatted on endlessly, promising to tell all her friends how satisfactory Henderson's had proven to be.

Claire interrupted the woman long enough to tell Arthur to begin the walk home, assuring him she would be following them directly. She watched as her coworkers hurriedly started walking down the cobbled road, all hoping to reach home before the rain began again, all of them expecting her to be no more than a few steps behind. It was more than the few minutes she had anticipated before Claire found herself at last free of Mrs. Grant. She stepped onto the footpath, looking up at the forbidding sky and the deserted road. *Even Betty has forgotten about me, she's been so distracted lately with her gentleman caller, Mr. James Forrester.*

Shivering in the evening's chill, she hugged her woolen shawl closer and began walking, watching the growing shadows warily. So intent on avoiding the puddles that were becoming increasingly harder to see in the fading light, she wasn't aware of a wagon approaching until she heard her name being called repeatedly.

"Mrs. St. Martin." The voice paused, waiting for a response before calling again. "Mrs. St. Martin."

Turning, Claire spied the oversized wagon that belonged to Henderson's Domestics. Looking up, she observed Mr. Smith, wrapped in a bulky cloak and muffler. Tipping his hat when he saw he at last had her attention, he brought the wagon to a halt. "Might I offer you a ride, madam?"

Claire, wondering whether the feeling of gratitude or trepidation was the stronger, nodded her head and stepped toward the wagon, unsure how she was going to climb up and keep her dignity intact, but the driver had already jumped down. Feeling that he was standing nearer to her than was necessary, she clambered up with the aid of his gloved hand. She was amazed at the transformation in the man from the previous day when he had been introduced to Braxton. He had changed from a clumsy, surly creature to a man who had nimbly regained his seat, all the while chatting, almost cheerfully and nonstop, to his unexpected passenger.

As she settled into her seat, he proffered a dingy grey cloth, which held a bunch of grapes upon which he had been nibbling. "No, thank you, Mr. Smith."

Somewhat surprised, he sat back and looked at her. "Most ladies are quite fond of grapes, Mrs. St. Martin…and I must confess it is a vice I am a slave to. I am not one to imbibe spirits or tobacco,"—he hesitated before resuming his brief tirade—"truly odious habits."

"I must agree with you in part, Mr. Smith, about the evils of tobacco, but surely a glass of wine…"

Ignoring her gentle protest, he snapped his whip at the horses, startling them into a trot, the rumbling of the omnibus shattering the stillness of the night.

Oh Wicked Escort

The silence loomed between them like a heavy mist until she once more found her voice. "It was a most fortunate coincidence that you were travelling down this road."

She barely heard his muffled chuckle and knew even in the darkness that his eyes were on her. "It was no coincidence, madam. I was unsure what time you would finish at Gainsby Hall but I thought I would try anyway, and when I saw the others leave and you weren't among them, I decided to wait, knowing you most likely wouldn't be too long."

Again, there was almost no trace of the lisp that usually haunted his speech as he peppered her with questions. "Why were you walking alone, ma'am? You could become the victim of some creature lurking in the shadows, waiting for a sweet morsel such as yourself to happen by. Was I mistakenly under the wrong impression that Mrs. Henderson expected everyone to stay together, and under no circumstances were there to be any stragglers?" His dark eyes seemed to bore into her as she reservedly answered his probing inquiries.

"Yes, Mr. Smith, those were Mrs. Henderson's instructions, but I told Mr. Tucker to start walking, sure that I would be finished with Mrs. Grant and the garden party before they got too far ahead. In their haste to get home before the rain began again, they just forgot that I hadn't caught up with them." She pulled her shawl tighter about her shoulders, unsure whether the chill she felt was the result of the weather or the man sitting beside her.

Chapter Fourteen

Unwilling to let him continue questioning her, she changed the subject abruptly. "And how did your funeral go, Mr. Smith? The poor creature—did she have any family or friends mourning her demise?" She paused, waiting for answers but he had returned to his usual sullen grunts that passed as conversation. Far from being offended, she could only feel a sense of relief that their exchange of dialogue seemed to be at an end.

As the wagon lumbered down the bumpy road, Claire noticed there was almost no one abroad, whether in carriages or on the footpaths. She couldn't stop herself from edging further away from the driver, huddling like a frightened mouse on the outermost corner of the seat. Little wisps of fog drifted eerily upward, blending with the smoke that curled lazily from chimneys. Somewhere in the distance, a dog howled, adding its mournful cry to the ghostly atmosphere. The wagon rumbled noisily through the hushed silence of the streets.

Apprehension coursed through her whenever Mr. Smith glanced sideways, his expression unreadable in the gloom of the night. She almost cried in relief when she spied a familiar structure looming just ahead, the building that housed her and the rest of the staff of Henderson's. She couldn't help wondering why she had been so nervous. She had always prided herself on not being one of those silly creatures that fainted or carried on when a situation grew tense or unpleasant. Turning the horses into the narrow courtyard, Mr. Smith slowed the omnibus, stopping as he at last drew near to the door. Before he had a chance to alight and offer her assistance, Claire had clambered awkwardly down, slipping clumsily on the damp ground before righting herself.

"Thank you for coming to my rescue, Mr. Smith." Before the man could reply, she was scurrying around the wagon toward the front entrance, and more importantly, a safe haven.

Unbeknownst to Claire, Mrs. Henderson, upon returning from visiting an elderly maiden aunt, soon learned that one of her employees had been left behind to make her own way from Gainsby Hall to home. She refused to accept the fact that Claire herself had told them to leave, assuring Mr. Tucker she would catch up with them. Haranguing her staff as she strode angrily back and forth, she reminded them they were supposed to return together, not piecemeal. The Tucker brothers had reluctantly volunteered to go in search of Claire, anything rather than listen to Eloise Henderson reminding them, for the third time in less than an hour, that there was danger on the streets of Whitechapel, especially for any woman walking alone. Just as the two men were making ready to leave, the door opened, revealing Claire, flushed but thankful to be inside, safe and warm.

Giving a brief account of Mr. Smith happening by, she excused herself and hurried to her room to freshen up before anyone could raise any further questions. With a final harrumph, Mrs. Henderson left them to their dinner, requesting that Claire be told she was to give an account of the day's events when she had finished eating.

Both Friday and Saturday, though busy, were days that Claire appreciated. There were no untoward events at either the Friday birthday celebration honoring a Mrs. Horace Waldham or the masked ball held on Saturday evening at the manor of Lord and Lady Lexington.

Braxton hadn't returned to disturb her peace of mind, although she seemed powerless to stop looking for him, chastising herself for the wave of disappointment washing over her when he didn't appear. She did see Billy Marple twice as he was going about the business of delivering goods, but there was no opportunity for more than a wave.

It wasn't until after church on Sunday that they heard the first rumblings of another murder. Small groups of parishioners, a few standing on the steps of St. Bartholomew's and a number on the footpath, some talking, others listening, as the news of a second grisly slaying in Whitechapel spread through the congregation.

D. L. Robinson

Eloise Henderson, after listening impatiently to the bits and pieces of news swirling about, gathered her staff and saw them safely onto the omnibus. Once they were all seated and hopefully out of hearing of their employer, they were soon whispering back and forth about the murder that taken place on the same night they had been serving at Lord and Lady Lexington's masked ball.

The cook, Mrs. Kenley, the only employee who worked strictly at Henderson's, stated matter-of-factly that she for one was glad she didn't have to be out and about whilst such a beast was free to roam the streets of Whitechapel. Her words soon quieted the other passengers as they all considered their own vulnerability.

There was a light drizzle falling off and on Monday morning but not heavy enough to keep Arthur Tucker from planning his stroll, knowing the man he was seeking was out of his shop until mid-morning. It was just after eleven o'clock that he found the opportunity to nip off and visit his friend Ollie, the well-informed butcher of Old Montague Street.

Claire busied herself with small tasks, trying unsuccessfully to banish all thoughts of Braxton Kane from her head. Still, she couldn't help but wonder where he was. She hadn't seen him since the fifth of September—five days ago. She tossed her head in irritation as she remembered what he had said before they parted that day. *"Oh no, my dear Claire, I am just as certain that we are meant to share not only the present but the future."* She sniffed, annoyed with herself. *If that doesn't sound like he'll be back, full of himself, haunting my steps until...what? What was he after?*

Frustrated, she went down for lunch, surprised to see Arthur Tucker just returning from his news-gathering. It was obvious from the expression on his face that he had been rewarded for his amble in the rain.

He waited, gloatingly patient, as his fellow diners quickly passed the salt and buttered slices of bread, all waiting anxiously to hear what news he had. The occasional scrape of a metal utensil on crockery was the only sound to be heard as he cleared his throat, obviously enjoying his sojourn as king of the hill. As usual, Mr. Smith sat slightly apart but listened as raptly as the others.

"As you all know, I set off this morning to see Ollie, in the 'ope of finding out about this latest murder and, might I say 'ere and now, 'e didn't disappoint me." Smiling puckishly, he paused, savoring the moment. "Well, t'was another 'unfortunate'." Ignoring the hiss of censure from Bessie, he continued. "This one 'ad 'er throat slit, she did, same as t'other one. But this time, 'e took something along with 'im…'er womb." With this latest crumb of information, it wasn't only the women who gasped in horror. "An' the copper what's been put in charge 'asn't got a bleeding clue."

As Claire had expected, conversation at dinner wasn't very different than that at lunch. Arthur Tucker held sway, deemed by all within their little household, even the practical no-nonsense Eloise Henderson, to be an authority on the murders of the two prostitutes. No one stirred outside as darkness fell, and bedtime was greeted with a certain reluctance by those leery of darkened rooms.

The following afternoon, after returning home from the tea they had been hired to serve at, Arthur took himself off in search of new gossip, and once again, he wasn't to be disappointed. It was while they were gathered around the dinner table that he dropped his newest tidbit that both horrified and fascinated everyone.

"There's been a bit of a stir in these 'ere parts. A bloke by the name of Leather Apron was nabbed today." A sigh of relief could be heard from his tiny audience, none noticing how pale Mr. Smith had become as he stopped to listen to the gossip.

Arthur continued with his news. "The coppers questioned 'im but 'ad to let 'im go. But still, some people think the police are 'elpless to protect them. A chap by the name of George Lusk 'as formed something called 'Mile End Vigilance Committee'."

And once again Mr. Tucker postured as all eyes turned to him, listening intently as he voiced his own opinion on the happenings of East London.

But as must happen with the passage of time and no new murders, the second slaying, although not forgotten, failed to rule any longer as mealtime conversation. Henderson's Domestics were occupied for the next two weeks with teas, charity bazaars, and another masked ball. It wasn't until Friday that Mrs. Henderson entered the dining room just as they were finishing breakfast.

"Everyone, if I might have your attention…"

All eyes turned to the imposing figure of their employer, waiting patiently while she cleared her throat. "Mr. Smith has once again volunteered to drive the funeral wagon for the poor unfortunate who was so brutally slain last Saturday, a Miss Annie Chapman, whose burial is this morning at nine o'clock." All eyes turned and glanced curiously at Mr. Smith before turning their attention back to Mrs. Henderson. "He promises to return in plenty of time to escort you to and from the Charity Bazaar and Tea at St. Eustace Church since the ladies in charge of organizing it assure me you won't be needed until late morning."

She nodded her head in dismissal and everyone slowly dispersed, going about their business, whatever that business might be.

Braxton Kane had indeed kept to his plan of not going anywhere near Whitechapel for a few days and was glad of it when he spotted one of Ben's footmen on two separate occasions, clumsily following him as he moved about the great city. He was once again out and about on Friday morning, having just left his tailor's shop, when a vagrant stepped out of the shadows, blocking his path. About to move around the man, he quickly drew back when the man reached out and attempted to grab at his arm.

"What a coincidence I should run into you here. I was beginning to think you were avoiding me."

Startled, Braxton took a long careful look at the man, trying to hide his shock. Ben, a man who had always taken such pride in presenting an elegant figure to society, now looked decidedly unkempt. His eyes were bloodshot and the stubble on his chin testified to the fact that he hadn't shaved for at least two days. Large smudges of dirt were evident on his fawn-colored pants, and both jacket and shirt were creased and torn. Despite being outdoors, the stench of stale perfume clung to his person, and fumes of liquor seemed to ooze through his very pores. Braxton, looking about, spied a coffeehouse across the avenue and began walking toward it, the shabbily-dressed Bennett Kirkwood quickly falling into step with him.

"Ben! What's happened to you? You look like hell! When was the last time you slept? And let's drop the pretense of this meeting being an accident. I've been aware of your men following me for days."

The other man laughed, but a slight flush of embarrassment crept up his neck and onto his cheeks. He held up his hands in mock surrender. "I must plead guilty, and it's your fault for being so close-mouthed about the woman you've secreted away somewhere...but you're right, I haven't been home for a day or two. The servants have probably had the police round by now."

He barely finished his sentence when Braxton, with a snort of disgust, walked faster, as if he wanted to put distance between them. Desperation and annoyance were barely concealed as Ben tried to keep in step with the man he had always considered the one person he could always count on, no matter what.

"Braxton, show me some pity. The whole of London society despises me..."

Hearing the words and the pleading note in his voice, Braxton relented and slowed his pace. Once inside the coffeehouse, he chose a corner table, furthest away from anyone who might recognize either of them.

Ben stared into the cold grey eyes, almost recoiling from the contempt he read there. "It's as I've said—all of London society, at least the part that matters, has heard the story of my wedding night, thanks to that gossipy bitch, Letitia Penrod, and her appalling offspring. They have bandied the story about until no one will have anything to do with me." He rubbed his unshaven stubble in irritation. "Mordock Peckworthy has certainly had his pound of flesh and more!"

Braxton, staring at the broken man across the table from him, could feel only the barest vestige of pity. "I'm sorry for my part in the whole sordid affair, Ben. Perhaps if I'd held out, it wouldn't have come to this."

The other man's eyes began to well up, alarming Braxton more than words could ever do. "Pull yourself together, Ben. Have you made any effort to find...?"

The self-pity disappeared instantly, replaced by snarling abhorrence. His response held a note of annoyed impatience. "And where would that lead, Braxton? I told you that I'm already a pariah in polite society. No, she's gone and good riddance, I say. I have my lawyer drawing up a Bill of Divorcement since she has seen fit to abandon me."

Braxton shook his head in disbelief at the other's determination to place the guilt anywhere but on himself. Rising, he looked with pity at the man and could see what might have been and what was.

Claire had been right to follow her instincts when she left her husband, and he was determined to tell her that very thing as soon as he judged it safe to see her. Although, if he was truthful, he wanted nothing more than to hold her in his arms, letting the scent that was hers alone tantalize him, tease, and remind him of the night they had spent together, albeit with her husband's permission, if not his blessing.

Chapter Fifteen

The staff of Henderson's Domestics found their time thoroughly filled serving at teas, dinners, balls, and the like. On the days following Annie Chapman's murder, whilst travelling through the familiar streets of Whitechapel, Arthur Tucker shrewdly pointed out that most women were being escorted by male companions, presumably husbands or sons. None but the very desperate dared venture out alone. Most walked in pairs at the very least as they went about their daily business along the cobbled roads and footpaths, adopting a mien that glared distrustfully at any lone male passing within their proximity. Even the raucous banter of shopkeepers advertising their wares along with the customary strident tones of a multitude of languages seemed somewhat restrained.

It was on the following Sunday, after returning from church, that Betty and her young man, James Forrester, invited Claire to join them for the day visiting Hyde Park. Politely protesting that she would be a deterrent to their time together, they both amiably assured her she would be most welcome and soon had her dashing up the stairs to fetch her bonnet, eager to walk about in the sun after the past few gloomy days.

The three strolled down Brick Lane toward Whitechapel Road, planning to ride a public omnibus to Hyde Park. Arriving at the top of the road, the three looked about, unsure just when such a conveyance would appear until James gave an excited shout, pointing at the omnibus that was slowly trundling down the road toward them. Waving their hands at the driver, the oversized carriage stopped and the three boarded, smiling broadly at such an auspicious beginning to their day. As they took their seats, Claire glanced out the window and spied a familiar carriage turning onto Brick Lane. *Well, Mr. Braxton Kane, you've arrived too late to upset my day.* She might, perhaps, have been more sympathetic had she but known the circuitous route he had taken to lose anyone that might be following him.

The ride to Hyde Park proved to be long, and after the third change of carriage, both Claire and Betty were beginning to look a little wilted, but James, ever the optimist, gave a glad shout as he spied their destination just ahead. They disembarked and stood admiring the Grand Entrance until James, taking the arms of both his sweetheart and her friend, walked slowly through the entrance, marveling at the majestic columns and archways.

Strolling leisurely down the footpath, they passed the Rose Garden, admiring the flowers and enjoying the warmth of the day. Reaching the Serpentine, James suggested they hire a rowing boat and travel by water for a change. Both Betty and Claire enthusiastically agreed, and the three walked around the waterway until they found the small pier that had several wooden boats tied to it.

As they stood there, a carriage halted a few feet away. Claire, her vision blocked by James and Betty, didn't see the tall and very handsome man alight, but he had recognized Betty and was walking purposefully in their direction.

It was Betty who saw him first, gasping in surprise and holding tightly to both Claire and James as Braxton Kane made his way toward them, moving with an easy grace, his smile revealing even, white teeth. Reaching them, his grey eyes warmed as they settled on Claire.

Tendrils of dark hair fell across his forehead, and Claire had to restrain herself from reaching up and brushing it back. His voice, when he at last spoke, was low and smooth.

"Well, I've found you." An irresistibly devastating grin crossed his face, his eyes resting on the one he had been seeking.

It was Claire's turn to gasp at his impudence. "Were you searching for us, Mr. Kane? And might one ask for what purpose?"

Grey eyes twinkling merrily, a chuckle escaped him before he answered. "Well, Mrs. St. Martin, I felt that you surely must be missing me, at least a little, after so many days having passed without sight of my dashing good looks, sparkling wit, and manly physique. I went round to Henderson's this morning, only to be told by that dear lady that you had set off for Hyde Park with Betty and her intended, who I assume must be this gentleman." He extended his hand to James. "I trust you'll forgive the intrusion, Mr...?"

James grasped the proffered hand and shook it eagerly. "It's James, James Forrester, sir. And no, your company is quite welcome, not an intrusion at all. We were just about to hire a rowing boat—it's just a shilling for an hour. Would you care to join us?"

"And I, sir, am Braxton Kane of Pennygrove Hall." He looked about and immediately began a slight reorganization of Mr. Forrester's plans. "Might I suggest, sir, that we each hire a boat to take the young ladies out onto the water? It's my understanding that four in a boat could lead to an unbalanced load."

Betty, still in shock at the turn of events, looked questioningly at Claire, wondering at the wisdom of letting Mr. Kane have her former mistress alone.

Braxton, as if reading her mind, smiled. "Please, Miss Sims...Betty, have no fear. After all, we'll all be on the water, in plain sight of each other—what could possibly happen?" He gave her his most disarming smile, putting her fears to rest for the time being anyway.

Claire wanted to shout in protest that he was doing it again, managing her life as if she were a mindless doll, but the thought of boating along the Serpentine was too tempting, and if she was to be completely honest with herself, she didn't find Braxton Kane quite as repugnant as she once had.

The two boats set out with Braxton soon outdistancing James Forrester. As the wooden boat glided along, Claire, sitting in the prow, enjoyed the tranquility of the moment. Glancing up, she saw he was watching her, a brooding look in his eyes. Sighing lightly, he looked about, ensuring they were out of anyone's hearing before he smiled at her.

"Claire, I must speak to you about Bennett."

Shock rendered her speechless for a moment, her whole body stiffening. "I refuse to entertain any thought of returning to Silverwood House and Mr. Bennett Kirkwood, so you might as well save your breath." There was icy defiance in her words as she lifted her chin, meeting his gaze straight on.

"You're jumping to the wrong conclusion, Claire. Bennett has his solicitor working on a Bill of Divorcement. He's claiming you deserted him."

The heavy lashes that shadowed her cheeks flew up in astonishment. "Divorce! Is such a thing possible?" She took a quick, sharp breath. "Does that mean I would be free? I could stop hiding?" Her mind reeled in confusion.

"I don't have answers to your questions yet, my love." He paused, thinking quickly. When he spoke again, his voice was tender, almost a murmur. "If you wish, I can contact my own solicitor and ask these questions for you."

There was a tremor in her voice when next she spoke. "Yes, please, Braxton, if it's no trouble."

"For you, my love, I would do whatever your bidding might be." He rowed in silence, both of them lost in their own thoughts. It was the sound of Betty laughing that brought them back to the present.

"Come on, you two. Our time is almost up."

Braxton smiled at the other couple, who'd drawn near in their boat. "James, I wager I can beat you back to the dock."

"You're on, Mr. Kane." At the formality of address, Braxton looked across at Betty and her young man.

"Please, both of you, if we're to be friends, we must address each other by our given names." The occupants of the other boat looked at each other, unsure of this familiarity but James, taking the lead, smiled broadly.

"You're on, Braxton, but I must warn you, I was the rowing champion of my village before coming to London."

All four were soon laughing as they skimmed across the water, an occasional oar splashing droplets of water over the two women who shouted encouragement at both men as they rowed toward shore. Short minutes later, they were all standing on dry land suddenly unsure of what was to follow.

"Might I offer all of you the comfort of my carriage?" He took Claire's arm and led the way. "This park is far too large for walking the whole of it."

And before anyone had time to think, they were all comfortably ensconced in the brougham, contentedly looking at the rest of the sights the park had to offer, pausing to listen to the music being played on one of the new bandstands that had become so popular in London's parks. It was quite some time later that they began to feel the chill of the evening air. Braxton invited them to be his guests for dinner at a pub where, he had heard it whispered even the Prince of Wales was known to be a frequent patron.

When a tired but lighthearted Claire and Betty at last arrived at the door of their building, it was a tight-lipped Mrs. Henderson who let them in, all other occupants having long since gone to bed. Apologizing for keeping her up so late, the girls quietly climbed the stairs, hoping not to wake anyone, especially Bessie Marigold, easily the most cantankerous person in their little circle.

Everyone was already gathered around the breakfast table when Claire and Betty joined the group the following morning. Mr. Smith, sitting in his self-imposed isolation, was staring morosely at the steaming pot of lumpy oatmeal the cook had just set down, and Bessie, at their appearance, grumbled loudly about the hours being kept by some people. The rest of the staff smiled at the two girls, enjoying their youthful exuberance.

Arthur Tucker, being the most outspoken of the group, was the first to speak. "And what exactly did you young ladies get up to yesterday? Did that Kane bloke find you?" At the mention of Braxton's name, Mr. Smith sat up a little straighter, unable to conceal his interest in the conversation, had anyone been watching him.

It was Betty who, rather pertly, answered Arthur's question. "Yes, Mr. Tucker, he found us and we had a lovely time. The weather was most agreeable, and Mr. Kane, for those of you who might have formed a different opinion of him, was a perfect gentleman. Why, he even invited James and me to address him by his given name." She nodded her head for added emphasis, obviously enjoying her moment of superiority, but Claire wished her former maid would say less about anything concerning either herself or Braxton.

Enjoying ruffling the usually quiet Betty's feathers, Arthur, blue eyes twinkling mischievously, smiled brightly, revealing his yellowish and slightly protruding teeth. "Cor, luv, 'e must be a right old toff! Bit odd though, 'im 'angin' about with the workin' class." He looked at his audience before speaking again. "What exactly is this bloke after, I wonder?"

Curious eyes turned and studied Claire who, blushing, smiled enigmatically at the circle of faces. The harsh scraping of a chair caught everyone's attention as Mr. Smith, with a look of cold fury in his dark eyes, cast a hateful glance in her direction before stomping from the room. They all sat in stunned silence as the slamming of the door resounded throughout both the dining room and kitchen.

Arthur was the first to speak. "Well, 'e left in a bit of a temper, didn't 'e?" Some giggled but others continued to ponder the cause of the man's bad temper. Looking at Claire, Arthur laughed.

"Don't look so surprised, missy. It's no secret that 'e's been sweet on you since you came 'ere." Claire paled at the thoughtless remark until she looked about her and realized they were all of the same opinion.

"But I've never encouraged him..." She could hardly lift her voice above a whisper.

Arthur shook his head, suddenly feeling fatherly toward the beautiful woman who sat in the dining room of Henderson's Domestics. "That don't matter a bit, darlin' ... 'e decided the first day you stepped through the door that you was the one. And then today 'e 'ears you been out gallivantin' with another man...now I ask you, luv, can you blame 'im?"

Stunned, Claire stared at him, at all of them, before turning on her heel in answer to a timely summons from Eloise Henderson.

The days following the Hyde Park outing would prove to be rather routine inasmuch as Henderson's Domestics was fast becoming a popular solution to those in need of temporary servants. The employees of the agency were all kept busy at teas and bazaars during the week, but at the week's end, balls and other entertainments assured Mrs. Henderson of a steady income.

Braxton anxiously reviewed the happenings of the day. Could he have been followed? It was unlikely but still the possibility existed. Just as his carriage was turning down the road to Pennygrove Hall, he had spotted Mordock Peckworthy's hireling, Leopold, skulking behind some shrubbery, a carriage and driver, presumably his, waiting nearby.

Why would that despicable troll be watching him? Obviously, Peckworthy had ordered his minion to do so, but why? And after that debacle of a wedding night, the man had paid Ben's debts as had been agreed. And when he and Ben had gone to Peckworthy's home after Claire had fled, there had been no doubt in Braxton's mind that the man knew nothing of her disappearance. So why would he be interested now? Perhaps he was looking for a way to torture Ben further.

And then there had been Ben's man lurking in the shrubbery outside Pennygrove Hall, although that hadn't surprised Braxton all that much. Once Bennett Kirkwood learned part of any story that interested him, he refused to rest until he had all the details. Knowing Braxton had "met somebody" who he refused to name must have driven Ben over the edge, so he had resorted to spying on the man he purported to be his best and oldest friend.

Ben's man had been easy to spot in the waning light, but had he been outside Pennygrove Hall the entire day, thinking Braxton at home? He must have been disappointed when the carriage returned home and the owner of the manor stepped out. The whole situation would have been laughable if Braxton hadn't been so alarmed, not for himself but for Claire.

Meeting his housekeeper at the door, he told her he was in need of someone who could slip out of the house to post a letter. She immediately saw an opportunity to put her grandson forward, but Braxton held up his hand, stopping her before she had time to mention the boy's name.

"This might be a difficult task, Mrs. Henfield. There are two men watching the house, but I somehow doubt either knows of the other's existence. It's imperative they know nothing of my comings and goings and most especially of a letter I must post with all speed."

The housekeeper gasped, a shiver of uneasiness causing her to pull her shawl closer about her plump shoulders, her eyes turning unwillingly toward the windows. "Should I have Thomas or one of the other men chase them away, sir?"

Braxton, his eyes studying the curtained windows, at last shook his head. "No, Mrs. Henfield, we'll let them continue to think we know nothing of their presence, but perhaps you could alert Thomas and the other male servants, discretely mind you, that they're about. And have someone check that all doors and windows are locked."

"Mr. Kane, you wanted someone to post a letter for you…my grandson Ethan is the very one you need, sir. He can nip out and be back before anyone knows he's gone, with no one ever being the wiser."

Braxton nodded, relieved the problem was to be so easily solved. "You fetch the lad, Mrs. Henfield, whilst I dash off a letter. I'll join you back in the kitchen."

The two separated, each determined to be first back but when he returned with the letter in hand, Braxton found his housekeeper and her grandson waiting, the lad's cap clenched in his hand. Sizing up the boy, Braxton felt confident his mission would be ably carried out. After introducing her grandson, the housekeeper watched Ethan secrete the letter into a pocket in his jacket before plunking his cap on his head, nodding confidently to both his grandmother and employer before slipping out the door.

As the minutes ticked away, Braxton anxiously paced the length of the library with long, purposeful strides, muttering to himself about the gall of those who dared spy on him. He paused long enough to pour himself a small brandy, his expression clouded with anger. He had barely sipped his drink when he heard a small cough at the door of the sitting room. Looking up, he saw Ethan, cap in hand, and a broad smile on his young face.

"It's done sir, with no one the wiser."

Braxton smiled, relieved. He pulled coins from his pocket and handed them to the youngster. His voice was gruff when he spoke. "Be sure to buy your grandmother something as well as yourself, Ethan. Well done, my boy."

Braxton returned to the library and poured a second brandy. Sitting behind his desk, he pondered the situation. What could Peckworthy's motive be for sending his minion to spy on him? Did he have any suspicions about Claire's whereabouts? And Ben! Was it simple curiosity about a possible love interest of Braxton's or did he too suspect something? His mind whirled with possible answers. Standing, he drained his glass and stretched his arms.

I'll call on Ben tomorrow, before I visit Higgins. Peckworthy? What should I do about Peckworthy? Perhaps I'll have some idea of what to do about him after I've seen Ben.

❀ ❀ ❀

On Monday, Claire once again became the focus of everyone's attention. A letter addressed to her arrived in the morning post, an occurrence she had never experienced before. Hugging the envelope to her breast, she skipped up the stairs. On reaching the haven of her bedroom, excitement caused her hand to tremble as she pulled a single sheet of paper from the envelope and read the short missive, written in a strong bold hand.

My love, he wrote, *it is of the utmost importance that I don't see you—for at least a week, possibly longer. I apologize for sounding so mysterious, but I'll explain everything when next we meet.* The signature was little more than a scrawl but she could just decipher his name. There was a postscript following his signature. *I would remind you that London, and most especially Whitechapel, can be dangerous places. Never, never venture out alone!*

Puzzled at the mysterious tone of the letter, Claire tucked it away, surprised at the disappointment his words brought her. Lost in thought, she slowly made her way downstairs to join her fellow employees who were already seated inside the omnibus, all patiently awaiting her arrival.

They had been hired to serve at another charity bazaar and luncheon that afternoon. Feeling everyone watching as she approached the front of the wagon, she steeled herself to occupy the seat beside Mr. Smith, but her apprehension soon disappeared. The man once again assisted her up, being most prudent to have minimal physical contact with her. Uncomfortable in the silence between them, Claire remarked about the weather but elicited no response beyond a grunt. She gave up on him at that point and retreated into her own silent reverie, dwelling on the letter from Braxton. The day was uneventful as were the string of days that followed.

Chapter Sixteen

As Braxton was ushered into the small breakfast room where Ben sat sipping his coffee, he sighed, recalling that the last time he'd been here was the day after Claire disappeared. It seemed like an eternity had passed, and yet it really wasn't that long ago, a few weeks more or less. He steeled himself...no looking back now. Claire's safety depended on how credible he could be in the next few minutes.

Ben looked up, not really very surprised to see who his visitor was, his tone becoming condescending. "Ah, Braxton, I knew you'd come calling sooner or later. Coffee?"

At the shake of his head, Ben tensed. He had thought something amiss the last time they had spoken. *I shouldn't have gone to see him that day—he had a chance to see how far I had fallen.*

"And how is your mysterious lady love, Braxton? Are you ready to introduce me to her?" Studying the familiar face, he paused before his lips twisted into a skeptical smile. "Is something amiss, old man? Surely she hasn't grown tired of you already?"

Braxton shrugged as if he was hiding a great hurt. "She's gone, Ben, back to Paris." Meeting the eyes of the other man, he measured him with a cool appraising look, wondering if this would be enough for him to call off his man.

"Oh, I am sorry." Ben studied his friend thoughtfully for a moment before speaking, as if weighing his words. "But no matter, old chum—it simply means you're free now and can join us tonight for a bit of gaming and whatever else we might get up to." Seeing a question in Braxton's grey eyes, he hesitated, his voice suddenly guarded. "Myself, Julius, and Teddy Chambers, that's all. Oh, come on, Braxton, let bygones be bygones. Teddy is truly sorry for his part in the whole sordid affair."

Braxton stood, suddenly anxious to be out in the fresh air. "Sorry Ben, I already have tentative plans. I might be going away for a couple of weeks."

Braxton felt a twinge of disappointment mixed with sadness as he looked across the table, wondering if it would ever be possible to return to their former easy camaraderie. "Well, I must be off. Don't bother seeing me out, Ben, I know the way."

Nodding his head, Braxton took his leave, wondering at this unexpected ability to lie so convincingly to one who had always known him so well, but if, hopefully, it rid him of an unwelcome shadow, then so be it.

Braxton's next stop was at Albert Higgins' law office, nestled in a rabbit warren of law offices situated near the Old Bailey Courthouse. Albert Higgins had been the family solicitor when his father was still alive, and Braxton had never had reason to seek legal counsel elsewhere.

The day was pleasantly cool and so, on entering his solicitor's office, he was immediately struck by the dry, papery smell of the outer office, a drab, windowless room containing three high desks pushed together. Three clerks, perched atop high wooden stools, were busily scratching entries in large, cumbersome journals. As Braxton closed the door, one of the three looked up from the book in which he had been writing, a questioning look forming on his pale, bespectacled face. Recognizing the visitor, he smiled as he quickly climbed down and approached one of the three doors, pausing to knock softly before entering the office of Mr. Higgins, senior partner. He returned almost immediately, smiling and bobbing his head as he ushered the visitor into his employer's office.

A portly man stood waiting in front of a small fireplace, a welcoming smile on his cherubic face. Wisps of grey hair had been combed neatly over his nearly hairless head, as if trying to conceal the baldness that resided there. A luxuriant grey moustache attempted to distract the eye from the veined bulbous nose that dominated the round face.

"Braxton, my boy, so good to see you." The two men shook hands and Braxton took the seat indicated. "Tea, or perhaps something stronger?"

"Nothing, thank you, Albert." Braxton fidgeted nervously under the older man's penetrating gaze. "I apologize for calling so unexpectedly, but it's a matter of some urgency. I'm hoping to clear up a matter that's been troubling me…it's just a few questions, actually."

Taking the chair opposite, Albert Higgins, recognizing that his visitor was trying to make light of a matter that to him was obviously a very serious affair, allowed him to take the lead. He nodded his head in understanding as he fussed with his pipe, lighting it as Braxton, staring at a spot on the floor, laid out the reason for the visit. He had barely gotten into the facts when the older man interrupted.

"You wouldn't be speaking of Bennett Kirkwood and his despicable behavior toward his bride, a Miss Claire St. Martin, would you?"

Braxton raised his head, astonishment in his eyes. "You've heard?"

"It's all over London, young man. Why are you here, asking about…?" He paused, his voice suddenly containing a strong suggestion of reproach. "Braxton Kane, are you the 'proxy bridegroom' in this sorry muddle?"

The younger man hung his head, shame weighing him down. "I didn't go into it willingly, Albert."

The two men sat quietly as Braxton explained Peckworthy's financial hold over Bennett Kirkwood and his threat to throw him into debtor's prison, plus the man's uncanny knowledge of Braxton's own brother, Patrick Kane, murderer and monster, with a promise to see that he remained imprisoned on the other side of the world if Braxton fell in with his plan.

Mention of Patrick Kane's name brought back a memory of Braxton sitting in that very chair many months ago, frantic to give his older half-brother a second chance. Between Braxton and Albert Higgins, they had arranged for Patrick's share of the Kane estate to be deposited in a bank in America with the understanding he would never return to England. Higgins, out of long years of affection and loyalty toward Braxton and his father, had helped convince the courts of that fact.

Braxton explained that somehow Peckworthy had discovered Patrick had killed a woman on the other side of the Atlantic, was now

Oh Wicked Escort

languishing in a jail cell in New Orleans, and would remain there as long as he, Braxton, went along with Peckworthy's plan. Braxton cursed his own weakness for agreeing to act the role of bridegroom on Bennett's wedding night, but Higgins merely sat listening, giving no hint of judgment or censure in this very peculiar matter.

"Well, my boy, I can neither condemn nor forgive you. That is something only the much abused Miss St. Martin, or should I say Mrs. Kirkwood, can do. Which brings me to ask the question—why exactly are you here?"

Taking a deep breath, Braxton quickly told of the hoax being discovered and subsequently revealed by one Letitia Penrod and Claire's impetuous flight to Whitechapel where she had found employment as a domestic. He assured Higgins that her whereabouts were unknown to anyone but himself. The man looked skeptically at the troubled young man, wondering what was still to be revealed.

"I knew, even before she fled, how utterly selfish I had been, sparing no thought as to her feelings, caring more about my brother, the same brother that others would call a monster." He stopped talking, pausing to collect his thoughts before continuing. "By chance, I met Ben a few days ago. He told me he was seeking a Bill of Divorcement, claiming Claire had deserted him." The lawyer sat quietly, busily depositing all the facts into the neat little cubbyholes of his mind.

Albert rose and walked over to a cupboard that sat unobtrusively under the window. Unlocking the small door of the cabinet, he poured two glasses of amber whiskey and handed one to Braxton.

"What is it exactly that you want from me, my boy?"

Braxton stood, glass in hand, and began pacing. "I promised Claire I would speak to you and find out exactly what this Bill of Divorcement will mean to her. Her main concern is would she be free and could she come out of hiding? It's my understanding that she plans to leave the country, sailing to either America or Australia, as soon as she had enough money saved, to begin life anew."

"Well, this is one for the books. I'll give you my opinion, Braxton, but that's all it will be, my opinion. I am not overly familiar with divorce laws." He drained his glass, clearing his throat before speaking.

"The law always favors the husband, but," he held up a hand to stop the interruption he saw coming, "in this case, I am not so sure it would. As I said, gossip was rife some weeks after the wedding, but I believe the court's sympathy would lie with the present Mrs. Kirkwood, or if you prefer, the former Miss St. Martin. And whether they ever shared a bed would be a further determining point. It's my understanding that her father died the day following the wedding, and her husband very thoughtfully left her to mourn undisturbed, so to speak." Braxton nodded, following the lawyer's words closely.

"Most likely the powers that be would decide a divorce unnecessary and grant an annulment. Again, gossip claimed that when they married, Miss St. Martin's father and Bennett Kirkwood were both laboring under the mistaken belief the other had money. Obviously, there would be no property to squabble over, nor any children as a result of the union. Am I correct in assuming this to be the case?" He looked sharply at the younger man, who nodded his agreement.

"She would be free to go on with her life, doing as she saw fit, whether that involved leaving England or staying, it would be her choice. Someday she might even wish to marry again. But, and I can't stress this too strongly, I don't know what polite society would make of her after such an event. She could be ostracized..."

An air of buoyancy had suddenly taken hold of Braxton. Claire would be free! He grasped the older man's hand and started to shake it but the look in the other's eyes stopped him. He braced himself, sensing a bucket of cold water was about to be thrown on him.

"What is it, Albert?"

"My boy, you know what else has to be done. Your brother Patrick must pay for his crime." Sensing Braxton's withdrawal, he looked up. Seeing the pain in the younger man's eyes, the old man's voice softened. "Braxton, it's the right thing to do. Perhaps the American legal system will find him insane and condemn him to life in an asylum. It's possible he might avoid the gallows."

Braxton nodded his head numbly. *And what if I do nothing and he kills again? I can't have that on my conscience.* "Oh course, Albert. What should be done?"

"I'll take it from here. You said he was in a New Orleans jail, I believe." Braxton nodded his head in confirmation. "I'll send a telegram outlining the details of attempted murder of a prostitute here in London. I must caution you that it will probably guarantee an even harsher sentence than if we did nothing."

The lawyer donned his hat and coat and the two left his office, each promising to contact the other if any new development occurred.

❀ ❀ ❀

Braxton's horse moved restively as he awaited a command, but Braxton continued to stare off into space, debating with himself whether to see Peckworthy or not. By seeing him, would he possibly make the man not only more suspicious but increase his determination to discover what he was hiding? And if he mentioned seeing Leopold lurking in the shadows so close to his home, would that possibly just send the man deeper into hiding?

And since he had already decided not to seek out Claire for at least a week or so, there was no danger of her whereabouts being exposed. Let the creature follow him, he'd soon grow bored with the game he was playing.

Feeling at peace with his actions of the morning, he turned his horse toward Pennygrove Hall.

❀ ❀ ❀

Claire bustled quickly down the hallway to the back entrance, aware that everyone was waiting for her. She had been delayed by Mrs. Henderson, who was anxious about today's engagement at Lady Willoughby's granddaughter's bridal tea and had been giving her some last-minute advice and instructions. As she made her way to the omnibus and her fellow employees, she wondered once more about Braxton's letter. He had said he would not be able to see her for a week or more and thus far he had been true to his word. *Oh, well, he'll soon appear out of nowhere, just as he has before, and then I'll demand an explanation, if not for his disappearance, at least for the mystery of it all.*

As she approached the omnibus, she saw Mr. Smith leaning patiently against the wagon, waiting to assist her up to her seat. She had finally reached the stage where she took little or no notice of the man and his surliness. Since his abrupt departure from the table on learning she had been spending time with Braxton, he had kept his distance, not only from her but the others also. He no longer joined them for meals, seeming to prefer the company of horses instead. The other women had at various times confided to her that they felt easier if he remained their driver, a remote and enigmatic figure that really had little influence on their lives, rather than someone they sat with during meals.

It did bother her that the man had taken to standing too close and holding her arm a trifle longer than he should have on those occasions when he was escorting them to their engagement of the day. They rode to and from the various locations around the city with few words exchanged, which was fine with her. *Why don't I just ride with the others?* she often asked herself? *It would be warmer and certainly friendlier.* But she refused to be intimidated by the man. The problem was his, not hers. If he chose to be distant, she felt quite capable of returning the same coolness to him.

As they rode along, she determinedly stopped her musings about the churlish Mr. Smith and turned her thoughts to the tiny pile of coins she had secreted away in the room she shared with Betty. Each month she had added to it but yesterday, when she had counted her pile, her plan of sailing away from England didn't seem quite so pressing. Braxton's face appeared in her reverie as she recalled the kisses they had shared on that ill-fated night long ago. She shook her head impatiently. She wasn't ready to forgive his part in the deception, at least not yet.

Everything went well at the tea and even the tidying up afterward presented no particular problem or delay. Lady Willoughby herself came to the kitchen, seeking out Claire to compliment both her and the staff of Henderson's on their flawless service, surreptitiously pressing extra coins into Claire's hand, murmuring that it was in recognition of her fine work.

The ride home was as subdued as the ride there, save for the clatter of the carriage wheels on the uneven cobblestones. Mr. Smith outdid himself in surliness, both to Claire and the others. She could hear the man muttering as he maneuvered the wagon through the narrow streets and knew she would have to report him to Eloise Henderson before the staff went, en masse, to their employer.

It was later in the day, after giving a full report of the afternoon tea, Claire hesitantly broached the subject of the driver. Eloise Henderson sighed as she leaned back in her chair. "I know the man can be rude and obnoxious, but I promised my husband that Mr. Smith would always find employment and a home here."

At Claire's curious look, the older woman sighed again. "The man saved Charlie's life some years back, and it was a debt Charlie never forgot. Smith himself disappeared, and I had forgotten all about him until some months ago when he came knocking at the door. I needed a driver for the omnibus, and he fit the bill. Please, Claire, I would consider it a personal favor if you could find a way to keep the staff happy and Mr. Smith at least somewhat content."

Smiling, Claire assured Mrs. Henderson she would seek a solution. "Would there be any problem if I rode with the others? It seems to be me that's setting him off." At her nod of approval, Claire left the room, hopeful that a change in the seating arrangements would be enough to mollify the man.

Claire climbed the stairs, anxious to change her clothes before dinner was served. Just as she reached the door to her room, it was flung open and a breathless Betty almost knocked her down, laughing apologetically as she caught Claire's arm. Mystified, she saw her friend was wearing her second-best dress, covered by a warm shawl.

"Claire, I'm so glad you're here." Her words ran into each other in her excitement. "James is waiting for me downstairs. He says he has some wonderful news! He's taking me out for a bite of supper and then a stroll, a long stroll." Cheeks flushed, she gave Claire a quick peck on the cheek before rushing down the stairs to the man who stood waiting patiently at the door.

Much bemused, Claire watched her friend hastening toward the man she loved. She sighed but then thought she was beginning to sound a bit like Eloise Henderson. Laughing at herself, she changed her clothes and then went to join the others for the evening meal, hoping her solution to the problem of Mr. Smith would meet with their approval. The man, muttering his vexation with the world, was just leaving the dining room as she entered, carrying his plate out to the stable, with only the horses as dining companions.

D. L. Robinson

It was hours later that Claire felt her arm being shaken and Betty's voice begging her to wake up. Opening sleep-filled eyes, she saw that Betty, still dressed and with a candle in hand, was hovering over her. Sitting up, Claire looked closely at her friend. Joy bubbled in Betty's laugh and shone through her eyes.

"Oh Claire, I'm sorry to wake you, but I simply couldn't wait till morning. James has proposed! And what's more, we're sailing to Australia in less than two weeks." Her head bobbed up and down, setting her blond curls bouncing.

Claire couldn't quite take in the meaning of her words. "You're leaving…in two weeks." She hesitated before speaking again, not wanting to spoil the moment. She stood up, dazed, but one look at her friend's joyful vibrancy brought her back to reality.

"Betty, I'm so very happy for you. Tell me everything—don't leave a thing out." She hugged her friend warmly. Claire smiled as she watched Betty who, unable to sit still, circled the room. Even her walk had a sunny cheerfulness about it.

"James had an uncle who sailed to Australia years ago when James was just a little boy, he barely remembers him. But now it seems this uncle, who never married by the way, has died and left James, who is his only living relative, a sheep station." She hesitated briefly before rushing on with her story. "It's a sort of sheep farm, I think. Anyway, his uncle's solicitor, a Mr. O'Connor of Sydney, has arranged for James, along with his wife and family, to return on the same ship that brought the news." She blushed prettily at the thought of being James' wife. "James says there's enough for the two of us, and most importantly, for my sister and nephew to sail with us."

She danced from sheer delight about the room before falling onto her own bed. "Oh Claire, I've never been so happy."

Claire smiled at her friend whose happiness was so contagious. "Betty, what will I do without you?" A sudden pall fell on the two women as they both remembered the precariousness of Claire's situation.

Betty suddenly sat up. "Your savings, Claire! Have you enough to sail with us?"

Smiling fondly at the woman who had once been her maid and was now her best friend, Claire shook her head. "My little hoard of coins hasn't grown that quickly, Betty. It'll be several months before I can sail anywhere."

The girls continued to talk until there was a sudden thumping on the wall, signaling that they were disturbing others, Bessie Marigold in particular. Having changed into her nightgown while they were talking, Betty blew out the candle and snuggled under the covers, smiling at Claire who was climbing back into her own bed.

"Tomorrow, Claire, we'll talk tomorrow." Her voice trailed off, slumber already claiming her.

✿ ✿ ✿

The sun was just starting to peep through the window when Claire opened her eyes. Stretching, she glanced across the small room and saw Betty was not only up but had made her bed before leaving their shared quarters. How could she have slept so soundly?

As she descended the stairs, she could hear animated voices coming from the dining room. Pausing in the doorway, she knew in an instant that an excited Betty had shared her good news with everyone. Mrs. Henderson stood and beamed at the high spirits of her young employee.

"It'll be just like a daughter getting married. What plans have you made, love?"

Betty glanced at the woman, unsure what was meant by the question. "I've already told you that we'll be leaving in two weeks, sailing to Australia."

"No, no, my girl, I mean the wedding. There's not a lot of time to make plans but if it means only a few extra, why, I think we could all squeeze in here and have a wedding luncheon. I've already checked the calendar, and Henderson's has no bookings for that date. You did say October ninth, a Tuesday, didn't you? Come to my office after breakfast and we'll discuss what's to be served."

"Oh, Mrs. Henderson, that's so very kind of you." Her eyes filled with tears at such an unexpected gesture. "Yes, we'll wed on October ninth and sail on the eleventh." Spying Claire, she crossed the room and hugged her friend.

"Did you hear Mrs. Henderson's offer? James will be so pleased." Drawing Claire into the hallway, she lowered her voice to almost a whisper. "Claire, would it be too cheeky if I invited your Mr. Kane...I mean, Braxton?"

A sudden loud snort sounded in the dining room. Turning, they watched as a thoroughly disgruntled Mr. Smith, having listened to all the chattering, carried his steaming bowl of oatmeal toward the door, muttering his opinion of women in general, and swearing profusely as he declared all of the fairer sex to be the downfall of man.

Mrs. Henderson's deep voice rang out. "That will be enough, Mr. Smith." Casting a black, glowering look at the woman who employed him, he pushed the door open, intent on escaping to his own private world.

Claire, stunned by the driver's remarks, blushed but refused to allow it to spoil Betty's day. She turned her friend's question quickly over in her mind. *Why not invite Braxton? And if for some reason he chooses not to come, well then, good riddance, I say.* She smiled at Betty somewhat tremulously before nodding her agreement. Their employer's voice rang out, interrupting them.

"Betty, come to my office, my dear, and we'll discuss the menu right now and also any guests you might wish to invite." Betty, with a startled look at Claire at suddenly becoming 'my dear', hurried to the woman's side, obediently falling in beside her as the two started walking together, chatting as if they had always been the best of friends.

Pausing just as they reached the door, Mrs. Henderson's voice carried over the chatter that had slowly resumed after their driver's dramatic exit. "And don't forget, everyone, including you Betty, we have another bridal tea this afternoon, not to mention a charity bazaar tomorrow afternoon and a ball at the American Embassy on Saturday, the twenty-ninth."

Her words caused everyone to suddenly stir from the table, carrying dishes to the kitchen and hurrying to their assigned duties, accompanied by good-natured laughing and teasing. The bell over the front door tinkled, a noise barely noticed over the din of everyone moving about, until Mrs. Henderson appeared in the doorway.

"Claire, you have a caller."

Blushing as the others glanced, first at her and then down the hallway toward the door, Claire's quick steps carried her away from their speculative looks. Reaching the front office, she saw Billy Marple, cap in hand and elbows leaning on the counter, his cheeky grin widening as he spied her hastening toward him.

She stopped at the wooden barrier, a warm smile on her face. "Billy! Whatever are you doing here?" Leaning across the countertop, she grasped his work-roughened hands and gave them an affectionate squeeze.

"Well now, missus, there you be. Old Billy got to wonderin' exactly how you been farin' and so I thinks to meself, the best way to find out is to ask you direct-like and so here I am, oh my yes."

Claire laughed, delighted to see a friend who had become so dear to her in such a short time. "Oh Billy, how kind of you to ask. I'm fine. How's Maybelle?"

About to answer her, they were interrupted by Betty. "Mr. Marple." She extended her hand, and Billy, unsure if she expected him to kiss it or shake it, chose the wiser course and shook it.

"I know you probably don't remember me, Mr. Marple, but I'm Betty Sims. Claire has told me how you came to her rescue, helping her to find me, and then fetching her baggage and all. Oh yes, I've heard all about you." Her blond curls bounced as she spoke. "And I've also heard about the lovely tea your wife prepared for Claire and Mr. Kane." She paused, more surprised than anyone else in the room at her own effusiveness, for Eloise Henderson had also been listening to the conversation.

Blushing at the words pouring from her, she hesitated, smiling at Claire before plunging on. "Would you and Mrs. Marple like to attend my wedding? It's next Tuesday, the ninth. I know we haven't been officially introduced but I feel like I know you, and since the only family I have is my sister and nephew..." Her words trailed off as she looked about, suddenly uncertain.

Both Claire and Mrs. Henderson stood, astonished at the sudden blossoming of the usually quiet Betty. Claire stepped toward her friend and gave her a warm hug. "Oh Betty, that's the sweetest thing I've ever heard." She turned and looked at Mrs. Henderson, unsure how the idea of two more guests was being received, but her employer just stood there, a tiny smile on her face.

Billy was silent, perhaps being the most flabbergasted of them all. "Why, miss, I'd be honored. But my Maybelle, she's off visitin' our youngest. About to have a baby of her own, she is, all the way up in Yorkshire. No, Maybelle's not likely to be back for a few weeks, but oh my yes, I'd be honored, miss."

The man, flustered at this unexpected attention, began to retreat toward the door until a third female voice stopped him. "Mr. Marple."

Looking about, he realized it was the owner herself, the formidable Mrs. Henderson, and that fact halted him in his tracks. "You deliver goods, don't you, Mr. Marple. Am I correct in thinking that, and so I can assume you know the city well?"

Nodding his head, he waited, expecting a crate or something equally unwieldy being thrust his way.

"I wonder, Mr. Marple, if we might impose on you, or rather on your knowledge of London. Mrs. St. Martin knows that Mr. Kane resides at Pennygrove Hall. What I'm wondering is, since you've made the acquaintance of that gentleman, if you know the whereabouts of Pennygrove Hall. Unfortunately, she doesn't have any further address, and Miss Sims wishes to invite Mr. Kane to her wedding. In your travels about the city, have you perhaps noted such a place?"

Claire looked intently at both women who now appeared slightly uncertain how this bit of meddling might be interpreted. Her first impulse was to stop anyone interfering in her life, something she had sworn to never allow again, but just as suddenly, she had second thoughts. *Surely, an invitation to a wedding wouldn't be taken amiss and whoever or whatever he's hiding from, well...*

Billy smiled, cheeky grin once more in place. "Why, I'd be pleased to do that for the young leddy, especially since Mr. Kane did tell me the whereabouts of Pennygrove Hall. You go and write your letter, missy, and I'll wait right here for it. Once it's in my hands, you can consider it delivered."

At a nod from Mrs. Henderson, the younger woman flew to the desk in search of paper and pen. Betty would have preferred more time in which to compose the invitation, but she didn't want to tempt fate by pushing Mrs. Henderson too far. Blotting the ink hurriedly before stuffing the letter into an envelope, she hastened back to where the others stood chatting amiably, as if they were all old friends rather than recent acquaintances.

Taking the cream-colored envelope from the girl, Billy doffed his hat to the three women, promising to deliver it before the day was out.

❦   ❦   ❦

The day, although busy, was not quite uneventful. Walking toward the omnibus, Claire, her heart racing, held up a gloved hand as the driver made a movement toward her. "Mr. Smith, both Mrs. Henderson and I feel it would be better if I rode inside with the others."

She smiled anxiously as he glared coldly at her before turning, clambering quickly into the driver's seat, muttering unintelligibly all the while. His passengers cringed at the sound of the whip cracking over the horses' backs, but the unfortunate beasts could go no faster on the narrow and crowded streets, further frustrating the omnibus driver.

When their destination was finally reached, a slightly shaken company stepped down. Arthur Tucker, backed by his brother Gordon and the youngest footman, Harley Stroud, walked to the front of the bus, intending to have a sharp word or two with the errant driver, but the man was already striding angrily down the road. Shrugging their shoulders, they turned and followed the women through the servants' entrance, sparing no further thought for the man.

The day did not improve. The bride, a thin, fluttery young woman, fussed constantly with the table settings, causing both the permanent and temporary staff to determinedly set everything back to rights whenever she turned to speak to her mother, which was often. Mrs. Chester Gooday, a forceful woman, not only dominated her daughter but questioned every decision and instruction Claire made, certain that she was being overcharged and worrying aloud that these temporary servants would probably steal anything that would fit in their pockets. The day seemed interminable but it did at last end.

A very subdued Mr. Smith sat in his driver's box while his fellow employees wordlessly boarded the bus. Arthur, intending to speak sharply to the man, turned toward the front of the wagon, but Claire, sensing his intention, shook her head, quietly urging him to let Mrs. Henderson handle the matter. Reluctantly, Arthur gave up his quest, helping Claire step up and as soon all were seated, Mr. Smith flicked the reins, gently urging the horses to take them all home. Surprised looks were exchanged at the startling change in the man, but weariness had taken hold of them and they sat quietly, hoping it wouldn't prove to be the calm before the storm.

※ ※ ※

Arthur Tucker, as was occasionally his habit, stepped off the omnibus at the top of the road, stopping to talk to friends and acquaintances alike, tucking a copy of the daily newspaper under his arm as he strolled toward his friend Ollie's butcher shop for a bit of gossip. Less than an hour later, he stepped back onto the path, eager to return to what had become his home and the people who shared it with him he now considered friends.

The mouth-watering aroma of Mrs. Kenley's lamb stew wafted through the air, greeting him as he opened the door, which led into the kitchen. Everyone was gathered around the table, waiting for the cook to set the pot on the table as Arthur hurried upstairs to hang his coat and wash his hands.

Taking his seat at the table, Arthur nodded companionably to all, including Mr. Smith who lurked in the shadows of the dimly lit kitchen. As the diners finished the hearty meal, they sat back, sipping their tea and chatting quietly. It was then that Arthur, hurriedly swallowing his last mouthful, delivered his latest bit of gossip.

"The murderer 'as 'ad the cheek to send a letter to one of the newspapers!" Perhaps it was the tone of his voice or perhaps the accuracy of the gossip he had gleaned about the recent murders that caused the others to give him their full attention. He sat back, smiling, happy to be in the limelight once more.

"How do you know your friend's information is correct, Mr. Tucker?" Mrs. Henderson's voice rang out, affirming that she was as anxious as the others about the murders.

Arthur smiled, ready to meet the challenge. "A chap what works at the paper told me mate Ollie and 'e told me. The paper 'as already sent it on to the coppers. And what's more, the bloke 'ad the cheek to sign the letter." Fast becoming a master storyteller, he paused, letting everyone digest what he had so far revealed. "It was signed *Jack the Ripper!*"

Gasps were heard all around the table, and bits of conversation begun and stopped as the faceless monster suddenly became a person, someone who hungered for blood. The women shuddered, pulling their shawls tighter about their shoulders as the men, trying to hide their own uneasiness, huddled close. No one noticed the stocky figure of the omnibus driver as he crept from the kitchen, his fingers twisting one end of his mustache, an arrogant smirk playing about his thin lips.

※ ※ ※

The following day unfolded much as any other day. The employees of Henderson's Domestics had been engaged to serve at a charity bazaar, which was being held further afield than they normally travelled. An anxious Claire, on approaching the bus, was relieved to see Mr. Smith already sitting in the driver's box, thereby avoiding any upsetting confrontation.

The bazaar itself ran smoothly, and Claire was asked by many of the ladies in attendance about Henderson's Domestics. Mrs. Henderson, an astute businesswoman, had foreseen such a possibility and had had more business cards printed, cards which Claire was able to hand out with each inquiry made.

They arrived home, wanting only their supper and their beds. Tomorrow was the American Embassy Ball, a day they knew from experience would be long and tiring. Even the effusive Arthur Tucker was content to seek his bed.

As Claire and Betty were about to climb the stairs, Eloise Henderson called to them. Exchanging curious looks, they walked toward the desk that was strewn with papers and ledgers, their harried but smiling employer sitting behind it.

"Good news, ladies. While you were gone, Mr. Marple stopped by with the welcome news that both he and Mr. Braxton Kane will be in attendance next Tuesday at the wedding. Including you and your groom, Betty, that will be a total of twenty people." She started to turn but suddenly remembered something. "Claire, I almost forgot. Mr. Kane has sent a note to you through Mr. Marple." Claire, fingers trembling, quickly seized the envelope, murmuring her thanks to Eloise Henderson.

Claire felt herself blush as she stood there clutching the letter, while she watched Betty hug first a surprised Mrs. Henderson and then Claire herself. Satisfaction pursed Betty's mouth as she exclaimed that now everything would be perfect, squeezing Claire's hand as she spoke.

Claire exhaled a long sigh of contentment as she hugged the letter to her breast, feeling a warm glow flow through her body. Her step was light as she turned toward the staircase, blissfully happy and feeling fully alive. She ran up the stairs, daintily holding her skirt up. Once safely ensconced in her room, she eagerly opened the envelope and unfolded the single sheet of paper within, recognizing his scrawled signature.

My darling Claire. I've never been so eager to attend a wedding. Stay safe. I have some news about your situation—I'll tell you everything on the ninth.

He's coming! He's coming! Tonight there would be no shadows on her heart. She finally admitted to herself that her feelings toward Braxton had definitely changed. He was no longer the villain, only a dupe like her caught in the machinations of Bennett Kirkwood and that master puppeteer, Mordock Peckworthy.

The day was gloomy with a threat of rain when Claire and Betty made their way to the dining room and a subdued breakfast. There was some desultory conversation regarding the gossip that Arthur Tucker had brought home from his friend Ollie, some speculating as to whether the letter signed "Jack the Ripper" and sent to a newspaper was genuine or a hoax, but the main topic was the Embassy Ball. Expecting the evening to last into the wee hours of the morning, everyone went quietly about their duties, content to stay indoors until it was time to leave for Grosvenor Square and the American Embassy Ball.

Rain had begun to fall in the early afternoon, forming small puddles on the path from the building to the welcome refuge of Mr. Smith's omnibus. He guided the horses through the mostly deserted streets, the residents of London venturing out into the damp cold on only the most urgent of matters.

Reaching the rear entrance of the Embassy, Mr. Smith quickly jumped down and positioned himself a short distance from the door, waiting as everyone stepped from the bus. As Claire emerged, he beckoned to her. "Might I have a quick word, Mrs. St. Martin?"

Steeling herself, Claire took a hesitant step forward, slowly becoming aware that Arthur Tucker was standing protectively beside her. Giving him an appreciative glance, the two stood, quietly waiting for Mr. Smith to speak.

Surprised at the uninvited presence of Arthur Tucker, Mr. Smith hesitated, his thin lips pressed tightly together in something akin to disapproval. "The driveway will soon be very crowded with carriages, Mrs. St. Martin. Perhaps it would be better, with your approval of course, if I took this cumbersome wagon to a less travelled road, returning sometime after the hour has struck one, to fetch you."

Claire, feeling somewhat at a loss, faced the man, uncomfortably aware of the murky depths of his dark eyes. "What does Mrs. Henderson usually have you do in a situation such as this? Would she not want you to return home and wait there?"

Shaking his head as if the suggestion was a foolish one, the man lowered his eyes. "Mrs. Henderson is off visiting a lady friend this evening, and the cook will already be tucked up in bed with a cup of cocoa. There's no waking that one up, and it's a cold night to be spending it in the stable. Mrs. Henderson usually lets me go off on my own. I stop here and there, enjoying a pint of ale before moving on. And I've never been late returning, no ma'am."

Claire, unwilling to give any more time to the matter and anxious to seek shelter from the cold rain, turned to Arthur for support. The man nodded, as eager as she to get indoors. "Very well, Mr. Smith, but see that you're not late returning."

Dismissing him from her thoughts, she turned to the welcoming warmth of the embassy kitchen, rubbing her cold hands together to warm them, and thus she never saw the look of loathing that crossed the face of the driver, the man they all knew only as Mr. Smith.

The efficient Henderson employees were already moving about, pouring wine into goblets and helping the embassy servants set out tiny canapés. Claire, making contact with the butler, had a quick tour of the ballroom, dining room, and various sitting rooms before returning to the kitchen where she began directing her small group of well-trained domestics to their posts just as the first guests began to arrive.

The evening proceeded much as such other evenings had. Guests whirled about the ballroom, the ladies' jewels and gowns blending into a kaleidoscope of colors, the men at their most striking in white shirts and dinner jackets. Glasses of wine were unobtrusively served to chattering, laughing guests, while strains of violin music drifted about the room. Many hours later, a late supper was served in the grand salon.

Claire knew, as dirty dishes began arriving in the kitchen, that the evening would soon start winding down. Guests with full bellies, light-headed from the wine and other spirits, would soon be yawning with the eldest, impatient for their cozy beds, being the first to leave while the younger ones struggled to keep the evening from ending.

It was less than an hour later that the last dishes were carried into the kitchen. The butler, accompanied by the housekeeper, were both singing praises of the domestic agency and her management of the staff as they escorted Claire to the back door, watching as she made her way to the waiting omnibus and its passengers. Finding a seat just as the bus began to move, Claire noted that everyone was aboard and that most were already nodding off, their heads bobbing with the movement of the wagon. The lateness of the hour and little or no traffic hopefully guaranteed a swift return to their home.

In the dim light of the flickering carriage lamp, she saw that Arthur Tucker, sitting directly across from her, was awake and watching her. Smiling, she turned her head and looked out into the damp gloom of the night, his voice startling her when he spoke.

"You know, young miss, when you was first 'ired on, I thought old Eloise was making a big mistake. Most of us knew at a glance you 'ad never 'eld a position, and we didn't expect you to last the week. But we was all wrong! Look at you, keeping everything running nice and smooth- like." They both glanced toward the unseen driver, and as if he was reading her thoughts, he spoke again. "Oh, don't worry about old Smith. "E's an odd bloke right enough, but I'm watching out for you."

Blushing, Claire could just make out his face in the dim light. "Thank you, Arthur, for your kind words and the reassurance of knowing you're there should I find myself in need of assistance."

He was about to speak again when they felt the carriage slowly come to a stop. Shouting voices could be heard, and men carrying lanterns to dispel the inky blackness of the night were moving up and down the road, peering down dark lanes and into shadowy corners. The others on the bus began to stir, confused at the unfamiliar surroundings. Arthur spoke reassuringly to them while trying to discern what was happening outside. A voice called out to Mr. Smith, inquiring about his reason for being abroad at such a late hour. He mumbled an answer, but the person questioning him decided to look for himself.

The dim light cast by the lantern he carried preceded a rather tall man wearing a police uniform as he stepped onto the bus. Shining the light around to see all of the passengers, he stood there, somewhat perplexed as to what should be done next. A second man stepped inside, clearly the first man's superior.

"Johnson, what have you got here?" The man's tone was brusque, his manner bumptious. Turning to the startled commuters, his eyes fell on Claire, but he was distracted with the sound of Arthur Tucker clearing his throat.

"What seems to be the trouble, cap'n?"

The man bristled at being the one questioned. "And who might you be, Mr...?"

"Arthur Tucker, cap'n. And this young leddy is Mrs. St. Martin, what's in charge of all of us 'ere. We is all employees of Henderson's Domestics."

Snarling, the man barked at Arthur. "Don't address me as Captain. I am Sergeant Adams." Turning to Claire, the man held up his lantern. "And you, I presume, are Mrs. St. Martin." He suddenly seemed to have lost his power of speech as he found himself lost in her deep brown eyes.

"Yes, sergeant. Can you please explain why you've stopped us? We've been serving all evening at the American Embassy and are just now returning."

Seeming to regain his senses, he drew himself to his full height but still his hapless assistant, Constable Johnson, towered over him. "Murder has been committed, madam, and this time the madman has killed not just one but two prostitutes...er...women, both butchered." At his words, everyone gasped. Fearfully, a few peered through the windows, worried the killer might still be lurking about.

Aware that he had shocked everyone, he once more faced Claire. "I take it that you were all at the American Embassy this evening and are only now returning to…" He hesitated, and Constable Johnson, having noted the legend on the side of the omnibus, quickly stepped forward, his back ramrod stiff and his mouth set in a grim line.

"Henderson's Domestics, located in Brick Lane in Whitechapel, Sergeant Adams!"

Dark mustache twitching in annoyance, Sergeant Adams admitted to himself that it was unlikely the occupants of the omnibus harbored a murderer. He stiffly wished them a good night, needlessly admonishing them to go directly home.

All signs of drowsiness gone, the occupants speculated about the identity of the fellow, this Jack the Ripper, as the wagon plodded along until at last they drew up to the familiar building that housed them. Weariness set in once more, as they made their way to their respective beds, content to let the world spin without their active participation for the next few hours.

Uncharacteristically, Mrs. Henderson didn't rouse them for the early service at St. Bartholomew's, allowing them to sleep in a bit, choosing to attend the second service instead.

They were just finishing lunch when Arthur strolled in, once again wearing a self-satisfied smile. All conversations came to a close as they waited expectantly to hear what he had learned from his friend, the very well-informed Ollie. Even the reclusive Mr. Smith, who had been about to return to his horses, stood waiting, quietly blowing on his tea as Arthur took the floor.

"Well, it's like the good sergeant told us last night, t'was a double murder. Two prostitutes…I mean two unfortunates! The first one 'ad 'er throat slit good and proper. 'Er body was found in Dutfield's Yard on Berner Street. The coppers think 'e was interrupted and 'ad to run." He stopped talking long enough to have a sip of the tea Bessie Marigold had poured for him before continuing his narrative.

"The second one, she was found on Mitre Square, not 'alf-mile from Berner Street. Well, 'e got 'er good and proper. 'Er face was cut up just

Oh Wicked Escort

'orrible, 'er throat was slit, and the coppers say the bloke stole some of 'er insides."

It wasn't only the women who paled at his description, but no one spoke, all of them too horrified with the mutilation but at the same time, all seemed incapable of walking away before learning all the gruesome details of the grisly murders.

"But," Arthur paused, relishing his power, temporary though it might be, "this time 'e might 'ave been seen. The coppers are talking to some blokes who was in the area around the time of the murders." He paused, gathering his thoughts. "The coppers 'as found evidence that she 'ad some grapes to eat—maybe the madman gave them to her."

Standing up to be heard, the timid voice of one of the footmen, John Ackerly, intruded on Arthur's oration. "With so much cutting, don't you think the monster would be covered in blood?"

Arthur considered the question, pleased at being asked for his opinion. He moved toward the man, who was a slightly built fellow, all eyes following Arthur, watching his every move. He stepped behind the unsuspecting footman, his arm suddenly shooting out and grasping the smaller man around the throat.

"Blimey, John, you just reminded me. The coppers think 'e 'ad to be standing behind 'er, choking 'er first and then slitting 'er throat. That way, any blood there is spurts onto 'er, not on 'im." Nervous laughter broke out at his words. He paused again. "And anyway, in this 'ere neighborhood, with all the slaughterhouses about, a bloke could be covered in blood and no one would take a blind bit of notice." Nods of agreement followed this shrewd reasoning.

Eloise Henderson's voice rang out before Arthur could say anymore. "I needn't remind everyone that we're serving tonight at the Charity Tea for Maimed and Blind Sailors."

Everyone rose at the reminder and started clearing the table. Mrs. Henderson looked around at her staff, smiling at their well-trained efficiency. "And we've been hired every day for the next week. Our reputation grows."

❀ ❀ ❀

It wasn't until they were having their evening meal that Arthur returned, having left the omnibus on Whitechapel Road as they were making their way home from their latest engagement. He hadn't named his destination, but all of his fellow workers knew he was seeking out the well-informed Ollie.

On his return, Mrs. Kenley placed a steaming bowl of soup before him while Bessie Marigold buttered a thick slice of bread and laid it beside his bowl. Smiling his thanks to the two women, he noisily slurped his way through the hearty dish, refusing seconds when offered. Leaning back in his chair, he scanned the faces of his audience, noting that even Eloise Henderson seemed eager to hear of any new developments.

"Well, the city itself 'as put up a reward of £500." His listeners sat back, most of them unable to imagine such a princely sum. "And that's just for information, mind you, you don't even 'ave to catch the bloke. What's more, 'e left a message on the wall of a building what's on Goulston Street but the coppers 'ave washed it off. It said something about the Jews being responsible. Scared of 'aving a riot on their 'ands, they are. Ollie says the witnesses' accounts were still being looked into."

Claire and Betty, satisfied that they had heard all Arthur had to offer, made their way up to the room they shared, talking more about Betty's swiftly approaching wedding than the lunatic that roamed the streets of Whitechapel.

The remaining days leading up to Betty's wedding were relatively uneventful. The omnibus deftly traversed the streets of London, weaving through the traffic to whatever social event the domestics had been hired to serve at and at the end of their day transported them home. And the madman that had terrorized all of London seemed to have vanished, at least for the time being.

Arthur, feeling duty-bound to keep his friends up-to-date, confidently repeated Ollie's gossip, passing on the doings of the Metropolitan Police in relation to Jack the Ripper. He nattered on about the police finally releasing the letter, ostensibly written by Jack the Ripper, allowing all of London to read the missive that had originally been sent to the Central News Agency on September twenty-seventh.

When pressed by Arthur, Ollie admitted to being so well informed because he had regular customers from the police force and a few in the newspaper business. Ollie had also told Arthur that a card, postmarked October first but most likely written just after the murders on the twenty-ninth, had also been sent to the Central News Agency. Ollie said the writer of the card had promised a "double event," which as Arthur quickly pointed out, had happened on the night of the Embassy Ball.

Chapter Seventeen

Claire and Betty ventured out one bright afternoon to visit Betty's sister and nephew. The two women, happy to be out in the sunshine, chatted companionably as they threaded their way through the congested footpaths, with Betty stopping to buy bread and cheese for the only family she had. They saw that no woman walked alone and took comfort in each other's presence.

As they made their way toward the lodging house that Rosie and her son were living in, they became aware of a commotion on the other side of Whitechapel Road. Slowing their steps, they watched as a horse and rider, who had obviously been travelling in one direction, were now trying to change course, but the traffic along the road was too congested to allow such a maneuver. Other pedestrians had also slowed, enjoying the discomfort and frustration of someone who was obviously a member of the upper classes.

Shouting from across the way attracted Claire's attention, her eyes eventually falling on the horse and rider responsible for the commotion. Her hand suddenly reached out and clutched Betty's arm, drawing the other's attention to her.

"What's wrong, Claire, what is it?" Betty's voice was sharp with concern for her friend, whose face was now deathly pale, her brown eyes wide with shock and dismay. Wordlessly, Claire continued to stare across the street at the man who was her husband and who now returned her gaze, a look of stunned disbelief on his face.

Claire, who momentarily turned toward the buildings that lined the street, squeezed her friend's hand. "Look at that rider, Betty, the one causing the commotion! Can you make out his face?"

Anxiously, Betty peered over the heads and shoulders of the throng of people that milled about, searching for whoever it was her friend had seen. At last she found him and her blood ran cold. Bennett Kirkwood! And it was obvious he'd seen Claire which was adding to the tumult. He was now attempting to reach their side of the road, but so far no one had given way to him.

Seizing Claire's arm, Betty pulled her along, as they started moving hastily down the road, away from her former employer but also further from the safe haven of Henderson's. They had to reach Rosie's lodgings before he was able to cross the road. Their steps quickened as they pushed their way through the crowded walkway, at last ducking into the questionable refuge of a narrow alleyway.

Betty no longer had to drag Claire along as both of them used their elbows to clear a path, for even here the foot traffic was thick. Long minutes later, they reached the street that housed Betty's sister, and looking back to ensure no one had followed them, Betty led the way into Rosie's rooming house, a dilapidated building sadly in need of repair.

The two rushed through the doorway, climbing a dingy, creaking staircase to the second floor, and hopefully out of harm's way, at least for the time being. Rosie, having heard their footsteps, stood waiting in the doorway of her cheerless and squalid furnished room. Seeing the panic in their faces as they reached the landing, Rosie, never one to question needlessly, stood aside as the two women spilled into her room. Handing over the bread and cheese she had purchased, Betty gave a quick hello to her sister and smiled reassuringly at her nephew who stood by a tiny table, before purposefully crossing the room to the tiny window and peering through well-scrubbed but threadbare lace curtains.

Cautiously pushing one of the curtains slightly aside, Betty stared down at the road below. She continued to stand motionless for some time before she gasped and stepped quickly away from the window. Claire rushed over but Betty quickly blocked the way. "Don't look out, Claire, he might see you. He's searching around, I'm positive he doesn't know which direction we went."

Turning to her sister, Betty smiled. "I apologize, my sweet Rosie, for my rudeness. This is my friend, Claire, who you've already heard so much about." Both women nodded a friendly greeting, Rosie casting a puzzled look at her sister.

"Don't worry, Rosie dear. A man who's been searching for Claire spied her as we were making our way to see you. He'll be gone soon." She glanced out the window and smiled.

"Ah yes, there he goes, in the opposite direction." Anticipating the question, Betty spoke again. "He was Claire's husband, Rosie, but she left him, for reasons of her own. And that's quite good enough for me." She shot her sister a challenging look.

"Well, Betty, if you find no wrong with her, neither shall I." Turning to her young son, she held out her arms and he ran into them, cuddling close to his own safe haven.

"Bertie, where are your manners? Say hello to your Aunt Betty and to this pretty lady… I'm sorry Claire, but I don't know your last name."

Smiling at the boy who continued to hide in his mother's arms, she spoke softly. "Couldn't I also be Bertie's aunt, Aunt Claire?"

Smiling widely at the suggestion of a brand new aunt, Bertie allowed himself to be coaxed to her side where the two sat talking quietly about the excitement of sailing so far away, while Betty and her sister discussed the upcoming wedding and the practical aspects of their voyage to Australia.

Anxious to be on their way, Betty glanced out the window and smiled. "I see no sign of him, Claire."

Before she could reply, Rosie jumped up and faced them. "Mr. Bothwell, my landlord, leaves every day about this time to buy up any bargains that didn't sell at market. Perhaps he'd let you ride in the back of his wagon, at least as far as Brick Lane."

At their hesitant nods, Rosie raced from the room, her feet barely touching the wooden stairs as she ran down to see her landlord. A moment later, a male voice grated harshly against the quietness of the house, drifting up the stairwell, although no words were distinguishable.

At last, Rosie's light footsteps could be heard as she ran back up the stairs. Her smile gave them the welcome news—they could take refuge in Mr. Bothwell's wagon, but he had stressed to Rosie that he was leaving immediately and couldn't wait for stragglers. No other words were needed. Kisses and hugs were exchanged, and then there was only the sound of hasty footsteps running down the stairs and outside to where Mr. Bothwell sat on his wagon. Impatiently he indicated they had better hop on as waiting for them was not part of his plan.

Clumsily they hoisted themselves up onto the dusty wagon bed, peering nervously about as the wagon started to pull onto the road for hopefully an uneventful journey home. The streets were rapidly emptying, and the thumping sound of shutters being hung by shopkeepers closing their shops for the day echoed through the streets. The two women had pulled their shawls over their heads, huddling together as the wagon lumbered its way down the road until the wagon slowed and the driver announced they were at the top of Brick Lane.

❂   ❂   ❂

It was the following day that Braxton received a short note summoning him to Albert Higgins' law office *"on a matter most urgent,"* but just as he was leaving Pennygrove Hall, Bennett Kirkwood arrived. Braxton sighed, hoping the man would be brief for he didn't care for the tenor of the note from his solicitor. He dismounted, motioning Ben to follow him into the manor.

The housekeeper met them at the door, certain that Braxton had forgotten something until she spied Bennett Kirkwood following immediately behind him. Sniffing disdainfully, she turned to her employer.

"Coffee please, Mrs. Henfield." He led the way into the library, and upon shutting the door, looked closely at the man who had arrived, unannounced and sadly, unwelcome.

"You look pleased with yourself, Ben. Do you care to share whatever it is that has you grinning like a Cheshire cat?"

"Let's wait for the coffee, Braxton. I don't want to be interrupted." He prowled restlessly about the room, humming softly.

Braxton, although normally not a believer in portents of doom, began to feel a tinge of unease as to just what Ben's news might be. His fingers drummed uneasily on the polished surface of his desk as the other man paused in front of the window, glancing briefly outside before resuming his restless pacing. They exchanged news of mutual friends, but Braxton's attempts at conversation were half-hearted at best.

A sharp rap on the door announced the arrival of Mrs. Henfield and the coffee. Braxton took the tray and watched as she closed the door behind her. Two leather chairs with a small table between them faced the fireplace where a small fire already burned. Pouring the steaming liquid into two cups, Braxton sat in one chair and gestured to Ben to occupy the other.

Taking a hasty sip from the cup, Ben turned and looked intently at the other man. "I've found her!"

Despite his suspicion that this was what Ben had come to tell him, Braxton looked at Ben in shock. Trying to slow the sudden racing of his heart, he took a deep breath before croaking out a question.

"I take it you're referring to Claire?"

"Of course I'm talking about Claire. I saw her yesterday, late in the afternoon in Whitechapel. I was making my way to a new gaming house that I had heard about and simply got caught up in the congestion that one always finds on Whitechapel Road, horses and wagons going in all directions, and the people! Well, I was trapped, couldn't move in any direction, and suddenly there she was, across the road, walking with some woman. I tried to extricate myself but the harder I tried, the worse things got…but I'm sure she saw me. One minute she was there, the next—poof—gone! I roamed around a bit but couldn't find any trace of her."

Braxton laughed. "Surely Ben, a glimpse of someone who reminded you of…"

The other man paused, momentarily doubting himself, but then shook his head impatiently, grinding the words out between his teeth. "No, Braxton, I'm telling you, it was her!"

With deceptive calm, Braxton asked the question that was foremost in his thoughts. "If it was actually Claire you saw, what do you intend to do, Ben?"

The question brought Ben up short. He ran his hands through his hair and looked wildly about the room. "Do! I intend to find her bolt-hole and when I do, I'll expose her to all of London society as a runaway wife. Let her be the villain in this farce of a marriage!"

Braxton's next words were spoken with staid calmness. "Ben, all of London society has heard the circumstances of your marriage, thanks to that scandalmonger Letitia Penrod. Claire has been judged an innocent victim, and that is where society's sympathy lies. You wouldn't be exposing a villain, you'd only be holding yourself up to more ridicule."

Ben stood up and pushed his hands deep into his pockets. "And Braxton Kane, do you think society doesn't know your part in all of this?" His tone was belligerent.

Rising, Braxton faced the man. "I accept responsibility for my role; in fact, I'll never forgive myself for going along with such a crack-brained scheme."

Bennett Kirkwood stood, suddenly aloof, his blue eyes darkening dangerously as he stared at the man he had once called friend. There was a silken thread of warning in his voice as he attempted to face down Braxton. "I will find her, without any help from you." There was a slight hesitation in his hawk-like eyes when suddenly he stiffened as if he'd been struck.

"You do fancy her, don't you?" His tone became sneering. "You sly dog, you're worried that I'll find her. I don't need to remind you that I'm still her husband." Curses fell from his mouth as he made his way to the front door. Reaching for the door handle, he stopped and turned, facing his former friend.

"I'll find her and drag her back to Silverwood, by her hair if I have to. Silverwood is her home, and I can only repeat that I'm still her husband." He spat the words out contemptuously before slamming the door behind him. The sound reverberated through the house, bringing Mrs. Henfield hurrying from the kitchen.

"Is everything all right, Mr. Kane?"

Turning to his housekeeper, he smiled grimly. "Hopefully it will be, Mrs. Henfield." His hand closed around the doorknob. "I'll be out for most of the day." As he left, he took care to close the heavy door softly so as not to alarm the poor woman any further.

On entering the lawyer's office, Braxton thought that perhaps time stood still in this particular room, for the three clerks were still perched atop their wooden stools, scratching entries into journals. The same clerk who had escorted him into Albert Higgins' office some days earlier once again jumped down from his stool and alerted his employer to the visitor who waited in the outer office. Albert Higgins himself emerged and waved Braxton into his chamber.

"My boy, how have you been keeping?" Without waiting for an answer, he sat down and gestured to the other chair. "Bad news, my boy, bad news! I think a splash of whiskey is needed." Saying that, he once more unlocked his liquor cabinet and poured the same fiery amber liquid they had drunk on Braxton's earlier visit.

Facing Braxton, Albert Higgins hesitated before speaking. "I sent a telegram to New Orleans as promised, dear boy, and only received a reply yesterday."

Braxton braced himself, knowing from the man's actions that the news must be very grim indeed.

"It seems your brother escaped from his cell some months ago and has disappeared completely."

Braxton sank back into the chair, at first too stunned to say anything. Tense silence filled the room. "How…I don't understand, Albert."

Taking pity on his client, the lawyer patted his shoulder consolingly. "The telegram doesn't give too much information, just that he escaped earlier this year, and there's now a reward offered for him. I'm sorry the news couldn't be happier, Braxton."

Rising, Braxton drained his glass. Pensively he stared out the window a moment before giving Albert a half-hearted smile. "I know it's wrong but I hope he stays on that side of the Atlantic. Let the law find him there and mete out their justice."

Sighing, the shorter man also rose. "I understand your sentiment, my boy. As to that other matter…" He paused. "I'm afraid I have nothing to report yet. I've consulted with an old school chum who has some experience in these matters, and he's now looking into it. I'll be in touch the minute I hear anything."

After briefly shaking the other's hand, Braxton left the office, lost in thought as he walked slowly down the footpath, torn by conflicting emotions. He mounted his horse and slowly made his way home.

At last, the ninth of October dawned. Betty and Claire had washed each other's hair the night before, and now, with breakfast finished, they hurried up the stairs to change. Because of repairs being done to the roof of St. Bartholomew's, thus making the church unsuitable for the service, the vicar had agreed to conduct the ceremony at Henderson's.

Betty, a bundle of nerves, found it difficult to sit still as Claire arranged her hair into a becoming crown of blond curls. Slipping her best gown over her head, she nervously smoothed nonexistent wrinkles from the skirt. The faint tinkle of the bell that hung over the door could be heard occasionally, with a new voice added to the ones already waiting downstairs. Betty's sister Rosie was sent upstairs by Eloise Henderson to lend assistance to the bride, if indeed any help was needed.

Rosie, pale cheeks flushed with excitement for her sister, reported that everyone was quite taken with young Bertie, especially a tall gentleman with sparkling grey eyes. Blushing, Claire glanced at Betty, a small smile of enchantment touching her lips.

At that moment there was a tap at the door, and Eloise Henderson poked her head into the room, letting them know all of those invited had arrived and were seated downstairs, waiting on the bride. Her footsteps echoed on the wooden stairs as she returned to the guests. Betty, eyes shining brightly, smiled tremulously at her sister, and Claire, hugging them both just as Arthur appeared in the doorway, wearing his best suit and a nervous smile, eager to escort the bride to her waiting groom.

Claire and Rosie followed the two down the stairs to what had once been Mrs. Henderson's office but was now, thanks to the concerted efforts of the staff of Henderson's, transformed into a chapel, decorated with late-blooming fall flowers. Chairs and benches had been carried in from the dining room, most of them already occupied. Rosie sat down next to her son, who was being kept amused by Billy Marple. Looking up, Billy gave Claire his cheekiest grin, nodding toward a figure hovering just inside the room.

Determined not to reveal her joy at seeing him, she couldn't control the racing of her heart as Braxton stepped out, his smile as intimate as a kiss. She met the smile and the hand that was offered, feeling blissfully happy and fully alive. He lifted her slender hand to his lips and brushed the fingertips with a soft kiss. Fleetingly, she again wrestled with the thoughts that still came to her, unbidden, in the early hours of the morning, before anyone else in the house stirred. *Am I ready to leave the past behind and even more importantly, can I?*

Taking her arm, he escorted her to where two chairs waited, and together they sat down just as the ceremony began. Claire found his nearness both disturbing and exciting, making it difficult to concentrate on the vows being exchanged by Betty and James but was soon brought back to the present as everyone stood, congratulating the newlyweds.

As unobtrusively as possible, the Henderson men carried the chairs and benches back to the dining room, arranging them for the wedding luncheon that was about to be served.

Braxton, although impatient to have Claire alone, soon realized he was receiving almost as much attention as the bride and groom, for most of the guests had never hobnobbed with a member of the upper classes before. He reconciled himself to chatting companionably with the other guests after congratulating the buoyantly happy couple. A giggling Molly seemed intent on attracting his attention but soon resigned herself to the fact that he had eyes for no one but Mrs. St. Martin, a fact that Bessie Marigold and the cook, Mrs. Kenley, laughingly pointed out to her as the three moved toward the kitchen and the task of filling the serving bowls for the hungry guests.

The chatter halted a few minutes later as a smiling Eloise Henderson somehow made herself heard above the cheerful din of the crowd. "Lunch is about to be served, if everyone will just move down the hall to the dining room." Nodding their agreement, the company slowly began to follow the mouth-watering aromas that were drifting through from the kitchen.

Billy Marple, with Rosie's son Bertie in tow, joined Claire and Braxton at the far end of the table. Before the meal was served, ribaldry ruled as toasts were made to the happy couple, most of the gathering remembering to include Rosie and Bertie as they wished them well when they all set sail for Australia in two days time. Conversation faded as all present consumed the delicious meats and pastries that the talented Mrs. Kenley had prepared.

At last, the bridal couple slipped away, James having arranged for a room at a nearby inn until it was time to board their ship. Arthur Tucker and his brother Gordon accompanied Rosie and Bertie through the perilous streets of Whitechapel to their lodging, promising to return for them on the day they were to board the ship. Billy, the last guest except for Braxton to leave, stood holding Claire's slim hands between his two large ones. He smiled down at her, the warmth of his smile echoing in his voice.

"Young leddy, I can see you're a good deal happier than you were some weeks ago, and that eases my mind, oh my yes it does. You're a real looker, you are, and your fella' is a handsome bloke. Oh, my Maybelle is going to be some disappointed missin' this little gatherin', oh my yes. Well, I've said my thank you's to everyone and now I must be off." Smiling, he placed his cap on his head and stepped outside, whistling a jaunty tune as he set off down the path toward home.

Seeing that at last he had her to himself, Braxton led her to a corner of the office, a dimly lit room still decorated with flowers, where two chairs sat as if awaiting them. "At last I have you alone, Claire. There is much I have to tell you…"

Claire, suddenly reminded of her brush with disaster just a few days ago, was just as eager to talk to him. Her heart fluttered, remembering the fear of that day, but she knew she was safe with him by her side.

"Braxton, I saw Bennett!"

Braxton stiffened at her words. "I know, Claire. He came to see me the day after…and somehow guessed how I feel about you." He rose from the chair and began worriedly pacing. "Oh, he doesn't realize the depth of my feelings, not yet at any rate. He was raving and went from seeking a divorce to dragging you back to Silverwood, by your hair, if need be."

Fear, stark and vivid, glittered in her brown eyes, and she trembled as fearful images grew in her mind. "Oh, Braxton, what am I to do?"

"Nothing, my love. Heed the advice in my first note to you. Stay indoors unless you're with all the staff of Henderson's, and never, ever venture out alone. He's certain you're in Whitechapel somewhere and likely has men out looking for you."

Her head bowed, she remained in an attitude of frozen stillness until he dropped down beside her once more.

"And now for some positive news. I've been to my solicitor, and while he cautions me that he's not an expert in these matters, he feels that the court's decision will probably be to grant you an annulment. There's no property or children, and the two of you have never shared a marriage bed." A delicate blush suffused Claire's cheeks at the reminder of her wedding night and the man who had spent it with her.

Tendrils of black hair fell on his forehead, and again Claire was tempted to brush them back, but just as her hand reached out, his own hand clasped hers and lingered.

It was at that moment that Eloise Henderson appeared and they sprang guiltily apart. Flustered, the older woman looked at them. "Oh Claire, I didn't know you were in here…" She stood there for a moment as if deciding what her course of action should be. "Well, I'll just leave you two alone." She hastily retreated back to the dining room, the ghost of a smile playing about her lips.

Braxton stood and with his powerful hands pulled her to her feet. His handsome face smiled warmly at her. "My beautiful, beautiful love, I must leave before Mrs. Henderson thinks she's harboring a harlot under her roof." He kissed her lips softly, his willpower sorely tested by such restraint.

"Claire, I can't promise when I'll be back—Ben is having my home watched." At her gasp of surprise, he smiled cynically. "Oh yes, my dove, he's had his man lurking in the shrubbery around Pennygrove, not to mention the esteemed Mordock Peckworthy, who for his own twisted reason is also having me watched." He paused, thinking for a moment. "Although I somehow think Peckworthy is doing it more out of curiosity than malice."

He opened the door and peered out, but no one seemed to be about. He smiled at her and then was gone. Claire hastily closed the door, less confident when Braxton was no longer beside her.

She slowly climbed the stairs to the room she had shared with Betty but now was hers alone, and at least for the present, she welcomed the solitude.

Betty and her new husband, along with Rosie and Bertie, stopped by on their last day in London to bid farewell to all of Henderson's Domestics, especially Claire and Eloise Henderson. Tears were shed as they left, but Betty promised she would write as soon as they were settled. Many of the staff, charmed by young Bertie at his aunt's wedding, had bought small toys for him to pass the time on the long voyage, but Claire, unwilling to risk going out, gave him a shilling from her small horde of coins to spend on anything he wanted.

After the excitement of the wedding, tranquility reigned in the building on Brick Lane. All of Henderson's commitments seemed to be teas and bazaars, and all were held in the afternoon. As they were returning from an engagement one Saturday afternoon, Arthur Tucker, with a wave of his hand, bid everyone his customary farewell as he jumped from the omnibus and went in search of Ollie, his friend and source of gossip and news.

They were just finishing dinner when Arthur returned home. He smiled enigmatically, apologizing for keeping everyone in the dining room and kitchen waiting whilst he slurped up a hearty serving of beef stew. Everyone knew he would say nothing until he had eaten, so they cleared the table and started tidying the kitchen, waiting for him to lay down his knife and fork. At last, sighing as he sat back, replete, Arthur smiled at his audience, pausing long enough to sip his tea. He was once more Arthur Tucker, keeper of secrets and purveyor of news.

"The news, my friends, is skimpy. Old Jack seems to be on 'oliday. Central News Agency 'ad another letter and the coppers 'ave 'ung copies of it outside all the stations, 'oping someone could say just 'oo wrote it, but they think it all a 'oax. And Mr. George Lusk what was elected 'ead of the Mile End Vigilance Committee 'as also 'ad a letter from old Jack. The 'andwriting looks like the first letter from 'im."

With no horror stories of murder and mayhem, the conversation around the table soon began to repeat itself. Theories were offered, but eventually they all grew bored with guessing games and began to drift off to their beds.

Claire followed behind the other women as they slowly climbed the stairs, all trying to put off retiring for the night while the madman was still so prevalent in their minds. Reaching the second floor, one by one the women gathered around Claire's open door, staring at the bouquet of flowers lying on her bed.

Molly, still irked at being ignored by Braxton Kane at the wedding, was the first to speak. "Ooh, Mrs. St. Martin, looks like your fella' was 'ere and dropped these 'ere posies off."

Claire paled, remembering the rose that had been left on her bed so many weeks ago, shot the girl a scathing look. "Don't be silly, Molly. Obviously, Mrs. Henderson accepted the flowers this afternoon while we were gone and forgot to mention it. They might not even be for me—I don't see a note."

Picking up the bouquet, she looked around the room but couldn't see that anything had been disturbed. Her feet flew down the stairs, her mind in turmoil. Knocking on her employer's bedroom door, she quickly inspected the flowers once more, hoping she had missed a card or letter but there was nothing to say who had sent them or, more importantly, who they were meant for.

As the bedroom door opened, Claire's hands trembled. *It's just a silly mistake, they're meant for someone else, not me.*

Eloise Henderson stood in the doorway, surprised to be disturbed in her private quarters, but a glance at Claire's ashen face told her the matter had to be of the utmost importance. Opening the door wider, she gestured Claire inside, hastily pulling a wooden chair away from a small table that stood in a corner of the room.

"Eloise, did someone deliver these flowers today? They were lying on my bed and my door stood open."

"On your bed!" She paused, pondering the seriousness of the matter. "There were no deliveries of any kind today, Claire. Is there a note? Perhaps they were meant for one of the others…"

"No! We all went upstairs at the same time. I was the last to reach the top. Everyone was gathered around my open door. Molly thought perhaps you had accepted them…"

"No, my dear, it's as I said. There were no deliveries today. Perhaps one of the men has his eye on Molly or one of the other ladies and didn't know which door was hers, although I thought I had made it clear to everyone, men and women alike, that there was to be no consorting if they valued their jobs." She pursed her lips, mentally reviewing each member of her staff.

"Claire, you did lock your door when you left your room this morning, didn't you?"

"Of course I did." She stopped, suddenly unsure. *Did I? How can I know for sure?*

Oh Wicked Escort

Hesitantly, Claire spoke again. "I know it's unfair, but what about Mr. Smith? Does he have a room on the men's floor?"

Meeting the younger woman's eyes, Eloise shook her head. "He does have a room but he rarely uses it. He seems to prefer the company of horses—a most peculiar man." She looked at Claire sharply. "What about the man you were running from when I hired you?"

Biting her lip, Claire looked away, her face even paler and clouded with uneasiness. When at last she replied, her voice was barely a whisper, causing Eloise Henderson to lean forward to catch her words.

"You're right, of course. I was fleeing both a bad marriage and a bad husband. He was despicable. I won't bother you with the details, the only thing that's certain is I will never go back to him, never! And by chance he saw me last week, when Betty and I went to visit Rosie. So now he has some inkling of where I am." Her finely arched eyebrows drew together in an agonized expression, and taking a deep, unsteady breath, she leaned back in the chair.

"But really, Eloise, I can't see Bennett sending me flowers. He told Braxton that if he found me, he'd drag me back to Silverwood House, by my hair if he had to, and I have no difficulty believing him capable of such a deed."

Eloise's eyebrows lifted inquiringly at the mention of Braxton's name, but she kept her questions and her thoughts to herself. Searching for a plausible explanation where there was none, Eloise once again leaned back in her chair. "Well, my dear, it's too late now, but tomorrow I promise I will ask everyone if they've noticed any strangers hanging about." She yawned, suddenly exhausted. Standing, she put her arm around the smaller woman's shoulders and gave her a gentle, motherly hug. "For now, Claire, go to bed. We have a busy day tomorrow."

Lost in thought, Claire climbed the stairs, hesitating before she opened her door. Shivering nervously, she undressed and jumped into her narrow bed, hugging the blankets tightly. *Tomorrow, she thought, tomorrow it will all make sense. Perhaps it's as we thought, one of the men fancies Molly or one of the other women and simply didn't know which room was hers.* Deciding it was definitely a mistake and would somehow sort itself out, she closed her eyes and eventually fell into a restless slumber.

D. L. Robinson

❦ ❦ ❦

Several curious glances were sent her way when she entered the dining room, but no words were exchanged beyond a good morning. Just as breakfast was finishing, Eloise Henderson came in, and as promised asked if anyone knew anything about the flowers left in Mrs. St. Martin's room or, if not, had anyone noticed any stranger hanging about. All shook their heads, directing inquisitive looks toward Claire once again as they moved busily about, performing their assigned housekeeping chores which kept Henderson's Domestics running smoothly.

Days passed with no other untoward events. There was no word from Braxton, but he had said he was being watched.

Mr. Smith, while polite, seemed to be keeping his distance, and for that, Claire was grateful. The other men were solicitous, all promising to keep their eyes peeled for any strangers that might be skulking about.

Thursday was a busier day than usual as they served at both the Autumn Tea for the Destitute in the afternoon and a small gathering at a supper meeting of the Planning Committee of the Royal Geographical Society, held in Exeter Hall, but they finished serving early, as agreed, and were making their way home before eight o'clock. Arthur, seeing the lights still on in Ollie's shop as they passed, stepped off the omnibus with a cheery wave of his hand, promising to bring home any new gossip.

Mrs. Kenley, waiting on their arrival, soon had the company seated and was serving them a hot meal with the promise of a treacle pudding for dessert, when Arthur walked in. He quickly joined them, refusing to impart any gossip until the meal was done, including the washing up, adding that he had caught Ollie just as he was locking up, which in his opinion was a lucky thing in light of the news he had to share with them.

It took only the hint of new gossip to motivate a speedy washing up of the dishes, and soon they were all back in their chairs. Even the reclusive Mr. Smith had stayed, most sipping a second cup of tea while Arthur savored the moment.

Looking about him, he saw that the people he had come to know so well, in spite of looking tired after their long day, were sitting quietly, eager to learn what he knew while at the same time dreading it. He guessed that the discussion afterward would likely be a short one.

"Well, as I said, Ollie was just locking up and in a bit of a 'urry to get 'ome to 'is missus and the promise of a 'ot meal, so 'e wasn't in any mood to dally." He paused, enjoying the attention.

"It seems Mr. George Lusk of the Mile End Vigilance Committee received a letter on Tuesday, the envelope marked 'From Hell', and with it a package containing 'alf a kidney what is suspected to be from the poor unfortunate that was old Jack's last victim. And a doctor 'as already said it's a 'uman kidney."

Horrified, no one spoke for a moment, but suddenly there was a flood of opinions until at last, the long day took its toll, and they all drifted, singly and in pairs, up their respective staircases, wanting nothing more than their own cozy beds.

❀ ❀ ❀

On waking, Claire peeked out the tiny window of her bedroom and saw grey clouds scudding across the sky. Shivering in the coolness of the room, she quickly completed her toilette but as she was fastening her dress, she spied a small vase of flowers on the tiny table beside her bed. Her eyes widened in alarm as she instinctively checked the door, satisfying herself that the key was still in the lock, just as she had left it last night. Her hand reached out and her fingers slowly turned the knob, needing to confirm that the door was indeed locked. She looked about the room but nothing seemed disturbed.

Trembling, she looked closely at the four walls but could find nothing that even hinted at a second entrance. Glancing at the window, she knew that only a child could fit through that small opening, even if you overlooked the fact that her room was on the second floor. Suddenly, nothing seemed as important as making her way downstairs. As if she was waiting for her, Eloise Henderson stood off to one side of the bottom stair, excitedly waving an envelope at her but one look at the girl's ashen face wiped any other thought from her mind.

"Eloise!" Her voice was deceptively calm. "Someone has been in my bedroom, whoever it was has left more flowers."

Eloise Henderson's thick eyebrows lifted in surprise, already moving toward the staircase. "When did this happen? Was your door locked?"

Near tears, Claire's reply was sharp. "Of course it was locked…I checked it as soon as I saw the flowers."

Together they made their way upstairs and stood before the locked door. Eloise took the key from Claire's trembling fingers, both women standing in the hallway as the door swung open. The offending flowers sat, as if awaiting their fate, on the table, while both women looked down at them, seeking an explanation for their presence. Eloise looked around the room as Claire had, searching for a secondary access but found nothing.

Patting the younger woman's shoulder, she led her from the room, locking the door and handing the key back. "Is there any chance you failed to notice them last night, dear?"

Tears welling up in her eyes, Claire shook her head. "Even if I didn't notice them last night, how did anyone get into my room? All the bedroom doors are locked during the day."

Bewilderment was obvious in the older woman's face as she led the way down the stairs, depositing the offending vase and its contents on a corner of her desk. "All right, dear, I'll speak to everyone again, but for now come to the dining room and have breakfast. Perhaps you'll feel better after a cup of tea."

They had taken no more than a few steps when Eloise Henderson withdrew a letter from her pocket. "Claire, in all the hubbub, I forgot about this. A letter arrived for you in the early post, and I believe it's from your young man."

Claire rolled her eyes. "Really Eloise, he's not my 'young man' at all." Glancing at the handwriting, she knew at once it was from Braxton. Calling out her thanks, she turned around and climbed back up the stairs. The need to be alone, with no one asking questions or sending sly looks her way, seemed to outweigh her apprehension about returning to her bedroom. Sitting on her bed, she examined the cream-colored envelope, savoring the moment before she very carefully opened it.

> *My love—while I must assume I am still being watched, I can wait no longer to share at least an afternoon with you. Ask the very practical and obliging Mrs. Henderson if you might have a free afternoon soon*

and write to me by return post.
   Braxton

She sat there, dreaming romantic dreams as young women are wont to do, until she realized time was passing, swiftly and impatiently, and so she pulled her drifting thoughts together. Her feet fairly flew down the stairs and carried her to the side of Mrs. Henderson who, spectacles perched delicately on her nose, was poring over a ledger. Her eyebrows lifted in surprise as she looked at her employee. Claire, the words tumbling out of her mouth, begged the use of paper and pen, stopping long enough to determine that tomorrow was probably the only free day they would have until the following week.

Claire, with a quick glance at Eloise for permission to impose, sat down and quickly penned a reply that tomorrow was her only free day, and her next day off would not occur until sometime in the next week or so. As she sat pondering the dilemma of being discovered by Bennett, Mrs. Henderson removed her spectacles and stood up, walking to the corner of the table where Claire sat.

"Is there a problem, Claire?"

The younger woman stiffened, momentarily abashed. "Mr. Kane would like to meet me somewhere, possibly tomorrow afternoon."

Brow furrowed, the older woman patted her hand with affection as she turned and started walking toward the door but paused after a few steps. "Claire, I know it's none of my business, but I would be remiss if I said nothing. You're still a married woman. Is it wise to meet a man who is not your husband?"

Claire, blushing, cast her eyes downward. "I know that in the eyes of the law I'm still a married woman, but believe me when I say my husband and I never..." she stammered in mortification, "we never shared a bed." As she spoke, she tried to hide the annoyance she felt when she thought of the months they had shared a house and nothing else.

"A wife, especially a penniless one, seemed to be the last thing Bennett wanted. And a solicitor who has been consulted on my behalf feels that the law, given the circumstances, will annul this sham of a marriage that it was my misfortune to enter into."

"Oh my dear girl, I'm only trying to look out for your best interests. Both you and Betty seem like the daughters I never had." She absently rubbed the back of the chair, suddenly uncertain of what to say next.

She stood, indecision causing her to open her mouth and then close it firmly, twice, as if unwilling or uncertain what to say. Glancing at her, Claire recognized that whatever the matter was, the older woman was determined to have her say.

Starting once again, Eloise nervously rubbed the back of the chair again. Suddenly and decisively, she squared her shoulders, clearing her throat in the process. "Claire, please never think of me as the enemy or a nosy old busybody. I know what it is to be trapped in a bad marriage." She paused, dabbing at the moisture that had suddenly gathered in the corners of her eyes.

"No, my girl, it wasn't me... my Charlie made me very happy. It was my sister, Emily. She was five years older than me, and I just adored her. But then she met Mr. Banbury at the Saturday markets; by chance he was in London on business. Not long after that first meeting, she left our cottage to marry him and move to his home in Cornwall. She promised to write, but as the months passed, we only ever received two letters from her."

Eloise's eyes had a haunted look as she revisited the painful past. "When my parents could stand it no longer, we travelled to that small village in Cornwall, luckily finding the cottage where they resided. There we met him, obviously just returning from some errand. Surprised at finding us outside his home, he unexpectedly turned into a man we could barely recognize. He raged at us, blaming my parents for Emily's failure to be a proper wife. We could hear her sobbing inside, but he wouldn't let us see her. We returned to London but my parents were brokenhearted. Less than a year later, we received word that Emily had died, no explanation, nothing. My parents seemed to wither away before my very eyes and soon they followed her to their graves. That was all more than thirty years ago—times were different then."

Both women dabbed at their eyes at the end of Eloise's tale. Claire walked over to her friend and hugged her. The older woman began to speak again.

"Thankfully, by this time I had met Mr. Henderson, my Charlie, who as I said made me very happy. The one blight in our marriage was the lack of children, but thankfully he said I was enough for him." She dried the tears that had fallen and smiled shakily at the girl who stood in front of her, her deep brown eyes still bright with unshed tears.

Claire hugged the woman even harder a second time, trying to chase away her sadness. "Oh, Eloise, I'm so sorry for you and Emily. I wish she had had a happier life." She bent her head, studying her slender fingers, and when she spoke, there was a soft gentleness in her voice.

"I know you're concerned with my welfare. It's just that others have made all my decisions for me, and they weren't always in my best interests. But Braxton, he's doing everything possible to right a wrong. And Eloise, the truth of the matter is…I think I'm falling in love with him."

Silently, the two women faced each other for some seconds until Eloise suddenly straightened her shoulders and cleared her throat. "Well, my dear, if that's how you feel, you certainly have my blessing. I feel Mr. Kane is not only an honorable man but one who cares for you, very much so, in fact. So write your letter quickly now, for the post will be collected very soon." She turned away but then snapped her fingers as if she had just thought of something. "Claire, you might want to mention to Mr. Kane that if I can be of any service…" Her words trailed off as she left the room.

Claire finished her note, adding a postscript explaining that Mrs. Henderson had hinted she could be called on if ever any help was needed. She was sealing the envelope just as the postman appeared in the doorway.

It seemed like hours had passed but in truth the clock was only striking three when a letter was dropped through the mail slot. Glancing at the envelope as she picked it up, Eloise smiled, her eyes twinkling at the thought of the mischief she might be getting up to. She had been too wrapped up in business of late, and it was high time she added a bit of spice to her life.

Claire was in the kitchen, having just finished helping Mrs. Kenley with the washing up from lunch when Mrs. Henderson burst through the door holding a cream-colored envelope. "Claire, there's a letter for you."

An enigmatic smile passed between the two women as the letter was handed over, and Claire, without another word, escaped from the kitchen and flew up the stairs, leaving the other employees wondering what the envelope might contain.

Claire sat on her narrow bed, re-reading the short note. Tomorrow at one o'clock! There was a soft, hesitant knock at the door. Claire crossed the floor and cautiously opened the door, revealing Eloise Henderson standing in the hallway, her eyes absolutely sparkling with delight. Stepping into the room, she asked the pertinent question.

"Well, will Mr. Kane be calling for you tomorrow?"

Claire, unable to contain her excitement, nodded. "He's calling at one o'clock—in a hired carriage." This last was spoken with trepidation, a reminder that someone might be following him. "Oh, Eloise, what if he's followed?"

"Tush, girl. He's demonstrating his intelligence by hiring a carriage." The two women spent the next half hour planning what Claire would wear until they heard the other ladies coming up the stairs to change into their serving clothes. Eloise Henderson peeked at the small timepiece that was pinned to her ample bosom.

It was time for the staff of Henderson's to ready themselves to serve at a dinner and musical evening at the home of a Mr. & Mrs. Rubicorn of Chelsea, and demonstrate once again the talents of the domestic agency.

Late the following morning that there was a quiet tap at her door. On opening, she saw the ample figure of her employer standing there, wearing a mischievous expression and holding a striped hatbox in front of her. Giggling like a schoolgirl, Eloise placed the cumbersome box on the bed and opened it, revealing a black hat complete with heavy black veiling.

"I hope you still plan to wear your black gown, Claire. This hat will set it off beautifully. I wore it when my Charlie passed on. And now you can play the part of a grieving widow." Her smile was eager and alive with affection and delight.

Claire opened the armoire, taking out the dress she had worn when her father died. Undressing quickly, she pulled the black gown on. Eloise fussed with the folds of the skirt as it draped gracefully over Claire's slender figure. She took the hat that Eloise held out to her and placed it carefully on her head, gently tugging the veil down to cover her face. At last she felt ready, pirouetting in front of her fellow conspirator. Clapping her hands in glee, the older woman stood ready to do battle with anyone who might harm this beauty who was temporarily in her care.

"Oh Claire, I doubt there's anyone who would guess the identity of such a mysterious beauty."

Not wanting to wear the hat down the stairs, Claire clasped it in her hand, looking at the other questioningly. "Eloise, you flatter me. How could anyone tell what the person looks like under such a heavy veil?"

"Trust me, girl. You turn heads everywhere you go, and I doubt a veil will prove to be a hindrance. Surely you've noticed?"

Claire felt her cheeks grow warm at the question. "I never encourage anyone to look at me, Eloise."

The older woman laughed, affectionately hugging the blushing beauty. "Oh my dear, I know that. If I had had the slightest suspicion that you were any kind of a flirt, I would never have hired you. But now, enough talk. We had better be downstairs when your young man arrives."

They proceeded down the stairs, both remarking on the gloomy greyness of the day. Neither of them noticed the silhouette of a man who, on hearing their approach, stood just outside the door, preferring to lurk in the shadows. He listened as the unwary Eloise went into her private quarters for a moment while Claire, using the small mirror that hung on the wall, fussed with the hat until, finally satisfied, she anchored it with an ebony hatpin. A small rustling sound caught her attention, and she peered into the dimness as a figure stepped noiselessly from the unlit hallway into the bright office and reception room.

"Mr. Smith!" Recognizing the driver, Claire smiled nervously, wishing that Eloise would return from wherever she had disappeared to. The man's eyes caught and held hers, causing a flicker of apprehension to course through her. Trying to appear nonchalant, she drew back a step. "I…ah…I didn't see you there. Are you looking for Mrs. Henderson?

She'll be back any moment."

Clutching his hat in his gloved hands, Mr. Smith's eyes roamed boldly over the slight figure standing before him. Glancing at her outfit, he hesitated and then began edging closer to her.

"Are you going somewhere, Mrs. St. Martin? Do you want me to hitch up the horses?"

Eloise Henderson's authoritative voice rang out, making Claire jump. "Mrs. St. Martin is not in need of your services today, Mr. Smith, but thank you for offering. She is being called for. Now, was there a particular reason you wanted to see me?"

The man started mumbling about taking the afternoon off unless she needed him, but anxious to have him gone, the woman curtly said the day was his own, to do with as he pleased, and wished him a pleasant one. Resenting her brusque dismissal of him, he bowed his head in the direction of the two women, his dark eyes, although unseen by either of them, exhibited nothing but icy contempt.

Watching the man as he strode angrily down the length of the hallway, Mrs. Henderson sighed. *Could he be Claire's mysterious admirer? But how could he gain access to Claire's bedroom when the door was locked? No, the man was a recluse—he certainly wouldn't seek the company of a young girl, no matter how striking she might be.* Although this certainly wasn't the first time she had witnessed his disruptive influence over the staff, especially the women, she was mildly surprised that even Claire, usually a very coolheaded girl, was visibly shaken by the man's presence.

While Eloise absentmindedly continued to watch as the man retreated toward the kitchen, the sound of a carriage stopping outside the building caused Claire's heart to beat faster. As she peeked out the window, the sun chose that precise moment to burst through the clouds. She saw Braxton had meant what he said for he was indeed alighting from a hired carriage. He paused to speak to the driver before walking those few steps to the door, his knock echoing in the silence of the room. Eloise smiled broadly at her and was rewarded with a nervous but absolutely enchanting smile.

Claire, having imagined this moment since receiving his note, felt the rapid beating of her heart as Eloise Henderson opened the door and stepped back, graciously inviting Braxton inside. As he removed his hat, that irresistibly devastating grin crossed his handsome features as he lifted Claire's slim hand to his lips, a spark of some indefinable emotion in his grey eyes as he regarded her.

"Mrs. St. Martin."

A slight cough from Claire's employer reminded him there was a third person in the room. "And of course, the very lovely Mrs. Henderson." He lifted her hand to his lips, although the gesture had lost its intimacy.

Eloise delayed them long enough to ensure Braxton took her willingness to help them meet at any time seriously, and somewhat amazed at such an offer, he nodded his thanks. Waiting until Claire had her face covered with the veil, he took her elbow and escorted her out to his hired conveyance. The driver stood by the door, ready to assist his passengers, should such assistance prove necessary. But had any of them chosen that precise moment to glance toward the corner of the building, he or she would have been astonished to see the reclusive Mr. Smith watching them, a look of the blackest hatred etched indelibly across his features.

Sitting inside the carriage, it soon became evident what had attracted Braxton to it. There were faded green curtains, threadbare but still of one piece, covering each window. The once plush upholstery, also green though now frayed and worn, gave the impression that someone still cared enough to lend some semblance of upkeep and repair to the interior of the carriage.

Claire, aware of how concealed they were behind the curtains, smiled uncertainly at the man who sat across from her. His hoarse whisper broke the silence.

"Madam, remove that veil. It prevents me from feasting my eyes on the beauty which I have had to deny myself these many days."

Slowly Claire raised the veil, the warmth in her deep brown eyes beckoning to him irresistibly. He studied her with a curious and deep intensity. "Do you have any idea how beautiful you are and how much I have suffered not being able to see you?"

She found it impossible not to return his disarming smile. "I refuse to bear the blame for any suffering you might have endured."

He held up his hands in mock surrender. "You are right, my love, I alone must carry the responsibility for our present situation." She sobered at the reminder of her predicament.

The carriage had only moved a short distance down the road when there was a shout, followed quickly by the screaming of horses. Their carriage came to a sudden halt. Unable to stop herself, Claire was thrown from the seat. Braxton instinctively caught her, quickly gathering her protectively in his arms. Peering through the curtains in an attempt to find the cause for the stop, he smiled when he spied a tiny white dog making its way across the road, unconcerned and unaware of any disruption he might have caused. Their carriage slowly began to move forward again.

Reluctantly he released his hold on her, achingly aware that one of his hands rested on her breast and that a blush was now creeping into her cheeks. "I…I'm sorry, Claire, I didn't mean…"

His words washed over her like cold water. "Braxton, I…" She sat rigidly on the cushioned seat, her head whirling in confusion. "Perhaps today was a mistake." Her hand reached for the door handle but his own larger hand quickly covered hers, preventing the handle being turned.

"No, my love, don't say our being together is a mistake." His voice was thick and unsteady. "Claire, I've already told you I would do anything I could to change that night—but I can't simply wish it away. All I can say is that I'm sorry."

His words became a velvet murmur. "You must believe me when I say I love you…I adore you." There was a faint tremor in his voice as he continued. "I want to marry you and spend the rest of my life making you happy. And I vow that, in spite of what just happened, I will not cross that boundary again until we are wed, that is, if you'll have me?"

Claire wistfully grasped both of his hands in her own slender ones. "I…I don't know, Braxton. I admit that I love you, but it's impossible to think of the future until the past, namely Bennett Kirkwood, has been resolved."

He hesitated momentarily, afraid of frightening her but found he could resist no longer. Gathering her in his arms, his lips gently covered her mouth. Her mind relived the soft warmth of his kisses on her wedding night, shocking herself with her own eager response. Raising his mouth from hers, he gazed into her eyes. She quivered at the sweet tenderness of his kiss but then he sat back, still cradling her in his arms.

His voice was thick and unsteady. "Enough of that, my love, or my promise to respect your virtue will be sorely tried."

Not wanting the mood to be spoiled, Braxton straightened his shoulders before covering her dainty hands with his own. "Now, madam, I am whisking you off, far away from the environs of Whitechapel where unfriendly eyes might spy us out, to Hyde Park and a charming tea room which overlooks the Serpentine, and where, I am assured, we can sip tea and enjoy each other's company without interruption."

A thoughtful smile curved her mouth, presenting such a captivating picture Braxton had difficulty swallowing. Releasing her hands, he sat back and smiled tentatively.

"Claire, at Betty's wedding, it was difficult to talk to you, so many people interrupting. But none of that matters now. We're here, together, with nothing but time. But be warned, madam, if you keep looking at me like that, my mind will definitely turn to other activities that don't include sipping tea."

Claire, at first shocked at his words, giggled. "Braxton, behave yourself." She sobered, observing him through lowered black lashes. "All right, Mr. Kane, tell me everything that your barrister said. Don't leave anything out." She paused, dreading the answer to her next query. "And have you seen Bennett since Betty's wedding? What about your Mr. Peckworthy? Has his spy made another appearance?" Her questions tumbled over each other in her haste to remember everything she wanted to ask him.

There was a trace of laughter in his voice as he once again held up his hands in mock surrender. Answering all of her questions and discussing what course of action might be best occupied them so completely that they were stunned when the carriage came to a stop. Claire quickly pulled her veil down before accepting Braxton's arm as she alit from the carriage.

Braxton led the heavily veiled figure through what had once been a shop and was now a tearoom furnished with small lace-covered tables, all of which were already occupied. A woman, red hair piled atop her head and wearing a starched white blouse tucked primly into the waist of her black skirt, smiled and beckoned them over. She eyed Claire curiously before leading them toward a very narrow staircase, which was concealed behind a large potted fern, informing them their destination was on the second floor.

Lifting her skirt just enough to climb the shallow steps, Claire followed Braxton up the creakily protesting stairs, wondering exactly where they were going. Upon reaching the landing, she could no longer contain her curiosity and lifted a corner of her veil. Four more lace-covered tables came into her view which, although all proved to be unoccupied, were spaced just far enough apart to ensure the occupants of any of the tables some degree of privacy.

They had no sooner settled themselves than they heard footsteps climbing the stairs, allowing Claire enough time to pull the veil over her face. Hoping to see the face behind the veil, the proprietress appeared first, followed closely by a young serving girl bearing a tray laden with cups, teapot, and a plate of tiny cakes, her thin arms trembling under her burden. Braxton jumped up and relieved the servant, who with a grateful smile at Braxton and a curious glance at the mysteriously veiled woman, turned and made her way hastily down the stairs.

The owner of the tearoom continued to linger, casting an eye at Braxton who in turn smiled politely, ignoring the invitation he saw there. The two chatted for a moment, the woman barely able to contain her curiosity, but he pointedly ignored her hints for enlightenment and she soon drifted back downstairs.

Claire, her face once more uncovered, lifted the pot and poured out two steaming cups of tea, aware that his eyes followed her every move. As she stirred her tea, Braxton spoke.

"Claire, before your marriage…I mean all those days we were in each other's company…there were few opportunities to talk. I want to know everything about you. You must have had a multitude of suitors. Did you consider any of them seriously?"

At her trembling smile, his heart soared. He took her hands in his, exhaling a long sigh of contentment. When he spoke, there was a slight tinge of wonder in his voice. "You're so beautiful, my sweet, and I desire nothing more than to spend my life worshipping you."

Resting his chin on his hand, a bemused smile on his lips and a trace of laughter in his voice, he continued. "I meant it, Claire, when I said I want to know everything about you. What was your childhood like? Were you happy?"

Her mouth curved into an unconscious smile. "Oh Braxton, there's not much to tell. Both of my parents were descended from French émigrés who fled The Terror. A handful of these émigrés settled in Kent, always planning to one day return home to France, but as each generation was born, England became their home. In the beginning, the villagers barely tolerated them...I'm not sure that we were ever totally accepted. My father thought it was due to the rancor that has always existed between France and England, not a personal dislike."

Claire paused, took a sip of tea, and smiled shyly at the man who now occupied her thoughts every minute of every day.

Braxton spoke, his voice calm, his gaze steady. "Go on, my love."

"My mother died when I was born, leaving my father heartbroken and with a newborn to take care of. By this time, most of the 'foreigners' had either died or married into local farming families. A woman from the village cooked and cleaned for us, glad enough of the coins she earned. My Aunt Marie, a childless widow, moved in to help my father take care of me. As I grew up, she taught me the basics of managing a staff of servants and how to conduct myself among the rich and privileged. As it turned out, her lessons were of great value when I was hired to work at Henderson's Domestics. She died a year before we came to London."

She paused, sadly remembering those she had lost. "I only ever had one serious suitor, Edward Fisher, the son of one of the wealthiest farmers in Kent. He was ten years older than me but we used to see each other on market days. My father refused to allow Edward to court me, claiming I was *'destined for a much higher position in life than one spent milking cows and breeding babies'*. No other suitors came forward after that."

"Believe me, Braxton, I tried to reason with him. I told him that it was 1888, and people were marrying for love, not to please their families. He just patted me on the head, convinced I was reading too many of Miss Jane Austen's novels."

"After losing our home, we moved to the city and stayed with my father's friend, Lord Magnus Jennings, thereby gaining a respectable London address. Through him, we were swept into the social whirl of London society. Bennett and I met and…well, you know the rest. My father and Bennett each thought the other had money, and so we were married. If my father hadn't been so sick, I think I would have resisted going along with his plan. After all is said and done, he was only trying to assure my happiness." Her faint smile was tinged with sadness.

Braxton tenderly kissed her fingers, and when he spoke, his voice was tender, almost a murmur. "Think no more about the past, my love. I vow to spend the rest of my life making you happy." Hand in hand, they sat in silence, each momentarily lost in their own thoughts.

At last, drawing apart, they smiled and by unspoken agreement, put the past behind them. Looking through the window, Braxton observed people out strolling and enjoying the warmth of the day. Rising, he pulled Claire to her feet.

"Come, sweetheart. Let's stroll beside the Serpentine and plan our future." The warmth of his smile echoed in his voice.

Claire, rising, met his smile and the strong masculine hand that was offered. As he descended the noisily protesting staircase, she hastily pulled her veil down, causing much speculation amongst those dining on the main floor. The redheaded owner of the establishment, a woman who trusted no one, least of all her staff, stood waiting at the doorway to collect monies owed and to bid farewell to all departing patrons, was not disappointed with the coins Braxton dropped into her outstretched hand. Wistfully she watched the handsome man and his mysterious lady walking leisurely in the direction of the Serpentine.

The two ambled along, enjoying the warmth of the day, laughing and chatting as lovers are wont to do at such times. Claire, giggling at some buffoonery of Braxton's, halted suddenly.

"You're not being fair, Braxton Kane. You know all about me, but I know precious little of you other than you reside in London. I refuse to take another step until I have learned all there is to know about Mr. Braxton Kane of Pennygrove Hall." She sat down on one of the wooden benches that lined the path, arms crossed obstinately but an appealing smile on her lips. His mouth curved with tenderness as he faced her, and for a brief moment, he studied her. A muscle clenched along his jawline, making Claire suddenly regret her challenge to him.

"What is it, Braxton? What haven't you told me?" There was a gentle softness in her voice.

Sitting, he seized her hands, kissing both of them in turn. "Claire, I...I don't know where to begin." He stood abruptly and began to pace, as was his habit when anxious, glancing at her as she watched him, patiently waiting for him to explain what troubled him.

Well, if this is to become a love story with a happy ending, I have to be totally honest with her.

Resuming his seat, he gently took her hands in his. "Please, my love, this is not a pretty tale. It would be best if you let me speak without interruption." He shifted his weight on the bench, wondering if this course of action was the right one but at last cleared his throat to begin his woeful tale.

"Claire, I've declared my love for you—I would shout it from the rooftops if I could—and miraculously you return my love. And you must believe me when I say once more that if I could change that night, I would. But what I'm about to reveal doesn't concern that night. This is something much darker, and I know that I have to tell you before we can go any further."

His grey eyes had a burning, faraway look in them, and she shivered, suddenly dreading what he was about to reveal. She wished she could take back her challenge to him.

"I have a brother, or rather I have a half-brother, Patrick. He's a few years older than me. His mother died bringing him into this world. As my mother told it, my father was devastated with his first wife's death and shut himself away from his son and the world for a number of years, leaving servants to care for the boy."

Leaning forward, elbows resting on his knees, he continued his tale in a low, composed voice. "But at last his grieving came to an end. He met my mother and they married. She told me that even as a young boy, Patrick seemed cold, as though he was incapable of love. She tried to be a mother to him but was rejected time after time. In due course, I was born. Patrick, never having been exposed to another child, was quite fascinated with me for a time, and I of course wanted to follow him wherever he went, but that was something he rarely allowed. Even as a youngster, he liked to slip off into the woods on his own."

He shuddered slightly, seeming to impose an iron control on himself as he resumed his story. "The gardener was the first to present my father with a disturbing find—bodies of small animals. Their remains were scattered about the estate, mutilated and hacked to death. And I, like any small boy, had pets, but any animal unfortunate enough to become my pet was doomed."

After a long pause, he continued his painful narrative. "My father knew immediately who was responsible. His first wife, Patrick's mother, had had a brother, long since dead, who liked to cut up animals. Patrick must have inherited this fondness for blood and pain from him."

"Anyway, Father confronted him, and after a brutal beating, extracted a promise that it would happen no more."

He smiled at Claire, but his mind was lost in the past. "My father was a man who refused to accept failings in himself or others, especially if it proved to be his son. He beat Patrick mercilessly every time an animal was found. Patrick would take the beating without a whimper and then disappear. As he grew older, his disappearances lasted longer. This went on for years."

Claire looked up and saw tiny beads of perspiration on Braxton's brow. She took his hand and held it, sensing his disquiet and letting him know he wasn't alone. He caressed her cheek, smiling sadly, and then resumed his tale.

"The day came that Patrick received word he had been accepted at St. Guy's Medical School as an apprentice. Truth to tell, I think my father was relieved. Only a few short months later, my mother died, and a little more than a year later, my father followed her. Patrick didn't bother to attend either funeral. In fact, I didn't see him for more than two years, and then one day he just appeared. He told me the instructors were bumbling idiots, and he had no intention of ever returning to St. Guy's." His voice had drifted into a harsh whisper.

Braxton gazed across the water of the Serpentine, lost in thought for a brief moment. "He was furious that I was the administrator of the estate—after all, he was the firstborn son. He had no interest in living at Pennygrove Hall or at our country estate. He said he wanted no one watching his every move ever again. Anyway, he left Pennygrove, returning only to collect his monthly allowance—how that must have rankled, his younger brother controlling the purse strings. In spite of his anger, things continued peacefully for some months until one night, just after midnight, he showed up covered in blood, begging me to help him. He confessed to me that he had tried to murder a common prostitute, slashing her throat and leaving her for dead. But somehow this poor creature survived."

Claire looked up at him, her face pale, and her brown eyes never leaving his tortured face. His expression was one of utter wretchedness.

His voice broke miserably. "I went to the family solicitor, Albert Higgins, the same man who is looking into finding a way to end your sham of a marriage. Somehow, acting on his advice, I was able to convince the magistrate that Patrick would leave the country, never to return. And since his victim had no one to protest on her behalf, he was released into my custody. He was given his share of the estate, and we sailed immediately for the West Indies, where I planned to leave him, hoping I would never hear of, or from him again. Unfortunately, he jumped ship before we reached our destination. I was so relieved to be rid of him that I didn't bother to mount a search. Selfishly, I didn't care where he went as long as he didn't return to our shores."

He leaned back on the bench, exhausted from the telling of his tale but knowing he had to continue. He wanted no secrets between them. "Somehow Mordock Peckworthy learned that my brother, who had so narrowly escaped the hangman in England, had murdered a woman on the other side of the Atlantic and was in custody in New Orleans."

Stunned, she stared up at him, her heart pounding. "That's why you went along with Bennett's proposal! What did Mr. Peckworthy threaten you with…scandal?"

"Much worse than scandal, my love. Even now, I can hear his voice. *"Your brother is currently in jail in New Orleans, a city on the other side of the world. His freedom, or rather the lack of it, will depend on your cooperation in my little scheme."*

Her voice was fragile and shaking and tears flowed down her cheeks. "Oh, Braxton, my love, what a choice was forced on you. Bed a stranger or release a monster on an unsuspecting world."

His grey eyes seemed to bore into her very soul as he struggled to maintain an even tone. "There is one thing more, my love. Just a day or so before Betty's wedding, Albert Higgins sent word for me to come to his office *'on a matter most urgent'*. Upon my arrival, he told me he had received word from New Orleans that Patrick had escaped, and the authorities had no idea where he had fled."

In the silence that followed, Claire's love surrounded and enveloped him as she wrapped her arms around him, holding him close, ready to challenge any who would do him harm. Relief flooded through Braxton. *She knows the worst and loves me in spite of it. What did I do to deserve this angel, this marvelous woman whom I already love more than life itself?* Slowly he straightened his frame, the weight of the world having fallen from his shoulders.

They looked deeply into each other's eyes, where the bonds of love are so often forged. His lips pressed softly against hers, devouring the soft sweetness of her mouth. Claire was again surprised at her own fervent response, her calm shattered with the hunger of his kisses, the touch of his lips a delicious, dizzying sensation. At last, he broke away, and taking her slender hand in his, he looked about, realizing that the afternoon sun was sinking low on the horizon.

Braxton threw back his head and let out a great peal of laughter, throwing his hat high in the air, ready to take on the world. As he hugged her to him, Claire joined him, laughing in sheer joy of the moment. He tucked her hand into the crook of his arm and they slowly walked toward the hired carriage and the driver who waited so patiently to drive them home.

It was on the ride home, safely tucked away from the eyes of the world, that Braxton once again urged caution.

"I'll be the one who suffers most, my love, but it's better we don't meet for a few days, perhaps for as long as a week, possibly longer. I'll send word through the post—that seems to be the safest way."

Claire shuddered inwardly at the thought of not seeing him for a week or, unthinkably, even longer, but she knew their future together depended on being cautious now. "How am I to wait that long?"

Stretching out his long legs, he cradled her in his arms. "What's this? Has Cupid's arrow pierced Mrs. St. Martin's cold heart?"

Oh Wicked Escort

Claire pouted as he teased her. "Be serious, Braxton. A week will seem endless!"

He looked into her sparkling eyes. "My love, it has to be this way. You know that." His tone was gentle but his meaning unmistakable. She nodded, biting her lip as she looked away. They rode in silence for some distance, both contemplating the empty days ahead.

As the carriage came to a halt, Braxton peered cautiously out the window. "We've arrived, Claire."

Opening the carriage door reluctantly, Braxton stepped out, thankful that the street seemed deserted. He turned to assist the veiled beauty down, holding her close for a brief second, releasing her only when the door to Henderson's swung open, revealing a smiling Mrs. Henderson.

"Well, Mr. Kane, I was beginning to think you had run off with my star employee."

"I was sorely tempted, madam. And please, call me Braxton, as a friend would—for I understand you are truly in our corner..." His words trailed off.

The proprietor of Henderson's Domestics nodded, smiling her delight. "Only if you'll return the favor and call me Eloise."

"My dear Eloise, I would deem it a great honor."

Claire smiled at the two, the man she loved and the woman who was fast becoming a cherished friend. She saw Braxton watching the street, and knowing his uneasiness, stepped inside the building, obliging the other two to follow her inside. She removed the stifling veil and delighted at the warmth she saw in Braxton's grey eyes as he feasted his eyes on her once more.

Eloise turned to the younger woman. "Oh, Claire, good news. I've hired a replacement for Betty, which means you once again have a roommate. Her name is Ruby Goodspeed." She rambled on unconcernedly about this newest staff member, Braxton and Claire paying little heed until Braxton stiffened and interrupted her chatter.

"Excuse me, madam, but would you repeat what you just said."

Eloise, startled at his tone, looked about, trying to remember exactly what her last words had been. "Oh yes, I was just saying that Claire need have no more concerns about her mysterious admirer leaving bouquets of flowers and nosegays in her room."

His grey eyes, suddenly sharp and assessing, looked intently at Claire. "What is this about?"

A beguiling grin crossed her face. "It's nothing really. A rose was left on my bed months ago—the same day you first discovered my hiding place. I thought you had determined not only where I was living but which room was mine. And then, if you'll think back, you were carrying a flower, in fact it was a rose…"

He nodded his head as he recalled that meeting. "Well, it certainly wasn't me, Claire. I learned your whereabouts purely by chance, and up to this moment have been totally in the dark as to where you lay your head every night. But what is this about flowers in your bedchamber? And more importantly, why haven't you mentioned it before now?"

Confused, Claire shook her head. "Braxton, I'm sure these flowers were left for one of the other ladies. It's just a silly mix-up of doors and rooms, but I admit I will feel easier knowing another woman is sharing my room." Her tone became playfully chiding. "And sir, if you care to remember, we had more important things to discuss today than any silly flowers, whoever they were meant for."

He stiffened, momentarily abashed, his mouth curving into an unconscious smile. "Forgive me, my love. You're right. There were far more important matters to discuss than flowers." He saw Eloise's concern fade as she listened to two people she was becoming extraordinarily fond of, her relief evident at his bantering tone.

"Eloise, I know you concern yourself greatly with the safety of all of those under your care—I can only trust that it was indeed harmless, a simple error on the part of some love-smitten Romeo."

He bowed over Eloise's hand before turning to Claire, kissing her fingertips lightly. "Ladies, I must be away. I have kept the poor coach driver from his pipe and slippers long enough. Claire, watch the post. I'll send word as soon as possible."

As the door closed quietly behind him, Claire felt an unfamiliar emptiness. Eloise, putting her arm around the girl's slender shoulders, urged her up the stairs to meet her new roommate.

Chapter Eighteen

Claire spent the days following her outing with Braxton cushioned in the familiar routine of Henderson's—Sunday service at St. Bartholomew's and throughout the week filling the servant deficiency of London while always listening for the sound of mail being dropped through the letterbox.

It was at breakfast the following Thursday that Eloise asked Claire to come to her office. Mr. Smith, who seemed to grow scruffier with each passing day, had recently taken to eating with the staff again, scowling and muttering to himself as the two women left the dining room. Those still eating edged away from him, finding his person and his behavior not only offensive but disturbing.

Eloise led the way down the hall, leaving Claire to keep up as best she could. As they reached the front of the building that served as both office and reception, the taller woman held the door open until they were both inside the room, pulling the heavy door firmly closed behind them. Startled, Claire looked at her. She had never known Eloise to be this concerned about being overheard.

Ushering her over to the wooden desk, Eloise sat down, gesturing to Claire to do likewise. The older woman, seeking a way to begin a distasteful conversation, slammed her large hands on the desktop, causing Claire to jump.

"I have decided, Claire, after many complaints which I can no longer ignore, that Mr. Smith must go. I risk losing two other members of my staff if I don't act. The women are uneasy in his company, and unfairly or not, most are laying the blame of the flowers found in your room on him."

Sympathetically, Claire lightly squeezed her friend's hand. "Oh,

Eloise, I'm sorry you've been put in this position, but I can't pretend to be sorry to lose the man as our escort. Surely someone else could be found to do the job."

Standing, Eloise Henderson began to pace, her long legs carrying her quickly across the room, talking as she strode about. "That's just it though. That cumbersome omnibus is difficult to maneuver, especially down some of the narrow roads and lanes in the older parts of the city."

Temporarily downcast, she suddenly broke into an open, affable smile, grateful for the friendly ear but aware that the problem was ultimately hers alone. The two sat for a few minutes longer, discussing problems of the agency and finding solutions for most of the difficulties, minor hindrances though they might be.

Claire suddenly jumped up. "Eloise, we're forgetting about Billy Marple." At the other's uncomprehending look, she excitedly began talking, her infectious enthusiasm soon capturing her employer's attention.

"Billy Marple works as a freight driver at Dabney's Freighthouse. Perhaps if I sent him a note explaining our situation, he might know of someone capable of handling such an awkward wagon."

The older woman, who a few short minutes ago had been envisioning the end of her livelihood, reached for her notepaper and placed it squarely in front of Claire. "Do you think he might know someone?" She stood quietly for a few seconds, her face reflecting hope tempered by disbelief. "Quickly, my dear, write to him. The post will be picked up at any moment."

She smiled fondly at Claire as the girl dipped the tip of her pen into the inkwell, her neat handwriting quickly filling the page. "Oh, dear girl, you've indeed lightened my burden. Now all I have to do is cope with Mr. Smith."

Claire faced her employer, becoming aware that, despite her formidable size, she was still a woman, a woman who had the unpleasant task of dismissing a man. "Would you like me to stay with you, Eloise?"

Sitting down, she smiled at the girl who now stood beside her, a girl whose loyalty was beyond question. Patting the other's hand, she shook her head. "Thank you for your kind offer, Claire, but I think I might need more than you're capable of providing. You run along now but please ask Arthur Tucker to step in, and once he's on his way to me, would you send one of the men to summon Mr. Smith, assuming he's returned to the stable."

The hall clock had just chimed eleven when loud voices could be heard coming from the office. The occupants of the dining room paused before turning curiously toward the front of the building. On recognizing the voice of Mr. Smith, the more daring edged cautiously down the long hallway until the door to the office started to open, causing the eavesdroppers to hasten quickly back to the kitchen.

Claire, who had the task of washing up for the week, was just drying her hands when Mr. Smith came striding angrily into the room. Spying Claire, he stood menacingly in front of her, arms akimbo, his eyes as cold and dark as glacial ice. She looked at the man and suddenly knew how a mouse must feel when confronted by a cat.

Mr. Smith spat out the words in a voice that, though quiet, had an ominous quality and was filled with contempt. "You…this is your doing!"

Flecks of spittle formed in the corners of his mouth, his anger becoming a glowering mask of rage as he seized her by the wrist, raising his other hand to strike her. Claire, her heart hammering, struggled to escape his iron grip, bracing herself for the blow just as the voice of Eloise Henderson echoed down the length of the hall.

"Mr. Smith!"

Shock crossed his face at the audacity of anyone daring to order him about. He saw the flushed face of the woman who was no longer his employer but who was quickly closing the distance between them. Looking about, he saw the people he had escorted through the streets of London for so many months, their faces set in anger at his daring to threaten the woman they had not only grown fond of but respected. With an almost animal growl, he released Claire's wrist so violently she fell against the lean body of Arthur Tucker.

All eyes watched as the miscreant strode angrily out of the kitchen. Assuring everyone she was unharmed, Claire watched as Arthur and his brother followed Mr. Smith outside, the other men just steps behind them, ready to gang together should the need arise.

The men soon returned, assuring Mrs. Henderson and the other women that the man had gathered his few belongings and stormed from the property, vowing revenge on all who resided within.

❀ ❀ ❀

It was early the next morning that Billy appeared, his familiar cheeky grin in place and a prospective omnibus driver following closely behind him. Billy introduced the man as Mr. Alfred Downs or, to his friends, Alfie. He was a middle-aged man with straw-colored hair, pale blue eyes, and a shy smile playing about the corners of his mouth. His clothes were clean but well worn. Billy explained that Alfie was an old friend, a childless widower, and down on his luck since his employer had unexpectedly died, and his heirs had closed what was at best a struggling business.

Eloise Henderson sent Billy into the dining room while she spoke to Mr. Alfred Downs. It took only moments for the owner of Henderson Domestics to satisfy herself that he was a suitable replacement for the recently departed but definitely unlamented Mr. Smith, although she took the precaution to have Arthur accompany him on a trial omnibus ride to ensure he was indeed the man for the job.

Returning to the dining room moments later, she saw everyone gathered around the window, all watching the prospective driver as he very capably handled the oversized wagon, Arthur perched beside him, talking nonstop as they turned onto the main road. Eloise wasn't the only one to heave a sigh of relief as the wagon disappeared from view.

Billy Marple looked at the owner of the agency and smiled. "Well, missus, I think Alfie will fit in quite nicely at Henderson's. If you both be agreeable, I'll see to it that he fetches his belongings and returns here in time to get everyone to your next engagement which, Mrs. St. Martin has informed me, is this very evening."

❀ ❀ ❀

The next six days were filled with engagements for the staff of Henderson's Domestics, leaving Claire little time to brood about the seeming impossibility of her situation. Alfie proved to be very popular with everyone, always ready with a kind word or a helping hand, a welcome change from the disturbingly sinister Mr. Smith.

Braxton proved to be an enthusiastic letter writer, putting on paper what he planned for their future, proclaiming his love and devotion to her in every missive. He also wrote in some detail about his meeting with Albert Higgins, who believed that the law would definitely lean in her favor. Unfortunately, Mr. Higgins was not one to be hurried in this unfamiliar aspect of law and moved at what Braxton considered a speed a trifle slower than a snail.

The last line of every letter declared his impatience to see her, but caution always won out.

> *My darling—*
> *No matter in what manner I depart from Pennygrove Hall, whether by horse, buggy or on foot, there is always the sensation of someone just behind me. I daren't take the chance of leading Bennett to your very doorstep.*

And so she spent her time, when not working or sleeping, writing to Braxton and haunting the letterbox in the hope of finding an envelope in his strong, masculine hand addressed to her, all the while heeding his counsel to never venture out alone.

The fiend that all were now calling Jack the Ripper seemed to have abandoned his pursuit of the "unfortunates", those women who, in order to survive, walked a solitary path in Whitechapel nightly. In the lull, rumors abounded. Arthur Tucker returned from his frequent visits to Ollie the butcher with idle bits of gossip, making the residents of Brick Lane wonder at the audacity of some of the claims.

In the midst of an after-dinner conversation one rainy evening, Arthur shared the two accusations that had made him chuckle. "Would you believe it that Prince Eddy, our own Queen Victoria's grandson, 'as been touted to be old Jack?" At the collective gasps of surprise and small bursts of chatter, Arthur chuckled once more before holding up his hand for silence.

"Think of it—a member of the royal family walking the streets of Whitechapel! As one toffee-nosed politician put it," he paused, lifting his nose and pursing his lips for effect, *'absolutely absurd'."* All joined in the laughter at his spoof of the anonymous politician.

As quiet descended around the table once more, Arthur looked at his audience. "And if it isn't Prince Eddy, the 'experts' say, it 'as to be a doctor what's guilty. After all, 'asn't the blighter showed 'e 'as medical knowledge?"

Heads nodded in agreement as small pockets of conversation broke out once more. The cook, Mrs. Kenley, stood up, her hand covering a yawn, declared that her morning started out very early and she must say good night. Almost as one, they all rose, Arthur banking the embers in the small fireplace and the other men checking locks on all the doors and windows as good nights were called and lamps snuffed out. Claire, along with her new roommate, Ruby Goodspeed, trailed the other ladies up the stairs, all anxious for the warmth and coziness of their beds.

It was during the night, while everybody slept, that an intruder crept into the stables and caused minor havoc. Harnesses, bits, bridles, and other paraphernalia had been strewn about the floor and hay thrown atop the pile, leading Eloise Henderson and her staff to think the prowler might have intended to set a fire, but something or somebody must have scared him off. A half-eaten bunch of grapes was found near the stable door, calling to everyone's mind Mr. Smith's fondness for that fruit.

It was decided that two male employees would sleep in the stable each night, all taking it in turn until the miscreant was caught, or failing to be apprehended, at least until they felt he had fled to other climes. There was much speculation about the identity of the scoundrel, all thoughts turning to the recent departure of Mr. Smith.

The following morning, the mail fluttered through the letterbox just as Claire was passing by. Scooping up the envelopes, she quickly scanned them, searching for the now-familiar handwriting. Clutching one of the envelopes to her breast, she dropped the others into a surprised Eloise's hands and dashed upstairs, closing her bedroom door against any chance passerby.

Her deep brown eyes sparkled as she eagerly tore open the envelope, liberating several pages of cream-colored stationary. Excitedly, she began to read.

Oh Wicked Escort

My dearest love—

Time passes slowly, although I assure you I am filling the hours with seeing to Pennygrove Hall and my country estate, Mossdale. I don't believe I have ever paid as much attention to my holdings before, but without that distraction I would have found myself standing outside a certain building on Brick Lane, not caring who might have followed me there.

You will be more than a little shocked to learn that Mordock Peckworthy paid me a visit yesterday. He didn't seem too surprised that your whereabouts were still unknown, although he hinted that he thought I knew something. He said he hoped he would have the opportunity to beg your forgiveness for the part he played when he exacted his twisted revenge on Bennett. I must admit that I thought him sincere.

I've heard nothing from Bennett but his creatures have been seen lurking about. I can only hope I have bored them to death with the mediocrity of my life for the past weeks.

And now for the best news, my darling. Albert Higgins, my solicitor, has contacted me and asks if we could attend a meeting with himself and a solicitor more conversant with matters of divorce, a Mr. John Mallory, in his chambers, on Monday, November fifth.

I know you'll have to discuss it with Eloise first but hopefully she'll recognize that your days with Henderson's Domestics are numbered, perhaps as early as the new year!

I must close now, my love. Write by return post if you can and tell me that Eloise is agreeable with you being away on the fifth.

Love always and forever, Braxton

Claire hugged the letter to her breast, her heart singing with joy.

They were going to meet with Mr. Albert Higgins and a Mr. John Mallory. As she danced delightedly about the room, the sound of everyone downstairs making ready to leave for the bazaar and tea they were serving at in the afternoon reached her. Quickly squirreling the letter away with the others, she picked up her cloak and hat, hurrying down the stairs just as the others were making their way outside to the patiently waiting Alfie and the omnibus.

It was later that evening that Claire had an opportunity to approach her employer with a request for the day off on the fifth of November. Eloise studied the young girl's face and saw the happiness that now resided there and found it impossible not to return her disarming smile.

"Oh Claire, I am going to miss you." Tears sparkled in the older woman's eyes. Claire looked up, a surprised look in her eyes.

Eloise laughed. "You silly goose. Did you really think I couldn't foresee the eventual outcome…after you and Braxton get the legal difficulties out of the way, why, it's the most natural thing that you'd marry…and he certainly makes no secret about his feelings for you."

Blushing, her mouth curved into an unconscious smile as she turned and made her way upstairs to her room.

Chapter Nineteen

The sun was valiantly trying to peek through the clouds on the morning of November fifth, but even the overcast sky failed to dampen Claire's spirits. She hadn't seen Braxton in over two weeks, but in those long, empty days, he had never failed to send a letter, sometimes one in the morning and a second arriving with the last post of the day.

But today—today she would see him! She danced about her room in her chemise, not yet ready to start dressing. He wouldn't arrive for another hour, but the staff of Henderson's, including Eloise, would be leaving for their serving engagement in less than half an hour. Claire didn't want to raise anyone's curiosity regarding the widow's weeds she'd be wearing, including her borrowed hat with its thick veil. Both Braxton and Eloise had thought it best if she continued her masquerade of a grieving widow rather than risk a chance discovery, and she had grudgingly agreed with them, much as donning the hateful veil irritated her.

A short while later, there was a soft knock on her door. Opening it, Eloise smilingly nodded her head in approval of the black dress that Claire had donned. "You look very fetching, my dear. I just popped up to let you know that we're leaving now, including Mrs. Kenley. She's taking a holiday from her kitchen this morning and catching a ride with us up to the high street. From there she'll walk to her sister's for a cup of tea and a bit of a gossip, returning in plenty of time to prepare the evening meal." She turned to go and then abruptly spun around.

"I almost forgot, dear. The lock on the front door is a little tricky—you have to jiggle the key around a bit before the lock catches."

Smiling, Claire assured her she'd manage, and if there was a problem, she was sure Braxton could handle it. Eloise returned the smile before resuming her trip downstairs where the others were assembling.

Leaving the bedroom door open, Claire could hear murmurs of conversation drifting up the stairs until, a few short minutes later, the outside door closed with a forceful bang. As she continued to fuss with her hair, Claire slowly became aware of how deathly quiet everything seemed with everybody but her gone.

She had never been totally alone in the building since her arrival at Henderson's—there was always someone about. And now she could hear every creak and groan of the building. Glancing out the window, she could see the omnibus as it trundled down Brick Lane toward Whitechapel Road.

About to reach for her hat, she heard a grating sound as if someone had opened a heavy door deep within the bowels of the building, followed immediately by a loud thud. She froze, wondering what the sound was, and more importantly, where it had come from. Had it really been inside the building when she knew she was the only occupant? Seconds later, there was a muffled cough, closely followed by a squeaking floorboard. Instinctively she turned toward the wall where the wardrobe stood, her ears straining to hear any other noise. *That noise couldn't have come from the other side of this wall—there's nothing there.* As she listened, tense and anxious, she had the eerie sensation of being watched, the hairs on the back of her neck seeming to stand on end. She licked her lips, her eyes darting about the room, searching frantically for some reasonable explanation of the noises she had heard. After several minutes listening—waiting, and she heard no other sound, she thought, *Eloise is right. I am a silly goose, I know there's no one else here. I heard them all leave.*

Then the floorboard squeaked again, as if protesting the weight of someone as yet unseen but unquestionably nearby. Heart beating furiously, Claire glanced nervously about but found nothing to allay her fears, becoming aware of a crushing sense of panic that threatened to overwhelm her. Forgetting about the hat, she edged cautiously toward the bedroom door, her entire being trembling fearfully as horrendous images invaded her imagination.

Black gown trailing behind, her footsteps echoed noisily as she raced down the stairs, knowing no one was chasing her but unable to slow her steps. Once safely on the main floor, she shakily laughed at herself for she had never been a believer in ghosts and the like.

Crossing the room to stand beside the door leading to the outside, she couldn't stop her hand from resting on the doorknob, ready to flee should any sort of creature materialize. She suddenly realized she had forgotten her hat, but as she stood there knew she couldn't go back upstairs, at least not until her friends were back in residence.

A quiet knock at the door made her jump. She tried to push the feeling of near panic from her mind as she hastened to admit the man who, now and forever, every inch of her being totally loved and adored.

Opening the portal, her heart was beating so loudly she thought he must surely hear it. The warmth of his smile sent shivers down her spine until, his smile fading, he grasped her shoulders tightly.

"My love, are you ill? You're so pale…you look as if you've seen a ghost."

Confused, she looked up and saw nothing but his love and concern for her. "Oh, Braxton, I know it's my imagination, but I've had such a case of the jitters. You know how old buildings creak and groan, especially if you know you're the only one in it. It's just put my nerves on edge." She laughed but even to her own ears, her words sounded unconvincing and hollow.

His voice was calm, his gaze steady. "What kind of creaking and groaning? You've never struck me as the nervous sort, Claire." He quickly found her a chair and forced her to sit down, holding her hands in his. They stayed like that for what seemed like seconds but in fact were more than a few moments, as Braxton assured himself that she had come to no harm. He smiled as he released her hands and in three long strides reached the open door and the staircase that led to the ladies' floor. He stood there for a moment, listening intently but hearing nothing. Turning again to Claire, he spoke in a soft, soothing voice.

"Which room is yours, sweet? Is the door locked?" He waited patiently for her reply.

"It's the first door at the top of the stairs, but I don't think I even closed the door, never mind locking it. Oh, Braxton, I even forgot my hat, I was so frightened." She reached into the pocket of her dress and retrieved her key, wordlessly handing it to him. She started to speak but realized he had already turned away, striding upward, unafraid, his long legs taking two stairs at a time.

As the minutes ticked by, Claire sat, tensely listening to the sound of his boots roaming about her room, and just when she thought she couldn't wait a second longer, he was making his way down the stairs.

He gave her a reassuring smile as he reached the bottom stair, her hat dangling from his long fingers. "I could find nothing out of place, my love, but remembering the flowers you found in your chamber, I looked about for some kind of secret opening in the walls and discovered nothing. I guess you're right, it's just an old building protesting rather noisily about the cold weather."

"Thank you for looking, Braxton." There was a gentle softness to her voice as she looked up at him.

The clock chimed the hour, reminding both of them that they had best be off. Braxton smiled, enjoying just being in her company. "Madam, your chariot awaits you. But first, there is one very necessary thing I really must attend to." She gazed up at him, a puzzled look in her eyes until he enfolded her in his arms, her soft curves molding to the contours of his lean body. His mouth covered hers hungrily, his tongue sending shivers of desire racing through her until at last he raised his lips from hers and gazed into the velvety depths of her brown eyes.

"Madam, as much as it tears me apart to say it, we really must be on our way. I gave you my word that I wouldn't cross this particular boundary again until we are wed, and I mean to keep my promise, but if you keep looking at me like that, I can guarantee nothing. Put that cursed hat and veil on so we can be off to our appointment with Albert Higgins and this Mr. Mallory."

As they left the building, Braxton did indeed have to jiggle the key to lock the door just as Mrs. Henderson had predicted, but scant minutes later they were safely ensconced in the same hired carriage they had used on their previous outing. Once the carriage door closed, Claire swept the heavy veil upward, meeting the infectious grin of her beloved. Neither they nor their driver noticed the ominous figure hugging the shadows of the building they had just left, nor did they hear his promise of a slow, painful death for the exquisitely beautiful but obviously evil harlot to whom Braxton Kane had given his heart.

Oh Wicked Escort

❦ ❦ ❦

The carriage stopped in front of a building that Braxton identified as the Old Bailey Law Courts. His solicitor, Albert Higgins, had asked that they meet in his office first so that he might be introduced to Claire before they met John Mallory. In truth, the solicitor wanted to meet the woman who not only had, albeit unknowingly, gained such notoriety but seemed to have cast a spell over his client, Braxton Kane, a man who had always seemed so sensible. They quickly crossed the cobbled footpath, ducking their heads as a cold rain began to fall.

Spying Braxton ushering a veiled woman through the front door of his chambers, a stout man left the warmth of the small fireplace in his private office, curiosity in his twinkling eyes and a welcoming smile on his face. As he hurried over to them, Claire had scant seconds to study the portly figure, his nearly bald head and bulbous nose almost going unnoticed as she eyed the flourishing grey mustache that dominated his round face. He politely ushered them into his office.

"Braxton, my boy, good to see you. And this, I assume, is Mrs. Kirkwood." His watchful eyes saw her stiffen at the unwelcome reminder of her marriage. "I do apologize, my dear, would you prefer that I address you as Miss St. Martin?" He led them to a table near the fire.

Claire lifted her veil, and in spite of reports of her startling beauty, Albert Higgins was taken aback at the exquisiteness of her entire being. Glancing at Braxton, the two men eyed each other, the solicitor at last understanding how the younger man had allowed himself to be part of that whole ridiculous wedding night farce.

Claire looked at Braxton, suddenly hesitant. His tight expression relaxed into a smile, reassuring her. She turned and faced the lawyer, her smile finding its way through a mask of uncertainty. "The staff at Henderson's knows me as *Mrs.* St. Martin, Mr. Higgins. They believe me to be recently widowed."

His pale eyes widened in astonishment, his thoughts momentarily suspended. *Whatever I might have expected, this girl is not going to be pushed around by anyone.* He paused, weighing his words carefully.

"Legally, my dear girl, you are Mrs. Bennett Kirkwood, but I can understand your aversion to that particular title. For the time being, let's continue with *Miss* St. Martin. Will that suit you?"

She offered him a small, shy smile. "That would be most agreeable, Mr. Higgins."

The three sat at Albert Higgins' desk, the solicitor explaining what he expected to happen when they met with Mr. Mallory, who had already been given the particulars of their tale. Both Claire and Braxton wanted a guarantee that the outcome would see the marriage between Bennett Kirkwood and Claire St. Martin dissolved. Whether that was accomplished by an annulment or divorce wasn't important at this point. Unable to give any assurance of the outcome, Mr. Higgins, checking his pocket watch, stood up, declaring it time to meet the other solicitor and lay their case before him.

Claire paled, a wave of apprehension sweeping through her until she felt Braxton take her hand and squeeze it reassuringly. The rain had stopped, for the moment at least, as they followed behind Albert Higgins as he made his way to a neighboring building. It seemed to Claire they had walked down miles of dimly lit corridors before he stopped abruptly in front of a door with the name *Mr. John Mallory, Solicitor*, lettered on it in gold. Claire lifted her veil as they entered the office.

The three were ushered into a second office that was a confusion of clutter and where a tall, barrel-chested man with a florid complexion and a shock of greying hair stood, hands clasped behind his back, peering through a dusty window as pedestrians hurried by. When he turned, Claire felt sharp eyes boring into her, as if seeking some sign that she was worthy of his time. Biting her lips nervously, she flushed, uncomfortable under his searching gaze.

Mr. Higgins hesitantly stepped forward and extended his hand. "John, so good of you to see us. May I introduce Claire St. Martin, wife of Bennett Kirkwood." He turned slightly and indicated the other visitor. "And this gentleman is Braxton Kane." He paused while Braxton and the other solicitor shook hands, the latter bowing his head in acknowledgement of Claire's presence.

John Mallory's deep baritone voice seemed to fill the room as he invited them to sit down on the three leather chairs which had been arranged in a semicircle before his desk, a desk that seemed to be a jumbled chaos of books and papers that were unceremoniously pushed aside as he seated himself, nodding to Mr. Higgins that he had the floor.

Albert Higgins began his narrative. "It is Miss St. Martin who is seeking either a divorce or an annulment, as I indicated in my letter to you. Naturally, she would prefer an annulment. She has never shared a bed with Mr. Kirkwood while she lived under his roof, neither before, during, nor after the marriage ended, and is quite willing to testify to that effect."

John Mallory nodded as he plucked a sheaf of papers from a corner of his desk, looking at it briefly as he cleared his throat. "Miss St. Martin, gentlemen…since 1857, when the Divorce Act came into being, divorce has indeed been somewhat easier to acquire but…" He held his hand up, as if lecturing students. "It is still a complicated procedure and is generally more favorable to the husband than the wife. A man can petition for divorce on the grounds of adultery, but a woman is unable to petition on grounds of adultery alone—there has to be another aggravating factor such as rape or incest."

Noting that his clients were becoming restive at this unwelcome news, he smiled briefly before continuing. "But your case, Miss St. Martin, is without a doubt most extraordinary. Both your father and your husband thought the other wealthy, although Mr. Kirkwood will come into his inheritance in the course of time. For some reason which I cannot understand, your husband, Bennett Kirkwood, arranged for another man, his best friend in fact, to be his proxy so to speak, on your wedding night, with you somehow being none the wiser."

He cast a speculating look at Claire, ignoring Braxton who was angrily rising to his feet. "Sit down, Mr. Kane. It is not my intention to impugn the lady's reputation. I'm merely stating the facts as they have been presented to me."

John Mallory paused for a moment, rubbing his chin as he collected his thoughts. "Sadly, the day following your marriage, your father died. And Bennett Kirkwood, a young and presumably virile young man, still does not seek your bed at any time in the weeks following the funeral. I can only assume that was a precaution on his part so that, should there be a pregnancy as a result of the wedding night, there would be no doubt as to the sire. Am I correct?"

His cold blue eyes fell on Braxton, who nodded, miserably ashamed of his role once more. "There are too many unanswered questions here, young man. Obviously, Mr. Higgins is privy to your secrets but lacks my expertise, and if you want my expertise, you must be not only honest but open. What is said in this room will remain in this room, but without your full cooperation, I must regretfully bow out."

Braxton, with a hesitant but encouraging nod from Claire, motioned the man to return to his chair. Claire laid a reassuring hand on his, her eyes full of love, lending him the courage to lay bare the story of the past few months. The tale slowly unfolded, from Mordock Peckworthy's mad scheme of revenge on Bennett Kirkwood to Braxton's forced compliance with the plot, although, he admitted, he wasn't sure whether he was protecting his brother, admittedly a monster, or some unknown prostitute plying her trade in the darkest corners of a city somewhere on the other side of the world. At the mention of Letitia Penrod and the part she had played, Mr. Mallory raised his eyebrows, muttering something unintelligible to the others.

As he continued talking, John Mallory made copious notes, his brow furrowed and his lips pressed tightly together. Albert Higgins looked from one to the other, unsure whether the man would accept the case at this point.

Finally, ashen-faced, Braxton finished his tale, defiantly meeting the eyes of the man he hoped would help put this sorry muddle behind them.

Mr. Mallory, realizing Braxton's account was finished, looked at the three anxious faces who awaited his decision. "Well, I'll take the case." There was an almost spontaneous exhaling of breath and relieved grins all around the small circle.

"Firstly, I want to say that, although you callously went along with Mordock Peckworthy and Bennett Kirkwood, I feel you are sincerely repentant and would change your actions if you could. Also in your favor is that since you couldn't change what had already occurred, you searched and, against all odds, found Miss St. Martin, presumably to atone for your cavalier behavior. And, if I'm any judge, the two of you have fallen in love and hope to marry." His voice trailed off as he awaited confirmation of his suspicions.

Braxton could only manage to nod while Claire daintily dabbed her eyes with a white handkerchief. Albert Higgins pumped the younger man's hand vigorously, smiling joyfully at both of them.

Leaving the three to collect themselves, the large man left the office momentarily, explaining on his return that he had ordered tea. Sitting down, he scanned his notes quickly before looking at their eager faces.

"Miss St. Martin, I would advise you to go for the lesser of two evils—an annulment. I am certain the marriage would be ruled invalid, and since there are no children, always a problem in a divorce, and no wealth to speak of since your husband hasn't come into his inheritance yet, I foresee no problem."

Claire could only nod in dazed agreement as the man continued.

"Divorces are a messy business and are published in the newspapers, both parties thereby vilified. I feel, thanks to that vicious gossip, Letitia Penrod, that you have had enough notoriety to last a lifetime." He shook his head, as if trying to dislodge a memory. "I've met her—a truly dreadful woman! Now, you could sue her for slander, but that would only whet the public appetite for more gossip so I would advise you to do nothing on that front." He smiled at the three of them. "Least said, soonest mended, I believe."

There was a quiet knock at the door. Mr. Mallory crossed the floor quickly and accepted the tray from his clerk that he had requested and which was laden with teapot, cups, and saucers. Surprisingly deft, he filled the cups with the steaming liquid and passed them around. There was quiet appreciation as they sipped the hot brew, all musing on what had already transpired and what might still be coming. John Mallory put his empty cup down and broke the silence.

"Yes, annulment is probably the best path to follow, and I'm sure that with the facts I have to present your request will be granted without you ever appearing in a courtroom. And since Mr. Kirkwood has never publicly mounted any kind of search for you or demonstrated the least bit of concern as to your well-being, he will be looked on most unfavorably. I have already had a man poking about, and from what he was able to gather in a short space of time, your husband has become something of a social outcast because of his behavior toward you. No one will receive him, and he's been drinking heavily, spending all of his time in either brothels or gaming houses."

Braxton bowed his head, saddened by the news of the downfall of a man who had once been a boon companion. Unable to feel any pity for the man she had wed, Claire squeezed her beloved's hand, wishing she could magically make all the badness in their lives disappear. He lifted her hand, kissing her fingers gently as a smile found its way through the uncertainty that was so evident on his face. The intimacy and sentiment of the gesture wasn't lost on either of the older occupants of the room, strengthening their determination to have the chaos that was presently ruling the young couple's lives disappear and arrive at a happy conclusion.

❀   ❀   ❀

It was late afternoon before the two lawyers felt they were prepared for any possible occurrence. Albert Higgins returned to his office, leaving Claire and Braxton to dine alone at a small tavern just on the outermost perimeter of Whitechapel. Although they continued to practice caution, they were happily aware that such distasteful subterfuge was coming to an end.

Night was fast approaching when Eloise Henderson greeted them at the door, thus assuring Claire that the building was now fully occupied. After chatting with Eloise for a few moments, Braxton took his leave, promising to be in touch with Claire if he had any news. The two women made their way to the kitchen where they shared a pot of tea as they caught each other up on the happenings of the day. Claire, somewhat reluctantly, told her employer of her attack of nerves earlier that day and Eloise who, although concerned, reluctantly agreed that it was most likely nothing more than finding herself totally alone with an active imagination.

Claire, with some trepidation, mounted the stairs to her room, taking comfort in the knowledge that her roommate, Ruby Goodspeed, was already there. On entering the shared bedroom, the two exchanged pleasantries as Claire moved about, making herself ready for the night. It wasn't until she was about to turn the bed down that she spied the small bunch of dark purple grapes, lying unnoticed against the dark coverlet until that moment. Her hand clutched at the wooden bed frame, her legs suddenly weak.

She could barely croak out the words. "Ruby, did you put these grapes on my bed?"

Ruby stirred, yawning and reluctant to leave her cozy bed. "Grapes! No, Claire, I've left nothing on your bed." Suddenly she realized the implication of the question and scrambled from her warm nest to stand beside Claire, both staring at the innocuous fruit, both too frightened to speak.

Claire at last turned her head toward Ruby, her voice seeming to come from a long way off. "Ruby, fetch Mrs. Henderson!" Accustomed to obeying without question, Ruby pulled the door open, her bare feet rapidly descending the dimly lit staircase, her voice shrill with panic as she called her employer's name.

Claire, after what seemed an eternity, heard Eloise Henderson's heavy frame climbing the wooden stairs, her voice echoing in the stairwell as she questioned Ruby who followed closely behind her. Bedroom doors began to open, the other occupants of the ladies' floor questioning each other about the unusual commotion. As Eloise reached the landing, all eyes turned to the doorway that stood open, watching as their employer entered the room. Ever so slowly, all of them began to edge closer, wanting to know the cause of the clamor.

Eloise met Claire's frightened eyes as she moved toward the bed and the offending fruit. They both held their candles aloft, examining the walls much as Braxton had done hours earlier. Their voices were low as Eloise, with Claire's frightened approval, made some rapid decisions. She turned to the nightgowned figures hovering in the hallway and was about to speak when the thumping of many footsteps hurrying down the men's staircase to the main floor could be heard.

Arthur Tucker's voice seemed to float eerily up the stairs. "Mrs. 'enderson! What's all the to-do about? Do you ladies need our 'elp? Should we come up?"

Eloise moved to the top of the stairs and looked down at the small circle of men standing by the door, ready and almost willing to do battle.

"Give us a few moments, Mr. Tucker. We'll need your help but not immediately. I'm going to send Mrs. Kenley down in a few moments to make us all a cup of tea."

Turning back to her female staff, she met their stares and began to speak in what she hoped was a reassuring voice.

"Ladies, we have an emergency of sorts. Someone has once again entered Mrs. St. Martin's private bedchamber, and this time the cheeky devil has left a bunch of grapes on her bed. How this person is gaining entry is a mystery but for tonight at least, we must all pull together!"

She paced nervously in the confined space, wondering at the events of the past few days. As she looked at the faces gathered around her, all displaying varying degrees of apprehension, she hoped her words offered some comfort as she resumed speaking.

"As a temporary solution, I will offer my own bedroom as a haven for Mrs. St. Martin and trust that two of you will find it in your hearts to share your room with Miss Goodspeed, and yes, I do realize you will be most crowded. In a few moments, I will invite the men up to move the two beds to their new quarters and, when that task has been accomplished, I'm inviting all of you downstairs for a cup of tea, and for those whose nerves might be feeling a bit frayed, something a little stronger."

Excited chatter broke out at this most unusual and unheard of invitation, accompanied by a few giggles, the unknown intruder momentarily forgotten. The cook, Mrs. Kenley, and her roommate Molly Garfield, were the first to speak up and invite Ruby Goodspeed to share their bedchamber, cramped though it would be.

"Ruby, Claire, take what you'll need for tomorrow morning. When we go downstairs, we'll all discuss what has to be done to solve this mystery. And ladies, as I'm about to summon the men up, might I suggest you all put on your dressing gowns."

There was an excited flutter as everyone departed for the said garments, animated chatter following them into their individual chambers. Ruby and Claire also sprang into action, thankful to have a task to occupy their thoughts as they bustled about the suddenly empty room, collecting what they would need for the morning. Eloise moved toward the top of the stairs and looked down at the men's upturned and curious faces.

"Mr. Tucker, if you gentlemen would come up and move the two beds to other rooms, it would be greatly appreciated."

The words were barely out of her mouth when there was a rush for the stairs, the men not only curious about the night's events but also about the women's quarters, forbidden territory to them until this moment.

Waiting for the oldest and slowest, Mr. Hargrove, to at last reach the second-story landing, they stood quietly, listening to the unwelcome discovery of the grapes left on Mrs. St. Martin's bed. They all remembered the flowers that had been left just as mysteriously.

"…and so, gentlemen, if you would move the two beds, each to their respective new quarters, it would be much appreciated, and as a gesture of gratitude, we'll all go downstairs for a cup of tea or, if you prefer, something a little stronger."

Her words were met with a murmur of enthusiastic anticipation. The Tucker brothers stepped toward Claire's bed and removed the bedding before starting carefully down the narrow staircase with the bed frame. A third man picked up the thin mattress, blanket, and pillow, transporting all unceremoniously down to Eloise Henderson's room with Claire following closely behind him, carrying what she would need for the next day or so. Two others stepped forward, and since Ruby's bed was only being taken to a room on the same floor, they carried it, bedding intact, down the hall to where Mrs. Kenley stood patiently awaiting their arrival.

As soon as Ruby's bed was fitted into the room, Mrs. Kenley, with Molly in tow for company, made their way to the kitchen. Slowly the second floor emptied as the tired employees noisily made their way down to the dining room for a cup of tea and most especially for the promised tipple.

As they all sat around the dining room table, no one could come up with a feasible theory as to how someone was gaining entry to Claire's chamber, although they all agreed it had to be in the hours between Claire's departure and their own return. She told of her fear, before Braxton had arrived, of squeaking floorboards, some unseen person coughing, and the sensation of being watched. Arthur Tucker, with a nod from Eloise Henderson, quietly returned to the room of mystery but came back with a puzzled look on his face.

"I 'ad a good look round, luv, but couldn't see any sign of a way in except through the door."

At his words, Eloise Henderson joined the conversation. "I've decided to call that builder with offices just down the road, Mr. Thrupp, to come by and have a look. If I remember correctly, it was his father who converted this building many years ago from stable to factory—that was before my own dear husband purchased it. And who knows, perhaps he'll be able to shed some light on the situation."

Tiredly, everybody began to stand. The small tipple of whiskey had apparently done its work. As they filed out, moving to their respective stairways, Mrs. Henderson gave them leave to sleep in if they could, reminding them that their engagement tomorrow was a business dinner, beginning in late afternoon and ending, hopefully, in the early evening.

Eloise Henderson put an arm around Claire's drooping shoulders and led her to the only bedchamber on the main floor. Wordlessly they made up her bed, and exhausted, Claire allowed herself to be tucked in and was already entering the welcoming arms of Morpheus before Eloise had extinguished her candle.

With great puffs of smoke drifting upward from his pipe, Mr. Thrupp arrived while everyone was still at breakfast, allowing the owner of the building to show him the room in question with no onlookers giving their opinions to the builder. He looked around for some time in silence, scratching the stubble on his chin as he thought of his long-dead father, trying to recall anything the old man might have said about this particular job.

The stillness of the room was broken by the sudden clapping of the man's hands together, causing Eloise to jump at the unexpectedness of the noise. "I remember now!" He smiled at Mrs. Henderson as he walked directly to the wall that the wardrobe stood in front of. Laying his pipe down, he opened the cupboard door, and pushing past the hanging garments and moving shoes and boxes aside, he knelt down and peered intently at the back wall of the oversized cupboard.

Eloise listened as he began tapping the walls, all the while muttering to himself until there was the sound of something wooden being pushed aside. At last Mr. Thrupp's head reappeared, a very satisfied smile on his thin face.

"My old dad told me about it. I never actually had a hand in the building of it. And it's intended to open nearer to the floor. Most people, if they were to search, would only look across, rarely would their eyes travel downward." At her blank expression, he smiled. "The 'special visitors' door!" He smiled smugly at her blank and uncomprehending expression. He stepped away so she could examine for herself the discovery that had so delighted him.

Kneeling down, Eloise saw that the lower quarter of the back wall of the wardrobe had been pushed aside, leaving a gap just large enough for an adult to climb through. Ever so cautiously, she poked her head into the opening but the blackness of the space beyond the wall exuded a musty odor and she nervously backed out.

Laughing, Mr. Thrupp relit his pipe, starting to recollect the circumstances of such a strange hidey-hole. "If you recall, Mrs. Henderson, when your husband bought this building, the second and third floors was only used for storage." He smiled happily when she nodded her head.

"But," he said, waggling his finger at her, a knowing smile playing about his mouth, "the old gentleman what owned the factory had this very room built and kept it locked, with him having the only key, very private-like, for the occasional visit from one of the 'ladies' he liked to entertain." He winked at her as he recalled his father laughingly telling him of the owner's peccadilloes.

"His wife, though, she was a bit of a Tartar. The woman was so convinced that her husband was up to something, she would drop by without warning, hoping to catch him 'in the act' so to speak. He persuaded himself that he was justified having this secret entrance built. The 'lady' what might be visiting could come and go with nary a soul being any the wiser." He chuckled at the foibles of the unnamed couple.

Pausing, he took another look at the black opening he had uncovered. "If I remember correctly, there was a set of stairs leading down to a small door at the side of the building." Holding a lantern in front of him, his voice trailed off as he squirmed through the wardrobe. A delighted cry was soon heard and then scrambling noises as he wriggled back into the room. "The stairs are still there and appear to be sound." He disappeared again, this time taking a little longer before reappearing. His face wore a troubled look when he re-emerged.

D. L. Robinson

"Someone's been using the bit of floor what's in there to spy on whoever occupied this room. A hole's been poked through the wall, giving the dirty beggar a view of the room and whoever was in it. The plaster what fell isn't too dirty so it wasn't very long ago." He stood back and gazed at the offending wall, suddenly taking a step forward and pointing. Signaling Eloise, they both approached an almost invisible spy-hole to the left of the wardrobe. Turning, Mr. Thrupp attempted to move the oversized cupboard, but it couldn't be budged. Bending, he soon found cleverly hidden nails that anchored it in place. "Someone didn't want this cupboard moved."

Eloise Henderson clapped her hands together, delighted that the mystery was solved but angry that her trust had been so abused. *It had to be that man Smith! There was no other explanation, but how was one to prove it? He hadn't been seen on the property since his dismissal.* Oh well, at least she had some news to carry to those waiting downstairs.

About to leave the room, Eloise turned to the builder. "How do you think Smith came to know about this secret entrance?"

The man stared at her and slowly scratched his head in bafflement. "Is that the name of the man who you suspect? Wasn't he the one who drove that omnibus of yours?" She nodded her head excitedly.

"Let's have a peek at the outside of the building, missus. Maybe there's a logical explanation."

She led Mr. Thrupp down to the main floor and through to the kitchen, offering no explanation to her staff whose curiosity could barely be contained. The more daring of them gathered around the window and watched as Mrs. Henderson and the builder strode to the back of the property and then turned, both intently studying the brick structure.

Mr. Thrupp determinedly paced the width of the building, silently scrutinizing it until, with a loud *aha*, he marched toward the far side of the building and a narrow strip of neglected land that lay between Henderson's and the neighboring structure. Excitedly he motioned his temporary assistant to follow him. Approaching the thick growth of weeds, the builder carefully inspected the brick wall. With a perplexed look on his face, he knelt down and studied the weeds. His excitement was evident as he moved into the overgrowth a few feet before kneeling down again, tapping at the bricks until a small door swung outward.

"Here's how the filthy beggar got in. Easy enough to see if you look where the weeds were flattened. I'm guessing that over time this tiny door must've come loose and eventually swung open, at least enough to attract his attention. He discovered the stairway and where it led, but now his shameful secret has been discovered."

Standing with Eloise Henderson at the front door of the building a few moments later, the builder promised to send a couple of his lads over first thing in the morning to board up both the entrance into the building and the concealed opening in the wardrobe.

"For the time being, have your lads pile a few cans—whatever they can come up with that's noisy—in front of the door, enough to make him think twice about trying to open it if he dares to return. That should keep him away." He grinned at her, thanking her for the opportunity to recall memories of his old dad. Winking, he tipped his cap and started down the path, whistling cheerfully as he made his way to the main road.

The owner of Henderson's Domestics walked thoughtfully into the dining room. A hush fell over everyone as she approached, and all eyes turned in her direction. Catching Claire's eyes, she smiled before turning to the room at large.

"Well, as you all know, Mr. Thrupp, the builder, has been here and had a good look around the bedroom in question. Most importantly, he's solved the mystery of the anonymous delivery of flowers and grapes. I know, Mr. Tucker, you examined the room, looking for a secret opening, but it was as I'd hoped. Mr. Thrupp did indeed have inside knowledge. His father, who was also a builder, did the actual work." There was a buzz of conversation at that bit of information, and then all fell silent.

"There's a secret panel inside the wardrobe that slides across, just enough to let someone wiggle through. It's very cleverly hidden on the lower part of the back wall, which according to Mr. Thrupp, is a place most people wouldn't notice if seeking a concealed door. Beyond that opening is a staircase, still sound according to Mr. Thrupp, leading down to a second hidden door, which opens to the outside. And in case you're wondering why no one has ever noticed the entrance from the outside, it's on that weedy strip of land between our building and the next, and is quite overgrown with weeds." Looking at her staff, she saw most of their faces registering surprise and concern.

"I assure you there's nothing to be worried about. Mr. Thrupp advised me to have anything that will clatter noisily piled in front of the outside opening, just for tonight. His men will be by tomorrow morning to permanently seal both the outside entrance and the wardrobe access in Mrs. St. Martin and Miss Goodspeed's bedroom."

Smiles of relief slowly appeared on all their faces, and several of them started to shuffle from the room until Arthur spoke. "I know what bloke it was, even if you won't name 'im. It was that Smith, a strange chap if ever there was one. Evil in 'is 'eart, there is!" Subdued muttering was heard, most agreeing with his shrewd judgment.

The buzz of conversation subsided when Claire stood up, after all, it was her bedroom that had attracted the attention of the fiend in the first place. Claire nervously cleared her throat before speaking. "Was Mr. Smith or whoever it was able to spy inside the room? I've told you of the fright I had yesterday afternoon when it felt as if someone was watching. My hair felt like it was standing on end!"

It was a fair question but one Eloise Henderson had been dreading. She reluctantly faced Claire, although she addressed the entire room. "Mr. Thrupp uncovered a peephole in the wall where someone could have stood and watched the occupants of the room." After the initial shocked gasps, the women demanded to know if these peepholes were in every room.

"As far as I know, it was only in Mrs. St. Martin's room. Now please, don't let your imaginations run away with you. Miss Goodspeed and Mrs. St. Martin will remain in their temporary quarters until after Mr. Thrupp's men have made the necessary repairs. And now, Mr. Tucker, if you'll attend to blocking that small doorway on the outside of the building, we can all begin to get on with our day."

Satisfied with her handling of the matter, she turned and started to walk toward her office until Arthur Tucker's voice stopped her. "Mrs. 'enderson, we'd like to revisit the ladies' floor and see this secret entrance for ourselves…if you don't 'ave no objection?"

She turned slowly, her thoughts churning wildly in her head. *If I allow everyone to have a peek, their curiosity will be satisfied. If I don't, they'll be creeping in there at all hours, imaginations running wild, and it would probably be even worse for Claire and Ruby.*

"Of course, Mr. Tucker, I should have thought of it myself. I'll leave it up to you to take care no one ventures beyond the wardrobe itself. Mr. Thrupp thought the stairs still sound but one never knows…" Her words trailed off as she resumed her walk down the hallway toward her office, a satisfied smile on her face.

Just as the door to the ladies' stairway was flung open, she called Arthur Tucker and Claire over for a cautionary word while pointing to the clock. "Just a quick look, please. We've just enough time for lunch before everyone has to make their preparations to leave for that business dinner. According to our new driver, the very satisfactory Alfie Downs, it's quite some distance from here."

Nodding their heads, they returned to the others who stood waiting at the stairway, each of them reluctant to be the first up the stairs. It took some minutes before all had trooped upward, their footsteps echoing through the building. Taking the lead, Arthur unlocked the door and edged over to the now infamous wardrobe. Carefully opening the cupboard door and bending, he peered inside. Unable to see into the blackness beyond the wall, he backed out and ushered Claire and then Ruby to be next.

Curiosity somewhat satisfied, each staff member left the room to prepare for lunch and the evening ahead. Bringing up the rear was old Morley Hargrove who had a quick look before a now impatient Arthur ushered him out. Arthur carefully locked the door before slowly following the elderly fellow as he trudged down the ladies' stairs, turned, and breathlessly puffed up the second set of stairs to the men's floor.

A short while later, Claire emerged from Eloise's bedroom, dressed and ready to meet the challenges of the business dinner the staff had been hired to serve at that evening. Knowing she had a few minutes, she sat at Eloise's desk and dashed off a hasty note to Braxton, recounting the discovery of the grapes on her bed and the hiring of the builder, Mr. Thrupp, who by chance was the son of the builder who had done the renovations years earlier. She wrote that the very clever Mr. Thrupp had uncovered the hidden entrance into her room. Hearing many footsteps on both sets of stairs, Claire ended her note, sealing it just as the postman arrived for the final collection of the day.

Mrs. Henderson had everybody up early the following morning, wanting the ladies especially to be washed and dressed before Mr. Thrupp's men arrived and invaded the second floor.

All of the staff were carrying out their assigned housekeeping chores, most just finishing up when a resounding knock on the door echoed through the building. Eloise jumped up, certain the men from Mr. Thrupp had arrived, but when she opened the door, it was Braxton Kane who greeted her.

"Eloise, I apologize most sincerely for calling at this early hour, unannounced and unexpected, but I received a note from Claire in the early post, giving me an abbreviated version of the happenings here since we parted yesterday. I must see her, if only for a moment, just to reassure myself that all is well."

The woman, almost as tall as Braxton and near to him in size, chortled inwardly as she turned his words over in her mind. "Braxton Kane, I'm willing to bet a shilling that in times gone by you've probably bragged to your friends that no bit of fluff would ever have you jumping through hoops, no matter how pretty she might be. And now look at you, totally enthralled by a slip of a girl." Unexpectedly she hugged him, overcome by feelings of almost motherly fondness at his look of discomfiture.

Eloise, on her way to fetch Claire from the kitchen, was unaware that her words had triggered a memory of that night so many months ago at Silverwood House, an evening of revelry spent with his friends, Bennett Kirkwood and the Chambers brothers. *My God,* he thought, *I did spout some nonsense about being content with my bachelorhood...the same night Mordock Peckworthy re-entered all of our lives and started this insane chain of events.*

He pushed the memory aside and exhaled a long sigh of contentment as he watched Claire walking down the hallway toward him, his mouth curving into an unconscious smile. She met the smile and took the hand he offered, the seconds ticking away as they lost themselves in the nearness of the other.

His words tumbled from his lips. "Claire, your note arrived this morning...I'm sorry to call without warning, but I had to be sure you were safe."

Laughing softly, she gazed into his grey eyes, seeing his love reflected there. "I didn't mean to alarm you, Braxton, but you did say you wanted to know if anything unusual happened." She turned away and saw Eloise watching them from the doorway, a wistful look in her eyes.

"Eloise, would it be all right if I showed Braxton the wardrobe and its hidden passageway? Perhaps one of the others could accompany us…?" Her words trailed off into uncertainty.

"I'm sure no chaperone is needed, Claire, but once again I must remind you that there's not much time before you have to leave for today's engagement. And I'm sure Mr. Thrupp's men will be arriving soon."

Nodding, Claire took Braxton's hand and led him up the ladies' staircase, their footsteps barely echoing as they slowly climbed the creaking wooden stairs.

Once inside her room, Claire found herself encircled by his arms, her calm shattered with the hunger of his kisses. Pushing herself away, she laughingly protested, reminding him of his promise to wait for the marriage vows to be spoken. Mentally he cursed his honorable intentions as his hands slipped up her arms, drawing her closer until at last, with a very deep sigh, he reluctantly released her.

He looked around the room until his grey eyes fastened on the offending wardrobe and the secret hidden within. Hesitantly they stood in front of it before he pulled the door open, revealing the small sliding door. And just as Mr. Thrupp and the staff of Henderson's had done before him, Braxton knelt down and peered into the silent blackness. The sound of many shoes tramping up the stairs interrupted his deliberations and he stood up, brushing self-consciously at the knees of his trousers.

Eloise was the first to cross the threshold, followed closely by a tall, thin man puffing on a pipe, who nodded offhandedly at Braxton and Claire. Two more men entered the room and stopped abruptly, their mouths hanging open as their eyes fell on Claire. It was Mr. Thrupp noisily clearing his throat that brought their attention back to him, although neither failed to notice the stranger that was now towering over them, a fleeting shadow of jealous anger sweeping across his face. Both stepped closer to their employer, studiously ignoring the dazzling creature that had moved to the doorway, unaware of the furor that was whirling about her as she awaited Braxton to join her.

Eloise, a smile ruffling her mouth, introduced Braxton to the builder. The two shook hands, Braxton struggling to hide the unexpected surge of jealousy he had felt only moments earlier. Wisely, Eloise, having no wish to impede Mr. Thrupp in his area of expertise, joined Claire and Braxton as they made their way down the stairs.

Bidding the young man good-bye, the older woman moved toward the dining room where everyone was gathered, waiting for Alfie and the omnibus to transport them to their late afternoon engagement.

The young couple stood outside the front entrance, exchanging a chaste kiss. As the woman turned to go back inside, he called out to her. She nodded her head in agreement, both waving until, deep in thought, he mounted his horse and trotted down the road. Neither of them noticed the man who stood just a few feet away, shivering in the chill November air, reflecting on the young couple's tender farewell.

As the hireling made his way back to his master, he puzzled over what the man had called out to the woman. Shaking his head, he kicked the nag he rode, hastening toward Silverwood House where he hoped the information he carried would earn him a few bob more. That had been the agreement. *Find the woman and the reward would be more generous than he had ever dreamed possible.*

A cloud of steam hissed in the fireplace, the consequence of a cup of coffee being thrown petulantly into the flames, slivers of broken china scattered about the hearth. Bennett Kirkwood, a crumpled piece of paper in his hand, paced the length of the room in long, angry strides, his muffled voice calling down curses on some unseen soul. He was unaware that his housekeeper, recently hired to replace that treacherous Mrs. Dixon, scurried past the door toward the questionable sanctuary of the kitchen. She had heard the anger contained in the barely audible curses and was fearful that her employer would unleash his foul temper on her.

Finally ceasing his tirade, he poured himself a large glass of whiskey, downing half of it in a single swallow. He loosened his grip on the letter he held, smoothing out the creases before reading it once more.

How dare she—the black-hearted bitch! Hiring a solicitor in the hopes of securing an annulment! And I know just where she got the money for that. That bastard I once called friend, Braxton Kane. They've made me the laughingstock of London. I'll kill both of them. I'll shoot them right through their wicked and immoral hearts!

He threw the letter into the fire and watched the flames devour it, taking a second pull on the drink he held as he watched the paper burn away to nothing. Running long fingers over the lower part of his face, he felt the stubble there. Surprised, he realized it had probably been at least two days since he had last shaved or even washed. He looked down at his clothes, stained, wrinkled, and probably reeking.

His shoddy appearance was her fault too! He had once been well-groomed, welcomed into the highest circles of society and now...now nobody invited him anywhere. In fact, servants had been instructed to turn him away. Even the Chambers brothers wanted nothing to do with him. He looked at his glass, astonished to see it empty. Lifting the bottle to pour another, he heard a timid knock.

Snarling, he crossed the room, flinging the door open to reveal his trembling housekeeper and that creature, that insect he had hired, somebody Boile, to find Claire.

"Yes, what is it? Boile, isn't it? Well, what news?" Seeing the man open his mouth to speak, he quickly stepped aside, admitting the scoundrel into his refuge, his private sanctuary, before hastily closing the door on his housekeeper as she furtively attempted to peer inside.

Mr. Boile, cap in hand, twisted it about fretfully for a moment, watching as his employer lurched back to his desk. *This bloke is drunk...and at this time of the morning.*

Boile stood waiting, licking his lips hungrily as he watched Bennett refill his glass and then, more frustrated than disappointed, saw the man carelessly spill some of the golden liquid as he stumbled clumsily to a chair near the fire. Nodding at Boile, he leaned forward, trying to focus on the man's words.

"Mr. Kirkwood, sir, we did just like you told us, me and my mate, Dick Trout, and two other lads, twenty-four hours a day, every day. We stayed hid outside that Pennygrove Hall, and whenever this Kane fellow left, we was right on his tail. He had no idea we was there."

"Do you have news or not, man?" Bennett's tone was impatient, his words slurring together.

"Yes, your honor, yes sir. This morning he takes off, real early it was. I follows behind him cautious-like but he don't notice nothing, he just rides out to the east end of the city as if the devil was on his tail. He knows where he's going, no hesitating or nothing."

Bennett slowly sat up straighter, his heart beginning to race with excitement. *This is it! All those months, waiting for word of her and now…"*

"Anyways, he stops in front of a brick building and starts banging at the door. A woman, not old, not young, but very tall and big-boned, a real armful, opens up the door. They speaks a few words, and she hugs him before she lets him in. And while I stands outside in the cold for a fair bit, waiting patiently mind you, three men arrive, builders by the looks of them. They go in and I'm still waiting. At last, the door opens again and your bloke steps out, but he's not alone. This little bit of a woman steps out with him, and oh my lord, she's a looker. I've never seen such a beauty. They have a quick cuddle, and just as she's turning to go back inside, he calls to her, but I couldn't quite catch what he said. They grins at each other and then they're both gone, her inside and him heading home, leastways that's where I think he went. I came straight here."

Bennett Kirkwood studied the man Boile, watching as he shifted from one foot to the other, uncomfortable under such close scrutiny. "Think, man, what do you suppose he said? Did he speak of their next tryst?" At the man's puzzled look, Bennett rephrased his question, unable to hide his irritation as his voice rose in volume.

"Did he mention their next meeting?" The words seemed to bounce off the walls.

Boile, still clutching his grubby cap, scratched his head. "No, your honor, t'wasn't nothing like that. It was something…iluvucara…I couldn't make it out." He shrugged his shoulders, a nervous look on his grizzled face.

Bennett's dark eyebrows slanted in a frown as he turned the garbled phrase over in his mind. "Claire! Could he have been saying Claire?"

Ned Boile's mouth turned into a pleased grin, revealing blackened stubs of rotting teeth. "That's it. He said '*I love you Claire*'."

He drew back, suddenly unsure whether he had been wise to reveal the words of his employer's former friend. Bennett Kirkwood momentarily looked like he wanted to strangle somebody, anybody, but instead burst into high-pitched maniacal laughter.

"How very wonderful! He loves her! And did she return the sentiment? Oh, Mr. Boile, you have just confirmed the justness of my plans for that...that wife-stealing bastard and the harlot that was once my wife!"

Bennett stood there, silently contemplating that unfortunate couple's demise, until he suddenly remembered his hireling's presence. Putting his hand on the man's back, he led him to an array of liquor bottles. "Pour yourself a drink, Mr. Boile, while I mull over the situation."

Somewhat taken aback by the lightning-swift change of mood, Ned Boile poured himself a very generous glass of whiskey, marveling at the number of bottles while he wordlessly pondered the privileged lives of the wealthy. Sipping the rich amber liquid, he sat down, determined to enjoy the sudden, albeit temporary, turn his fortunes had taken.

Lighting a cigar, Bennett looked at the shabbily-clothed individual sitting opposite him. "Call your men off Pennygrove Hall. Set them watching..." He paused briefly. "Where exactly did you say my wife is living?"

Boile looked up, not yet ready to depart the lavish surroundings he found himself in. "Brick Lane, Henderson's Domestics on Brick Lane in Whitechapel."

Bennett Kirkwood considered the answer before once again breaking into maniacal laughter. "Do you mean she's taken employment, working as some sort of domestic?" The look on his face was one of disbelief.

Boile rubbed his grizzled chin, ponderously considering his answer. "I don't know what she gets up to, she just stepped outside to say good-bye to the toff." His tone bordered on the impertinent, no doubt fueled by the whiskey.

Distracted, Bennett looked at the man. "Yes, of course." Chuckling, he began sauntering about the room, picturing the delicate hands of his beautiful wife scrubbing floors or her slender form wrestling a scuttle of coal up from the cellar to warm the feet of her betters, bits of soot clinging to her now-pale cheeks.

"Delightful, just delightful." He returned to the collection of bottles, a question in his eyes as he held up one of them to his temporary drinking companion. A second glass was thrust toward him, and Bennett poured until both glasses were full. No words were exchanged as the two sat, lost in quiet contemplation as the fiery liquid warmed their bellies.

❁   ❁   ❁

The staff of Henderson's Domestics journeyed to two halls the following day, serving at a charity luncheon for orphans and later in the afternoon at a tea for disabled soldiers. Soon they returned home, tired and ready for their evening meal, which had been prepared by the talented Mrs. Kenley.

Arthur Tucker, in spite of his frequent stopovers at his friend Ollie's butcher shop, found all news, whether fact, gossip, or speculation regarding the madman Jack the Ripper, had almost dried up. The fiend hadn't struck in more than a month and the residents of London were sitting back, breathing a collective sigh of relief, most convinced he was either dead or had moved on to new hunting grounds.

It was just before midnight on Thursday, the staff of Henderson's all tucked cozily into their beds, that the eldest resident, Morley Hargrove, was awoken by a muffled thumping coming from the outside of the building. Somewhere a dog howled, sending other dogs into a frenzy of barking. Cool night air swirled around Morley's bare legs as he peered sleepily through his third-story window into the black nothingness of night. The two men sharing his room heard him stirring about and would settle for nothing less than lighting a candle and traipsing downstairs to check the windows and doors on the main floor.

As they cautiously crept down the squeaking staircase, the flames of their candles danced in the slight breeze they created, casting eerie shapes on the walls. The three huddled together, none willing to take the lead. They had just reached the halfway mark when an angry howl filled the air, swirling about their ears as if some crazed creature was baying at the moon. Regretting their foolhardy plan, the three turned, wanting nothing more than the welcoming safety of their beds, but the spine-chilling wail had woken the others. Bedroom doors began to open, and pale, fearful faces cautiously peered out, whispering anxious questions, which no one could answer. The furious yowling of dogs seemed to increase by the second.

Arthur Tucker, always a sound sleeper, was the last to appear, white hair rumpled and eyes still sleep-filled. Impatiently he pushed his way down the stairs, trying to make sense of the jumbled voices, which were all trying to account for the sinister noises in the night.

The door at the foot of the stairs slowly creaked open, throwing the men, young and old alike, into a state of confusion, unable to decide if they should charge ahead or retreat up to the safety of the third floor.

A candle revealed Eloise Henderson and Claire, trepidation evident on their pale faces as the men suddenly began jostling each other in their haste to reach the bottom stair. Lighter footsteps could be heard descending the ladies' staircase, and soon all were once more gathered in the kitchen, spilling into the dining room.

It was one of those moments, when all had fallen silent, that a sneeze was heard from the other side of the kitchen door, quickly followed by the sound of heavy boots scraping and running across the cobbles, causing timorous hearts inside the building to beat even faster. Arthur, bolder than most, rushed to the door but even as he pulled it open, the unknown entity could be heard racing toward the front road and the shadowy recesses afforded by neighboring buildings and alleyways.

After very little discussion, the men decided they couldn't sit inside so, clustered tightly together, they cautiously stepped outside, all holding candles or lanterns aloft. They soon returned to the kitchen, able to reassure the ladies who stood huddled inside the kitchen door that whoever had been outside had fled. Arthur and his brother Gordon determinedly walked to the far side of the building, soon spying the prowler's efforts to open the once secret but now sealed entrance which had led up to Claire and Ruby's bedchamber.

Eloise Henderson, once again recognizing a need, had Mrs. Kenley brewing up a pot of tea while she unlocked a small cupboard, extracting a bottle of brandy from within. Returning to the dining room where they were now seated, she followed behind the cook as the tea was poured, smiling as she added a generous dollop to each cup.

The chatter around the table was muted, eyes turned often to the blackness of the night beyond the glass of the windows, all wondering what was to come. At last, Mrs. Henderson clapped her hands to gain everyone's attention.

"I wonder, Mr. Tucker, if tomorrow you would be so kind as to go round to the police, alerting them to our prowler. Perhaps one of them could patrol the building and grounds of Henderson's, at least for a while. Who knows, perhaps it would even scare the scoundrel away."

Arthur Tucker nodded his agreement, and Mrs. Henderson smiled her gratitude at him. "But for now, everyone, I think we should go back to bed. The miscreant appears to have fled, and we have a wedding to serve at tomorrow, so it will be rather a long day."

Slowly they all filed out, grateful for the fact that they all shared a room with at least one other person. Calling out their good nights, footsteps could be heard trudging tiredly up both staircases, and one by one, the muffled sounds of bedroom doors closing. Eloise and Claire retired to the room they were sharing, chatting quietly about the day to come, deliberately avoiding mention of the night and its happenings. As Claire closed her eyes, she reminded herself that Braxton had yet to be told of the happenings on Brick Lane. *I'll write him tomorrow,* she thought, *nothing would be accomplished by writing a letter tonight.*

Claire, true to her promise, wrote a letter to Braxton on the morrow and had it ready and waiting before the first post was collected and, unsurprisingly, Braxton's reply arrived that afternoon. Claire, intent on finding a quiet corner to read it, didn't see the fond smiles on most of the faces gathered around the table on a very bleak Friday although, amongst two or three of the women, there was whispering that such goings-on had never happened until after the arrival of the mysterious Mrs. St. Martin. It was the sharp-eared Mrs. Kenley who soon had the gossips shamefacedly leave the room, cheeks burning at the tongue-lashing they received from the usually mild-mannered cook.

Claire settled herself by the front window, eagerly opening the letter and not entirely surprised by the contents.

Oh Wicked Escort

My love...

What you wrote this morning confirms my suspicions that you are in danger on more than one front. Not only Ben, but it seems the mysterious Mr. Smith has anything but your best interests at heart. Before writing to you, I took it upon myself to write to your Lord Magnus Jennings of Romford House, requesting that the three of us meet. Ben once mentioned that he had called upon you—that was after you disappeared. I hope he'll be agreeable to offering you a safe haven, at least until we have disposed of your marriage to Ben. I would much prefer you to be under my roof at Pennygrove Hall, but the gossipmongers will have enough to deal with when your marriage is dissolved. I know you're serving at a wedding today so I will assume you'll always be surrounded by people and safe. Remember—never venture anywhere alone.

I also had a note this morning from John Mallory advising me that Bennett Kirkwood has been served notice that you have filed a petition for the annulment of your marriage. He has yet to respond. As soon as I hear anything from either Lord Jennings or Mr. Mallory, I'll write. Love always and forever, Braxton.

The remainder of the morning was spent putting the living quarters of Henderson's in order. After the midday meal, everyone retired to their respective chambers to don their serving attire, reassembling in the dining room, all prepared to dash to the omnibus should the menacing grey clouds that hung over the city decide to release their contents. Mrs. Henderson and Mrs. Kenley were staying home, lending stamina and fortitude to each other, something sorely needed after the night they had all spent.

As the cumbersome omnibus rumbled down Brick Lane, two riders slowly followed, knowing the slow-moving coach would be hard to lose, even in Whitechapel. And just as they rode unnoticed, so did a figure travelling on foot, muttering dark threats in the direction of the oversized coach.

Mr. Smith, knowing the staff of Henderson's would probably be hours at whatever event they had been hired to serve at, decided to stay within the environs of Whitechapel. His fingers caressed the cold steel of his knife, the urge to taste female flesh almost overwhelming in its suddenness. *My blade hungers! I'll hunt on Dorset Street—plenty of strumpets wandering about, all begging to feel my blade pierce their rotten hides. How I'll laugh as I watch the last spark of life dim in their disbelieving eyes.* He turned off, his boots scraping against the cobbles, no longer interested in the whereabouts of those employed by Eloise Henderson.

Chapter Twenty

Upon returning from their engagement, Eloise handed Claire a letter that had arrived with the last post of the day. She carried it to a quiet corner of the hallway, not venturing far from the others who were sitting in the dining room.

> *My darling,*
> *I've received word from Lord Jennings. He's been most anxious as to your whereabouts and is very agreeable to meeting us tomorrow, although I'm not sure how eager he is to meet me. He implies in his note that he has heard the gossip surrounding your marriage and my part in it but assures me he is reserving judgment until he has spoken with us.*
> *If you're agreeable, I'll call for you tomorrow for lunch. We'll meet Mr. Mallory at three o'clock, for he has also written, asking if you could come by to sign some legal papers. Lord Jennings has invited us to an informal dinner at six o'clock.*
> *My love, don't worry about wearing mourning clothes or that hateful veil. After all, Ben has been notified of your intent to apply for an annulment so the need for subterfuge is at an end. Love always and forever,*
> *Braxton.*

Claire tucked his letter into the pocket of her skirt and went into the dining room to join the others, for despite the lateness of the hour, all were willing to delay the climb up the stairs to their bedchambers.

Eloise Henderson, although loath to admit it even to herself, was happy to be sharing her room, the only bedroom on the main floor. Everyone lingered over the tasty light meal Mrs. Kenley had waiting for them on their return, most pouring a second cup of tea to postpone the evening's end.

Mrs. Henderson and Arthur made one last inspection of the windows and doors, assuring themselves that the building was as secure as it could possibly be. On their return, the men, yawning, made their way to the staircase leading to the third floor, calling out their good nights to the ladies. The ladies, seeing the men depart, decided that there was indeed safety in numbers and mounted their own set of stairs, wishing Claire and Mrs. Henderson a good night.

And for those who slept under the roof of Henderson's Domestics, it was a very quiet night indeed.

Arthur Tucker was pale and breathless when he returned from his morning walk. Passing the dining room window, he gave only a fleeting look at the people he had become so fond of as they lingered over their morning tea. Shedding his jacket, he caught his brother's eye, quietly sending him to fetch Mrs. Henderson, for his news, in spite of it being as yet unconfirmed, was of the greatest magnitude, and he knew she would want to partake in every aspect of the discussion that was sure to follow.

He looked at the circle of faces that gazed up at him, a few displaying mild curiosity while some, more perceptive than the others, reflected fear, as if already guessing the nature of his announcement. Eloise Henderson entered the room and took a chair, leaving the floor to Arthur.

He spoke with quiet emphasis, his demeanor solemn. "There's been another murder." Silence reigned for a few seconds while everyone took time to absorb what had been said before the room became a hodgepodge of voices, all asking questions and demanding answers. Arthur let them ramble on for a moment but then held up his hands and gradually the din faded into silence.

"The streets are abuzz with rumors but just outside Ollie's, I ran into a bloke what knows, 'e was almost there, at the murder, I mean. What 'e told me was that it was another prostitute but this one 'ad a room in Miller's Court off Dorset Street. 'Er name was Mary Kelly. 'E knew 'er since they 'ad lodgings in the same 'ouse."

He stopped talking and stood watching as his news was absorbed. Taking a deep breath, he plunged on. "Seems like the rent collector was making 'is rounds this morning and when 'e knocks at Mary Kelly's door, no one answers. 'E figures she's 'iding cause she don't 'ave the dosh, so 'e peeks through a broken window and sees a 'orrible sight. Blood and gore everywhere! 'E starts shouting *'murder, murder'* and before you knows what's 'appening, there's coppers all over the place."

His tale at an end, he waited for the questions that were sure to follow, but disappointingly there was only silence until Mrs. Kenley stood, placing the dirty cups and plates on a tray.

"I thought he was gone…disappeared, this beast, this Jack the Ripper, I truly did. And now we'll be afraid to venture out again." Still mumbling, she made her way into the kitchen, slowly followed by those whose turn it was to do the washing up.

One by one, the residents of Henderson's Domestics took up their duties, tidying and dusting, making the living quarters of Henderson's presentable. As Eloise Henderson quietly returned to her ledgers, she couldn't decide if it was a good thing or not that the agency had no engagements for either Saturday or Sunday, apart from church services Sunday morning. *They need something to distract them from all of the recent goings-on. Braxton will be calling for Claire soon—maybe the rest of us can stroll down to the pub for a pint. We've all been under such a strain lately, and perhaps we could even raise a glass in memory of the poor unfortunates who met such grisly ends.* She felt her spirits lift just contemplating such an outing.

Why, I haven't visited a pub since my Charlie was alive. She sighed, momentarily lost in her memories. Having made the decision, she marched down the hall, broaching the idea to those still in the dining room, even offering to buy the first round. Her proposal was met with broad smiles, and soon footsteps could be heard running up the stairs as the invitation was quickly carried to the rest of the staff.

D. L. Robinson

A bone-chilling dampness filled the air, seeming to seep into the very core of anyone unfortunate enough to be outside. Braxton, in his own brougham driven by his own man, arrived just after the clock had struck noon. Claire, garbed in a deep forest-green gown trimmed with black lace and a pert matching bonnet, was waiting for him in the reception area of Henderson's. The smile in his grey eyes contained a sensuous flame and she felt a warm glow flow through her. As he wrapped her woolen cloak about her shoulders, Eloise stepped into the room.

After exchanging mutually warm greetings, the three then discussed the latest murder, all expressing their distress and sympathy for the victim. Eloise filled Braxton in on the details that Arthur Tucker had garnered in his travels about Whitechapel. Braxton, commenting on his surprise at the restrained silence the staff was displaying, was quickly assured by Eloise it was more due to the shock and gruesome horror of the crime, coming just when everyone had foolishly begun to assume the monster had left, if not the country, at least London itself.

Standing in the open doorway, Braxton, mindful of the chill in the air, quickly outlined the day ahead to Eloise, including their dinner engagement with Lord Jennings, before ushering Claire from the building. Neither of them took any notice of a shabbily-dressed individual, known to his acquaintances as Ned Boile who, as the door to Henderson's had opened, quickly stooped to adjust the strap on one of his boots. He maneuvered himself to keep within earshot as good-byes were said, satisfying himself that the bloke at least was oblivious to the eyes that watched as he handed Claire into his brougham.

The carriage, under the skilled handling of Thomas, wheeled its way as best it could through the heavy traffic of Whitechapel, leaving the couple seated inside with nothing to think of but each other. Braxton gave Claire a smile that sent her pulses racing before he lowered his lips to hers, gently covering her eager mouth. They separated for a moment until his lips recaptured hers, more demanding this time. Claire was trembling when he at last released her.

"Once again, madam, I must caution you that I only have so much self-control and right now it's being sorely pressed protecting your virtue." His voice, deep and sensual, sent a ripple of awareness through her, his gaze as soft as a caress.

He took her hands in his and together they sat, content just to be in each other's company, letting the world pass them by as they rumbled down the road. "I thought we might lunch at The King's Head. It's a very old establishment and is usually quiet at this time of day. I've heard it said that Queen Elizabeth dined there on her way from the Tower." Claire smiled her approval, content to go anywhere as long as she was in Braxton's company.

As the brougham rattled down the cobbled road toward Whitechapel Road, a pair of scruffy horsemen, Ned Boile and his friend Dick Trout, followed discretely behind, staying back just far enough to avoid detection. A third man, riding a hired nag, eased himself from a narrow lane, keeping just close enough to keep both the coach and the riders in sight.

As usual, the traffic of Whitechapel was congested, and neither the pair of riders nor the third man had any trouble keeping the carriage in sight. Crossing the Thames, the carriage wound its way down a narrow lane, stopping in front of a small but fashionable restaurant.

The owner, a pompous individual with a swarthy complexion and a sliver of a moustache, met them at the door, immediately recognizing Braxton from previous visits. Turning slightly, he spied the delicate beauty standing beside Braxton, curling tendrils of dark hair escaping from beneath her bonnet, her deep brown eyes meeting his, and was instantly smitten.

He bowed low over Claire's slender hand, almost caressing it, until he felt the other man move restively behind him. Glancing up, the proprietor saw cold grey eyes staring intently at him and he quickly released her hand. Whirling around, he snapped his fingers and a waiter instantly came forward to lead the handsome couple to a table by the fire.

While Claire and Braxton dined inside, the disheveled Mr. Boile and Mr. Trout tied their horses nearby and huddled together in a doorway opposite the restaurant, shivering in the chill November air. Neither of them took any notice of the man who, unknown to them, had been following and who had now crept stealthily into an adjacent doorway. He stood quietly, listening to their complaints about the weather until one of the pair noticed a pub just a few doors down the road.

Ned Boile, the brighter of the two, was the first to speak. "I'm sure a gentleman such as Mr. Kirkwood is wouldn't want us to take a chill, Dickie, and I'm also certain he'd insist that, if we was to be fortunate enough to find a table in front of that window there what's facing this here restaurant, he'd congratulate us most heartily." Dick Trout nodded, drool escaping from his mouth as he smiled his agreement.

Having heard their plan and still unnoticed by either of them, their unseen shadow slunk away, and once past the concealing shadows of a few cottages, retrieved his horse and scurried nimbly down the lane. Arriving short minutes before his as yet unmet companions, he had the incredible good fortune to find a table that was not only vacant but was situated in front of the window facing the lane, ideal for observing the entrance of the restaurant.

After tying their horses next to the only other horse there, Boile and Trout stepped inside the drinking establishment and saw that the table they needed was already occupied. Approaching the table, they by gesture indicated they would like to share it with the man already sitting there. A nod of agreement was enough. Both men sat down, satisfying themselves that the brougham still waited outside the restaurant, thus it followed that the two lovers must be inside. Settling themselves for a bit of a wait, they ordered ale, magnanimously including one for the gentleman who had allowed them to share his table with them.

Watching the pair with interest, the other man sat slightly apart wondering, not for the first time, what their interest was in following the young lovers about the city. Skillfully, he steered the conversation around so they were soon telling of the oddities of the gentry. Ned Boile, the more talkative of the two, was soon whispering their reason for being out on such a night—the toff what had hired them claimed that some other bloke had somehow stolen his wife and he wanted her back! And what's more, he didn't care if anyone got themselves killed!

Mr. Smith pointed toward the brougham standing outside the restaurant. "That isn't the carriage you're following, is it?" At their suddenly guarded nods, Smith smiled scornfully but neither Boile nor Trout noticed. Before relating his own tissue of lies, Mr. Smith ordered a pitcher of ale, making the pair look on him almost as a benefactor.

He had lowered his voice, making the other two lean toward him. "Lads, this is most extraordinary! I've been following that very same carriage. The bloke owes me money and refuses to pay me. I've been trying to catch him alone, no witnesses, that sort of thing." He sat silently, tensely, waiting for some sort of reply, filling their mugs with the frothy ale.

Ned Boile, assured that the other was one of them, wiped his mouth on his sleeve before lowering his voice also. "I overheard the blighter and an older woman chatting about their plans for the day, which included lunch, a meeting with some bloke called Mallory, and then they was going on to dine with a Lord somebody, but I can't remember the toff's name."

Mr. Smith patted the other's arm, reassuring him that with the three of them following the carriage, they couldn't possibly go wrong. The pitcher was just about empty when Braxton and Claire finally emerged from the restaurant, and the three hurriedly left the pub, retrieving their horses from where they had tied them.

Having sent word to his driver that they were leaving, Braxton, feeling the cold dampness of the day, quickly helped Claire into the carriage. Thomas, who had been sheltering in the kitchen of the eating house, jumped nimbly up to the driver's box, and seizing the reins, soon had the horses trotting through the streets of the great city. But once again neither the driver nor Braxton noticed the entourage they had acquired.

After some miles through narrow and congested roads, the brougham once more came to a halt, this time in front of an old building, which contained solicitors' offices and was situated next to the Old Bailey Courthouse. Braxton, after assisting Claire from the brougham, turned to his driver and pointed to a tavern across the street. Flipping the man a coin, Braxton told Thomas to get out of the cold and have himself a pint, admonishing him to keep a sharp eye out for their return. The driver smiled as he secured the horses before crossing the road, not for the first time thinking Mr. Kane a most generous man.

The stealthy trio once more huddled in a darkened doorway and studied the situation. Mr. Smith, fearing more ale might create an awkward situation, confided that this stop was most likely a short one, and with the driver already in the tavern, it would probably be better if they hung back. Looking briefly at the sky, he started talking, his words so low the two struggled to hear his words.

"Look around, lads. The hour is already late. I doubt they'll tarry overlong in this place. They'll need time to reach the toff's manor." He stopped speaking as his devious mind worked out a plan of sorts. "Mr. Boile, it seems to me they'll be some hours before returning to Whitechapel. What were your instructions?"

Ned Boile studied the man, suddenly realizing he had relinquished his position as leader. Rubbing the stubble on his chin, he thought long and hard before he spoke. "When we knows they've settled someplace for the evening, one of us is to fetch Mr. Kirkwood and bring him to wherever we is waiting."

"Good plan, Ned. I think it would be wise if you didn't mention my interest in Mr. Kane to your employer. He probably wants the whole thing kept very quiet. When you leave to fetch him, I'll slip away at the same time. The carriage will have to cross the bridge to return to Whitechapel. I think that's where I'll wait. See if you can convince this Kirkwood chap to do the same. In this weather, there's not likely to be any foot traffic about, and very few carriages venture into Whitechapel after dark. Yes, an excellent place to waylay someone."

Just over an hour later, a door opened and Braxton and Claire emerged. Feeling the coolness of the wind, Claire hugged her woolen cloak tightly around her. Braxton, looking down the road, was rewarded with the sight of his driver hurrying toward them, holding his hat against the wind that threatened to lift it from his head. The two men nodded to each other as Braxton assisted Claire into the brougham before stepping in himself. A few short minutes later the carriage was clattering down the cobblestoned lane, three shadowy figures following as closely as they dared.

Both the carriage and foot traffic was lighter that late in the day, making the travelling much quicker. The trio of rogues, seeing the carriage slow down before turning into a wide drive, secreted themselves behind a hedge and watched as a beaming Lord Magnus Jennings personally greeted his guests, ushering them into the welcoming warmth

Oh Wicked Escort

of Romford House.

❈   ❈   ❈

Lord Jennings first embraced Claire and then held her away from him, studying the young woman who faced him, his lined face wreathed in smiles. He shook hands with Braxton, but his smile had become very reserved. After the initial greetings were over, he led them into his sitting room and closed the door, as much to prevent eavesdropping as to keep out any cold drafts, although a fire burned in the stone fireplace.

"Sir," the old man sputtered as he faced Braxton, "the only thing preventing me from calling you out is the look of happiness on this child's beautiful and beloved face. I swore, before you arrived, that if she displayed any sign of misery, well…" His voice trailed off.

Claire, taking Braxton's hand in her own, faced their host, a tremulous smile on her lips. "Please, my Lord, allow us to tell you our story. Braxton was as much a victim as I was."

He interrupted her, his temper suddenly flaring. "I tried to warn your father…just before the wedding, I had begun to hear rumblings about that young scoundrel Kirkwood, but Pierre was too sick, not to mention too stubborn, to listen. Don't bear him any grudge, dear girl, all that mattered to him was that you be happily settled and to ensure you would be taken care of."

He ran his fingers through his thinning strands of silver hair and then abruptly sat down, facing the young couple. "All right then, tell me your story, although I make no promise that I won't interrupt again."

Smiling tentatively, Claire faced the old gentleman. "You were right to be suspicious of Bennett but there were other villains, and as I said, other victims."

And so between them, Braxton and Claire related their tale, from the initial visit of Mordock Peckworthy and his threat of debtor's prison if Bennett didn't fall in with his plan to the suggestion that if Braxton chose not to cooperate, his brother, a depraved murderer, would be released from his cell on the other side of the world, free to continue killing innocent people.

Claire almost cringed as she related the hoax visited on her on her wedding night, but she continued to hold Braxton's hand, a fact not lost on Lord Jennings. She told of Letitia Penrod's learning of the deception, which resulted in Claire's flight from Bennett Kirkwood and Silverwood.

At this, Lord Jennings sat up. "My dear, you should have returned to Romford House. I know I was away when you left your husband, but you would have found a safe haven here."

"I dared not take the chance of being turned away and Bennett finding me. By the greatest good fortune, Silverwood's housekeeper, Mrs. Dixon, had dismissed my maid, wrongly to be sure, but she was unaware that Betty had told me she had a sister living in Whitechapel. I simply walked out of the house one day and caught a ride with a Mr. Billy Marple, the driver of a freight wagon. He most reluctantly took me to Whitechapel, and by an incredible stroke of luck, Betty's path crossed ours at that very moment. She had just been hired on at Henderson's Domestics. Convincing her that I too needed to find employment was probably one of the most difficult things I had to do, but eventually she did lead me to Eloise Henderson, which is where I've been living all these months." She sat back, breathless, from her long tale.

Lord Jennings slapped his knee, laughing in both shock and delight at Claire's pluck and determination. "I launched a search for you but it was as if the earth had swallowed you up, not a trace could be found." He smiled and Claire noticed that his smile was, albeit reluctantly, starting to include Braxton.

"Braxton discovered my whereabouts by chance but never revealed my hideaway to anyone, including the man who had been his closest friend from their shared boyhood, Bennett Kirkwood."

She nodded to Braxton who cleared his throat and picked up the threads of the tale. "I came to realize that I was being watched by both Ben's and Mordock Peckworthy's men, although I don't think either of them was aware that the other existed. On the few occasions that Claire and I dared to venture out, I hired a coach and Claire wore widow's weeds with a thick veil to cover her face. Eventually we met with my own solicitor and a Mr. John Mallory, a solicitor who knows more than most about annulments and divorces. We've laid out the facts to him, including my own despicable part in it, and he's certain Claire will be granted an annulment, but it will take time."

Lord Jennings sat for a moment, digesting all that he had been told.

Just as he was about to speak, a servant entered the room and announced dinner. The three strolled into the dining room, chatting about the weather and such while the servants were about, for Lord Jennings was reluctant to have any gossip rekindled concerning the missing mistress of Silverwood House.

As they feasted on the bounty of Lord Jennings' pantry, they continued to chat of general matters, ignoring even Jack the Ripper's latest murder, both men reluctant to bring such horror to the table. The meal finally over, the three returned to the sitting room where a silver tea service awaited their attention. Settling back into the soft chairs, they sipped at the hot brew, content to reflect on the evening, all three knowing the telling of the tale was not yet at an end.

Lord Jennings was the first to speak. "At one point, young man, I would have had you horsewhipped, but having had the chance to observe you and see the...ah...the affection you seem to have for each other, I can only say, despicable though your actions were, I feel you have suffered greatly from the part you played. And I'm guessing that there is yet more to your tale, is there not?"

Claire and Braxton smiled at their host's astuteness. Braxton once more picked up the story where he had left off. "The final part of the story has nothing to do with Bennett Kirkwood but rather with a Mr. Smith, a former employee of Eloise Henderson." He quickly outlined the workings of Henderson's Domestics, the owner Eloise Henderson, her employees, and the former driver of the omnibus, Mr. Smith, a morose and extremely cantankerous man.

"She sounds like a fine figure of a woman, Claire. Perhaps I'll have the opportunity to thank her for the haven she provided in your hour of need."

Braxton smiled at both of them before he resumed his tale. "Claire found, on more than one occasion, flowers left on her bed. You must understand the employees of Henderson's were strictly separated—the men slept on the third floor and the women on the second, each with their own staircase—no overlap would be tolerated, ever. It would have meant instant dismissal. There was consternation amongst the ladies for no one could explain how this unseen admirer could have access to any of their rooms. Anyway, Eloise finally had to sack Mr. Smith or risk losing her other employees. The man left the property muttering threats and whatnot, but no one was too alarmed. There was nothing but relief at his departure."

Braxton was now moving restlessly about the room as he continued the tale. "The last incident was the undoing of the man. Days after he left Henderson's, a bunch of grapes were left on Claire's bed. This was the last straw for Eloise. She called in a builder whose father, by chance, was the man who had refurbished the building years earlier. He had constructed a secret passage for the owner's 'ladies' to come and go freely, without anyone's knowledge. Well, Mr. Thrupp soon uncovered the secret entrance leading into Claire's chamber, the staircase, and the concealed exit from the building. His men came round and sealed both entrances, but I find myself troubled by the man's ingenuity. What might this propel Mr. Smith to do? He's obviously obsessed with Claire." His voice was rough with anxiety as he regarded Lord Jennings, his eyes reflecting his fears.

"I don't know if he's gone away or merely planning his next move. How can I protect her?" The rich timbre of his voice was reduced to a hoarse whisper.

Lord Jennings felt the last of his doubts about Braxton disappear. "Chin up, my boy. We'll both protect her." The beginning of a smile tipped the corners of his mouth. Standing, he held out his hands to Claire, the warmth of his smile echoing in his voice.

"My dear, if you're in agreement, might I suggest you move here to Romford House. And you, dear boy, should consider doing the same. If, as you say, you're being watched, why not disappear, so to speak?"

All three were standing, their excitement building. There was a slight tinge of wonder in his voice when Braxton spoke. "I admit to hoping you would take Claire in, but I never gave a thought to myself." His words were filled with awe and respect.

"Then it's settled. I'll have my housekeeper make up your rooms."

Laughing, her dark eyes darting fondly between the two men, Claire held up a hand. "Stop, both of you. Lord Jennings, it's wonderful that you're willing to take both of us in, but I must return to Henderson's tonight and tell Eloise where I'm going." There was a soft gentleness in her voice. "Why, if I didn't let her know my whereabouts, she'd be sick with worry."

The old man looked at her, his face reflecting the worry he felt at the thought of her leaving the safety of Romford House. "Humph! Something tells me you'll prove to be as stubborn as your father."

She looked at them both, her smile beautifully radiant. "Eloise Henderson took me in and gave me more than a sanctuary, she gave me a home and has become a dear friend. I owe her the courtesy of an explanation. Braxton, you do understand, don't you?"

His tense expression relaxed into a warm smile. Sighing, he faced Lord Jennings. "Claire's right, sir. We both owe Eloise an explanation and peace of mind. Might we postpone this move until tomorrow morning? We've been out and about most of the day. If anyone did follow us, I'm sure they've long ago given up and gone to seek their beds. Should there be trouble, my driver is a marksman of the highest caliber."

Throwing his hands up in despair, the old man looked at both of them, his faint smile holding a touch of exasperation. "All right, I recognize defeat…I surrender. Braxton, I know you will, but I must say it regardless." The two men faced each other. "Protect this jewel, son. She's precious to me, and if my suspicions are correct, she's even more precious to you." Braxton nodded, unwilling to attempt any words.

Claire, smiling through a mist of tears, hugged the old man. "Thank you so very much, you dear, dear man."

Braxton, listening to the clock chiming the hour, turned to Claire. "If we're going to leave, my sweet, it must be now, for the hour grows late." Turning to the other man, he bowed his head. "Thank you again, my lord. We'll return in the morning."

Calling for their carriage, they stood by the open door. The night sky was dark, the moon casting little light as ghostly fingers of fog drifted aimlessly through the cool night air. Claire shivered as she stepped hesitantly outside, suddenly unsure if they were doing the right thing by insisting on returning to Henderson's. *Silly goose,* she chided, *Braxton will be right beside you.*

Claire waved to Lord Jennings as the brougham pulled away from the manor, thankful for the travelling rug Braxton had draped over their legs. Shivering slightly, she found it impossible not to return his disarming smile...Braxton, her love, her life. Snuggling cozily together, they seemed to fly through the almost deserted streets, for the weather was keeping people indoors as much as the madman who seemed able to roam the eastern end of London with impunity.

❁   ❁   ❁

As the carriage crossed onto the bridge that would soon set them within the environs of Whitechapel, Braxton began to relax slightly until the driver, pulling hard on the reins, shouted down to Braxton that a carriage blocked the road leading off the bridge.

Inside the carriage, a wave of apprehension swept over Claire. Braxton squeezed her hand, trying to reassure her even as he drew a pistol that had been concealed behind a cushion. As the brougham cautiously approached the roadblock, Braxton quietly asked his driver if he was ready, and Thomas's voice, equally restrained, assured him that he was prepared for whatever was to come.

The wind whistled hauntingly through the fog that seemed to shroud the bridge and the horses, sensing the tension, whinnied nervously.

Thomas, still subdued, called down to Braxton. "The carriage seems deserted, sir. Perhaps whoever was in it went for help."

Braxton warily pushed the carriage door open and peered impatiently into the inky blackness of the night. "Stay up there, Thomas, and keep your pistol cocked." He guardedly stepped away from the brougham, his footsteps echoing on the cobbles as he cautiously approached the blockade, the horses of that carriage neighing nervously as he approached. He laid a comforting hand on the one, keeping his pistol aimed at the carriage door. Taking hold of the handle, he pulled the door open and glanced quickly inside but spied only emptiness. He heard a boot scrape on the cobbles just as cold metal touched the back of his neck.

"Drop your weapon, Braxton!" The voice was absolutely emotionless, chilling Braxton through his very being.

A shot rang out from the shadows, shattering the stillness of the night. Thomas cried out once, and then there was only silence. Ned Boile stepped from the shadows, his gun pointed at Thomas whose hand was now empty, blood trickling down from a wound on his forehead. As everyone watched, the driver slowly slid from the coach seat, his unconscious body wedging itself into the footrest. Boile stood there, his gun now pointed at Braxton.

As Braxton turned to face the man he had shared his youth with, he saw Claire at the window of his carriage. He heard her gasp of surprise as she recognized her husband's features. His stomach churned with anxiety and frustration. "Leave her alone, Ben."

Bennett Kirkwood lashed out angrily. "She's my wife, you arrogant, home-wrecking bastard. Did you really think you could steal a man's wife without reprisal?"

"I didn't steal her—you threw her away!" Braxton's voice was filled with contempt, his eyes conveying the growing fury within him.

Spying the gun Bennett held on Braxton, terror, stark and vivid, glittered in Claire's eyes. Suddenly fearless, she left the questionable safety of the brougham, stumbling awkwardly as her feet reached the ground. Quickly straightening herself, she stared defiantly at the man who had been her husband, icy fear twisting around her heart.

Dick Trout chose that moment to suddenly appear from behind the rear of the carriage, standing so near that Claire was soon breathing in his fetid odor. Her breath came in quick, shallow gasps as she desperately willed herself not to faint.

Bennett Kirkwood, a highly proficient shot, waved his gun threateningly as he snarled at Dick Trout to move away from his wife. Unluckily for Dick, he paid no heed to the man who was his employer, being too enthralled with the unexpected perfection of the woman who stood so near, a woman who would normally be unobtainable to the likes of him. A second shot rang out, and slowly, with a disbelieving look on his face, Dick Trout crumpled to the ground, a thin thread of drool flying through the air. With a tiny squeak of terror, Claire jumped away from his lifeless body. Bennett threw back his head and laughed before turning his gun on Braxton once more.

"Don't move, Kane, not if you value your life."

Stepping forward, Bennett seized Claire's wrist. "And now, my dear wife, we'll say good night to this little party. It's time we celebrated our marriage." He paused, thinking of the pleasures to come. "I know…we'll call this night our wedding night."

Glancing at the unmoving body of his friend, Boile watched as Bennett Kirkwood yanked Claire along the road, pausing just long enough to whisper in the hair-covered ear of his accomplice, *"Kill the bastard after we've gone and there'll be a few extra coins for you."*

Fury was choking Braxton, but fear for Claire prevented him from moving. He watched as she was dragged, screaming his name, to the other carriage, fighting desperately but no match against her captor's superior strength. Bennett had just managed to open the carriage door when an unknown voice rang out.

"Let her go!"

Spinning around, Bennett peered into the darkness. A shadowy figure stepped forward but it was one Bennett failed to recognize. At first glance, he had thought it was the police but looking at the shabbily dressed figure, he knew it couldn't be.

"And who might you be? Don't interfere or you'll sleep tonight with a bullet between your eyes."

Startled, Claire looked at the newcomer and gasped. "Mr. Smith!"

"Mrs. St. Martin or Mrs. Kirkwood, whatever your name is!" He bowed slightly before facing Bennett Kirkwood once more. "You still have hold of her, Kirkwood. I won't tell you again to let her go!" He spat out the words contemptuously, his lips thinning with rage.

Bennett turned to the woman who had been haunting his dreams for these many months. "Another conquest, Claire?"

She looked dazedly up at her husband. "Don't be foolish, Bennett. This man is...no, this man *was* the escort for Henderson's Domestics, until his wicked ways proved to be his undoing, and he was dismissed."

Braxton, standing a few feet away, stared at the man who had appeared out of nowhere. *Mr. Smith? How did Mr. Smith just happen to show up?*

Ned Boile stepped forward, a sheepish grin on his pale face. "It's all right, Smith. This be the man what hired me, Mr. Kirkwood, and that be his wife, the one what he wants back. This here bloke is the one you be after, the one what owes you money." His thumb pointed at Braxton who was watching the scene being played out, stunned disbelief written across his face.

In the tense silence, the sound of a pistol being cocked filled the night air. A shot rang out and Bennett Kirkwood staggered backward, no longer thinking of Claire, only of escape from the madman who had just put a bullet through his chest. His steps slowed as he staggered across the bridge toward Whitechapel, until another shot whistled through the air, ensuring he went no further.

Ned Boile, witnessing the unexpected turn of events, suddenly recognized the very great peril in which he found himself. His cold fingers dropped the pistol he held, suddenly, desperately, intent on nothing but escape. As he ran, he looked back and it was at that moment that another shot rang out and Ned Boile ceased to exist.

Mr. Smith stepped toward Braxton, who was now holding a trembling Claire in his arms. "Have you come to any harm, Mrs. St. Martin, or perhaps I could just call you Claire?" He waited patiently until she managed to shake her head.

"Who are you?" Braxton ground out the words between his teeth. In the distance, he could hear police whistles and the faint sound of running feet. *I have to stall for time until the police arrive.*

The man opposite him laughed as if he had been told a very amusing story. "Baby brother, don't you recognize me?"

Braxton squinted, trying to see the face clearly in the shadowy light. "Patrick?" He stared at this latest arrival, a war of emotions raging within him.

"You don't act as surprised as I thought you would, although when we met so unexpectedly at Henderson's, I wasn't certain that you hadn't seen through my little charade." He giggled fiendishly, neither of the men noticing Claire's look of incomprehension.

"I wondered, when I started ridding Whitechapel of its vermin, if you would put two and two together. You of all people would have known I was helpless to stop myself, as much a victim as the scum I was unable to resist ripping open. And then this pretty little thing appeared on the doorstep of Henderson's." His fingers reached out and caressed a strand of her hair that blew gently in the wind, and Claire willed herself not to shrink away from his touch.

"I heard the gossip, you know, about you and Kirkwood and this exquisite beauty. At first, I didn't realize who she was, but when you started sniffing around her skirts, I knew. And what a time I had! Scaring everyone at Henderson's with the mysterious flowers left in her room. I thought it a stroke of genius to leave grapes—I was sure she would know who had left them, but by then I no longer worried about discovery. I watched her, you know, undressing, brushing her hair, all the little things that women do before retiring for the night."

Braxton tensed, ready to spring, but his half-brother kept his gun aimed at Claire. "And now it's just the three of us, and you know what they say about three being a crowd." The barrel of his pistol suddenly pointed at Braxton's head. Claire was powerless to stop the scream that suddenly filled the still November night.

Lowering his pistol slightly, Patrick looked at Braxton, a fierce hatred burning in his eyes. "I've always hated you, brother. You had everything I wanted but never got—our father's love, a mother, and servants always fussing over you. And Father, when he discovered my unfortunate thirst for blood, asking me, *'why can't you be like your brother?'* When I was at St. Guy's studying medicine, I used to imagine it was you or that bitch you called Mother on my dissecting table." The sound of a pistol being cocked echoed in the cold stillness of the night as he once more pointed it at his brother's head, his lips twisted in a cynical smile.

A shot rang out, but it wasn't Braxton that fell. Thomas, so very, very stealthily, had retrieved his pistol from the floor of the driver's seat, the pistol no one had bothered to collect, and seeing his master threatened had without hesitation fired his gun.

Patrick Kane lurched about for an instant before reeling toward the balustrade of the bridge. Sending a final look of hatred at his half-brother and the woman they both loved, he stumbled over the barrier, dropping into the cold grey water that flowed under the bridge, the splash as he hit the water barely perceptible. Braxton ran to the side and looked over but was unable to distinguish anything as the watery grave closed over the body of his deeply troubled brother.

As Braxton wrapped his arms around Claire, holding her as tightly as she held him, they could hear the voices and footsteps of many men approaching.

As they were being questioned, it quickly became obvious to Braxton that Thomas had been unable to hear anything Patrick had said and was under the impression he had shot a man named Mr. Smith, a man who threatened his master with a pistol, an act which soon had Thomas being hailed as a hero by one and all.

For one wild moment, Braxton thought of protecting his family's name from the scandal that was sure to erupt. *Why say anything? No one would ever know the real identity of Jack the Ripper. Let everyone assume it was Mr. Smith who had plummeted into the Thames.*

❀ ❀ ❀

The police soon had the road cleared after the senior officer delegated two of his men to drive the carriages and the only three people still alive to the nearest police station.

Thomas, dried blood covering the shallow wound on his forehead, sat on the seat opposite Braxton and Claire. He watched as his employer fussed over the young lady who looked as though she might faint at any moment.

Still, Thomas mused as he studied them, *there was something very strange about the whole incident, one of the gentry claiming to be Miss St. Martin's husband. Maybe there was something to that tale I heard about Mr. Kane and his friend Kirkwood deceiving some society beauty. I always put it down to petty gossip.* He leaned back against the plush seat and rubbed his throbbing head, watching as Braxton Kane continued to fret over his lady. *But she is absolutely stunning.*

The carriage slowed and Braxton found himself the object of intense curiosity. Meeting Thomas's eyes, he smiled. "You'll be rewarded handsomely for your part in all of this, Thomas."

The man smiled. "I'm just grateful that the man who shot me had such a bad aim, sir."

The carriage slowed, and looking out the window, Braxton saw they had arrived at the police station. Alighting from the carriage, they were hustled into the building where innumerable voices swirled around them, offering tea to the lady, firing questions at the gentleman, and patting Thomas on the back as one and all congratulated him on his bravery and fine marksmanship.

❀ ❀ ❀

Two of the policemen pulled up chairs beside Braxton, nodding politely to Claire, who still clung to Braxton's arm as if in need of reassurance that he was alive and well. Braxton admitted that the two rather shabby men had been strangers to him, but he gathered they had been employed by Bennett Kirkwood to watch his movements.

The older of the two officers looked at him sharply. "Why would anyone want to know what you were getting up to?"

"Because, gentlemen, he was trying to find his wife and thought I would lead him to her." He paused, reluctant to involve Claire but knowing there was no way around it, he rose and stood behind Claire's chair, his hands resting protectively on her shoulders. Facing his inquisitors, he looked at them, challengingly. "Allow me to introduce the woman who was married to Bennett Kirkwood but who prefers to be known by her maiden name, Miss Claire St. Martin."

At their questioning looks, he knew he wouldn't escape with anything less than a full explanation. "Miss St. Martin has engaged a solicitor for the purpose of having her marriage to Bennett Kirkwood annulled." Dumbfounded, the two men gazed at the delicate beauty in disbelief, for in their world no one escaped once the bonds of matrimony were tied. An unwelcome blush crept into Claire's cheeks.

The older officer, being the first to recover, puffed out his cheeks, perplexed at the goings-on of the gentry. "Very well, sir. Am I correct in assuming that the third body is this Bennett Kirkwood?"

"That's right. He was about to shoot me when my brother, my half-brother actually, Patrick Kane, appeared from out of nowhere. I heard one of Kirkwood's thugs try to assure his employer that it was all right, he...that is, Mr. Smith...was with them. But 'Mr. Smith' or 'Patrick Kane', whichever you prefer, fired his gun, killing Kirkwood but not before Kirkwood had killed the second of the thugs for standing too close to Miss St. Martin. It was at that point that the first thug tried to escape, but my brother shot him before he had gone very far. And you already know that my driver, seeing my life threatened, shot 'Mr. Smith', who tumbled over the balustrade of the bridge and has presumably been swept away in the Thames."

The two officers of the law looked at each other, both trying to follow the events as the gentleman related them.

"So why would this Smith or Kane want to murder you?"

Oh Wicked Escort

Braxton shuddered, flushing miserably. "That, gentlemen, is a long story." The evening became even longer as he gave a brief outline of the workings of Henderson's Domestics and the association Mr. Smith had with Miss St. Martin and his mad delusions. "And so you see, gentlemen, he saw me as a threat, brother or no." A look of dejection began to spread over his handsome features as he bowed his head in resignation.

"There's more. In his ranting, he claimed he was ridding Whitechapel of 'its vermin' and said he was 'unable to resist ripping his victims open'."

Both men snapped to attention, their interest fully engaged. "Are you claiming that he, your half-brother, was Jack the Ripper?"

Braxton's expression was haunted—he could do no more than nod. The older policeman saw him give a resigned shrug.

"Sir, are you aware that we have lunatics walking in here all the time, all confessing to be Jack the Ripper or some other notorious murderer? What makes you believe your brother was telling the truth?"

Confused, Braxton met the other's eyes. "Because, as a boy, he was always cutting up animals, including any pets I had. Even my father was unable to control him. And he hated me! He hated the fact that Claire..." He paused, uncertain whether to go on. "He was insanely jealous that Miss St. Martin was in love with me!"

Scratching his head, the older man laughed softly. "I can understand anyone envying you that, sir. And I do take your story seriously. As soon as it's light, I'll have men out combing the banks of the river for your brother's body, but that's a long shot at best."

He stood, brushing his jacket and smiling. "Take the young lady to Henderson's in Whitechapel or to this Lord Jennings, and then get yourself and your driver home. Come back tomorrow, and perhaps we'll have news of some sort. We will need you to identify at least the body of Bennett Kirkwood, although I don't know how we'll identify the other two. And I would advise the young lady to contact her solicitor."

Braxton's head swung around, but the man met his eyes with a small grin. "She won't need an annulment now, will she, sir? She's just become the Widow Kirkwood."

It was late the following morning when Braxton returned to the police station, an event he dreaded but knew it would solve nothing by procrastinating. He was directed to the morgue where he identified the body of Bennett Kirkwood, again denying any knowledge of who the other two dead men might be. Leaving the dismal place, he reflected that, although he was saddened by Bennett's death, he could feel no remorse for the man who had been a very real threat to Claire, not to mention almost killing him.

As he emerged from the building, he found a young police constable waiting for him. The lad quickly explained that Sergeant Stillwell would like a quick word. Nodding for him to lead the way, Braxton was quickly escorted to a small room in a neighboring building. The constable, pausing before a closed door, knocked softly, waiting until he heard a muffled voice. Opening the door, he stepped back and gestured Braxton inside.

The tiny room was reduced in size by the wheezing, corpulent man who occupied the space behind a cluttered desk, his foul breath permeating the very air. He thanked Braxton for coming as he motioned him to take the only other chair in the room.

"Have you found my brother's body?"

"Not as yet, sir, but we'll continue looking." He consulted a small notebook for a moment before returning it to his pocket.

"I've had a word with my superiors, Mr. Kane, and have passed on your suspicions concerning your brother and the story you told the two officers who attended you last night. Have you changed your mind about any of it, sir?"

"Of course I haven't changed my mind!" He was quickly becoming irritated with the man's intrusive manner. "Do you really think I would make such an accusation about my brother if I didn't believe it to be true?"

Sergeant Stillwell's reply was barely audible. "Yes, yes, quite right."

Braxton, unable to escape the man's breath, briefly held a white handkerchief to his nose, sighing at the futility of the conversation and wondering how the man had risen to the rank of sergeant.

"Now sir, we've never had either Patrick Kane or Mr. Smith in the station, willingly or not. No one has ever come forward and pointed a

Oh Wicked Escort

finger at him..." He hesitated for a second. "That is, until now. And believe me we've had some very high names bandied about." His voice became hushed and conspiratorial. "Would you believe that even Prince Albert Edward, Queen Victoria's very own grandson, has been suggested as the monster?" Braxton merely nodded, giving Sergeant Stillwell no satisfaction at all.

"No, no, my dear sir, it's unfortunate that your brother was such a ne're-do-well, but it does happen, even in the best of families. My superiors, while wishing your brother was the Ripper, thus ending this terror in Whitechapel, feel that there is no proof and that sadly, he was just another lunatic wanting attention."

There was a sharp rap at the door, and without invitation, a man stepped into the tiny room. Sergeant Stillwell stood up abruptly, his florid complexion deepening.

"Inspector Abberline! This is a surprise, sir. Indeed sir, it is an honor!" The sergeant had turned into a groveling sycophant.

"Good day...Stillwell, isn't it?" The heavyset man could only nod, wondering what a Scotland Yard inspector wanted with him.

"I take it this gentleman is Mr. Braxton Kane?" Another nod, but a wary expression had fallen across the sergeant's face.

"Would you mind, sergeant, if I had a few minutes alone with Mr. Kane?" Although his words were spoken softly, there was little doubt as to the outcome. Inspector Abberline, who had the appearance and quiet manner of a banker, held the door open, leaving the rotund sergeant with little choice but to leave the room.

As the door closed behind the banished officer, the inspector held out his hand, and Braxton, puzzled at what had just occurred, took the extended hand and shook it.

"Good morning, Mr. Kane. As you have no doubt gathered, I am Inspector Abberline of Scotland Yard. I was assigned to this Jack the Ripper case because of my expertise within the area of Whitechapel." He crossed to the recently vacated chair of Sergeant Stillwell and sat down.

"Mr. Kane, do you know how many murders occur in Whitechapel on any given night? And do you have any idea how many lunatics have shown up here confessing that they are Jack the Ripper?"

He leaned back, glancing up at the ceiling as he gathered his thoughts. "Granted, not all murders are as gruesome as the mutilations done by this Jack the Ripper fellow, but they can be quite ghastly. Why would you think your brother was this…this madman?"

"Did your officers tell you what he confessed just before my driver shot him? He said he was ridding Whitechapel of its vermin and that if I had put two and two together, I would know he was helpless and as much a victim as the ones he'd ripped open!"

"Yes sir, I can understand your reasoning. But last night, on the bridge leading into Whitechapel, there were a total of four men killed, although we have as yet to find your brother's body. Another man was wounded in the fracas, and yet you can only identify one body. What bizarre circumstances could lead to such an event?"

Braxton sighed, weary of repeating the tale but knew that an inspector from Scotland Yard would most likely accept nothing less. In a quiet voice, he once more told the story of Claire and the deception he and Ben Kirkwood had heartlessly carried out on her and her subsequent flight into Whitechapel.

Many minutes had ticked by on the small clock as the story reached its conclusion. Inspector Abberline stood, and placing his arm familiarly on Braxton's shoulder, escorted him from the room. "I suggest, sir, you return to your home. Take comfort in the fact that you and the little lady, who was also almost a victim, escaped unharmed. Please trust me when I say that should we find any trace of your brother, well, we'll of course notify you at once, sir, at once."

Chapter Twenty-One

More than a month had passed since the start of the new year. Eighteen eighty-nine! Claire hugged herself. Life was more than brilliant—and today she was exchanging marriage vows with Braxton Kane.

Sitting in the master bedroom of Pennygrove Hall, she reflected on the past year. If it hadn't been for Bennett and his selfish, lecherous ways, she and Braxton...well, who knows? She shuddered delicately. *No, don't dwell on those who had caused fear and sorrow. That time was the past.*

The police, search as they might, had never found Patrick Kane's body. True, the murders had stopped for more than a month once before but then the madman had struck again. Whitechapel and its residents were practicing caution this time. They would not believe the monster gone until a lot more time had elapsed.

Braxton had admitted to her that he had grave misgivings as to whether Patrick was truly dead. "What if he's still alive, Claire? What if he comes back...?" He couldn't finish the sentence.

Tongues had indeed wagged, just as they had known they would. Society seemed to have closed ranks against the young couple, judging them guilty of...what exactly? It didn't seem to matter. Vicious gossip flew across dinner tables and through salons, each story juicier in content than the last, fed by malicious scandalmongers such as Letitia Penrod and her daughters, Miranda and Minerva.

Braxton had waited less than a week after Bennett's death to formally propose, and after the initial flurry of excitement had passed, they had sat back and discussed the future—their future. He admitted it preyed upon his mind that she and any children they might have would be ostracized because of a moment of weakness and stupidity on his part.

And because the young lovers had been so much in the news, all of London was interested in their doings, and news of the engagement flew from one end of the city to the other, although they were still out of favor with society itself.

❁ ❁ ❁

It was just days before the wedding that a richly appointed carriage had drawn up in front of Pennygrove. The driver had climbed down and asked if Miss St. Martin or Mr. Kane were at home to Mr. Mordock Peckworthy.

It was a short time later that the three met in the drawing room of Pennygrove Hall. Claire was guarded, wondering what the man wanted, while Braxton, on the other hand, had been against even letting the man in. But Claire had won the argument.

The man had entered, dressed just as richly as when Braxton had first laid eyes on him in Ben's home so many months earlier. He refused offers of tea or something a little stronger, preferring, he said, to get down to business. Braxton saw at once that the man, always thin, was now almost skeletal.

Taking Claire's hand, Mordock Peckworthy drew it to his lips, kissing it softly. The niceties finished, he faced Braxton.

"Kane, I'm here to apologize…to both you and Miss St. Martin. I was a swine! So intent on satisfying my own twisted need for revenge, I cared nothing for those hurt along the way. Forgiveness might be too much to ask, Miss St. Martin, but I hope one day you may find it in your heart to do so."

He faced Braxton and smiled sadly. "Kane, don't bother thinking of killing me, for you see before you a dying man. I'll soon join my own beloved…that's all I ever really wanted."

Taking Claire's hand again, he patted it in a paternal manner. "You are every bit as beautiful as everyone says, both inside and out, from everything I've heard." He reached into a pocket and drew out a piece of paper.

"This is a bank draft—call it conscience money if you will—for everything you've been put through. If you don't want to accept it for yourself, give it to charity."

Claire looked at the paper and looked back at the man, her brown eyes wide with wonder. "Mr. Peckworthy, we can't accept this…"

Peckworthy's hand closed over hers. "Please, my dear, accept it. Without an heir, the remainder of my estate will go to a distant cousin, something I now find to be of little consequence."

He stepped away from her, and nodding to Braxton, picked up his coat and left the room with a subdued good-bye. Braxton and Claire stared at the door and then at each other, totally speechless over this most extraordinary and curious visit.

It was the following evening that Braxton, standing in front of the fire, had made a proposal of a different kind. "What if, my darling, we were to leave England, never to return? Neither of us has any family in England or anywhere else for that matter. We could leave this country and begin life anew. I could sell Pennygrove and my country estate. I had already sold my interests in the West Indies just before we met."

Claire studied his beloved face, thinking of all he would be leaving. She had no property or any belongings other than the wardrobe her father had bought to launch her into London society. All of Bennett's property, being entailed, had gone to an uncle, a younger brother of his father.

"My love, are you sure? You would give up everything, leave all of your friends and go *where*? Where would we go, Braxton?"

His mouth curved into an unconscious smile. He stopped to consider her question and then blurted out an answer. "What about Australia? We already know somebody who lives there, Betty and James."

Claire clapped her hands in excitement, mixed strongly with astonishment. "Are you certain you want to do such a thing, Braxton?"

He stood, his strong arms encircling her, and then his mouth moved over hers, devouring its softness. The touch of his lips was a delicious sensation that she couldn't get enough of, his kiss sending spirals of ecstasy through her until they broke apart, shaken by the passion they both felt. His lips slowly descended to meet hers once more in slow, shivery kisses, but too soon, he drew away from her.

"Again I must remind you, madam, that I'm only human. We only have a few days before we say our vows, and then all will be well."

They sat up till after midnight making their plans. As he prepared to bundle her off to bed, he admonished her to get a good night's sleep, for tomorrow they would start inquiring about booking passage on a ship bound for Australia.

Laughing, Claire lifted her skirts slightly, telling Braxton to stay right there as she skipped up the stairs. Wearing an impish grin when she returned, she made him close his eyes before placing her small store of coins in his hands. He frowned in puzzlement as he undid the cloth that held the money.

"That, sir, is the money I saved toward a passage to either Australia or America to escape Bennett."

He exchanged a smile with her and then shook his head. "You are amazing, my sweet. To think of all you did, alone…I love you, Claire, more than life itself." Standing, he took her arm as he escorted her to her bedchamber.

"Good night, my sweet, until tomorrow."

And now, their special day was here. They had decided to not give society the opportunity to snub them by refusing an invitation. Instead, they invited only those who they considered true friends.

She had heard the omnibus rumbling up the driveway, and peeking through the window, saw the staff of Henderson's Domestics alight, all dressed in their best finery, all wearing warm smiles.

Billy and Maybelle Marple had followed them up the drive in a black hansom cab. Maybelle was in her best frock, and Billy, despite his suit, still wore the cheeky grin that Claire had come to love. They greeted the Henderson staff, joining them as they walked to the front entrance as treasured guests do, receiving a warm greeting from Braxton.

Lord Jennings had arrived earlier than the others for Claire had asked him if he would walk her down the aisle. The warmth of his smile was all the answer she had needed.

And now it was time. Her heart was fluttering so quickly she wondered if she was capable of descending the staircase.

There was a soft knock on the door. "Claire, it's time." Lord

Oh Wicked Escort

Jennings' voice was low and composed, just as it had been that other time.

No, she thought *forget the past. This is the beginning of your new life. You're marrying the man you love, your dear friends are waiting downstairs to share your joy, and the monsters have all been cast out, never to rise up again.*

She opened the door and smiled at the elderly man who stood there. "You, my dear Claire, are so very beautiful…why, you take the breath away even from an old man like me. I know how very proud your father would be at this moment."

Smiling up at him, she took his arm and slowly, ever so regally, the two glided down the stairs, where her love and all her tomorrows awaited.

About the Author

D.L. Robinson is most passionate about writing, followed closely by a love of history, adventure, and romance. She has been married to her high school sweetheart and best friend for many years–traveling the world together and laughing as often as possible–even in those moments when life presents itself as being distinctly 'unfunny'.

She has researched her family's British ancestry as well as her husband's multi-faceted European background, finding the time to sign up for mini-courses as a 'mature' student to learn more about the lives and scandals of the European and Russian monarchies.

She is the author of *Banish the Dragon* and *Oh Wicked Escort* and is currently working on her third novel, *A Conspiracy of Mothers*.

She and her husband enjoy spending time with their children, grandchildren and close friends, always ready to hand round a plate of home-made cookies and a cup of tea to their treasured guests.

Author Contacts:

www.risforromance.net
https://www.facebook.com/risforromance.net